ACKNOWLEDGMENTS

Wow, what a ride! It seems that just yesterday I came up with this idea at my sixth-grade track camp. What a privilege it has been to be involved in this fantastic process. So many people helped, guided, and encouraged me along the way, without whom I would not have this story.

First, thank you to my family, especially my mom, who helped me with the LONG and arduous process of making sense of the writing of a twelve-year-old, and my dad, who helped me wade through all the financial decisions and provided a business perspective of publishing my writing. This has been an incredible journey, and I look forward to continuing it with you. I love you all!

Thank you to Mrs. Weed and Kate, my mentors, for taking time out of your busy lives for me and for the invaluable critiques and comments you provided.

Thank you to my best friends—Grace, Kalena, Alex, Molly, Hannah, Tyler, Mia, Jonathon, and Lauren—and the entire class of 2014 from Brentwood Christian School. Thank you for being the most amazing friends God could have ever given me; I love you all.

Thank you to Priscilla, Nicole, and Mrs. Peyton, without whom I would not have this wonderful story. You have inspired me countless times to keep going and keep dreaming, no matter how long I had writer's block. I love you, my sisters, mentors, and friends!

Thank you to everyone who inspired me, knowingly or not, for without you, this story would be a very different one indeed.

And thank you to my readers. Without you, this story would be nothing.

I look forward to continuing the journey with you all the next time around!

BOOK ONE OF SONS AND DAUGHTERS

YOUNG FALCON

*Elizabeth
Anne
McKinney*

ELIZABETH McKINNEY

BOOK PUBLISHERS NETWORK

Book Publishers Network
P.O. Box 2256
Bothell • WA • 98041
Ph • 425-483-3040
www.bookpublishersnetwork.com

10 9 8 7 6 5 4 3 2 1

Printed in the United States of America

LCCN   2011937367
ISBN   978-1-937454-04-3

Editor: Julie Scandora
Cover Designer: Laura Zugzda
Typographer: Stephanie Martindale
Dragons © Tanais-tanais | Dreamstime.com

To God, my guide and inspiration.

CONTENTS

PROLOGUE
HUMANS

"One, two."

Their makeshift wooden swords met in mid-air with a sharp clack, irritating Veryan's sensitive ears. He whirled around to meet Pyralus's second blow with his own sword, trying to keep up with the older boy's count. While the swords were only for sparring, they could still break bones and leave dark bruises if you were not quick enough to block them. No matter how fast he reacted when sparring with Pyralus, Veryan had been getting more than his share of bruises over the past few weeks.

"Good," Pyralus commented and thrust his sword up with a lightning-fast jab. Veryan threw up his own wooden blade to block the blow, and Pyralus's sword smacked loudly against Veryan's, "three."

Veryan, with a swift twist of his wrist, spun his sword around, intending to catch Pyralus off-guard. However, the more experienced and faster nineteen-year-old anticipated Veryan's next move, and their swords met again.

"Four," Pyralus said, smirking at Veryan.

Veryan frowned, feinted to the left, and then drove his sword toward Pyralus's arm. The older boy spun out of his reach and whacked Veryan across the back with the flat of the wooden blade, causing Veryan to wince.

"Five."

Pyralus then stabbed his sword at him several times in swift succession, the lean muscles in his arm springing and flexing with ease as he went through the practised motion. Veryan barely had time to block each blow before another demanded his attention, much to his alarm. Pyralus was so much faster than he that it was almost embarrassing, especially to a proud boy like Veryan, and he did not wish to be humiliated yet again by his friend. "Six, seven, eight, nine ..." With each strike against Veryan's sword, Pyralus called out another number. The last blow left Veryan with a stinging mark on his upper arm, and he let out a short hiss of frustration, annoyance building inside him.

Determined to hit Pyralus with his own blade and thus spare some of his honour and to save himself from getting a few more bruises, Veryan tried to return some of the thrusts, focusing hard on moving more quickly. He almost succeeded several times, but always Pyralus's sword met his. When Veryan tried to aim for Pyralus's shoulder, the older boy ducked down and delivered a smarting blow to Veryan's knee before straightening swiftly and continuing to parry. Pyralus's count continued to escalate each time his sword met Veryan's. Gritting his teeth in determination, Veryan feinted again, trying desperately to find an opening so he could actually hit Pyralus, but that only resulted in his receiving a smack on the wrist, another blow to his already wounded pride. He could not touch Pyralus.

Several more minutes of this ensued before, finally, Pyralus knocked the wooden sword from Veryan's hand and sped his own blade up to Veryan's neck, a conceited grin on his face. Veryan narrowed his eyes in good-natured bitterness, though truly, he was miffed that Pyralus had won this time as well, his feathers ruffled at the fact that he simply could not best Pyralus. "Beaten once again, Veryan," the older boy declared with an arrogant smile.

Veryan sighed. "I know, I know. But I *am* getting better." He rubbed his wrist thoughtfully, wishing that he could, just once, defeat Pyralus and restore some of his broken dignity. Where Veryan came from, one's honour mattered more than anything; one guarded this prized possession at all costs. Therefore, he did not appreciate being beaten time after time, especially seemingly without much effort on Pyralus's part.

Pyralus nodded in agreement, twirling the wooden sword in his hand deftly. "Yes. At least now, you can actually block my blows. A few weeks ago, the best you could do was take an occasional swipe at me, and I bashed you up pretty badly, even though I was going easy on you." He smirked again, sky-blue eyes amused.

Veryan tapped the already darkening bruise on his wrist. "I have more than enough of these by now."

Pyralus chuckled, his cunning grin widening, making some of Veryan's annoyance with his friend evaporate. "True … But can you keep from getting a few more?" He stabbed his makeshift sword toward Veryan's shoulder with a sharp jab. Veryan twisted away, and they resumed their frenzied parrying. The loud clacks of the wooden swords rang throughout the pine forest, disturbing the otherwise peaceful morning.

Veryan and Pyralus were soldiers for Queen Elisheiva's army. Both boys had been assigned to a troop that did little more than border patrols, scouting, and occasionally recruiting new soldiers for the military. Twelve years was the required term for any soldier who served in the army. Veryan had been in service for four years, and Pyralus for five. Veryan had come to this troop when he was merely eleven and had served as a page until he was old enough to join the army; he was eager to complete his service, even though he would have nowhere else to go when his time was ended. But he would cross that bridge when he came to it; now he just focused on bettering his fighting skills, schooled by Pyralus as often as the boys had time to depart from their military duties. Though neither of them was old enough—Veryan now only eighteen and Pyralus nineteen—to contribute significantly to the queen's army, their constant practise was making it possible for them to become stronger and more efficient with the blade.

Only three recorded battles had been fought in the recent history of Yaracina, the elven continent on which they lived, and it had been long before either of them was born—over six hundred years ago. Neither of the two boys would likely ever serve in a real battle, but regardless, the commander of their troop—a man by the name of Gornhelm—insisted on having the men train in preparation for a possible battle whenever they were not on the move. And for the two youths, "on the move" occupied most of their time. As soldiers of one of the patrol troops, Veryan and Pyralus had been to every city and town in Yaracina. And since they were the two youngest members of the patrol troop, they had naturally formed a friendship.

Pyralus slapped Veryan with the flat loudly on the side of his head and then laughed as Veryan complained, "You can't hit me there!" Veryan thrust back, trying in vain to land a hit on the older boy, but Pyralus evaded his attempt yet again. He whirled and twisted away from Veryan's wooden blade, and yet his sword was always there to meet Veryan's. It was frustrating Veryan endlessly.

All of their sessions were like this, but Veryan was becoming progressively better with his sword as he sparred with the older boy. Soon, he believed, he would truly give Pyralus a reason to duck away because, in reality, it was not as if he was actually going to hurt him anyway. He had asked Pyralus to tutor him when time allowed while the group travelled, since the older soldiers did not have much regard for him or Pyralus due to their youth, much less the time or patience to school them with the blade. Besides, Pyralus was probably as capable a fighter as many of the soldiers, if not better, even at his young age. The boy was fast, strong, and devious.

"Ow!" Veryan complained as Pyralus whacked him soundly on his left shoulder. "You're supposed to help me, not injure me!"

"I am helping you!" Pyralus countered and then struck him on the right side. "If you don't want to get hit, you have to move faster! If these were real swords, Veryan, you'd be long dead."

"Yes, I know, I know. *You* don't have to tell me that," he muttered. Veryan sighed and unenthusiastically blocked Pyralus's next blow, but he failed to stop the one after it, and it earned him another throbbing welt on his wrist.

"Come on," Pyralus taunted, grinning devilishly. "My little cousin can fight better than this, Veryan, and he's younger than you!"

The goad accomplished its intended purpose, and Veryan injected himself back into the mock fight. A few stinging cuffs later, he threw down the wooden sword in surrender. Pyralus crowed victoriously, "That's twice in one day!" His friend's blue eyes were alight with amusement.

Veryan, in spite of being disappointed with himself and more than a little frustrated, could not help but smile at the older boy. Pyralus tossed his sword from hand to hand, flourishing the wooden blade with a triumphant grin.

Suddenly a horn was winded in the distance, beckoning them back to camp. Pyralus's cocky grin dropped from his face and was replaced by an agitated scowl. Veryan understood his aggravation. Neither of the two boys enjoyed staying at the camp with the disagreeable older soldiers. They were young, after all, and wanted to be out doing something instead of sitting around listening to the older men talk, especially Gornhelm. The man had an incredible talent for being dislikeable.

"Come on," Pyralus said sourly, and he grudgingly began walking east toward the horn-call. Veryan followed slowly, wishing their sparring could have gone longer. He would like to have had a few more chances to land a hit on Pyralus.

⁓

Not far away, two young men watched the elves head back towards their camp, concealed by the shadows of the swaying trees, out of sight and hearing range of Pyralus and Veryan. They stood silent for a moment, waiting until the elves had disappeared from view and listening intently to the whisperings of the wind, and then the elder of the two said softly, "There's a troop of about twenty elven soldiers not far from here, to the north about half a mile or so. I don't think they'd be any threat to us, but then, I've been wrong about that before."

For several seconds, the younger, a black-haired boy of seventeen, contemplated in silence what the other had said. He crossed his arms over his chest and tipped his head back to study the sky, as if searching for answers amongst the never-ending canvas of blue, and the elder boy watched him impassively as he waited for a response.

Eventually, the black-haired boy said, "We won't attack the troop unless they give us a reason to do so, then, if you feel they're not a threat. I'd prefer our presence to be unknown here, but if one of them happens to see us, we can't let him spread the word that we're here."

"I agree," the other said, his fingers straying over the pommel of the sword belted at his hip. "But don't you think the others will wonder if one of them goes missing? What then?"

The younger shrugged, obviously unconcerned. "If that becomes the case, then Namarii will deal with them, I suppose," he answered, making the other shift uneasily, a grimace on his face.

"That's hardly fair, Lliam."

Lliam's face darkened as some unknown sentiment crossed his face at his scout's words, and anyone could see that his irritation had been aroused. "We've had this discussion before, Jakob, and you would do well to remember that. I know what you think of her and her methods, but you also know why it's necessary sometimes, don't you?"

There was an uncomfortable pause before Jakob replied, and Lliam sensed that the man's frustrations had also been provoked, even though he was astute enough to keep his anger inside. The long-simmering argument between them could be continued another time; right now, they had a task to do, and they needed to devote their energy to that instead of their quarrels. Lliam was too tired to want to argue with his friend now, anyway.

"Yes, I know," Jakob admitted heavily.

Lliam gazed out at the empty forest for another few minutes, calculating and considering where his men could head next; he had travelled through this forest once or twice, but not enough to be totally familiar with it and completely sure of where he was going. For sure, the contingent of Elisheiva's soldiers should be avoided as widely as possible; he did not want to get into any skirmishes just yet. Instructed that no one should know of their presence in Yaracina yet, Lliam would do his best to stick to those orders.

Decided, he told Jakob next, "Tell Roman to take the men northwest for about two miles; that should give us enough distance from the elves. We'll camp at the end of those miles tonight."

Jakob nodded his head in affirmation. "Anything else you want me to tell him?"

Lliam thought a moment and then replied slowly, "Tell him you're in charge until I get back." He knew Roman would not like that one bit, but such an appointment was necessary in Lliam's absences. Roman was too untried to be leading the men anywhere, even such a short distance, and Jakob, having been in the army far longer than both Lliam and Roman, was a natural leader and worked well with the soldiers assigned to Lliam, so he would entrust Jakob, not Roman, whilst he was scouting around the elven camp.

Jakob laughed dryly. "You know he won't like that."

Lliam snorted. "Since when have I cared what he thought about my orders? If he doesn't like it, he can go sulk in the back as he always does, but it won't change anything. Go on now; I'll catch up with you tonight once you've found a spot to camp."

Jakob dipped his head once and then hurried off back to where Lliam's troop was resting, a little less than a mile or so away from where Lliam now stood.

Lliam watched Jakob until his scout disappeared, still keeping an eye out for any wayward elven soldiers that might happen to see the man, and then he began walking towards the encampment, following the path he had seen the two young soldiers take earlier. It would not be hard for Lliam to find the elves' camp, he knew; Jakob had already given him precise enough directions that he would be able to navigate his way through the shady woods to find it. He also knew from his previous journeys through that forest that there was a large glen about a half-mile away, and that that was likely where the soldiers were camped. Lliam would observe the elves for a little while. If he believed that they would pose no threat to his men as they passed through, the elves could pass unharmed; but if they did represent a potential problem, he would send Jakob or another of his men to trail the elves as they continued to make sure they did not find Lliam's troop and to warn them if the elves came too close. As much as he wanted to protect his own, Lliam also had no desire to kill innocent people, even elves, and hoped they would just stay away from him and his troop.

⟡

A few minutes later, Pyralus and Veryan entered the edge of a glen surrounded by tall pines, which cast long, stiff shadows on the needle-draped ground and gave the impression that a fierce ring of ancient sentinels was keeping watch over the little band of men. In the shadows of the dark trees, soldiers were gathering from their scouting duties and various chores around the campsite to the centre of the glen where Gornhelm stood with his right-hand, Comundus. Veryan groaned softly when he realized that Gornhelm was intending to make one of his infamous announcements. Veryan hated them—always long, tedious, and repetitive.

Veryan reluctantly looked at Gornhelm as the man began speaking, automatically trying to tune the words out, but Gornhelm's gravelly voice reverberated around the camp loudly, making it nearly impossible to ignore. "At daybreak, we will head west to Orlena, near the coast. This trip will take about a week, give or take a day or two; we'll see how it goes. And we'll be travelling through the Salquessaé Plains. You know what that means; it'll be an easy trip for you. Once there, we will receive a specific assignment from our queen, may she live forever."

Veryan sighed in exasperation. Why did they never get any good assignments? It was always just border patrols, checkups with various governors, making sure everyone was doing what they were supposed to be doing, or even occasionally ferrying messages between cities, though usually Queen Elisheiva's messengers took care of that. There were never any genuinely interesting assignments given to Gornhelm's band. As Gornhelm began to drone on and on about the honour that was coupled with receiving this assignment, Veryan sighed and turned toward Pyralus and said softly, "It sounds like just another border patrol. Nothing exciting, as usual."

Pyralus agreed with a good-natured smirk. "Right. We never get assignments that are worth our getting up at the crack of dawn." But Veryan knew he was not really complaining; Pyralus naturally fell into the role of a servant more willingly than Veryan, who had grown up having to wake at the crack of dawn every morning of his life and found no reason to be happy about it. Pyralus was not what Veryan would refer to as someone who objected to hard work. At all. Pyralus rarely ever complained or protested about anything, no matter what it was, and as such, Gornhelm liked Pyralus far better than Veryan, who only did what he was supposed to do when forced to do so. Veryan did not like being told what to do by anyone at any time, and everyone in the troop knew it. Veryan was too proud to take orders or perform his assigned tasks willingly.

Veryan began listening to what Gornhelm was saying again, half-hoping that there might be something more to this project than the past ones they had been given.

"We will receive the details of our assignment from the queen's ambassador at the Tower of Orlena," Gornhelm said. "I believe, and this is only a guess, that she wants us to look for new recruits for the army. Some of her seamen have spotted tall black ships with flags bearing a blue dragon on the horizon west of the coast. We may need to be ready to defend ourselves, and as I'm sure you all know, our armies are inadequate and out of practice, to say the least. Queen Elisheiva will need all of us to help her defend Yaracina, and we can start by gathering soldiers for her. We'll need as many as we can get if these ships are truly a threat, but if they're not, it will be good for the army to reshape anyway. There may be more enemies we need to fend off in the future."

A frown flickered across Pyralus's brow momentarily, and then he lowered his eyes and looked at Veryan earnestly. "What do you think of that? Black ships? I haven't heard that one before," he said.

Veryan snorted, dismissing the story immediately as fiction. Black ships? Where would they be coming from? None of the islands had black ships, nor did any of the Yarans, and he knew they certainly did not come from his home. But seeing that Pyralus was serious, he said tactfully, "I don't know what to think. Stuff like that is always popping up, but every time, it's a false alarm. I don't think there's any cause for worry unless we actually see some of these ships," he said.

Pyralus said nothing.

Veryan stole a glance at his friend, wondering if he seriously believed these stories. Pyralus's clear blue eyes were searching the skies, a troubled look on his face, as if he was probing the pale shreds of cloud for answers. While Veryan could not pinpoint exactly what it was, something about the look in his friend's eyes bothered him greatly.

"Pyralus! Veryan!"

Veryan snapped his gaze from Pyralus to look at Gornhelm, a brief surge of dislike distracting him from thoughts of his friend and the black ships. The captain stood roughly seven feet from him, and his shadow covered Veryan completely, which made Veryan scowl in annoyance, though he said nothing and aimed his exasperated glare at the ground in front of his boots, waiting for Gornhelm's comment. "You two will be the rear guard," the captain said.

Pyralus dipped his head compliantly, his ready agreeability to Gornhelm's instructions irritating Veryan immensely. How could his friend be so willing to serve that man? Veryan was sure he would never be able to understand Pyralus completely, nor did he particularly want to do so.

"Yes, sir," Pyralus replied.

Veryan said nothing, his proud nature rising to give strength to his dislike of his captain. Swallowing his aversion, he focused intently on the ground.

However, his silence caught Gornhelm's attention, and Veryan could tangibly feel the tension rising in the air, like lightning waiting to strike. The captain raised his eyebrows as if expecting a response, but when Veryan remained mute, he demanded, "Well, boy? Are you going to respond to my order?"

Veryan raised his head and looked Gornhelm straight in the eyes, his insides squirming with rebellion. "No, sir," he said simply.

Gornhelm looked taken aback, and then he narrowed his eyes and walked off, saying something in a low voice to Comundus.

Pyralus grasped Veryan's arm and turned him around roughly. "Veryan, you shouldn't do things like that; he hates you enough already. You know he could have you whipped again, don't you?"

Veryan yanked his arm away, uncomfortably reminded of the time he had been punished when he was still a page for talking back to one of the older soldiers, who also happened to be one of Gornhelm's friends. He had been sentenced to seven lashes in front of the entire troop, which had damaged his pride more than anything else; the punishment had been relatively light as he had been only thirteen. But still, he was not eager to be punished in that way again, for now that he was eighteen, he knew the number of lashes would be much higher.

Pyralus continued, "If you keep acting like that, he will throw you out." His eyes were solemn and earnest, as if he wished Veryan would just listen to him for once and be sensible.

Veryan shrugged, trying not to show that the prospect did, indeed, frighten him for he truly would have nowhere else to go if he was ejected from the army. But he spoke flippantly, saying, "Let him; I could care less. In fact, I'd be happier if he did. Besides, he wouldn't; I'm too good an archer for him to lose." That, at least, was true. Gornhelm would never risk losing Veryan; he was not only the best archer in this troop but also one of the best among the others, as well.

He noticed Pyralus eyeing him disapprovingly, his friend's utter practicality showing clearly. "That may be, but don't let it go to your head," Pyralus warned.

Veryan bristled instinctively at the suggestion but knew Pyralus meant no harm, so he said nothing in reply.

Once they were dismissed, the boys walked toward the edge of the glen. Pyralus crossed his arms, tipped his head back to look at the sky, observed it for a long while, and then remarked softly, "I know you hate being a part of this troop, Veryan, but eventually you're going to have to accept that you are. You came here. You *asked* to join—"

"Don't tell me my past, Pyralus!" Veryan snapped harshly, annoyance blistering inside him along with a raging, consuming guilt. To be reminded of his past was to be reminded of something he should have never, ever agreed to do and something that had haunted him every day since he had. "I know it better than you."

Pyralus gave a short sigh of exasperation. "You're right, but I don't want you to get in trouble with Gornhelm. That's all." He paused by one of the pine trees and gazed up intently at its needled branches, looking as if he would very much like to climb it, but he made no move other than to reach out and brush his fingers through the spiny branches.

Veryan sighed and looked away, trying to suppress the remorse he felt for arguing with his oldest friend. It was not Pyralus's fault, after all, that Gornhelm hated him, and all Pyralus was trying to do was keep Veryan from being thrown out of the troop. He knew also that Veryan had nowhere else to go.

"What do you hope to gain by being so stubborn, anyway?" Pyralus asked, running his fingers lightly over the edge of one of the pine boughs.

Veryan sat down wearily, feeling frayed, and remained silent, tired of the argument; he hated fighting with Pyralus.

"Veryan?" There was a note of concern in his friend's voice.

He turned his head toward Pyralus, looking him over. Veryan knew he could not tell the older boy what had happened to make him come here and ask to be in the army and why he was always so angry and defensive. He could not tell Pyralus anything, not because he liked keeping secrets but because Pyralus would not—could not—understand. In fact, very few people could, and none that he knew of so far. And as for being stubborn … well, it was just in his nature. Veryan sighed heavily, drained from the constant weight of his past. He made no reply to Pyralus, other than rolling a twig between his fingers and snapping it.

Pyralus remained silent for a few minutes, his eyes scrutinising the forest with a look Veryan knew to mean he was listening, as he often did, to things Veryan could not hear. Pyralus had the most exceptional hearing of anyone he had ever met, and it was often very unsettling to Veryan. The boy could pick up on conversations from a great distance away and hear everything perfectly, which meant Veryan always had to be careful about what he said. Because of his ability, Gornhelm often used Pyralus as an invaluable scout, and the boy never failed him.

Pyralus turned to Veryan, hand on his dagger. "Want to go hunting in a little while?"

Even though he was feeling bone weary and sleep deprived, hunting sounded awfully good to Veryan just then; perhaps it would serve to keep his mind off things for a while, at least. However, at that present time, he did not think he could drag himself up, so he told Pyralus, tiredly, "Maybe in an hour or two. I just want to sleep right now, Pyralus."

Pyralus sighed but clapped his hand on Veryan's shoulder, saying, "Very well, then. I'll wake you soon."

⁂

Veryan gripped his bow tightly, his fingers pressed firmly against the wood, which was worn smooth from years of use, as he and Pyralus walked wordlessly through the forest, his dark eyes darting from tree to tree, scanning the forest for signs of anything unusual.

It was now late afternoon, and the sun cast long shadows on the forest floor. The trees were still, making it seem as if Pyralus and Veryan had walked into a painting. No breeze stirred their dry needles, and the air felt hot and heavy, as if a great storm was waiting to unleash its load. The thick air muffled their footsteps, making it seem as if they were walking on great swaths of heavy cloth, and made Veryan feel as if he was suffocating.

But he forced himself not to pay undue attention to the peculiar state of the motionless forest. It unnerved him, to be sure, and caused him to be a great deal edgier than normal, but he knew—or rather, he told himself—that there was nothing to be afraid of in the forest. They were the only ones there.

Pyralus sensed something too and seemed jumpy, constantly looking behind them and off to the sides as they walked. His eyes also searched the forest in front of them warily, roving back and forth as if examining guilty criminals, and his fist gripped tightly around his dagger. There was a suspicious, cagey look on his face, one Veryan understood to mean that Pyralus knew something more than he was telling him. What did his friend know that he did not?

"Pyralus," Veryan breathed, afraid to disturb the deafening silence, "what is it? Do you hear something?"

Pyralus looked irritably at Veryan, motioning for him to be quiet. His friend's eyes were veiled, and he looked as though he were listening intently, his head cocked slightly to one side. Veryan, impatient and beginning to feel nervous, hissed, "What is it?"

Suddenly a flock of crows took flight and cawed their alarm high above the trees, startling Veryan and bringing back violent, painful memories. He watched the black birds streak across the darkening sky, their wings pumping frantically as they hurried away, his mind racing back to similar birds and trees all those years ago …

Pyralus put his hand on Veryan's shoulder and said very softly, "Listen."

Veryan tried, standing as still as he could and letting himself become aware of everything around them. He could hear the dry rustling of the pines high above their heads; he could smell the rain in the air; he could feel the tension crackling in the stale air, like lightning waiting to strike. But he sensed nothing else out of the ordinary. What did Pyralus hear that he could not? "I don't hear anything," he told Pyralus quietly.

Pyralus cast another worried glance at the grey woods before them, silent and foreboding. Veryan began to feel agitated. What was it that Pyralus could hear that Veryan could not? "I think we should head back now," Pyralus said then, an edge of panic colouring his voice.

The instant they turned around, Veryan knew what it was that Pyralus had been sensing.

Seventeen soldiers and a small, hooded woman stood silently on the slopes of a bare, grassless knoll behind them and to their left. The warriors were garbed entirely in silver, including their armour and chain mail, with hair and eyes the colour of ravens' wings. Crossbows and quivers full of obsidian-tipped arrows peeked over their shoulders, and there were swords belted at each of their waists.

But their faces intimidated Veryan the most. Expressionless, stony and grave, their tanned faces looked as if they had just silently watched someone tortured and had not felt the slightest flicker of emotion. Their eyes remained blank, void of feeling, and yet contained a frightening hint of steel. They were dangerous, he knew, and it alarmed him how they simply stood, soundless and solemn, watching Pyralus and Veryan. Equally silent and cold stood the woman, her face shadowed by a velvet hood.

He heard Pyralus breathe a soft curse under his breath. Drawing Veryan's attention, however, was the soldier at the top of the low knoll, a boy a few years older than himself. The boy had no visible weapons, and his blue eyes and lighter skin made him stand out even more from the rest of them. But his face was no different. Unyielding and hard, it bore the signs of a well-worn soldier. No older than twenty at the most, he stood tall and straight, his head held high, as if some nobleman's wayward son, and he carried a certain air of dignity about him that made Veryan wonder why on earth he was there with such a group of common foot soldiers.

Clearly the soldiers' leader, he said something in a very low voice, not allowing Veryan to understand his words. Worried, Veryan glanced at Pyralus, who was staring at the men with eyes that held some kind of faint understanding, though coupled with a sort of uncertain awe, making Veryan speculate as to whether his friend knew these strange people. And if so, why had he not told Veryan about them?

The leader watched them for a long while, as if calculating, looking back and forth from Veryan to Pyralus, who stood frozen in place like deer found out by a determined hunter. Then the young man said to the men standing on the slope of the knoll behind him, "Kill them both. I want no one to know of our presence here."

Pyralus's blue eyes widened, and he instantly snapped at Veryan, "Go!"

The two boys turned and fled for the safety of the woods behind them, running as fast as they could will themselves to go, their legs pumping with elven muscle as they sprang over the pine needles littering their path. An obsidian-tipped arrow whistled past Pyralus, embedding itself into the trunk of the tree he had just passed. Pyralus cursed and stumbled but regained his footing almost instantly and with a rather uncanny air of grace.

Navigating through the forest swiftly was another matter entirely. It was tangled with low-hanging branches, dead limbs and twigs, and thick undergrowth in places. With all the obstacles, Pyralus and Veryan were slowed down to about the same pace as the soldiers, giving them no advantage and causing panic to rise in Veryan like a cauldron in danger of boiling over.

The men continued to shoot at them, missing mostly because the boys' movements were so much smoother and more fluid than their own that they could never quite predict where they would be a second later. Even so, Veryan kept thinking that at any moment he would feel an obsidian tip striking him from behind.

Suddenly, he felt his foot catch on something, and Veryan pitched forward into the dirt. He spat out a mouthful of dirt and quickly struggled to get back to his feet, ignoring his bleeding palms and stinging knees.

"Veryan!" Pyralus hissed, stopping to catch his arm and pulling Veryan up angrily and hurriedly. The nineteen-year-old looked behind them worriedly, and so did Veryan. The soldiers were close enough that Veryan could see the whites of their eyes now, and as he saw them run and began to piece everything together, he realized with a sickening flash that they were being pursued by *humans*.

Revulsion and hatred so strong it almost bowled him over rushed through Veryan's veins, heating his blood and making it roar in his ears. What on earth were *humans* doing here in Yaracina? How did they get here? But most important, *why* were they here? Veryan spat angrily at the ground, wishing he had enough time to fire a few arrows into each of their hearts. Humans were a lowly filth, in his opinion, on the same level as sewer rats, and it stung his dignity sorely to run away from such creatures.

Cursing once more, Pyralus shoved Veryan forward forcefully, and Veryan began to run again, hating himself for causing them to slow down. Pyralus was the faster runner, making Veryan have to sprint to keep up with him, and it was taxing him. Veryan's breaths began to come in short pants while Pyralus was still running strongly.

Suddenly Pyralus gave a hoarse cry and stumbled to the ground, falling to his hands and knees. Veryan pulled to a stop a few feet ahead, whirling around. Why had Pyralus fallen? Had he tripped? Veryan saw the answer protruding from Pyralus's side in the form of an obsidian-tipped arrow, the sight of which hit him as hard as if he had been struck himself. Stunned, Veryan just stared at him in a sort of frozen haze, his brain unable to process what was happening. Seconds later, another nicked Pyralus's leg enough to cause a shallow wound and made him gasp in pain from the combined injuries. At the same time, a torrent of memories, all excruciating and terrible, flooded into Veryan's mind. Numbed by the sight of the arrows, Veryan could only gape at Pyralus for a long moment, trying to regain himself, until a victorious cry from one of the approaching men drew him back to reality, banishing the recollections and forcing him to think about what was happening now. Fierce anger burned in Veryan's heart, fuelled subconsciously by his memories, and red dots swarmed over his vision, creating a violent set of mind. Veryan's quivering fingers nocked an arrow before he even realized he had moved, and he let it fly without thinking at one of the advancing men. It lodged in the man's throat, one of the few places not covered by armour, and he fell forward into the dirt with a rough cry, causing another to trip over his body.

"Veryan, what are you doing?" Pyralus snapped crossly, though his voice was coloured with pain. "Go! Get away from here!"

"Not without you!" Veryan retorted, furious that Pyralus would suggest such a thing. Did he think Veryan would just leave him there to die? Fighting as hard as he could to keep the memories of such a similar scene at bay and trembling from the effort, he tightened his grip around his bow as if that would give him the extra strength he needed to survive this fight.

"Veryan! Now's not the time for bravery! You'd be an idiot to stay here; do as I say, and *go!*" Pyralus said heatedly, his hand pressed against the wounds on his back, the red blood dripping down over his fingers and falling to wet the leaves below. "You've got to warn the others, Veryan. Please go."

"No!" Veryan protested angrily, nocking an arrow and shooting another soldier, who fell facedown to the forest floor. Anger and hate bloomed in his heart, and he fired them with every arrow, willing the darts to kill their intended targets. He could not think clearly for the red haze that was filling his mind, could not see anything but their silver armour glinting in the pale sunlight, could not feel anything but the burning anger streaming through his veins. He *needed* to kill these soldiers. How dare they shoot Pyralus in the back while they were running away! Only cowards killed their enemies from behind.

He gave a small gasp from the violence of his roiling emotions.

"Veryan, listen to me!" Pyralus snapped angrily, his blue eyes blazing. Veryan paused, slightly lowering his bow, the red haze dissipating slightly around his mind at the sound of Pyralus's voice. "You need to get back to camp and tell the rest of the men before these soldiers find them! Please!" Pyralus paused to suck in air, his chest heaving with the effort of trying to breathe with the arrow piercing his back. The sight of the crimson blood running over his friend's hand enraged Veryan, but he forced himself to relax the taut string of his bow, banishing the recollections from his mind and attempting to think logically, as the older boy so often did. *Think, Veryan*, he urged himself. *Think! What should you do?* Pyralus was right. But how could he leave Pyralus here to die? He was his only friend …

Veryan ducked out of the way of a flying obsidian arrow and cursed his situation. Pyralus had ordered him to leave him there, so he would have to do it; his upbringing and the past seven years he had spent as a soldier left no choice but to try to make it back to the camp. He glanced at his dying friend, whose breath was getting shallower. Veryan could only hope and pray now; he could do nothing more.

Veryan glanced at the approaching soldiers, then at Pyralus. How could he do this to his friend? Feeling torn, Veryan finally cursed once more and spun on his heel, sprinting off into the forest with twice the speed of a fleeing deer. He paid no mind to the twigs and branches that whipped across his face as he ran, not heeding the lines of blood that the wood caused to appear on his face when they smacked against his skin in his haste, nor paying any attention to his still-bleeding palms and skinned knees. He just had to get away. From the soldiers, from Pyralus, from the cowardly part of himself that was all too prominent now. He should not have left Pyralus. But he had no choice now; he had to keep running. He had to keep running.

꒰

Pyralus could not see well. The ground blurred before his eyes, mixing the colours of the dirt and grass together into one murky blob, making him want to vomit with the dizziness that was overtaking him. Agonisingly sharp jolts of pain vibrated in his ribs every few seconds, making involuntary tears spring to his eyes and instinctive gasps of pain leave his lips. One hand was pressed feebly over his wound, and he could feel the hot, dark liquid flowing down over his fingers; the other was weakly supporting him, keeping him from falling face down against the forest floor. He was completely disoriented. The world seemed to spin around him, making him feel even worse.

A violent kick in his wounded side sent him crashing to the earth. The pain was so intense that Pyralus let himself succumb to unconsciousness for a moment, glad for the momentary relief. But when his eyes fluttered open a few seconds later, he was met with a quite dreadful sight. One of the stone-faced humans stood over him, another black-tipped arrow pointed at his heart. The man's black eyes stared into Pyralus's blue ones with fiery disgust and Pyralus knew the man would not hesitate to release the dart, thus ending his life.

Pyralus sagged helplessly against the ground, closing his eyes wearily and waiting for the pain and darkness that would come with the final arrow. It would be a relief from the excruciating pain that was sweeping over him in violent waves now, anyway.

Instead, Pyralus heard the young leader say hurriedly to his soldier in a low voice, "Leave him, Jakob; he'll die on his own. We still need to kill the other one, and he's nearly out of sight." And then came the sound of the men continuing on past Pyralus, their worn leather boots making dull, soft sounds on the forest floor. Soon, their footsteps faded into the distance, leaving Pyralus wounded, bleeding, and dying on the forest floor.

He closed his eyes, feeling a dull stiffness beginning to drape over his limbs. The searing fire in his side remained, but if he lay totally still, he could numb it and, maybe, almost without pain, drift off. He knew death would come, so he did not try to get up and make it back to camp; it would likely only kill him more painfully. Instead, Pyralus lay on the forest floor, in a pool of his own blood, until night fell over the world, and he passed into the realm of dreams.

INTENTIONS

I lowered my bow after my last shot, a frown creasing my brow as I eyed my shot critically. The arrow was barely touching the innermost white ring painted on the tree's trunk. It was a small reward for the past two hours I had spent, nocking, releasing, and fetching over and over again.

Frustrated, I stalked up to the trees and yanked the arrow out, my fingers trembling. The stone point was beginning to dull from the past hours of practise, and I grudgingly switched to a fresh, sharp arrow. The two fingers I used to pull back the string were aching, the muscles under my skin feeling worn and tender, but I pulled the cord back to my cheek resolutely, determined that I would hit my target.

I practised my archery every day for two hours with the goal of becoming a more accurate archer than my current status—quite terrible. Only in the past week had I succeeded in hitting the target at all. I was in no way a skilled archer, but my efficiency lay more with the bow than with the sword. With a sword in my hand, I was much more likely to hurt myself than anyone else. My reflexes much too slow for me to fight well with a sword, my twin sister, Malitha, insisted on sparring with me every few nights in an attempt to hone my skills with the blade, but so far, she had wasted her time upon me.

I let the arrow fly. It zipped through the air and lodged in the tree about two inches from the innermost white circle this time, farther away from my target than the last shot.

Cross and tired, I gave up, not even bothering to retrieve my arrow. I sullenly sat down on the mass of convoluted tree roots that sprung from the earth under our home in the trees. I craned my neck back in order to see it. It was a three-story house built of silverwood, the kind of tree that was native to my home in Aseamir, and it was fixed in between a fork in the tree's branches, almost two hundred feet off the forest floor. The silverwood staircase wound around the tree's massive trunk, its circumference wide enough to be encircled by seventy men with outstretched arms. Our city had the largest and tallest trees on our entire continent, but only the families on the outskirts of the walled city actually lived in them. The rest of the Aseamirians lived inside the forty-foot stone walls that protected the borders of the large city. My family was about half a mile into the forest, and my mother, Aubryn, often sent Malitha and me into the city to buy the things we could not produce at home.

I dropped my gaze from our house and wearily leaned back against the roots, flexing my aching fingers, trying to work out some of the pain.

"I say, Elysia. Two hours of practise, and you *still* can't hit the centre?" I heard my sister say nearby, and I rolled my eyes. As the older twin, I had the advantage—however slight—of age, which made Malitha competitive and childish, often berating me for things she could not do any better and preferring to tell me about the boy in town that had caught her eye that day.

"You can't do any better, Malitha," I retorted, glaring at my younger sister crossly.

She tossed her golden hair flippantly and sat down beside me primly. "I know, but at least I dedicate my time to … more important things than pursuing a sport I'm no good at, Elysia. You're not getting any better, I promise you that."

My irritation arose, fanned by two hours' worth of blisters on my fingers and knowing that what Malitha said was true. But instead of retorting with an equally insulting remark, I simply took my bow and ascended the stairs, leaving Malitha and her exasperating talk behind.

Malitha and I had once been best friends, never arguing, never contradicting, never cruel. We had done everything together, always concurrent, as twins should be. But once Malitha and I had turned sixteen, she had decided that she was better than I was. She had begun to exclude herself from me and our younger sister, Lillian, preferring to stay inside with Aubryn and help her with the housework. She also loved to go into town, just to visit her friends. She never had time for Lillian or me anymore, and she treated Lillian as though she were a bothersome little pest, even though Lillian was fourteen years old.

We were both seventeen now, and things were only getting worse. Malitha thought she was terribly superior to me and treated me with snobbish disdain that made me want both to kill her and to curl up and just cry. I missed my old sister dreadfully, wishing that she would regain her senses and realize that I was her sister and her twin, not her slave. Mother told me that this phase would pass, but I was not entirely sure. It had been going on for a long time, and I was worried that it would never end.

I came to the top of the stairs and opened the door to our home, stepping inside. Lillian was sitting by a bookshelf, a large, dusty book in her lap. Her golden hair, so different from my own dark red, glinted like strands of gold in the light that was spilling through the window by the bookshelf. Lillian looked up, her brown eyes sparkling as she saw me and greeted me fondly. I returned the greeting, smiling at her, and then asked where our mother was. Lillian directed me to the top floor.

I walked up the stairs to the third floor, the one of the three levels that we girls only rarely used. Aubryn often came up here, however, sometimes disappearing for hours behind the closed door. I wondered what she did up there, all by herself, but I had never found the courage to ask her; it was probably nothing very exciting, anyway. I knocked lightly and pushed the door open, it sliding smoothly across the worn floor.

Aubryn was rifling intently through some grimy old scrolls and books, as if she were searching desperately for something but could not find it. Engrossed as she was in her frantic hunt, she did not hear me come inside.

I waited for a moment, watching her, and then cleared my throat. Aubryn jerked up, brown eyes finding mine instantly. Her golden hair was tangled about her face, having come loose from its tie, and her eyes looked faintly frenetic. However, upon seeing me there, all of the lines of worry eased from her face, and she gave a relaxed smile, but I knew the anxiety of her search had not left her.

Aubryn waded through the books, scrolls, and other unused items on the floor over to me, stepping lithely with elven grace around the obstacles. "Hello, my dear," she said, smiling fondly at me, her British accent still very heavy, even though it had been many years since she had left that ancient country. In a moment, she stood before me, beaming with a motherly smile. "How are you? I've hardly seen you at all today."

I forced myself to smile, still wondering what she had been looking for, but not intending to ask her. "I'm fine, Mother. I've just been practising my archery for a few hours, and I came in once Malitha started criticising me again." I frowned at her, all my previous irritation re-arising, and absentmindedly rubbed my sore fingers, the pain in my hand distracting me from the pain in my heart. Why did my sister have to treat me so?

Aubryn sighed, well aware of my twin's tendency to do so. "I'm sorry, Elysia," she said apologetically, "but I believe this will all pass in a few months. Malitha's just growing up; that's all." She gave a reassuring smile, but I was not convinced.

"If she's growing up, then why is she acting like a child more than ever?" I asked imploringly.

Aubryn sighed again. "I don't know, dear. I just don't know. But come; let's not ruin this beautiful day with talk of your sister's pettiness." As she said this, she stepped over a few more books and led me back down the stairs, closing the door to the third floor behind us, sealing away whatever secret she had been searching for.

We came back to the first floor, where Lillian was still reading. My youngest sister glanced up briefly and then continued reading. Aubryn went over to the small iron stove and pulled out an iron pot from a cabinet. "Lillian, would you fill this with water, please?" she asked, and Lillian bounced up, abandoning her book to do what Aubryn asked.

"Of course," Lillian said, smiling at her mother as she took the pot and hurried out the door to fill the pot with water from the large brook that flowed past our house. I smiled as I leaned against the windowsill, watching my little sister, who was so much like Malitha had been before she turned sixteen, jog quickly down the winding staircase. Lillian and I had become closer than ever since Malitha's stubborn persistence in segregating herself from us had begun, and she was perhaps dearer to me now than Malitha had ever been. Bright and lively, Lillian was a perfect copy of Malitha, only without the pettiness and immaturity. Malitha and I were so different, especially for twins, that I often wondered how we could even be sisters.

"Elysia, would you mind terribly going into town for me in a few days?" Aubryn asked as she began slicing vegetables. "The Midsummer's Eve Festival is coming up, you know, and there are some things I'm going to need. You can get some new arrows while there, too. I know you're down to only three."

"Of course. It's been terribly boring around here lately anyway," I replied with a smile, still watching Lillian down at the river. Our father was away on business in one of the southern cities, Rielture, and would not be returning for a few more weeks. Aubryn relied on me as the oldest to help her get things done while Father was gone, and while I was happy enough to help, I wished that Malitha would help me with the chores as well, as Lillian did, and not try to coerce me into doing hers for her. We used to work as a team, back when she was not so immature, and I missed doing our household jobs together.

But I hardly counted going into town for my mother a chore; I greatly enjoyed it. Two of my closest friends, Laela and her younger brother, Garrett, lived within the walls, and I loved seeing them every chance I could. Garrett ran the archery shop in town, and he was the one who had gotten me interested in archery in the first place. Laela and I had been good friends ever since I could remember, and I was pleased that I would be able to see them soon.

"What do you need?" I asked my mother.

She gave me a long list, and I felt my heart sink as it went on and on. Perhaps I would not have time to see my friends, after all. Even though I knew where everyone's booths were, Aseamir was not a particularly small city, and it took a good amount of time to meander through the crowds and find everything. It could also be especially difficult if the booth-tenders had run out of something, for then one had to track it down somewhere else, and there was never any guarantee that the needed item could be found.

I pursed my lips. "Why can't I just go today?" I asked when my mother was done.

Aubryn paused to wipe her knife on her apron. "Well," she said, "it's Saturday, and you know the markets are most crowded on Saturday. Wait until Tuesday when it's more likely the things I need will be there. Is that all right? I suppose you could go today if you really wanted to, but—"

"No, I'll wait," I sighed. I had forgotten today was Saturday. I loathed big crowds, especially in a market, for there were so many shouts and angry voices and people tripping all over each other … I could wait to see my friends. It was only a few days more, besides.

"Oh, and Elysia," Aubryn went on, "I forgot to tell you, but your father needs you to do something for him. He was planning to travel on to Hartford City from Rielture to pick up some important papers he needs, but he's been delayed and won't be able to get them in time."

That piqued my interest. "What does he need them for?" I asked, turning around to face my mother and leaning against the windowsill. I had an interest in many of the other cities in Yaracina, especially Hartford City, which was the capital, because I had never been to any of them, and for as long as I could remember, I had dreamed of visiting these large, sophisticated places where the women wore elegant dresses and the men were dashingly polite. So had Laela and Malitha, and we still did, occasionally. But the only one who ever got to see those grand places was our father, though I had often begged him to take me with him when I was younger, and laughing, he had kissed my cheek and told me that when I was older he would take me to all the grand parties and places my sisters and I had dreamed of as children.

"For some business he's doing with a couple of his colleagues," Aubryn answered, measuring a spice carefully before adding it to the bowl before her.

Considering this, I was silent for a while. "So … he wants me to go and fetch papers for him?" I asked, trying to figure the situation out whilst also trying not to let myself get too excited.

"Yes."

"Where will I get them? Is there someone there that has them for Father?" My heart began to beat faster.

Aubryn nodded. "Yes. His name is William Ar-Braidan; he's a friend of your father's, and he's got the papers. All you'll have to do is ask for him at the Melbourne Inn, get the papers, and bring them home. It'll be a long but easy journey, and you'll be able to get out and see some of the world, as you've always wanted."

I hid a pleased smile, secretly bursting with excitement but trying to be mature about it all. "All right, then; I'll go. When should I leave?" I asked, proud that my voice showed no hint of my inner exhilaration.

Aubryn thought about it for a long moment, the only sound in the kitchen that of her small knife slicing through a wild onion. "Thursday," she said after a while. "That will give you time to get everything together after you get back from town, and there won't be many people on the roads this early. The festival's still far enough away that travellers won't be leaving yet. Is that all right?"

"I suppose … That's all he wants me to do? Find William Ar-Braidan and bring the papers back?" I asked, just to make sure.

"Yes. That's all … Elysia—" Aubryn started, but right then Lillian came back inside, the pot full of water. She smiled cheerfully at Aubryn and me, her sweet face brightening, and she set the pot dutifully on the stove. Then she returned to her book by the shelf, her brown eyes bright with anticipation as she resumed reading.

Aubryn bit her lip and fell silent, her dark eyes unsure. I knew she had been about to say something else, and I wondered what it was. A little put out that Lillian had come in at the wrong moment, I turned back to face the window and leaned against it again, feeling the light breeze ruffle my hair and gently feather across my face, whispering rumours and fantasies of what was coming to me as I tried to collect everything and process it all.

After a while, I turned back to look at Lillian, examining my little sister absently, who was still poring over her storybook. Personally, I did not approve of her obsession with stories and fairy tales, such as the ones about humans, fire-tamers, and Apparates, knowing very well that they were not real. However, I must admit that the stories intrigued me as well, though I did not obsess over them as Lillian did.

When I was younger, I had asked Aubryn why my friends Laela and Garrett did not pronounce words the same way I did, and she had told me that it was because my sisters and I had British accents, having been brought up by parents who were born and raised in England. Naturally, that had intrigued me, and while I had been curious about stories about such faraway places for a time, now Aubryn told them only for Lillian's benefit.

"I'm going down to the stables for a bit," I said to Aubryn, and I opened the door and descended the stairs, feeling in need of some solitude.

⟳

Given to me by my father on my fifteenth birthday, Benthey was a roan Arabian stallion and a very beautiful one at that. A grey stallion called Xanthis had been gifted to Malitha. Sometimes my closest friend, Benthey would hear my most troubling concerns. I could count on him always just to listen and never argue or contradict. And with a bothersome sister like mine, making all her demands and complaining about every little thing, it was always nice just to come here and relax.

Benthey lifted his head when I came in, his brown eyes meeting mine. He shook his mane and then lowered his head, continuing to nibble on the hay at his feet, blowing out softly and scattering a few strands of grass from the pile. Xanthis, in a stall across from Benthey's, also lifted his head, inspected me, and then nickered softly, shaking his mane at me. I smiled at him as I walked to Benthey's stall.

Benthey lifted his head again as I came to a stop before him. He nudged my shoulder fondly, and I smiled and scratched his forelock. "Mother's asked me to go to Hartford City to bring back some documents for Father," I told him. "I think it's going to be quite boring, just going there and back, just fetching some old papers ..." Benthey eyed me disinterestedly.

"But, you know," I told him, "I'm actually very happy that I'm having to go all the way to Hartford City. Maybe I'll meet some interesting new people and see some new places ... That would be nice. You know, I've never even been out of Aseamir before ... It'll be a nice change, and maybe I'll get to go to one of those fancy parties I used to dream about when I was little. You think?" I said in a whisper, knowing full well that what I was saying was nothing more than child's talk. Benthey gave a low nicker, almost as if he were agreeing with me.

I smiled at him. "Would you like to get out of this old stable and take a ride with me?" I stroked his red mane fondly, and Benthey nudged my hand with his big nose.

I smiled again and took his bridle from a hook on the post of his stall and then unlatched the door. Benthey tossed his mane excitedly, knowing what was coming next. But when he walked out of his stall, he was limping, avoiding putting pressure on one of his hind hooves. Frowning, I knelt down and tapped his foot. He obediently lifted it for me. Once he had, I saw that his iron horseshoe was broken. Most of the shoe was missing, but a small piece of it was embedded in his hoof, no doubt making it hard and painful to walk.

I put my hands on the iron piece and tried to pry it out, but succeeded only in making my horse jerk his leg, nearly hitting my head. I fell back on my backside with a startled exclamation. Benthey snorted, and his leg muscles twitched. I got up and calmed the horse, stroking his nose, and thinking. *He can't keep that broken iron in his hoof. Even if I weren't going to Hartford City, he would still need to have it removed. But who …?* I tapped my fingers on Benthey's shoulder, trying to think of who in Aseamir could replace his horseshoe before I left. Frowning in displeasure at not being able to remember the name of the local blacksmith, I pushed my hair out of my eyes and tilted my head back, groaning. I knew I should know it, but every time I nearly had the name, it escaped my mind again. *Oh, I hate it when I can't remember something that's important!* Suddenly, I recalled the name as the person's face popped into my mind.

"Oh, Alqua! Right!" I wondered how I could have forgotten him. He lived in a modest, two-story house on the outskirts of Aseamir and worked in a forge behind his house. He was young at eighteen but, by far, the greatest smith I had ever known. His parents had died of a peculiar disease several winters ago after they had travelled to the southernmost part of Yaracina, which was said to be occupied with strange people with supernatural abilities. Orphaned at the age of fifteen, Alqua had been taken in by the city's previous blacksmith, Juro, as his young apprentice.

In only three years, Alqua had proved himself worthy of the trade, and Juro had since moved on to another town, Rhona, where the people were in need of an experienced blacksmith. A shy, quiet young man, Alqua kept mostly to himself. My father knew Alqua well, however, because of his horse-trading business and had great respect for him. Even though I greatly liked Alqua and thought he was an uncommonly skilled blacksmith for his age, people generally left him alone except when they needed his service. I also knew that Malitha fancied him, which I thought quite ridiculous.

Still frustrated with myself for forgetting the name, I turned the horse around, back into his stall and left, promising Benthey that his shoe would soon be replaced. He responded only by looking back at me with a solemn look in his deep brown eyes.

ᴥ

I returned to the house, pausing to watch Lillian struggling to shoot an arrow. The bow she was using was mine and too big for her. Once she had managed to pull the string back, she could not hold it long enough to get the arrow positioned and release it, as she spent most of her time reading and collecting plants, not practising with us. Frowning in frustration, Lillian kept trying but was not able to string the bow.

I smiled and walked up to her, saying, "Having some trouble with that?"

Lillian lowered the bow, relaxing the string and scowling at it, and looked up at me. "Yes," she said, sounding a bit irritated with her lack of results.

"Well, for one thing, this bow's too big for you. You know you're not strong enough to be using mine yet; you don't practise enough. Where's yours?" I asked her.

Lillian shrugged. "I don't know. I couldn't find it, and I saw yours, so …"

"You lost your bow, Lillian?" I demanded disapprovingly. Father had made each of us a bow on our thirteenth birthdays, and while Malitha and I had outgrown and replaced ours, Lillian's was still the right size for her.

Lillian avoided my eyes sheepishly. "I'll find it," she promised me. "But I'm so close on this one! Could you just help me now, and then I'll go look for my bow? It won't take long."

I sighed, annoyed with Lillian because she had lost her bow, but she was right—she nearly had managed to shoot this one. All she needed was for me to advise her as she nocked the arrow, and with a few more tries, I knew she could do it. "All right," I agreed. "When you pull the string back, be sure to keep your grip strong and steady; don't shake, if you can help it. Keep that arm straight."

Lillian did as I directed, fitting the arrow's nock firmly onto the string before pulling back, and to my relief, she was able to hold the bow for a few seconds more before she had to slacken the string. "Well, I'm almost there," she said decisively. "It just hurts the back of my arm."

"Keep trying," I encouraged her. "Once you get a little stronger, it'll be much easier. Just keep your muscles tight and hold on as long as you can."

She tried once more, and keeping the sting taut long enough, Lillian had time to aim in the general direction of the tree. She released the arrow quickly, and it struck the largest circle of the painted tree. "Yes!" she exclaimed, a happy grin lighting up her face.

"Well done!" I told her. "See? Just a few more tries was all you needed."

My sister smiled at me. "Thanks, Elysia. I'll keep practising, and—"

"First, go find your bow," I reminded her, and with a laugh that told me she had already forgotten it, she darted off to the house, leaving my bow on the ground. Shaking my head and smiling, I picked it up and carried it with me back to the house.

Bounding up the steps, I poked my head inside before entering. Aubryn was there, stirring a simmering pot of stew. She looked up in surprise as I came into the room, and I hung my bow on its hook in the hallway. Setting down the spoon, she wiped her hands on a clean cloth as I came into the kitchen, saying, "Do you have anything I could use to trade?"

"Why? Are you going somewhere? I thought you weren't going to leave for Asea—"

"I'm going to Alqua's. Benthey has a broken horseshoe, and I need to get it replaced before I go to town on Tuesday."

Aubryn frowned. She watched me for several minutes, her brow creased in thought. "Come up to the second floor; I'll see what I have." I followed her up the steps.

When we reached the second floor, Aubryn asked me, "How long will you be gone?" I almost laughed at the unneeded concern in my mother's voice.

"I don't know, but I'll have to stay until Alqua finishes the horseshoe. Benthey will get nervous if I'm not there when he's in an unfamiliar place."

Aubryn raised her eyebrows, looking as if she were about to question my sanity.

"He's a *horse*," Aubryn said tactfully.

"Yes, I'm aware of that," I muttered, retrieving my deerskin pack from under my bed. Aubryn handed me several items to trade to Alqua in return for the horseshoe. I was acutely aware of two brown eyes intensely watching my every move as I began filling my pack.

When finished, I sat back on my bed and looked up at my mother. Aubryn blinked and waved her hand. "Just don't be gone a long time. I'm going to need your help preparing for the festival," she reminded me.

I nodded and shouldered my pack.

"I'm ready," I said.

∽

The leather tied smoothly under my fingers as I knotted my pack straps to Benthey's saddle. The red roan tossed his mane and eyed me with a bored expression, obviously not very eager to leave the stables. I patted his neck as I finished tying my pack. In addition to the pack, I also tied a bedroll onto the saddle, in case I should have to be gone overnight. Aubryn, Lillian, and Malitha stood at the base of the silverwood tree, waiting to see me off. The sun was a blinding disc high in the sky.

I took a deep breath and exhaled slowly. Though I knew I would have to come back before leaving for Hartford City, I could not help feeling that this was the start of my adventure. In the depths of my mind, I had a growing feeling that my trip to Hartford City would involve much more than a routine trip to pick up papers for Father. I sensed that something far greater was being interwoven into my destiny, and this, my first step, marked the new beginning and the exodus of my old life.

After saying a hurried goodbye to my sisters and mother, I led Benthey through the silverwood trees, the sun glinting on the dagger belted at my waist. Without looking back, I headed away from Aseamir toward Alqua's home about ten or fifteen miles away in the forest at the edge of the Salquessaé Plains. I had been there a number of times before with my father and was fairly certain I would be able to find it on my own. I would have to go slowly, though, since

Benthey was already limping, and I did not want to cause serious damage to his hoof.

After half an hour, I stopped for a quick rest and a bite of food. I picketed Benthey near a patch of lush grass, and then dug an apple out of my pack. Relaxing, I sat on a large, flat rock in a tiny clearing as birds twittered and spiralled overhead in the clear, azure sky.

The beauty and simplicity of the natural world enchanted my mind, and I loved spending every second that I could enjoying it. I breathed deeply, letting the aromatic smell flood my senses. I closed my eyes.

A few minutes later, I got up and gave the remainder of my apple to Benthey. I also poured several handfuls of water from my waterskin for the horse to drink. Then checking to make sure no straps had come loose on the saddle, I mounted the roan and rode on slowly towards Alqua's home.

A couple of hours passed, and then the line of trees gently dipped inward, as if a bite had been taken out of the foliage. I could now see the tan grasses of the Salquessaé through the web of tree branches and white clouds floating lazily in the soaring heights of the sky above. I murmured, "Whoa," to Benthey and reined him to a halt. The roan stallion snorted and came to a stop. I shaded my eyes to shield the sun as I inspected Alqua's house.

The simple two-story building was built on the ground underneath the shade of the silverwood trees. A barn was barely visible through the trees to the side of the house, and Alqua's workshop was located in a clearing behind the house. The sun slanted through the vibrantly bright leaves to illuminate a distant figure moving about the clearing.

I smiled and dismounted. Benthey pawed the ground and followed me, limping even more now after the ride. As we entered under the green canopy, leafy shadows fell on the two of us.

A pair of foxes darted in front of Benthey, and he startled, rearing back slightly. I tightened my grasp on his reins and said soothingly, "Hey, whoa, boy. They won't hurt you, all right? Easy, now." Benthey calmed at the sound of my voice and tossed his mane.

I turned my eyes back to the scene in front of me. By now, Alqua had seen us and was walking toward us, wiping his hands on a dingy cloth. His startlingly dark eyes probed me thoughtfully as he stopped in front of me. I dipped my head and put my hand on Benthey's shoulder. For a long, awkward moment, the only sound was the twittering of the birds and Benthey's heavy breathing. Then Alqua turned and motioned with his hand for me to follow.

ALQUA

 seated myself across from Alqua on a stump that had been fashioned into a seat. The tanned smith silently offered me a cup of spring water. I took it slowly and drank, uncomfortably conscious of his searching eyes on my face.

When the last drop was gone, I set the cup down on the ground and turned my attention to Alqua, who was gazing around the forest.

Finally, he broke the silence between us: "Where is your father?" Alqua's voice was so soft, I had to strain my ears to hear it. His voice sounded worn and tired, as if he had used it too much, although living alone out here in the forest, I wondered how that could be possible. I shifted my gaze to Benthey, who was grazing on a patch of grass, before answering.

"My father left several weeks ago for Rielture and won't be back for a few more. My horse, Benthey, has a hind horseshoe that's broken and a piece of it has embedded into his hoof. I'm going to be travelling to Hartford City during the Midsummer's Eve Festival, and he needs to be fit for the trip. I—"

"And I suppose you want me to replace his shoe?" Alqua snapped, his eyes narrowed slightly. I clamped my mouth shut, taken aback. *This isn't like him. He's usually willing to help. I wonder what's wrong today.*

I chose my words carefully. "Yes, if it's not too much trouble. You've always helped my family before, and I'd be honoured if you'd help us again. I brought some things to trade …."

Alqua grunted and stood up tiredly. He turned and slowly headed toward his barn. I scrambled to my feet and trotted after him. Alqua entered the barn and walked to the far end. There he stopped and leaned against the doorframe, his back facing me and his arms crossed. He seemed to be lost in thought. I paused behind him. It did not seem wise to break the silence just yet.

I continued to wait without a word as Alqua stared into the depths of the lush forest through the open door. The seconds stretched into minutes before he began to speak. When he did, he said quietly, "I'm sorry I was so curt, Elysia. Your family has always traded generously for my services, and for that I should be grateful." He turned and walked over to me. Though his eyes gleamed in the sunlight, there was a look of despair in them. Alqua's shoulders dropped as he sighed. "Business has been scant these past months on account of the rumours people have been hearing. They're too frightened to leave the city to come all the way out here, and I've gotten frustrated trying to work everything out on my own, but that's no excuse to treat you badly." He paused and looked away briefly before continuing, "Come; let's take a look at your horse's hoof." The smith proceeded to walk past me and out the other door. I was confused about what had just happened. *One minute, he's snapping at me, and the next, he's apologising to me?* I exhaled heavily and shook my head, hurrying after Alqua.

꙳

"I'll have to remove the embedded piece, clean the wound, and wrap his hoof for a while. It'll bleed when I take it out," Alqua announced as he inspected Benthey's injured hoof. I stood over Alqua, watching his every move. I did not want Benthey accidentally kicking Alqua if the smith did something that hurt my horse.

Alqua stood up, wiping his hands on his leather pants. "All right," he said, "bring him into the barn." He strode across the clearing into his workshop, leaving me to lead Benthey. The horse held his hoof in the air, hobbling after me on three legs. Having to make the trip from Aseamir with the broken piece in his hoof had obviously made Benthey's foot even more tender, and I watched him with concern. However, the horse seemed steady enough to make it to the barn.

Once there, I led Benthey to an unused stall next to a sorrel mare. I absently stroked the stallion's velvety nose and allowed my thoughts to wander until Alqua came. The smith had a hoof pick in one hand and fresh bandages in the other.

But as I continued to stand and look over his shoulder, Alqua turned his piercing gaze onto me with a look that I interpreted to mean he did not want me there. I meekly exited the stall and sat on a stool outside, but positioned myself where I could watch. Alqua knelt beside Benthey and grasped his hind hoof. The roan tried to jerk his foot back, but Alqua held it firmly. The horse surrendered when he realized he was under the smith's control.

Alqua examined Benthey's hoof carefully before continuing. Then he laid his tanned hand on the iron piece that was implanted in Benthey's hoof. I noticed that blood stained the area that surrounded it, and I curled my lip in distaste at the sight.

Alqua hesitated before attempting to remove the rooted shard. He turned his dark eyes on me with an unreadable look. "Could you possibly …," he paused as he thought of the right words, "not be here for this? I … I need to do something for the horse that I don't want you to see." Alqua seemed troubled and a small edge of urgency crept into his voice.

I frowned. I had wanted to make sure that Benthey would be all right and did not want to leave him. *Alqua must have a good reason for not wanting me here*, I determined, but I was still reluctant to part with my stallion. I exhaled and forced myself to say, "All right. Where do you want me to go?"

Surprise flitted over Alqua's face quickly, so quickly I wondered if it had been there at all. Amusement followed an instant later as I realized Alqua had not expected me to agree so readily. The smith ran his fingers through his dark hair before answering. I noticed he seemed very nervous and anxious for me to leave.

"Wherever you want. Just stay out of the house," he replied shortly.

I turned and walked out of the barn, trying hard to ignore my curiosity and concern. I forced myself to remove all thoughts of going back. Instead, I focused my attention on the forest, which seemed to beckon me into its relaxed and carefree surroundings.

～

I woke with a start, wondering how long I had been there. My forehead was beaded with sweat, and my hands were clammy. Still breathing heavily, I attempted to calm myself, as vivid images of my dream flooded my mind.

I saw a red sky with smoke curling into its four corners. Dead bodies of a great army populated the ashen field beneath the sky. Blood stained the ground, as though a crimson river had flooded the war field. Crows and vultures perched in scrubby bushes, preparing to devour the bloodied corpses, their beady eyes eagerly scrutinizing the dead … Then I saw a lone figure standing amongst the dead. He clutched a long sword with a ruby in its pommel, and he had dark hair, but his face was hidden. The young soldier looked around the field, spotted something, and ran over to a motionless body. Trembling, he touched his fingers to the person's face and then let out an anguished cry, collapsing to his knees on the blood-drenched ground. Tears streamed down his face as he knelt over the body before him, his shoulders shaking with silent sobs.

Suddenly I saw another person, a girl who I recognized to be myself, standing not far away, watching the boy weep. A tormented and aggrieved expression painted her face, and even as I watched, a tear rolled down her cheek. After a moment, she went to the dark-haired boy and put an arm around his shoulders, and they sat there together, tears falling down both their faces.

I shuddered. I had had premonitions before, and I knew that they were not like other dreams, simply to be taken lightly or ignored. In my experience, premonitions had startling clarity and had proven almost always to be entirely accurate. I used to have them fairly often, but they were not so common anymore, and this one was the first in a long while.

I shook my head. *That couldn't have been a premonition. There've been so few wars in our history, and our only enemies are extinct. Maybe it was just a dream,* I tried to assure myself. But it had seemed so real …

I let out a shuddering breath and leaped down from the tree in which I had been sleeping. I headed back towards Alqua's barn.

౫

"Is he all right?" I queried as I leaned down to inspect Benthey's hoof. As he lifted his foot, I let out a gasp. The hoof where the broken horse-shoe had been firmly rooted showed no sign that it had ever been injured, and only unmarked skin covered the area between the edges of his new shoe. It looked just as perfect as it had before Benthey's injury. *How could that be?* I wondered silently.

I frowned and looked at Alqua. His face was pale and drawn. His usually luminous eyes were markedly dull. "What did you do?" I asked him suspiciously, standing upright. Though I was slightly alarmed at his unusual appearance, I was also very curious to know what Alqua had done to heal Benthey so completely.

Alqua sighed and leaned against the door. "I used magic, Elysia, to heal your horse," he said tiredly and then continued hesitantly. "I went with my parents down south several times when I was younger, and someone there taught me how to use it." Alqua ran his fingers through his black hair, looking fatigued.

Confused, I cocked my head. *What does he mean, magic? What is magic?* I looked again at Benthey's miraculously healed hoof. Frowning, I turned back to Alqua. He was watching my face anxiously.

"What is magic, Alqua? Is it dangerous? Of course, I've heard Malitha mention something about it once or twice to my mother, but I never asked what it was," I said, curious yet cautious.

Alqua sighed again and shook his head. "It's not something you need to get into, Elysia. Magic is … well, it's *magic*. I don't know how to describe it, but it's not dangerous unless you use it in the wrong way or use too much of it at one time. Healing Benthey's foot was probably more than I should have done at one time." As if to coincide with his words, Alqua wobbled, and he sank onto the stool where I had been sitting earlier.

Concerned, I enquired, "Does it take energy from your body when you use magic?" Alqua's lips lifted in grim amusement. "Only when you use too much at a time." His eyes flickered to my face. "I don't want you using magic. If you're not strong enough and you use too much, it would kill you. I shouldn't have even told you about it. And," he said, eyeing me, "I don't think you could use it, anyway."

Alqua leaned his head against the stall and closed his eyes. I frowned and looked at Benthey. The horse tossed his mane and whinnied. I was curious about this new concept but not unduly so. Several times, Malitha had said something about it to Aubryn, and somehow, it seemed Alqua had always turned up in the conversation. But since I did not really know Alqua very well, or care, I had never questioned Malitha about it. But now I wanted to know. "How do you use magic?"

A long sigh preceded Alqua's answer. "Elysia, I think it's time you were heading home. I'm not going to tell you anything more about magic except this: *Forget about it*. It's not worth it."

I looked at him unhappily. "Fine," I said grudgingly. I untied my pack from Benthey's saddle, which was straddling a stall door, and tossed it to Alqua. He caught it and looked at it with an odd expression. "Take what you want," I muttered. Alqua's refusal to tell me about magic had put me in a foul mood. I crossed my arms as I watched Alqua stare blankly at the pack. Then he threw the bag back to me. Surprise emanated from my voice as I said, "You don't want anything?"

A shadow crossed across Alqua's face, and an odd note resounded in his quiet voice. "No. It's free of charge. I—" He stopped himself and waved his hand. "Go on. It's time you got home. Your sister will be worried about you." And with that, he left the barn.

⟫

I mounted Benthey with a reluctant feeling in my heart. I was not ready to leave Alqua's house yet, but night was approaching. I felt that our conversation had ended on a bad note and that I had frustrated Alqua even more than he had been earlier. With a parting glance at the wood house in the glade, I clucked to Benthey and gently kicked his sides. I directed the roan toward the open field that blanketed the edge of the forest in order to make the most of the remaining daylight. Benthey sprang forward, taking full advantage of his healed foot by bolting through the Salquessaé, and the plain passed by in an auburn blur.

It was not long before the sun disappeared beneath the horizon, and I stopped to make camp for the night in a small glen along the forest's edge where I knew there was a small stream. I tiredly unsaddled Benthey and let the horse graze and drink from the stream. I ate some of the food I had left in my pack and gathered wood for a fire in the morning. I then arranged my bedding on the ground and threw myself on it, falling asleep as soon as my head hit the blanket. Stirred by the night breeze, the leaves of the silverwoods whispered softly in my ears as I sank into a deep sleep.

ᣟ

The fire crackled and spit flames in the early morning light, sending up brilliant shoots of orange energy. I sat staring into the fire without seeing it, my arms wrapped around my knees. My mind was full of the images of my premonition. It had visited me again during the night with such lucidity and realism that I feared going to sleep ever again. I shook my head and stood up, dusting my palms on my dress. After dousing the fire with water from the stream, I quickly ate a hard roll from my pack for breakfast and then prepared Benthey for the short trip home. With the night's rest, he seemed eager to be off to home again, and I was too. I just had a few days before I would leave Aseamir for the first time in my life, and as the day was getting closer, I was getting more excited. The things I was going to see! The people, the places, the experiences … I closed my eyes and just shivered with excitement.

Benthey bumped my shoulder with his nose, and I opened my eyes with a smile. "All right, boy, let's go," I said softly. I mounted my horse, and we began riding towards home.

Soon the familiar landmarks of Aseamir began peeking through the tall silver trees to my left. I reined Benthey to a stop and turned to look over my shoulder in the direction from which we had come. The tan fields stretched endlessly before my eyes, with the trees growing smaller as they got farther away on the right side of the auburn sea.

I turned my eyes back to Aseamir, exhaled heavily, and lightly nudged Benthey's sides. The roan sensed my reluctance to go on and went forward at a slow pace. I peered up at the sky as dark, cool shadows flew over me. Black clouds were gathering over the morning sun, growing slowly taller and darker. I spurred Benthey on with a new eagerness to get home. The horse seemed puzzled by my sudden change of attitude but quickly picked up speed, sensing my urgency.

By the time the storm broke, I was dismounting in front of my house. Large raindrops pounded down on me as I hurriedly led Benthey to the stable, his eyes wide with fear. After removing his saddle and bridle and settling Benthey in his stall with hay and water, I turned and ran as quickly as I could through the driving rain to my house. I bounded up the steps, the winds tearing at my clothes and stinging drops pounding into my back. I slipped on the steps twice, but finally, I pulled myself into the house and slammed the door with all my strength. Panting heavily in my drenched clothes, I lay like a dead thing inside the house. A few minutes passed as I tried to regain warmth in my body. Listening to the furious elements howling outside, I shuddered to think that only wood nailed together was protecting us from the wailing storm. Pulling myself up into a sitting position, I looked around for my family. The candles were lit upstairs, and I could hear Aubryn and Malitha's voices floating down. The house swayed intermittently with the force of the ravenous wind.

Shivering violently, I stood up, leaning against the wall to support myself. I needed to get out of these wet clothes; my feet and fingers were numb. Inching my way to the stairs, I could feel the vibrations of the rain pounding on the wood house through my feet.

I came up the stairs slowly, greeting Aubryn and Malitha with a small wave, saying hoarsely, "I'm back."

Aubryn's initial smile turned to concern as she saw how very wet I was and how I was shivering from the damp. "Oh, we must get you out of those wet things!" she cried, scurrying about to find me some dry clothes.

I sat down on my bed next to Malitha and waited as my mother searched. I half expected Malitha to ask me how Alqua was, but to my relief and surprise, she said nothing. After a few, silent moments, she simply got up and left the room, leaving me feeling both resentful and concerned.

"Here we are," Aubryn said, coming over to me and handing me a dry dress and underclothes. After helping me into them and seeing I was warm and comfortable, my mother left me alone in the room, the storm pounding wildly against the walls. Though only mid-morning, the skies had been turned dark by the clouds, and a single candle flickered on the nightstand, casting a pale halo of light into the darkness.

I sat on my bed for a long while, staring at the ceiling blankly, wondering about my trip to Hartford City. I would be leaving in four days. What if I could not find the right road? What if I got lost? What if I could not find the Melbourne Inn? What if …? I sighed; there were so many things that could go wrong, but I did not want to dwell upon them and ruin the excitement of my trip.

Frowning, I turned over on my side, uneasy. However, I was distracted from my anxious thoughts when I heard the door creak open.

A moment later, someone sat down on my bed, and turning to face her, I saw that it was Malitha. In the candlelight, I noticed my sister's pale and drawn face and dull eyes.

"What's wrong, Malitha?" I said softly, watching my sister closely, hoping she would not snap at me. Malitha blinked, and her eyes focused on me as if withdrawing from a trance. She shook her head, causing strands of honey-blond hair to spray across her shoulders. "Nothing, Elysia," she replied, her voice sounding faded and worn.

I rolled my eyes in frustration. "I don't appreciate your lying to me, Malitha. I know *something* is wrong. Saying 'nothing' only supports my guess that something's bothering you. Come now; what is it?" I said gently. Malitha sighed and shuffled her feet. I knew that to be a sign that my sister was thinking about what to say. I was pleased that Malitha was giving up without much of a fight. *She must be desperate to tell someone,* I realized as I noticed a panicked look in Malitha's eyes. Finally, she surrendered.

"I—I keep thinking about Alqua. I saw him here the other day, and we talked. And now I can't stop thinking about him. You know I've fancied him for years, and he's so …" She trailed off and looked away, embarrassed.

I blinked in surprise. *What? This is what's bothering her?* I puzzled. I had known that Malitha admired Alqua, but I did not realize she was at all serious about him. Instead of trying to get to the core of the problem first, I asked, "Why was Alqua here? He usually doesn't come here unless he has business with Father."

"He came to see me," Malitha admitted, avoiding my eyes. *That explains it,* I thought dryly.

I changed tactics. "So why do you keep thinking about him? If you know he likes you, then what's to worry about?" I asked, genuinely curious.

Malitha took a long time to answer. When she did, she said, "That Mother won't approve of us wanting to be together. You know what she thinks about his use of magic? That he's some kind of sorcerer. She thinks it isn't safe for me to be around him! She's forbidden me to see him again," Malitha said in an urgent whisper.

I could see her tearful eyes glistening and knew that Malitha had a serious dilemma. If she defied Aubryn and continued to see Alqua, then not only would she feel guilty, but also it might lead to the destruction of her relationship with Aubryn. However, if Malitha obeyed Aubryn, she would risk losing Alqua and possibly become embittered toward our mother forever. All the same, I was not entirely convinced my childish, immature sister really was interested in Alqua, and this might just be something that would blow over soon. But still … I had not seen her look this vulnerable in a long time, and she never talked to me like this anymore. Maybe she really was feeling conflicted.

I frowned. I was not sure this was something I knew how to deal with since I had no experience in matters of the heart. Sighing, I looked up at the ceiling while Malitha watched me miserably. "What should I do, Elysia? I can't obey Mother *and* still see Alqua!" She groaned and covered her face with her hands. I did not know what else to do, so I lay there awkwardly as Malitha cried softly.

‹৵›

I sat down and shifted on the knotted root to get more comfortable. Aubryn sat beside me, and we watched Malitha teach Lillian how to shoot an arrow with the yew bow that belonged to Malitha. Lillian fared better with Malitha's smaller bow than she had with mine and succeeded in hitting the circle just below the bull's-eye, which caused her to grin victoriously. "I'm doing much better today, Elysia!" she told me proudly, and I assumed that she must have worked hard while I was away, for she seemed much more confident than previously.

"Well done," I praised her. "If you keep practising, you'll be hitting the middle every time!"

She laughed. "Yes, and then maybe I can teach *you* how to hit the bull's-eye!"

Malitha rolled her eyes with annoyance as she watched our younger sister bounce and chatter in excitement. I narrowed my eyes in disapproval at her childishness. Could she not be happy for Lillian instead of being so exasperated?

We stayed outside all day and into early evening, enjoying the time together. As the sky began to darken, Aubryn went inside to prepare dinner. Eventually, Malitha, Lillian, and I headed back indoors, and after assisting Aubryn, we sat down at the table to eat our dinner.

‹৵›

Later, I lay stretched out on my bed, the feather-quill pen I held scratching across the parchment. Writing always helped me fend off boredom, and I enjoyed seeing the inky letters dance across my mind's eye. I was in the middle of writing a little story that I had come up with recently: that of a girl who had lived inside a giant maze all her life and knew nothing of the world outside of her confinement. It had been partly inspired by Lillian, who had showed me a picture of a giant maze in one of her books.

Unlike Lillian, however, I hated reading and preferred only to write.

I paused and set my pen down on the small nightstand beside my bed and stretched my fingers, which were cramped from grasping the pen for such a long time. I rolled onto my back, careful not to brush against the wet ink. I studied the ceiling for a long while, no particular thoughts filling my mind, and I relaxed completely. I closed my eyes and let the familiar blackness of my mind envelope me.

A few minutes later, I felt the edge of the bed sink as someone sat down beside me. I opened my eyes, lifted my head, and stared into Malitha's dark brown eyes. "Yes?" I said politely, in too good a mood to turn her down.

Malitha toyed with her golden hair, which was braided over her shoulder, before answering. "I've been thinking, and I've decided that being with Alqua is more important than obeying Mother. I know she will be furious with me if I continue to see him, but I ..." She faltered briefly, her voice dropping to a low whisper, "I love him."

I groaned inwardly and laid my head back on the bed. *Wonderful. Just what we need—Malitha and Alqua defying Mother's wishes and being together*, I thought with a small sigh. Malitha watched me anxiously. "You ... you won't tell Mother, will you, Elysia? I know I'll be disobeying her, but that doesn't mean I'll enjoy it. Just don't tell her, and we'll see how it goes, all right?" Malitha seemed almost to be pleading with me, hoping I would agree. As hard as it was for me, I knew I could not do this. *If I keep the secret from Mother, we'll both be in deep trouble*, I reflected sullenly. And frankly, this was bizarre. Malitha had not talked to me like this—like a sister—in a very long time, and it made me suspicious.

"I can't agree to this, Malitha. I'm sorry, but I can't go behind Mother's back and help you when she's specifically told you *not* to continue seeing Alqua. You'll have to swim this ocean yourself," I said reluctantly. Seeing Malitha's reaction almost made me want to take back what I had said and help my forlorn sister, but common sense overruled. *That wouldn't help at all*, I told myself.

Malitha's shoulders sagged, and she lowered her head, defeated. Her big brown eyes closed in disappointment. She gave a heavy sigh and muttered softly, "All right. I appreciate your honesty, Elysia. That's more than you can say for me." And with another miserable sigh, Malitha left the room.

Rumours and Obstacles

T he next morning came with a brilliant dawn and a turquoise
sky that stretched endlessly in every direction, like a great blue
bolt of cloth stretched across a table in preparation for stitching.

After feeding the four horses and three chickens, Malitha and I
gathered our packs and prepared to go into town. It was finally time
to go to Aseamir. Malitha was coming too, probably because she
wanted a chance to see Alqua. Lillian stayed home with Aubryn to
help with the gardening, something she enjoyed doing and we older
girls disliked. She also relished having Aubryn all to herself for the day.

After we said goodbye to Aubryn and Lillian, we walked across
to the stable where we had harnessed our horses to a small wagon
earlier that morning. I mounted Benthey, and Malitha swung up on
Xanthis, her speckled grey stallion. We waved goodbye to Aubryn
and Lillian as we exited the stable area and headed to Aseamir. The
horses pounded down the road, venting their excitement in every
step. The sylvan trees soon became thicker, and more elves began
appearing as we drew closer to the western gate of Aseamir a mile
or so away. High stone walls surrounded the city, and two black iron
gates, one at the eastern end of Aseamir and one at the western end,
gave a commanding presence to the entrances of the city. My family
was one of only a few who did not reside within the city walls, but

the governor of Aseamir, a woman named Viveca, had graciously agreed to grant protection and safety to those of us outside the shelter of the stone walls.

Aseamir was one of the smaller cities in Yaracina, which was a landmass surrounded on all sides by the sea. There were lands across the sea, such as another elven continent called Eshen that was nearly twice the size of Yaracina, as well as hundreds of islands around both the elven lands, but few Yarans ever ventured to the other nations, as our navy ships were small and not well equipped for frequently making such long trips. And although many isles surrounded us, their people rarely came to the mainland except to get supplies that were unavailable there.

Soon Malitha and I made our way inside the gate and led the horses and cart through the crowded streets of Aseamir. All around us, women hurried to catch their rambunctious children, and men laughed heartily with friends or traded for a needed item.

We slowly manoeuvred through the crowds to Seppho's booth and tethered the horses to a nearby post. The black-haired woman was a colourful trader who came to Aseamir every few months with news from other cities and towns in Yaracina. She mainly traded small animals such as chickens and goats for grain, fruit, and other small necessities. Her booth was devoid of customers at the moment, so Malitha and I approached the small stand.

Seppho looked up with an immediate, jovial smile from the grain bags she was sorting behind the stand, tucking a stray strand of hair behind her ear. Her icy blue eyes were so light that they were nearly white and had always disturbed me mildly when I looked at them. She dusted her palms on her aqua skirt and said, "Malitha and Elysia! Good to see you, girls! How are your mother and father? Doing well, I hope?" Seppho bent down to rearrange something behind the wooden stand. She reappeared a second later, the small golden discs on the circlet above her brow jangling as she moved. With her bright shawl and skirt, as well as her curly dark hair and the headpiece she wore, she very much resembled a gypsy. Seppho bent forward with a mischievous look on her face that reminded me of a little girl eager to share a particularly good secret.

"Have you heard about the black ships along the coast? Queen Elisheiva's men spotted them about a week ago, sailing offshore from Port Jasmine. They said the ships were flying a flag with a blue dragon on it. Sounds interesting, hmm? What do you think of it?" Seppho's icy eyes glittered with anticipation as she waited for my reply.

"Do you know anything else about it?"

Seppho tilted her head back with a knowing expression. "In fact I do! Elisheiva's men have reported that the men on those ships are ...," she leaned forward to emphasise her words, "*humans*. Humans are sailing our waters!"

I glanced at Malitha, not wanting her to see that my curiosity had been aroused. She did not particularly care for foolish stories about humans and dragons and other such fantastical creatures, but I rather found them fascinating, as did my friend Garrett. Malitha was not paying any attention to me but was, rather, staring at something in the distance behind us, so I answered Seppho, "It does sound terribly exciting, but it can't be true, sadly. Humans aren't real. It's probably just elves from some of the nearby islands, sailing in for supplies. I almost wish it was really humans, though. I'd like to see one and finally have something exciting happen around here."

Malitha caught my last few words and looked at me, frowning. I shrugged self-consciously and watched as Malitha set two large bags of apples on Seppho's stand. "Have anything to trade?" she enquired in a less-than-friendly tone that suggested she wanted to get on with business.

Seppho's eyes twinkled, and she bent down to retrieve a caged chicken that was squawking insolently at being removed from her shady canopy under the stand. Seppho took the grain and pushed the chicken toward me. I smiled apologetically at Seppho for my sister's rude behaviour.

I handed the chicken to Malitha, who was shifting anxiously. She took the cage and hurried back to put it in the wagon and then turned and stared at me with an expression that I knew meant she wanted me to hurry. I guessed she had seen Alqua. Turning back to Seppho, I thanked the raven-haired woman and headed over to the wagon.

When I reached the wagon, Malitha was still there, shifting impatiently. As I approached, Malitha hissed, "Come on! I promised Alqua I'd see him before we left!" Her brown eyes flashed with annoyance.

I tried to hide my exasperation as I spoke. "Oh? And what am I supposed to do? Correct me if I'm wrong, but I doubt you want me there while you're speaking to him."

Malitha eyed me carefully before answering me. "Right. You can do whatever you want. Look at the horses or something; I don't care as long as you don't disturb us."

"What will you be doing?" My voice came out sharper than I had intended, and Malitha responded in kind, her eyes narrowing.

"Talking," she said bitingly.

I frowned but nodded. "All right. Go on." Malitha gave me an insolent smirk and darted off through the streets.

I shook my head, scowling, and left the wagon, proceeding to walk down the street, eyeing the traders' wares appreciatively. Many of their booths offered small trinkets that were tempting to own for one's pleasure but, unfortunately, not items our family could afford to barter for. Others proffered practical items, like tools, clothing, and an assortment of foods. As I made my way farther down the streets, more of the booths and shops presented animals, some for food, some as beasts of burden for farming. One booth had rat-killing cats for trade.

I took my time wandering through the city, gathering the things my mother had asked for as I came across them. I happened across just the person I was looking for, my friend Laela, whom I had not seen in several weeks because her mother had come down with a fever and needed constant attention. She also confirmed what Seppho had told me of the black ships off the coast of Port Jasmine.

"Is your mother still going to let you go to Hartford City?" Laela asked in concern. I had told her of Aubryn's strange proposition from my father and how I was going to have to go all the way to Hartford City just to retrieve some papers for him.

I put a reassuring hand on her arm and said, "The road I'm taking is long but easy, Laela. You needn't worry about me. And I'll have my dagger and my bow with me. You know I can at least fight with a dagger, though I'm not too good with the bow." I gave her a grin.

At that, Laela grinned back widely, and she reminded me, "Well, I remember that time you beat my brother in a contest when you were but twelve years old."

"Yes, but Garrett's improved greatly since then; I doubt I could hope to beat him again."

After several more minutes of conversing, I bade farewell to Laela and continued to meander through the busy cobbled streets.

As I walked, I noticed a small group of men moving through the streets nearby. There were only seven of them—and a young, golden-haired woman, to my surprise—but it was their appearance that made me watch them more closely. I paused, pretending that something at one of the booths had caught my fancy, but I watched them out of the corner of my eye carefully.

With unusually dark hair as black as ravens' wings—and dressed in ragged clothes that spoke of hardships and long journeys, the seven young men and the woman moved warily through the crowds, apparently ill at ease. I noticed then that I was not the only one watching them. I heard whispers floating around me, and many eyes followed the group's path.

Their dark skin spoke of many days in the sun, and their unfamiliar features were exotic but strangely handsome, but there was one who looked different. A younger man towards the edge of the small group had lighter skin, lighter even than mine. He seemed very uncomfortable, even more so than the others, for where they smiled and laughed occasionally, looking around with fascination at my city, he did not join in. One of them would notice something, nudge another, and point it out to him. Then they would stop and marvel at another item in a booth. But this man never smiled nor laughed nor looked around in awe. He kept his eyes to what was right in front of him and never spoke to any of the men but one.

I noticed that another one of the younger men appeared to be even younger than I. He had the darkest skin, seemed to be the liveliest of the group, and smiled constantly. He had a cheerful white smile, and his black eyes glimmered with a youthful spark. He seemed interested in everything and even went so far as to attempt conversation with some of the booth tenders. The young woman stayed close to him, and though they looked little alike, I wondered if she were his older sister from the way she hovered over him. The young, silent man, however, looked unduly frustrated with the younger boy.

Totally engrossed, I leaned back against a booth having only a few customers and watched them under the shade of the tarpaulin above. But then I found myself walking closer, too curious to observe from the concealment of the booth. When I was in hearing range, I stopped and pretended to browse at a booth. It was then that I saw something that previously I had only seen in books: armour. It was just leather jerkins, greaves, and bracers, but I suddenly felt a tightness in the pit of my stomach. They were soldiers. But what on earth were they doing here? Then I noticed that there were swords too, hidden beneath the folds of their dark blue cloaks, visible only from the hilt, but they were there. Soldiers ... since when had Queen Elisheiva approved men from her army to be in our city? For what reason were they here?

"I don't like this," I heard the lighter-skinned man say. I glanced briefly at him. In that split second, all I saw were his eyes. They were coloured a deep blue that reminded me of a sky with a gathering storm.

The soldier next to him, the only one he spoke to, replied softly with a thick, odd accent, "I don't either ... He shouldn't have sent us here. What use could he possibly have for this old town?" As quietly as he spoke, it was difficult for me to make out exactly what the man said, but if I strained my ears, I could catch most of his words.

"The walls," the other answered, glancing at the towering, ancient stone walls that surrounded Aseamir. "This would make a fine fort if we should ever need one."

"Apparently not," the accented one countered. "Not if we got in so easily."

"We would be more careful, Jakob. Our guards are not so lax as these. They weren't even armed." He said it contemptuously, as if disgusted by the fact that they had been permitted inside the city.

My mind started racing. What were these men doing here? Why were they talking about the guards of Aseamir as if they were not in the same army? My fingers brushed over the leather book covers at the booth where I was standing, my eyes scanning over the titles without comprehending them.

"Jakob, could I have some money?" the youngest soldier, the one with the contagious smile, asked then. I instantly liked him, just from the sound of his voice. It was warm and cheerful, as though he was glad to be here.

"I have no money, Haidan," Jakob, the one with the odd accent, said. "Ask someone else."

There was a heavy sigh from Haidan. "Do *you* have any money?" he grudgingly asked the disagreeable, blue-eyed young man.

"If I did, I wouldn't give it to you," he answered.

"I'm shocked," Haidan said dryly and moved away from him and Jakob. I noticed that the young woman handed him some bright silver discs, which I had never seen before. What was money? Those little silver discs? What was he going to do with those? I watched, intrigued, as Haidan gave the booth tender the discs and took something from the booth. *How odd*, I mused. *Exchanging those little discs for items? Well, I suppose they must be of some value.*

"Roman," Jakob said in a disapproving voice. "Haidan's your cousin. Why are you so rude to him?"

Roman answered ill-temperedly, "He may be my cousin, but he is no family of mine, Jakob." And with that, he stalked off, melting into the crowd. Jakob sighed, looking after him—as did the young woman—and then rejoined the small group of soldiers, who were crowded around Haidan, looking at what he had traded for at the booth.

I lingered at the booth for a moment longer, and then I remembered that I had not yet seen my aunt, Laurielle. She bred horses for a living, and she had been the one who had sold Xanthis and Benthey to our father, who had given them to Malitha and me on our twelfth birthdays.

I hurried off in the direction of the horse pens, all thoughts of the soldiers leaving my head.

Finally, the horses came into view. A powerful stallion and two sleek mares were grazing in a large wooden enclosure. Several men were clustered around the horse dealer, Laurielle. She wore a brown, Greek-style tunic, and her hair fell in bouncing golden curls down her back. She was busily engaged in serious negotiation with one of the interested traders as he attempted to barter with her for one of the mares. I was fairly sure that she had not noticed me as I walked past the group to the gate that led into the horses' pen and glanced around quickly. Here at the far eastern edge of Aseamir, there were fewer people, and it provided more solitude than the crowded main marketplace.

When I had finished making a quick sweep of the area around the pen, I focused my attention on the gate's lock. It was made of iron, no doubt fashioned by Alqua, and locked firmly. I pulled a small silver key from the satchel at my side and slipped it into the keyhole. Laurielle had given me the extra key and permission to visit the horses whenever I wanted to because she was my aunt, the only sister of my father, Damir. I put down my satchel, which contained the things I had gotten for Aubryn, before I entered the pen, leaving it next to the gatepost.

I walked through the gate, and Benthey's sister, a brown roan named Abenaki, trotted up and greeted me. I had chosen Benthey instead of Abenaki when Laurielle had given me the choice, so the mare had stayed with my aunt.

Abenaki tossed her mane and whinnied to announce my arrival to the other horses. A few of them looked up, but none came over.

I stroked Abenaki's shoulder, marvelling at the rippling muscles in the horse's legs. Then I looked over my shoulder at Laurielle and her customers, several of whom were now standing by the fence, watching Abenaki. Laurielle was engaged in a heated conversation with a man who apparently disagreed with her over the worth of the horse he was interested in owning.

I looked back at Abenaki, frowning. The horse stared at me with deep brown eyes that mirrored my face. I peered around Abenaki at the other horses, all of whom were grazing nonchalantly at the far end of the pen.

I patted Abenaki one more time before exiting the corral, but before I could get to Laurielle, a young man of about nineteen beckoned me. I recognised him as Laith, a friend of Malitha's.

Laith flicked his gaze over me before saying, "Good day, Elysia. Is Malitha here?" The boy's light eyes were friendly, but he seemed tense.

I laughed in my mind. *Ha! Wait till I tell Malitha that Laith wanted to see her!* I knew she disliked him quite a lot, despite his rather obvious affections for her. However, I concealed my amusement behind a friendly face, not wanting to give Laith the impression that I thought him humorous. "She is, but I'm afraid I don't know where she is right now. I'm sorry, Laith. Could I give her a message for you?"

Laith had looked disappointed when I had said I did not know where my sister was, but then he brightened. "Yes! Could you tell her …" He pondered what he wanted to say for a moment. "Could you tell her I'd like to see her soon? There's something I want to ask her." Laith paused and looked at me.

I nodded pleasantly. "Yes. I will."

Laith looked relieved and thanked me before leaving. Laughing softly, I meandered over to Laurielle, walking slowly so I could watch a trader attempt to barter a white hen to a flustered-looking woman. The woman firmly refused and continued on her way, walking a little faster to escape his eager appeal.

Amused, I stood behind the man and my aunt, still arguing over the horse's worth.

"If you don't like my terms, you don't have to trade for the horse! I'm tired of haggling with you, and I'm sure there are others who aren't so dense as to turn their nose up at a perfectly good bargain! Have you ever thought of that?" Laurielle snapped. Stifling a laugh at the absurdity of it all, I listened to my sharp-tongued aunt speak.

The customer, a young man whose very face seemed to emanate wealth, was glaring furiously at Laurielle. He crossed his arms and spat, "Well, fine! If you don't want what I'm offering, then don't take it. I'm sure I can find something better to trade my jewellery on than an old, run-down horse!" And with that, the young man stomped away, leaving Laurielle looking rather indignant.

I hurried over to my aunt. "Why didn't you just accept what he was willing to trade?" I enquired. "Now you've lost a customer over a silly argument. Isn't some jewellery better than nothing?"

To my surprise, Laurielle laughed. "Oh, I suppose. But the main reason I didn't give in was that I'm not ready to sell my 'old, run-down horse' yet, and I didn't want her to belong to someone who didn't realize her value, so it worked out the way I wanted."

I cocked an eyebrow but did not comment on my aunt's logic. Instead, I changed the subject. "You have heard that Malitha and Alqua are seeing each other? Apparently it's been going on for some time."

Laurielle laughed like a delighted child. "Yes, and against your mother's will, too! Oh my! That girl is so headstrong! She's just like your father, you know. When we were younger, he would always disobey our parents and get into the worst sorts of trouble!" Laughing again at her memories, Laurielle motioned me to follow her to her tent.

Once inside, my aunt sat on a round carved stool and gestured for me to do the same. "So!" she said, pulling out a little flask, which I guessed contained spiced wine, my aunt's favourite drink, "I hear you're off to Hartford City come festival time, eh? That right?"

I nodded and brushed back a lock of auburn hair. "Yes. Have you ever been there?"

"Oh, once or twice. You know, people there love to bargain! Did I ever tell you that once I spent two hours haggling with a man? And over what? A catfish. A *catfish*! Yes, it was big, but two hours! Oh, it was so ridiculous! But eventually, I did get a piglet for it, so I suppose it wasn't *completely* pointless." By the time Laurielle had finished, her mouth was curved into a broad grin, and I was laughing hard. We laughed together a few moments more, until we finally calmed ourselves and picked up the conversation again.

"Besides the people's love of haggling, what did you think of their city?" I asked.

"Oh, I suppose it was rather dismal. So many people there! Never get a moment's rest! Somebody's always after you, trying to get you to trade for something. The scenery is absolutely breathtaking, in spite of all the cluttered streets and marketplaces, and I very much enjoyed seeing some of the historic sites from the city's first days. Did you know that there is still a building standing where Yara was said to have dwelled for a time?"

My interest redoubled. Perhaps this city did not sound so gloomy after all. "Really?" I asked, trying to imagine the city back when there were fewer people, and … Yara. What had she looked like? Was she really how the stories had described her? I had often wondered about the lady of our greatest legend, the lady, from whom, it was said we were all descended. Had she known, when she had first come to Yaracina's shores, that one day this entire land mass would bear her name and we would call ourselves Yarans in honour of her?

Then reality reminded me that Yara was only a story. That tale was not true; it was only part of our culture's mythology. But it was exciting to think about, the fact that—if she had been real—Yara certainly might have stayed in that ancient building for a time. Smiling to myself at my naiveté and fanciful imagination, I listened to Laurielle respond, "Oh yes! You know, I remember when your mother—" Then she cut herself off and suddenly grew sombre. This sparked my interest, and I pressed, "When my mother what?"

But Laurielle's face clouded, and she dismissed the subject by saying, "I shouldn't have said anything. Forgive me.

"Well, it's getting late," she went on, forcing a smile, "and I expect Malitha will be back by now. If not, get something to eat, and then wait a little while longer. If she doesn't show up by the seventh hour, come back here, and I'll tell you how to find her." Disgruntled and upset by my aunt's closure on the subject of what Aubryn had done, I also put on a half-smile, but it did not come out entirely how I intended. Laurielle gave me a genuine smile now, the warmth and gentleness returning, and she said, "Dear one, I held my tongue because your mother might not want me to share such a …" Her smile turned pained. "Such a silly thing, really. If you truly want to know, ask her when you return home." I smiled reluctantly and then bade my aunt a fond farewell.

After pushing, shoving, and dodging my way back through the heavy crowds that still clogged the marketplace, I reached the wagon, thoroughly exhausted. Malitha was not there.

Slumping against the wagon's oaken side, I looked around wearily. Spying Laryssa, the owner of The Golden Apple, heading down the street, a small barrel of fine wine in tow, I abruptly realized that I was hungry, and even from here, I could detect the aromatic scents of the eatery wafting down the street. I stepped back out into the busy street and intentionally followed the tantalizing smells. Breaking free from the masses when The Golden Apple's sign appeared above the heads of the passing townspeople, I entered the eatery, famous with both visitors and the locals for its excellent food and drinks. Warm, delicious aromas of food cooking, as well as a faint smoky odour, tickled my nose as I manoeuvred around several exiting people and sat on a high stool at the marble bar. I noticed that six of the soldiers I had seen earlier were in there; the blue-eyed one was missing.

Laryssa, who had been busy stocking the wine barrel in a store-room behind the counter, spied me and came out, a broad smile on her face. Her glossy brown hair was braided neatly over her shoulder, and her soft grey eyes twinkled as they focused on me.

"Hello, child. It's good to see you again. It *is* you, Elysia, isn't it? It's been awhile since I've seen you. My, but you've grown into such a *lovely* young woman! Any boys come calling yet?" Laryssa said, her eyes sparkling in the dim light.

I smiled back awkwardly at the woman. "No … How's business?" I asked, changing the subject but not sure what else to ask her. After all, she was Aubryn's friend, and I did not know much about Laryssa.

"Oh, it's just grand! How're your mother and father doing?"

"My mother is well, and my father should be coming back home in a few weeks. He's on a business trip to Rielture. He left about three weeks ago." Laryssa nodded thoughtfully. Silence followed, and the two of us looked peacefully around the noisy eatery.

Then, "Anything I could get you, love? Would you like something to eat?"

"Oh, yes, please. Anything would be fine. Whatever's easy for you," I replied, not particularly caring what Laryssa gave me to eat, as long as it filled my stomach.

Laryssa's smile deepened, and she said, "You're just like your mother. Always so polite and caring about what's all right with other people." She went into the little kitchen behind the counter.

Embarrassed that my comment had not been taken the way I had meant it, I felt my cheeks warm and ducked my head, not wanting Laryssa to see.

I tapped my fingers on the marble, noting how the light that shone on it made the tiny, thin veins of colour seem as though they were floating in the marble. *They're flying*, I thought, smiling. How I wished I could fly. How I wished that I could spread a pair of brilliant white wings that would sprout from between my shoulder blades, feel the wind ruffle the soft, snowy feathers, and let myself stretch the wing muscles and pump them strongly, soaring gloriously above the green forests and sparkling seas, flying into the sunset …

Laryssa returned with a platter of food, interrupting my far-fetched daydream. Shaking my head a little to clear my thoughts, I began eating the salt pork and fresh vegetables slowly, still contemplating my day. After a moment, I glanced around the eatery curiously. I had never really studied it too carefully, but now that I did, I saw that it was fairly nice. However, when my gaze passed over the six soldiers sitting in the corner, I suddenly lost my appetite. I stared down at my food broodingly, my brow creased in thought, wondering about them. Maybe Seppho was right … Maybe the rumours about the ships on the coast were true. I shook my head. *Impossible*, I thought. *Humans are extinct and have been for nearly seven hundred years.* I glanced at the men again, too curious to worry about Seppho's silly rumours. The youngest one, the one who was always smiling, noticed me. His smile dimmed for a moment and then reappeared in a friendly grin. I quickly looked away.

Then I noticed it was getting dark outside. Frowning, I hurriedly finished my meal, even though I had lost what appetite I had had, and left the eatery, thanking Laryssa for the food and paying her with a small glass bead bracelet that my mother had given to me to trade. Letting the general current of the crowds sweep me along, I headed for the wagon. But before I returned to it, I stopped by the archery shop to replenish my arrow supply and to see my friend Garrett.

He was hanging a yew bow on a peg on the back wall as I came in the shop. He looked over his shoulder to see who had come in, and a lazy half-grin lit up his face when he saw me. "Hey, Elysia," Garrett said, adjusting the bow minutely on its hook before coming over to me, his grin even wider now.

"Hello, Garrett," I said with a smile. "How's business?"

"Oh, it's good," he said cheerfully, thrusting his hands into his pockets. "So. My sister tells me you're off to Hartford City next week, hmm?"

I nodded, wandering over to where Garrett's supply of stone-tipped arrows were neatly displayed. I picked one up and reverently ran the tip of my finger over the apex. Garrett made the finest arrows I had ever seen of those who made arrows in Aseamir, and for that reason, I always got my supply from him.

He came over to where I was inspecting the stone-tipped shafts, crossed his arms, and smiled. "Sounds fun," he said, his green eyes twinkling merrily, and I smiled at him fondly.

"Yes, I think it will be," I replied, twirling an arrow nimbly. "Perhaps I'll hear some new tales or stories there, and I can tell them to you when I get back." I wandered back to where the bows were hung on wall pegs, running my fingers gently over the curved wood.

Garrett and I shared a love of myths and tales, most notably those of the fire-tamers and Apparates, and if ever either of us heard a new fable or story, we would tell it to the other as soon as we could. However, Garrett loathed any stories with humans in them with an uncommon ferocity, often not even consenting to stay in the same room with someone who was speaking of them. I had never understood his abhorrence of humans, and he had told me that he did not either, but it seemed so deeply ingrained in him and his sister that it appeared irreversible.

He grinned. "I'd like that," he said, adjusting a bow on its hooks as he followed me along the wall.

"Have you heard the rumours?" I asked, looking over my shoulder at him. "About the black ships on the coast and that humans are supposed to be sailing them?"

Garrett snorted. "Of course, I've heard them, but I don't believe a single word of any of them; humans aren't real—everyone knows that."

I hesitated, not willing to voice my thought that maybe they *were* real ... After all, those soldiers I had seen in the streets did not look like any elves I had ever seen. I lapsed into a thoughtful re-evaluation of the seven young soldiers I had seen in the streets. Their dark skin and hair and exotic faces certainly made me wonder where they were from, and while there was a deep, almost totally buried suspicion beginning to burrow its way into my chest, I chose to ignore it for now; after all, I was not sure I really *wanted* to know where those men had come from.

"I saw some men in the street," I said softly, dropping my hand from the bow it had been resting on. "They looked ... like they weren't from here. They had dark hair and skin ... I've never seen anyone that looked like them before."

Garrett's face darkened, as did his eyes, as he wandered over to the counter at the back of the store, and he replied, "So? You've never been outside of Aseamir before; they could just be travellers from some of the southern cities."

I was silent, choosing to let the case rest. *Humans aren't real*, I assured myself reluctantly. *They never have been, and they never will be.*

I then took sixteen stone-tipped arrows and said to Garrett, "What do you want for these?" as I rummaged through my satchel to find something to trade for them.

Garrett looked up from behind the counter and briefly inspected the arrows, then waved his hand, saying cheerfully, "Nah, they're free of charge. With business as good as it is, I can afford to let those pass."

Surprised, I asked, "Really? Sixteen of them?"

He grinned and affirmed, "Yes, Elysia, every last one of them." Garrett picked up a box of arrowheads and carried them to a different spot as he continued: "In return,"—he paused as he set the box down,—"you can have a safe trip to Hartford City for me."

I smiled at him fondly. "Well, if that's to be your payment, I'll certainly try." I set my new arrows at the bottom of my satchel carefully, the tips resting against my whetting stone, so that they would not tear a hole in my bag. "Thank you, Garrett."

"Ah, don't mention it," he said nonchalantly, though I could tell he was glad that I was pleased. He began pulling out a few arrows that did not yet have arrowheads fixed on them and set them down on the floor beside the box, his fingers dexterous and quick as he began to work.

I watched him for a while and then shifted my gaze to the bustling streets outside his shop's windows, looking without really seeing. Even though I would be coming back fairly soon, I realized that I would miss Aseamir once I left. It really was a beautiful city, and I loved it, despite my deeply embedded longing to travel and see the world. Even as a young child, I had wanted to go to other places and be exposed to other cultures and all the interesting people and things there were to see there. It was almost as if I was intended to leave this place, meant to be … somewhere else. I could not fully describe the feeling, but like a thorn in my heart, it stuck, having lodged there the day I was born, and I knew it would stay till the day the world ended …

"So!" Garrett said, pausing and looking up at me. "Laela said you're going to Hartford City just to fetch some papers for your father?" He said it as if he found the very idea of making a trip to the capital especially for papers very absurd, and I laughed at his expression.

"Yes, that's right," I agreed, coming to stand behind him as he attached the arrowheads to the shafts carefully, his fingers flying over the arrowheads. I knelt down beside Garrett, staring at the long, slender arrow shafts with a sigh.

Garrett smirked at me. "Couldn't your father fetch his own papers?"

"He's in Rielture," I answered with a grin. "And he's been delayed, so he's requested that I fetch them for him."

He rolled his eyes, but I could tell that he was going to let the case rest. "I bet you're excited, hmm?"

"Yes … and no. I wish I was getting to leave for a more exciting reason," I said musingly. "Though I should be grateful I'm getting to go at all, I suppose. Maybe someday … I'll get to go back there when I can stay longer and have more time to see everything."

Garrett nodded understandingly, brushing a few strands of his dark blond hair out of his eyes. "Be sure to remember everything so that you can tell me when you get back," he said then with a smile, pausing to look at me.

I nodded, suddenly having another intense feeling of longing to stay in Aseamir swell up inside me. After all … I had never been away from home before. What did I know of the world and the way it worked? For all I knew, everything I knew, everything I *thought* I knew … could be totally wrong. All of a sudden, I felt wildly frightened about leaving everything familiar behind and venturing out into the world, but the feeling wore off fairly quickly when I began to consider all the good things that could come from my trip. I smiled a little to myself at my own naiveté.

"I have to go," I said to Garrett then, but as I started to leave, he protested by saying, "Wait a moment," and he came over and gave me a big hug. I smiled as he released me and said, "You didn't honestly think you could get away that easily, now, did you?" He grinned widely at me, and I laughed. "Silly me," I replied, hugging him once again.

And after thanking him once more for my arrows, I shouldered my satchel and headed back to the streets of Aseamir.

⁘

To my relief, Malitha was back, leaning heavily against the oaken side of the wagon when I returned to Seppho's booth.

"Hello," she muttered, avoiding my eyes.

"Well, how's your prince?" I asked, a note of mockery colouring my voice. Malitha flinched and did not answer. *I wonder what happened*, I thought, the general disapproval in my mind turning to concern. I studied her for a minute before continuing. "Malitha, is everything okay? Alqua all right and everything?"

"Oh, yes, he's fine, it's just ... well ..." She broke off, and took a heavy breath as if to reassure herself before going on, "H-he wants to talk to Father about ... marriage when he comes back from Rielture." Her news told, Malitha slumped to the ground and buried her face in her hands. "I don't know what to do! I know Mother won't allow us to be together, but I love him, and I want to marry him. Ohhh," she moaned miserably.

I stood beside my sister and held her while she sobbed dramatically, feeling lost and helpless inside.

COMPLICATIONS

As Malitha and I unsaddled Xanthis and Benthey in the stable back at home, Aubryn came out to greet us. Helping Malitha with Xanthis, she could not help but notice her daughter's forlorn expression.

"Malitha, dear, are you feeling all right? You look a little pale," Aubryn said in concern. Malitha put a reassuring hand on her mother's shoulder.

"I'm fine, Mother. I'm just a little tired. That's all," Malitha promised. I looked on in disapproval, knowing my sister was lying to Aubryn.

I eyed the buckles on the saddle darkly as I unfastened them. Their pure, polished silver glistened like my sister's tears over the man she supposedly loved, and I loathed the buckles for reminding me of Malitha's predicament. *So many tears and so much heartache over a man. Why would anyone want to be married anyway?* I had begun rather to dislike Alqua for all the pain he had brought to my sister, especially when I considered that this relationship was probably borne merely of physical attraction and would most likely not survive the test of time.

I freed Benthey from his tack and led him and Xanthis out to graze. Then I followed my mother and sister back to the house, my bow and quiver still strapped to my back. My soft leather boots were stained with mud, I noticed, as I removed them at the doorway. I wriggled my bare toes, feeling the fresh air rush over them as they were freed from the confines of my footwear.

Lillian was asleep on a papyrus mat in the corner, her golden hair splayed out across her shoulders in waves. I smiled as I climbed the stairs to my room, trailing Malitha. Lillian had lately taken to sleeping on the floor instead of her bed because she insisted that some group of people—called the Egyptians—slept on papyrus mats at night. *Who knows what kind of stories she's getting in her head from those silly books,* I thought with affection. I had never cared for myths and legends and stories from other places; I cared to hear only Yaran stories.

Malitha and I walked to the window once inside the room, and she leaned against the frame of the window, sighing heavily. I stared out at the silver forest below me and said nothing because I knew there was nothing to say.

ॐ

The next day was spent hurriedly preparing food for the Midsummer's Eve Festival. Malitha and I dutifully helped Aubryn cook, but grudgingly on my part, for most of the day. When I found the time, I packed for my trip to Hartford City. Little food items, such as cheese, apples, and bread, began to disappear from Aubryn's store and turn up in my pack.

Malitha became more and more nervous as the festival approached. There was no doubt in my mind that she was planning to talk to Aubryn about marrying Alqua. I could only imagine Malitha's face when Aubryn firmly denied her proposition. What was she getting herself into?

ॐ

That night at supper, Malitha spoke up, looking hesitant but obstinate. She said, "Mother, while Elysia and I were in the city, I ... saw Alqua."

Aubryn looked up sharply. "Alqua? Malitha, you know I've said—"

"I know, Mother! But let me finish!" Malitha snapped. I set down my fork and leaned back in my chair, convinced that my sitting between the two could prove dangerous in this conversation. Lillian watched with hooded eyes, looking uncomfortable.

Aubryn's mouth tightened, but she allowed Malitha to continue. Looking relieved, my sister plunged into her story.

"H-he spoke to me, and we … discussed marriage. But, please, Mother, before you say anything, let *me* say this: I love Alqua, and I *will* marry him with or without your blessing," Malitha finished, her lower lip trembling slightly. I could see how much she hated speaking to her mother like that, but I agreed it was necessary if Malitha hoped to marry Alqua.

Aubryn sat back in her chair, looking rather bewildered. She was silent for a long time, so long, in fact, that Lillian and I finished eating, cleared the table, and went upstairs, leaving Aubryn and Malitha to talk.

꒳

"Elysia," Lillian said as she sat down on her mat, "Will Malitha get to marry Alqua? Or will Mother forbid her?" Her large brown eyes were inquisitive, and I knew from experience that I could not hide the truth from those huge, innocent eyes.

I sighed and motioned for Lillian to lie down. "I don't know, Lillian. I don't know."

꒳

Falling back into the pillow, I stared miserably at the ceiling. I closed my eyes and just relaxed for a while, breathing softy. In. Out. In. Out. My mind wandered for a while, from how my father was faring on his trip to what Aubryn had said to Malitha about Alqua's offer of marriage. I snorted softly. I knew my sister was immature and petty and she had broken many a boy's heart before, but this was simply ridiculous! She had hardly even known Alqua before she was fifteen, and since then, Father had rarely taken her with him when he went there. How on earth—and *why*—did she become attracted to him? And marriage, at age seventeen! Surely this was the stupidest thing my sister had ever done.

Tired of thinking about it, I got up and went to my window, exhaling deeply. I crossed my arms and let the warm night air caress my shoulders and face, and closing my eyes, I let my mind drift again.

Tomorrow, my journey would begin. A faint feeling had been nagging at my heart lately, whenever I thought about this trip: doubt. For some reason, I felt that this voyage would consist of much more than a mere journey to a city to fetch papers. I seemed to know what was going to happen as if I had already made it but just could not retrieve the exact details out of my tangled subconscious.

I stared out at the graceful expanse of silver trees that made up the forest in which I lived. The spindly, dew-webbed leaves swayed gently in the breeze, and the warm air spiralled into my room, filling it with balmy forest scents. The familiar aromas soothed my anxiety and loosened the ball of tension that had formed in my gut. But, the general mood of unease that had crept into my mind remained.

I had always—somewhere deep inside—known my life would be more than this: merely helping my sisters with chores; making trips into Aseamir to trade for things we needed; riding my horse away from home for a few hours to escape the boring dullness of life while knowing that I would have to come back when night fell. Life held more for me than the simple, ordinary existence I had here. When I contemplated my future, I often felt that threads of something grand stretched out alongside the timeline of my life, but what they could be, I did not know. However, I did know for certain that there was more for me than this.

The gentle sound of feet on the wooden floor behind me interrupted my musings, and I turned to see my mother, pale and shaken. Alarmed, I hurried over to her and guided her to my bed, where she sat down slowly, looking as if she were in an unbelieving trance. "Mother?" I asked, my voice shaking, suspicions whirling through my mind. "What is it? What's wrong?"

Aubryn did not answer for a long, tense moment. Then she gradually lifted her eyes to meet mine. They were full of hurt and fear. "Malitha's gone," she answered in a choked whisper. "Alqua … She's gone …"

Dread and irritation with my sister drowned out all my previous concern, and I shook my head ruefully. *Why did you do that, Malitha?* I asked her silently in my head, thinking with dismay at the grief this would bring our family. All because she did not have enough sense and patience to work this out in a way that would not hurt us all.

I Must Go

Morning came swiftly. I felt excited, anxious, and frightened all at once as I gazed out at the pale morning sun, illuminating the forest before me. My bow and quiver were slung across my back, my dagger was belted at my waist, and I clenched its pommel tightly to reassure myself. Aubryn stood at the base of the tree, her face still tear-streaked because of Malitha's determined departure. We both knew that she had gone in search of Alqua.

I absently fingered the straps on Benthey's pack while purposely waiting for the sun to rise completely before setting off on the road to Hartford City. I was reluctant to leave. Sighing, I thought, *I guess I hoped Malitha would be here when I left, but now that she's gone, I hate to leave without seeing her.* I rubbed my forehead and looked back at Aubryn and Lillian. My youngest sister gave me a sombre half-smile and waved ruefully, but Aubryn did not move. With her still in shock from Malitha's sudden elopement, my leaving for Hartford City could not have come at a worse time, and though I was reluctant to leave my mother in such a state, I knew my father was counting on me to get his documents for him.

Benthey snorted and pawed the ground in an uncharacteristic display of impatience. I patted his neck and leaned my head against his. The horse calmed after a few moments and stopped fidgeting. I closed my eyes and focused on my breathing, waiting for the sun to rise and enjoying the feel of what few rays fell on my skin.

Finally, the sun rose fully above the treetops, and it was time for me to leave. Exhaling deeply, I turned to Aubryn and said, "Good bye, for now. I'll be back soon," trying to be reassuring.

Aubryn gave only a grim smile. "You don't have to leave, Elysia," she whispered, her voice pleading. "There are dangers out there, people who would harm you … Elysia, there are things I've never told you … that I think I should have before you reached this age—"

"Mother," I sighed, cutting her off. I looked at her with gentle chastisement, and Aubryn pressed her lips together in a hard line. "Perhaps it's better you didn't know … not yet …"

"I must go," I said, and I embraced her. We held each other for a long moment before backing away. I lowered my eyes, doubts spiralling through my mind. What did she mean, things she had never told me?

Aubryn wiped her eyes. After a moment of consideration, she relented, "If you are decided, then. I'm so proud of you, Elysia. You are a true credit to your family."

I smiled and then looked to Lillian. The younger girl smiled affectionately and waved mournfully after I released her. "Thank you for agreeing to take over for me while I'm gone, Lillian," I told her. "I know Mother is glad that you'll still be here to help her. You were always a better worker than Malitha and I, anyway."

Through mournful eyes, Lillian's still smiled. "Don't be gone too long, Elysia," she warned me, and I chuckled.

"I'll do my best," I assured Lillian, embracing her with a heart overflowing with love for my little sister, and then turned back to my stallion.

I mounted Benthey and spurred the horse into an even trot. The summer sunlight fell across my face and arms, and a cool wind tugged at my hair as we rode through the silverwood forest. I did not look back once my home was out of sight, so thrilled was I finally to be leaving Aseamir for the first time in my life.

Home is behind. The world is ahead. But right then, I had no idea how true those words would be.

༈

Several hours later, I slowed Benthey to a stop and let the roan graze while I searched for a stream. I found a tiny tributary only a few yards from where Benthey stood, and though it was indeed very small, its waters looked clear and pure. The small gurgling brook flowed through the golden-brown grasses of the plains, carving a jagged break in the prairie. I sat down next to the rivulet, stretching my cramped legs, and skimmed my fingers through the clear, cool water, loving the feel of the stream on my skin.

After a while, I unscrewed the cap of my waterskin and dunked it into the stream, filling it to the brim with water. I examined the brook a moment and then took a long drink from the container, thirsty from the mid-morning heat. It never got particularly hot this far north, only very humid and sticky, and I did not like the summer months much for that reason. No, I much preferred the cool crisp air of winter and the snow that came with it.

The water was cooler than I had expected, and after swallowing quickly, I gasped and rubbed my temple, trying to lessen the ache that the water had caused in my head. Once it was gone, I took another, slower drink, and even as it flowed down, I could feel the water seep into my tired muscles and lift some of their aching.

I stood a moment later and walked over to Benthey, and taking his reins, I lead him to the stream. He sniffed at the water once or twice and then began to drink, flicking his ears to ward off some small insects. I filled my waterskin once more as my horse drank, and then we began riding again.

༈

After waiting for almost an hour and a half in the tall grass and scoring three missed shots, I managed to shoot a young rabbit and carried it back to my selected campsite for the night. We had ridden far that day, nearly thirty-five miles, and while I wanted to continue, it was getting dark and would not be safe for Benthey, as he might catch his hoof on something.

As I began skinning the rabbit I had shot, the knife scraped smoothly over the rabbit's tawny fur, making a soft, comforting noise with which I was well familiar. Looking up absently, I caught a glimpse of figures moving along the horizon, silhouetted against the sinking sun. Curious, I strained my eyes to see better, but it was so far off that even my eyes could not make out very good details. But this I could tell: It was a line of soldiers, filing slowly across the sky's length, looking worn out, their shoulders hunched as they walked. Several of them held spears, and most of them had a sword belted to their waists. One soldier was smaller than all the others and lagged at the back of the line. It looked as though it was taking much effort and energy for him to keep up with the rest of the men.

Pain stabbed into my wrist. Sucking in air sharply, I looked down to see blood oozing from a superficial cut on my wrist just below my palm. When I had looked up, the unexpected appearance of the soldiers had distracted me, and my knife had slipped in my hand and cut me. Sucking in my breath, I reached into my pack and drew out a strip of clean gauze. Before wrapping it around my cut to stop the bleeding, I hastily dipped it in the spring water and got it nicely wet, and the coolness temporarily deadened the pain.

꒰ঌ

A little while later, I looked ruefully at the tiny loaf of bread and rabbit meat that was to be my supper. Quirking my lips, I picked up the bread and bit into it. It was somewhat stale, but it tasted all right. The rabbit was still cooking, its savoury scents wafting pleasantly around me, and my stomach ached for the meat instead of the old bread.

Benthey moved closer to the fire now that the sun had gone down, still grazing amiably on the prairie grass. Wolves howled around us, but I knew that we were not far enough into the wilder part of the Salquessaé Plains to encounter any that could be of danger to us, but just in case, I would keep the fire going through the night.

I could see the moon beginning to show in the pale sky, shedding silver rays across the plains and casting everything in a muted shade of grey. I smiled a little; I had always preferred day to night, but tonight was so especially beautiful that I could not help but wish it could go on forever.

I finished my meal and then unpacked my bedroll. I was careful not to put it too close to the fire, but I lay fairly close to the flames, having always felt safe around and comforted by fires. I wrapped up in my blanket and watched the stars for a long time before falling asleep, wondering about Malitha and what she had been thinking when she had run off to Alqua's. How could she do such a thing? Did she not realize all the consequences that could—and would—come with her impulsive actions? And what would happen if she found she did not really love Alqua or he not really love her? I sighed deeply and thought, *I shall never get married, and it would have to be someone extremely extraordinary even to tempt me into falling in love.*

ॐ

Veryan felt terrible. The pain in his foot made it impossible to keep up with the others, and they all jeered at him for being weak. *And with good reason,* he thought sourly. *I am weak. I'm awful at fighting, my blasted temper makes me vulnerable, and it's my fault that my only friend is dead. All because I was* stupid *enough and* clumsy *enough to trip while we were running away … Pyralus was killed because of me, because I'm just a eighteen-year-old* boy *who shouldn't be here and certainly is not wanted here.* Fuming, angry with himself and with the world, he kept trying to go faster to prove to himself and the men that he could keep pace with them. But it was becoming increasingly difficult, and they all knew it.

Gornhelm had refused him a horse to ride on and had made him stay at the back as the guard, even though they all knew Veryan was incapable of fighting in his condition with anything but a bow. And therefore, Veryan knew Gornhelm had done it to insult him. *Some guard I make. I'd be killed as soon as we were attacked,* he thought angrily. *We all know that.*

While Veryan had been running back to camp after leaving Pyralus to die, he had tripped on a large, jagged rock in the path and had fallen headlong on more sharp rocks. Now he had a hole in his foot the size of the tip of his thumb that bled continually because he had to keep walking with the troop. He could barely force himself to get up every day. The pain of losing his only friend as well as the tenderness of his injured foot had destroyed any zest for life, and he felt he was merely doing the minimum to get through to night. The constant jeers and spiteful laughter of the men, coupled with the various insults and demeaning comments over the past seven years, put even greater weight on Veryan's state of mind, making him feel unsafe and helpless.

Veryan soon began panting with the effort of trying to stay up with the others, and sweat was slick on his forehead, back, and sides. The morning sun beat down mercilessly on the soldiers, making Veryan feel as if he was suffocating in his leather armour.

Suddenly Veryan stumbled over a sudden dip in the prairie. He gave a muffled grunt of pain as his foot scraped over a rock, and he fell into the tan grass. His injured foot cramped, the muscles clenching in spasms, and a shuddering gasp left his lips as the dull throbs swept over his leg. Gritting his teeth to keep from crying out, Veryan struggled to get up before Gornhelm noticed him but to no avail. One of the soldiers in front of him happened to turn and see him and called, "Captain! We've got an idler back here!"

Rage filled Veryan, making a crimson flower of anger blossom in his chest. *I'm not being lazy!* he seethed in his head. *But right now, walking is out of the question.* As if to echo his thoughts, another painful spasm erupted in his foot.

Gornhelm called for the troop to stop and marched back to where Veryan was lying helplessly in the grass. Veryan felt all the humiliating and mocking gazes of the soldiers trained on him, and he bit his lip to keep from shouting something quite unkind at them.

Then Gornhelm kicked the boy in the ribs, his hobnailed shoes digging into Veryan's side powerfully. The force of the blow forced Veryan's ribs inward and crushed them against his lungs. The breath whooshed out of his body, and when it came back, he groaned as the sharp pulsing pain engulfed his ribcage. Involuntary tears flowed from his eyes, though he tried desperately to keep from showing it.

Gornhelm sneered and dragged Veryan up to his feet. Veryan winced as his foot scraped a rock and numbness and a constricting pain arched over his foot. He grimaced and leaned on his other leg, trying to keep his weight off his injured foot.

Gornhelm gave the boy a violent shake, unmistakably angry with him. "Get up!" he spat, "I'll stand for no idlers in this troop! When I recruit a soldier, I expect him to give me everything he's got and not decide to lie down and take a nap whenever he feels like it!" Gornhelm then threw Veryan down. He managed to catch himself before hitting the ground, trying not to let his foot hit anything as he fell. Leaning back on his hands, Veryan grimaced as the cramp in his foot moved up to his leg. It *hurt*, and as much as he wanted to shoot a furious reply back, Veryan could not focus on anything but the throbbing spasms in his leg. Even his fiery rage that had grown so great that it could burst his heart was lessened from the throbbing, but it was not put out entirely.

Then Veryan heard a scout ride up. The man dismounted, removed his helm, and said, "Captain! I've sighted a young girl and her horse nearby on the prairie. She doesn't look like a threat at all; she's probably just passing through."

"Very well, then. Let her pass," Gornhelm replied absently, his mind clearly elsewhere. The scout dipped his head and turned his horse around, about to ride off once more.

Veryan could feel the captain's eyes on him, and he groaned at his next words: "No, wait. Stop, soldier."

The scout turned back, his eyes puzzled. Gornhelm spoke again, his eyes still on Veryan. "You want a chance to prove yourself, boy? I'll give you one. Slaves are always in high demand down on the coast, and I'm sure the slavers would be very … pleased to receive a young girl. The troop needs some supplies, anyway, and we can get a fair amount for a slave. Capture her, and in return, I'll let you ride a horse." Gornhelm bent down and looked at Veryan.

Veryan, however, stared straight ahead, his eyes burning with resentment and fury. He wished with all his heart that he could plunge a dagger into the man's heart. But he would never kill again; he had sworn that a long time ago, and he would not break his vow for such a worthless kill as Gornhelm would be. Gornhelm lowered his voice and said, "But, if you fail, who knows? You might end up like your little friend back in the woods."

The threat could have been no clearer: Gornhelm intended to kill Veryan if he did not capture an innocent girl who had done the captain no harm. The mention of Pyralus and the implication that Gornhelm felt no grief over the loss of his soldier filled Veryan with sour remorse and hatred. The flower of rage in Veryan's heart grew, filling his thoughts and consuming him. Oh, how he longed to hurt Gornhelm! His fingers itched to draw an arrow back on the string, point it at the captain's heart, and let it fly …

He painfully shoved himself up, and though his legs nearly buckled under his weight, the cramp ceased a minute later, abating to a dull, aching throb. He managed to stay on his feet and glared with all his strength and anger at Gornhelm. The man wore a smug, victorious smirk, as if confident Veryan would fail. Veryan, in response, hissed, "I hope you won't be too disappointed when I bring her back to you."

The captain said haughtily, "I'll try not to make your death too quick. You deserve to suffer before you leave this world." Then he motioned for two others to join Veryan, and his cheeks flushed when he realized that Gornhelm had added two because he did not want him to try to escape while in the woods. Either Veryan would capture the girl, or he would fail, and Gornhelm would kill him.

Veryan drew his sword and, eyes burning with frightening rage, stood before the forest that held his soon-to-be captive. He would not lose this contest for his life.

⁂

I splashed cool water over my face, and then wiped a clean rag over my forehead and cheeks, savouring the feel of the water running over my skin. Benthey was picketed nearby, his reins looped and tied to the stub of a limb on a small twisted tree. The roan was resentfully grazing on the tall, dry, tasteless prairie grass, no doubt longing for the sweet, lush grass of Aseamir that he so often ate in the late evenings.

I slung my quiver on my back and slid the arm guard onto my left arm, positioning it so that it protected the underside of my forearm. My dagger was already belted to my waist; I did not even sleep without it out here.

Once Benthey's packs were ready, I mounted and clucked to the stallion, spurring the horse forward.

We rode for several minutes, and as it was a pleasant day, I did not hurry my horse along too much. We had time.

Benthey was making excellent time, trotting at a steady pace across the prairie floor, moving swiftly. We rode through the grasses for half an hour and then veered right into the forest beside us. Three miles north from it, we would take a road to begin our trip to Hartford City. Once we left this small forest, we would be completely out of Aseamir's territory and into the wild, uninhabited province of the Salquessaé Plains, until the road joined another, much larger and better-travelled road, which was the main road to Hartford City.

Abruptly, I was aware of the sound of thudding hooves, and the sound did not belong to Benthey. I looked over my shoulder, trying to find the source of the noise. I did not have to look hard or long.

Two horses were approaching me cautiously from behind at a steady gait, armed soldiers astride them. They slowed once they realized that I had noticed them and had stopped. One of the men's horses was a black Appaloosa and the other a light bay. Alarmed, I continued to watch for several more seconds to see what they were going to do. I discerned that they were headed for my horse and me, but why, I could not guess. Uneasiness accompanied this realization, and butterflies of anxiety began fluttering in my gut.

One of the men, the younger of the two raised a bow—strung with a black-tipped arrow—and called out, "You, there: Halt! Don't move!"

Frowning and feeling apprehension stir in my chest, I squeezed my heels against Benthey's sides lightly, letting him know he needed to be ready to run. The horse merely shook his mane and looked at the other horses uninterestedly, but as they slowly came closer, he began to become more restless.

The two men continued to approach me, more slowly now. The arrow was still pointed menacingly at me, and Benthey was clearly ill at ease. He twitched and fidgeted frequently, despite my murmured words of reassurance. But I was not so comforted myself.

Finally, as the soldiers got to be about two hundred yards away, I said in a voice that quavered slightly, "What do you want?"

The man with the bow said roughly, "Don't try to escape, girl. We're taking you back to our captain, and you're going to come willingly and without protest, understand?"

Now I knew something was definitely wrong. These men wanted to seize me and take me to their captain? *Why, and on whose orders?* I wondered.

As they approached even closer, I made a decision and kicked Benthey's sides, saying fearfully, "Benthey! Run!" The horse instantly bolted forward, his eagerness to get away evident with every pump of his muscular legs. Fear pounding in my heart, I looked back over my shoulder, wondering if the soldiers were going to give chase.

They did. Surging their mounts forward, the two men swiftly began gaining on Benthey and me. The forest slid by in a blur as I urged my stallion on faster, clutching the reins tightly as Benthey pounded down the path.

When I looked back again, one of the soldiers, the one on the Appaloosa, kicked his mare harder and began to pull up beside me on my right. He reached out a hand to seize Benthey's reins to stop the roan.

"Benthey!" I shouted, pulling Benthey's reins out of reach of the man's hand. I had no idea why these men were attacking me, but I was not about to let them accomplish what they had come to do.

The man astride the Appaloosa jerked his reins to the left, and with no choice but to obey, the mare then rammed into Benthey, crushing her weight against my leg. I stifled a groan of pain.

I slapped Benthey's reins against his neck again, still pressing my heels firmly into his side to keep him going faster, and he whipped his head into the Appaloosa's. She snorted angrily. The armoured soldier on my left steered his bay toward Benthey, trying to trap my horse in between the two of theirs.

I gasped as both my legs were pressed into Benthey's sides by the other horses' weights. Benthey swerved his head and bit the soldier's outstretched hand. With a cry, he reined his horse back. However, the Appaloosa's soldier pursued. I grunted and kicked Benthey.

A tree in the middle of the path loomed unexpectedly before us. Benthey swerved, missing the tree completely, but when the Appaloosa tried to do the same, she was off. Her rider's left leg and shoulder hit the tree, and he tumbled to the ground while his mare escaped unscathed.

Several hundred yards away, I reined the roan to a stop, looking over my shoulder, and patted his sides. He seemed proud that he had so skillfully evaded the riders and protected me, and I was glad he had done so.

But the bay's soldier, who was still clutching his wounded hand, rode up slowly toward me. I strung my bow and nocked an arrow, in case he should try to fight. But the soldier looked beyond me and grinned. Confused, I turned my head but felt only the cool sting of a sword on my neck.

CAPTURE

I slowly turned my head and stared at the young man at the end of the sword. His dark brown curls gave him an even younger look, and he appeared as if he was trying very hard to conceal his anger. His russet eyes, so dark they were almost black, showed fiery fury, which startled me. Why did he look so angry?

The other soldier, the one on the bay, came up behind me and shoved me hard with his uninjured hand. Caught off-guard, I slipped off Benthey and tumbled to the ground, landing on my outstretched wrist. I grimaced as pain lanced up my arm. Benthey, seeing that strangers were trying to harm me, reared in the direction of the young boy. To my shock, the boy stood fearlessly before my alarmed horse, not seeming to notice that at any second those flailing hooves could smash into him. After a moment, the boy reached out and took Benthey's reins casually, as if this were something he did every day. He held onto the leather reins very tightly and close to Benthey's mouth, and Benthey, sensing he was under the boy's control, reluctantly calmed and stood panting beside the boy.

I massaged my throbbing wrist as I watched with trepidation. I had never seen anyone who was so unafraid of a horse before.

The boy looped Benthey's reins around a tree limb and then stalked over to me. With a painfully strong grip on my upper arm, he dragged me to my feet. He pulled out a small, thin black cord and tied it tightly around my wrists, making my injured one throb all the more.

The boy turned me around, and I saw that there were more soldiers gathering around us, watching with amusement. A rather large, heavyset man at the head of the contingent crossed his arms and looked on with a sneer. The boy shoved me forward abruptly, and not expecting this, I stumbled and fell to my knees before the other soldiers. My wrist was aching so badly that I hardly cared. But I was curious nonetheless, and I looked around at the soldiers tentatively, trying to figure out why they had captured me.

The large man at the front, who I guessed was the leader of the troop, stepped forward slowly, eyeing me. The boy stalked past me, hissing murderously to the captain, "There is your prize; I hope you're not too disappointed." And then he disappeared into the crowd of gathered soldiers, leaving me wondering what on earth he meant by "your prize."

The captain tried to raise my chin so that I would look at him, but I flinched away, heart hammering in my chest painfully. In answer, the man slapped me across the face violently. I lost my balance and fell to the ground, feeling blood begin to ooze down my cheek. Stunned, I stared at the leaves just a few inches below my face, trembling. "Insolent brat," the captain muttered, and then he said to his soldiers, "Bring her with us. The slavers will have their prize."

One of the soldiers hauled me to my feet and shoved me on after the others. Two others tended to the injured soldiers and the bay, bringing them and Benthey after us a while later.

Still trembling and in pain because of my throbbing wrist, I fell into step with the soldiers as they continued to march through the woods, taking me away from my home forever.

⁓

We walked constantly, rarely stopping for food, drink, or rest. It was taking a toll on me because of both the pain of my injury and the brutal pace of the march. And as a prisoner, I was allowed less of everything, even rest. When we did happen to stop for a while, I had to remain standing while they all sat or reclined on the grass. I watched grudgingly from my spot while massaging my tender wrist.

We marched for three days through the Salquessaé until we entered an ancient, grey forest at sunset on the third day. Eerily silent, the trees, though large, were all dead. It seemed to me that an eternal, unseen winter had taken this forest captive forevermore, and its relentless grasp was visible even in the approaching darkness. I had never been so afraid to go to sleep before in my life. With the woods being so quiet, I could hear every single soft noise, and every one made my heart race with renewed speed. The spindly, spider-like shapes of the dead tree limbs silhouetted against the pale moon were especially frightening. I had never seen trees like this before, and frankly, they scared me.

A large forest, it took us nearly two days to reach the other side. I had no idea where we were going, but I did know we were travelling in almost the exact opposite direction of the road to Hartford City.

When we rested that night, the soldiers sat around the fire, and I was cast out to the edge of the glade as usual, far away from the safety and warmth of the flames. I huddled in front of a dead tree, getting what protection I could from the unusually bitter wind.

I could see the boy who had captured me by the fire, silent and stony faced. He seemed to be somewhat of an outcast in the troop; none of the men ever spoke to him nor even looked at him except when necessary. I wondered how old he was, for he looked only a few years older, at most, than Malitha and I.

Malitha. My family. What was I going to do? Had they any idea that I had never made it to the road and that I was now being taken who knows where by a group of soldiers? And why did there seem to be so many soldiers about lately? I sighed and sank down lower against the grey tree, feeling as though I could cry, for one more question was plaguing me, one that I was afraid to think about: What had I done wrong to deserve this?

ॐ

It was midnight when I saw him for the first time, only a few hours after I had been huddled up against that old dead tree. I was awakened by dull vibrations that shook the ground faintly beneath me. I opened my eyes uncertainly, not entirely convinced I was fully awake. But as I moved my eyes around the dim, shadowy depths of the forest, I became more confident that it was not a dream. There were horses nearby.

I pushed myself to a half-sitting position, listening hard. The quiet swishing of horses' manes and tails and the muted but audible thud of their hooves broke the silence of the night, and I could very faintly see large, moving shapes through the gloom of the night.

I looked over my shoulder, making sure no one had noticed my movement. None of the men stirred, and the fire had long since died, letting the creeping fog and chill steal over the campsite.

I carefully stood, holding my breath as I waited for someone to wake from my hesitant move, but when no one did, I gingerly took a few steps forward, still looking over my shoulder. My bound hands throbbed painfully, but I paid them no mind as I hurried into the dark woods.

Then, as the sound of hooves grew louder, I curiously turned my attention to the curtain of mist and fog before me, trying to make out any details or shapes. All I could see were occasional glimpses of moving black shapes, and I squinted slightly, wishing I could see better.

As I drew closer, the mist parted around me, letting me gain clearer sight of the horses and riders, moving—for the most part—silently through the forest, like a band of thieves stealing their way from the site of their crime. I began to be able to make out individual men astride the large horses, and I could tell they were wearing armour. Catching my breath, I moved quickly to where I was partially concealed by a thin grey tree. Pressed against the tree for suppression, I watched curiously as the long chain of horses and riders filed by slowly through the gloom.

The riders' heads were bowed, as were the horses', and the snaking mist curled around their hooves menacingly, as though it were warning the men that danger could befall them here. The horses were massive in size, barrel-chested, and with hooves that were as big as my head. Their thick tails dragged against the ground, making a soft, scratching noise against the dead leaves. I would have come up only to the horses' chests, had I been standing next to them. Astonished, I watched them with renewed interest.

I gazed at the men and their horses parading past for a few grey minutes, lulled by the soft sound of the horses' hooves on the ground and the gentle clinking of the men's armour. I relaxed against the tree, knowing that they could not see me.

Curious, I examined their faces briefly as each rode past. I knew, somewhere, deep inside my mind, that they were not elven kind, but I did not want to believe that any other races could exist. *There aren't any other kinds*, I reminded myself warningly, but even as I thought it, I knew it was not true.

I looked up then, suddenly feeling an odd compulsion to do so. My eyes met two storm-grey ones, and they belonged to a young man about my own age. He was looking at me as if he had known I was there all along and had been waiting for me to notice him. His eyes were the colour of the mist that veils the ocean on a stormy day, and they looked like two stars hidden behind the smoke of a soul-burning fire. *I know those eyes*, I realized with a jolt. Feeling a weird emotion flutter in my heart, I found I could not look away from those knowing blue-grey eyes. For they were mine.

The touch of a hand on my shoulder startled me, and I jumped away from the tree, whirling around.

The boy who had captured me stood behind me, one finger to his lips to signal for silence. I gaped at him for a moment, unable to believe he was here. I suddenly caught a short glimpse of a white bandage on his hand and another on one of his feet. A few pale streaks of dried blood were still visible on the linen strips. I had not known he had been injured, but he looked strong and determined, his russet eyes showing no signs of pain or weakness. There were dark circles under his eyes, however, and his face showed none of the characteristic softness of a young teenager. He looked hard and well worn, and that in turn made me feel vulnerable.

He slowly lowered his finger from his mouth, and then said in a low, rough whisper: "What are you doing out here? They might have seen you." He gestured at the passing horsemen.

I glanced over my shoulder, but to my dismay, the soldier whose eyes I had met was already gone. I did not know why I was so disappointed, but I had felt some strange, unexplainable connection to him, as if we were alike, he and I, in some, peculiar way ...

I slowly turned back to the waiting boy in front of me and answered him wearily, "I couldn't sleep, and I wanted to get away for a while, away from the others ... And I was curious."

His dark eyes flashed disapprovingly, and his mouth tightened. "About what?" he asked sharply, and I flinched back a little at the steel in his voice.

"The horsemen ... The sound of their horses' hooves woke me, and I wanted see who they were. Have I done wrong?"

His eyes darkened again, but he answered, "No. Just as long as none of them saw you." His gaze swept over my shoulder to where the last few soldiers were filing slowly by, their shapes partially obscured by the fog.

I looked away uncomfortably, thinking again of the soldier's blue-grey, knowing eyes and how I had felt I was looking into my own eyes. Fighting back a shudder, I exhaled unsteadily, my breath parting a thin screen of fog before me.

The boy said in a low and weary voice, "What's your name?"

"Elysia," I answered and then asked him the same. His eyes tightened temporarily, but he answered reluctantly, "Veryan."

I eyed him carefully, wondering why revealing his name would cause him such discomfort. In fact, our whole conversation seemed to be awkward for him, and he seemed very closed-off and aloof. His dark brown eyes appeared to be eternally cold and unemotional. Frowning, I studied him closer. Weariness lined every inch of his face, and his eyes had no youthful sparkle or hint of laughter. He looked as though he could collapse with fatigue at any moment. I suddenly felt very sorry for him and wondered, yet again, why he was here with all these older men and why he looked so exhausted.

Veryan looked around warily, as if he thought the soldiers were still nearby and could hear us speaking. Then he said frostily, "We should be getting back to camp, in case some of them happen to wake up." He turned and began walking through the thick mist back to the campsite, leaving me with no choice but to follow.

I glanced back once more, wishing I knew why I had such a sense of foreboding.

◊

Veryan was silent beside me as we marched, his brown eyes frosty and distant once more and his face impassive. He held the reins of a stallion, but he did not ride the animal, even though his foot was bound to be paining him. However, he showed no hint of ache or weakness.

Dark clouds, the colour of black smoke, were building in the west—the direction we were headed—and they looked as if they could burst at any moment. Thunder rumbled threateningly in the distance. Right now, I hoped it would rain, even though, later, I knew I would regret it. The air was hot and stuffy, and the stagnant breeze did nothing to alleviate the clogging heat of the surroundings. Strands of my hair clung to my forehead and my cheeks, and I brushed them back wearily, feeling the sweat of my brow come off on my hand. Longing for rain, I glanced up at the sky pensively.

"I hope it will rain soon. The air's hot enough to burn us alive," I murmured to Veryan, and he scowled in reply. Veryan did not seem to be in a particularly agreeable mood, and it showed on his weary face.

"Yes, the skies have not blessed us with rain in a long while," a new voice said on the other side of me; I found that it belonged to one of my friends, Marcis. He and I had had small conversations before, but we had not become anything more than acquaintances to each other. He, too, held the reins of a horse and walked beside us amiably. Veryan frowned again and pointedly looked away, staring straight ahead with steely indifference.

We walked silently beside each other for a long time in the stiff, hot air. I gazed up at the heavy clouds that looked so ready to burst and longed to feel the soft drumming of cool rain on my skin.

Suddenly I was aware of faint vibrations coming through the swaying grass. I felt it only very slightly, but it was there. I dropped my gaze from the sky and looked straight ahead, puzzled. There was nothing before me except the small line of soldiers and tan grasses that were swaying stiffly in the stuffy air. I listened closely again with my feet as well as my ears. The tremor was still there. I turned to Veryan and said in a low voice, "Do you hear something? Or feel a vibration?"

He looked at me slowly with an expression as unfathomable as it was chilling. An involuntary shudder tingled over my spine as his dark-brown eyes burned into mine. "Yes," he stated, and there was no emotion in that single, weighted word.

Unsure, I turned my gaze away, staring at the ground beneath my feet without seeing it, thinking.

The judders grew louder, and I became nervous. The vibrations were too hard and uneven to be a horse's gait, even a group of them, and something told me that these animals, or whatever they were, were large, larger than any animal I had encountered as of yet. I exhaled shakily.

Something moving out of the corner of my eye caught my attention, and I looked up. There were small, fast-moving specks on the horizon, and they were fast approaching. Narrowing my eyes, I tried to make out what exactly they were, but they were still too far away, even with my sharp vision. "What are they?" I mused softly, not truly intending to speak out loud.

There was a moment's hesitation, and then Veryan answered my question in an equally low voice, one that, again, contained no emotion: "Wolves. They're coming toward us for a reason." His russet eyes met mine, and I saw traces of doubt written in the bottomless brown depths.

The troop slowly drew to a halt as the soldiers sighted the wolves. Murmurs of unease rippled over them, and I vaguely heard the leader saying something in his deep, obnoxious voice. I unconsciously moved closer to Veryan so that our shoulders were touching and glanced at him with uncertainty. He exchanged a faintly nervous look with me.

Suddenly the wolves were much closer, and their sheer size astounded me. They were easily as big as the massive horses I had seen the soldiers riding the night I had met Veryan, which dwarfed every horse I had ever seen here in Yaracina, but these dogs were even several feet taller than the soldiers' horses. Had I been standing next to one, I would have only come up to the top of its front leg. Their eyes burned with a strange determination, and there seemed to be extraordinary intelligence mingled in with the purpose. I could have sworn that they knew what they were doing and why.

Half a second later, the first of the gargantuan wolves slammed into the troop, wiping out several men with one blow of its giant paw. The massive wolves were surprisingly swift and agile, and they dispatched many of the men without barely a glance at them. Wondering why on earth the soldiers did not rise again after they were knocked over, I stood inert in the midst of the confusion. My mind was bewildered, and I felt as if I should be doing something, but what, I did not know. Growls and sounds of claws tearing flesh sounded all around me, and dazed, I looked around for Veryan. I could not see him.

I took a few hesitant steps forward, looking around lethargically for Veryan. An immense grey wolf bounded past me, so close that I could feel the soft brush of its fur against my side, and snarling, closed its huge jaws around a man's shoulder. He did not rise again, and to my horror, I realized the man was dead. Never before had the death of an elf touched me, for although I knew of Alqua's parents dying, I had but heard vague stories of the circumstances. And because the elves had the potentiality to be immortal, our town never saw people's deaths, especially nothing like what I was witnessing now.

I suddenly tripped over something on the ground, and I fell backwards over a soldier's body. Horrified at the sight of his wide, empty eyes staring blankly into nothing, I scrambled back a few feet, heart pounding.

A low snarl caught my attention, and I looked up swiftly. My heart caught in my throat. A colossal russet wolf was crouched before me, just across the soldier's body, his intelligent black eyes watching me purposefully. I flinched back, startled. The wolf bared its teeth at me, inching forward unwaveringly.

I froze, unable to think or move with the shock of what could happen in the next few moments. My heart was beating so rapidly that I felt it could stop any moment, and my head felt dizzy with pounding adrenaline. My eyes locked with the wolf's, and I, yet again, noticed that there seemed to be undeniable intellect in the wolf's black eyes.

He took another few, slow steps forward, a low growl emanating from his throat. I caught a glimpse of sharp, white fangs glinting in the dim light.

Almost to myself, I murmured, "Why are you doing this?" I knew that the wolf could not understand, so I was not entirely sure why I had said it.

But, to my surprise, the wolf halted, his ears swivelling forward, a look of astonishment in his fathomless black eyes. He cocked his head curiously and took another step toward me. Now all the hostility was gone from his stance, and it was a step of pure inquisitiveness.

I unconsciously scooted back, heart still pounding and still light-headed. My hand scraped against the armour of another fallen man behind me, and with a terrified glance backwards at the body, I stopped, trapped.

But the wolf seemed to have no interest in killing me anymore. He was intently watching me, looking as though searching for something in my face. He cocked his head again.

Then he spun around and bounded away, lifting his jaws and letting loose a terrific howl that echoed across the plains and seeped into my bones. I felt something stir deep inside me at the sound, something I had never felt before …

All of the other wolves paused, spun their ears in his direction, and immediately loped away from the battered troop, following the russet wolf instinctively. I noticed that several of them halted briefly, casting an enquiring look in my direction, and then continued on after their leader.

I felt a hand on my arm and looked over my shoulder to see Veryan, staring after the wolves guardedly. Then he looked at me and asked, "Are you hurt?"

"No, no, Veryan, I'm fine … H-he understood me …," I said, half to myself, staring after the disappearing wolf pack with bewilderment, not entirely sure of what had just happened. Somehow, I knew the russet wolf had understood what I had said and had spared my life.

I do not know how on earth a wolf could comprehend what an elf says, but he did.

Veryan looked at me strangely, as if questioning my sanity, and flushing, I realized how ridiculous my words sounded. "Never mind, then," I replied softly, gazing after the wolves with a strange feeling in the pit of my stomach.

༈

Twelve of the original twenty soldiers did not rise again, and this bothered me. Surely their wounds were not so severe that they had died. Then the thought of the eyes of the man whom I had tripped over returned to my mind, and I shuddered involuntarily.

THE TOWER OF ORLENA

The clouds burst not long after the wolf attack, and heavy torrents of rain pounded down ruthlessly on the contingent, soaking them through with cool rain. Veryan pushed his hair out of his eyes yet again. He was glad now for the hot air preceding the storm because it still warmed them after the rain began to fall, creating a balmy cocoon of steamy air around them.

Elysia walked beside him, her twilight-blue eyes still gazing ahead at the horizon where the wolves had disappeared. He did not know why she seemed to be almost longing for their return. Veryan did not understand what she had told him when he had found her after the skirmish: *"He understood me …"* Did she think the wolf had known what she had said? He gave a mental shrug, not wanting to think about it at this time.

The wolf attack and the death of so many of the troop reminded him once again of Pyralus's death, only his death had been committed by the same humans he had found Elysia watching a few nights ago. Shaking his head miserably, Veryan wished with all his might that he could have saved Pyralus.

"Veryan …?" he heard Elysia tentatively ask, and he met her eyes, which were watching him enquiringly. "Veryan, where did you live before you joined the army?"

Anger blossomed in Veryan's chest, and without thinking, he snapped, "That's none of your concern!"

Stung, Elysia blinked a few times in hurt and then slowed her pace a little so that he was walking ahead of her. Guilt seeped through his resentment, but Veryan refused to acknowledge it. It infuriated him whenever his home and family were brought up. He knew it should not, but invariably it did.

Then he heard Elysia say softly, "Forgive me. I didn't know it was a sensitive subject." There was a bit of stubborn pride in her voice, and Veryan hid a smile.

Veryan wiped drops of rain from his brow. He knew that they were getting close to the tower now, and he also could tell from the way Gornhelm had been treating Elysia that she would be put in the prison with Yaron. *Yaron.* The memory made Veryan sigh and fervently wish he and Pyralus had been chosen for something else that night instead of setting the house on fire and taking the boy captive. Exhaling deeply, Veryan fought off the memories of the charred smell of the flaming wood, the dying screams of Yaron's parents, and Pyralus's unduly frightened eyes. He had always wondered why Pyralus had seemed so tense and scared that night when the house had come into view ...

Elysia asked, now back beside him, "What's the tower like?"

He raised an eyebrow at her, wondering why she would care to know, but all the same, he answered, "There are about seventy floors. Most of them are long abandoned and haven't been walked upon for many years. I imagine all the hallways and doors of those floors are rotting now. There are only about five stories that we actually use. One is a small armoury, where we have extra swords, armour, bows, spears, and the like, and the others are our quarters and the prison." *Where Gornhelm will no doubt put you*, he resisted the urge to add.

Elysia's brow furrowed. He knew she understood that important point as well. Her twilight-blue eyes darkened, and she scowled. "Are there any other prisoners?" she muttered, none too hopeful.

Panic flared in Veryan's chest, and he did not know what to say. *Should I tell her about him? Perhaps not.* He was quiet for a long moment, hoping she would draw an answer from his silence. And, he assumed, she did for her scowl deepened, but what answer, he did not know. Elysia sighed and brushed her wet hair out of her face.

"Elysia," he asked then, "where are you from?"

"Aseamir," she responded, and he noticed that her voice seemed strangely unemotional. With a quick glance at her eyes, he saw that it was because she was trying to hold back her emotion. Feeling lonely, he looked ahead, looking for the tower.

It did not take long for it to come into view. A massive, dark cylindrical shape springing out of the sea of tan grasses, it was imposing and sinister and always made Veryan feel as though it harboured some sleeping evil that only needed gentle prodding to be awakened.

Elysia commented upon seeing it, "*That's* the Tower of Orlena? It looks like a place of sin."

"Not far from it," Veryan replied grimly, mind flashing back to the night he and Pyralus had had to enter the burning house and bring Yaron out a captive.

With the black clouds that were mounted in the sky and the grey haze of the falling rain, the tower looked more than ever like a place of sin and regret. It held many unpleasant memories for Veryan, and he was not relishing the fact that he would soon have to revisit them.

⁂

The troop stopped not long after to eat something. Veryan could sense that the morale of the soldiers was perilously low, even though they were very close to the tower. The wolf attack had startled them, as well as slaughtered over half of the troop. Veryan had never seen wolves that monstrous. They were easily as large as the massive black horses of the soldiers he had seen and bigger than that, by several feet. Their eyes had burned with unquestionable intelligence, and they had followed their leader instantly and automatically. Veryan knew that they were more than just giant, brutish wolves who lived for killing. No, they had had an incentive for attacking the troop, and for some reason, something about Elysia had made the lead wolf call off his pack's attack. Veryan thought hard, trying to list all the possible reasons for it in his head, but none of them made any sense.

Elysia stood beside one of the horses, absentmindedly stroking its nose and staring up at the grey sky as the rain continued to fall. Her blue-grey eyes seemed to be seeing something Veryan could not, and her face had a curious expression on it, one that Veryan could not decode.

⸜

The tower grew closer with every passing minute, and so did Veryan's dread. By noon, even though the sun was hidden behind the weeping clouds, the tower was only a few hundred yards away, its massive, colossal stones cast with dim shadows, giving it a further feeling of darkness.

As the tower guards opened the ancient gates, which were forged of black iron, they began to creak, making a terrible, screeching sound that echoed over the plains. Veryan winced at the screaming noise that clawed so painfully at his ears.

A long, stone-cobbled path led up to the great doors that directed them into the tower. Veryan looked up, trying to find the top of the tower, but it was too high for him to see. The tower looked as though it were swaying against the gloomy sky, and Veryan dropped his head.

The grey gloom of the rain obscured the Salquessaé Plains around them, and Veryan could suddenly feel the gigantic pressure of the world crushing in around him, making him claustrophobic. Now he longed to get inside, away from the oppressive weight of the dark storm outside.

The mighty doors swung inward as Gornhelm and his lieutenant, Comundus, ascended the steps, and the rest of the soldiers followed hesitantly, uncomfortable in this foreboding place. Veryan tensed as he walked through the doors; it felt as if the tower was swallowing them and would never let them out, holding them prisoners forever.

To his surprise, he felt Elysia take his hand hesitantly, and he could feel the tension in her touch. She was intimidated as well, but Veryan yanked his hand away.

The men began ascending the stairs that would take them to the inadequate quarters that the tower provided and to tend the wounded. Veryan murmured, "Gornhelm will tell you where to go."

YARON

Alarmed at Veryan's departure, I stood staring blankly after him until he disappeared from sight with the others. Then, unwillingly, I turned to Gornhelm, who was watching me decisively, his black eyes narrowed. Heart sinking, I waited for his verdict.

He then gestured for me to walk in the direction of a smaller, darker stairwell, and loathingly, I complied. I knew he was going to put me in the prison.

The steps were dimly lit by dying torches, and they cast flickering shadows over us as we moved down the stairway. Gornhelm took one from its bracket before following me down the stairs.

I counted twenty-four steps. At the end of them was darkness; no more torches supplied light. Feeling anxiety at what could be waiting down there, I paused on the steps, unsure. But a prod from the tip of Gornhelm's sword pushed me on towards the darkness.

To my relief, Gornhelm walked ahead of me into the blackness with the torch he was holding, providing a small halo of light that pushed back the dark a bit. He pulled a silver key from a pouch on his belt and stuck it in the lock of a cell. He swung open the iron door and looked at me expectantly.

Filled with abhorrence and hatred for my circumstances, I walked in slowly, hating the feel of darkness sliding over my skin.

A sudden push made me pitch forward, and I crashed into a stone wall. I fell back, stunned, and landed on a pile of wet, mouldy hay, and I heard a mouse scurry by, squeaking its alarm at being disturbed.

Gornhelm laughed and swung the cell door shut. I could hear his heavy footsteps as he ascended the stairs. The torch he had been carrying went with him, leaving me surrounded by heavy gloom and blinding blackness.

؈

I woke that night to the sound of someone coughing. Listening hard, I finally determined that the noise came from several cells away. I said hoarsely, "Hello? Is anyone there?"

No one answered me, but I heard something, as if someone had shifted. Frowning, I squinted into the gloom, trying to pick out a person's shape in the blinding dark, but I could see nothing. I waited a few minutes and then decided that no one was going to answer, if there was anyone there at all.

I sighed and slowly lowered myself back to the floor. I lay on my back and stared dismally up into the darkness, wishing that I did not feel so alone and cut off from the rest of the world. I was captive in a stone prison in crushing darkness for an unknown reason, and I could do nothing to free myself.

The realization suddenly brought a lump to my throat and tears swam across my eyes. I gave a short sigh, blinked away the tears, and sniffed. I did not want to cry, not yet.

A long while later, I heard another small noise. I sat up, propping myself on one elbow, listening and strained my ears, trying to hear something—anything—else. I realized then that it was because I did not actually want to be so alone as I was feeling—I wanted someone else to suffer through this with me. However selfish that may seem, it would certainly make me feel much better if I knew someone else was going through the same torment I was.

"Hello?" I said again, softly.

Again, there was no answer.

I lay down again, closed my eyes, and let my weariness overtake me. A short while later, I drifted into a dreamless sleep.

ﹿ

Much later in the night, though not yet dawn, I heard another cough from the person in the cell down from me. It was hard and forceful, and it woke me from my light sleep.

I propped myself on one elbow again and waited, not saying anything. It was then that I noticed the light. The moonlight shimmered down through a tiny, jagged crack high up the wall, illuminating floating particles of dust, making them look like tiny, buoyant gems. I paused a moment to admire this glimpse of beauty amid the gloom, the little specks playing aloft. I supposed that the storm had finally passed, else I would have noticed the light before. I sighed, wishing for a large window through which I could see the stars. But the little light with which I was provided was so precious and magical that I did not mind not seeing the stars; the sparkling dust in the dark of that infernal cell was almost as wondrous.

Then I tried to see through the dark again, squinting. I hoped the light would help, but it did not much. I could faintly make out a shape darker than everything else in a murky corner of the prison, but I was not sure that it was anything more than a shadow. I rolled onto my stomach and went to sleep again.

ﹿ

The next morning, I wakened with a start. I sat up swiftly, unsure what had awakened me. I gazed around the prison with a darting glance, and seeing nothing unusual, I relaxed.

I absently massaged my right wrist, which was sore from when Gornhelm had shoved me in here and I had thrust my hand out to save myself from a fall. It was slightly purple and ached, but other than that, I was virtually unharmed from his rough push. My other wrist, the one that had been bruised from the fall during my capture, was mostly healed now.

I heard a small noise, and instantly my eyes found the source. I blinked in surprise.

A boy was partly concealed in shadows several cells down from me, out of the light. He looked only one or two years younger—if that—than I. He was sitting with his knees pulled up to his chest and his head down, his face obscured from view. His body was wiry and lean, but he looked muscular.

Baffled as to why a boy so young was locked up in here, I blinked a couple more times. *Why on earth …? But he's so young! Why would he be in here? He's obviously a captive, too, but … why would they want such a young boy? Surely he can't be of any use yet.*

I sat against the stone wall and tilted my head back, studying the ceiling. Then I gazed briefly at the small crack and finally back at the boy.

I started. Even in the dim light of the prison, I could see the boy's eyes locked on me. With a wildness to them, he looked as if he were a feral animal taken from his home and caged in a lightless world and left there to waste away, and I was his only hope of escape.

⁊

The rest of the day, I avoided looking his way, but the few times I did happen to glance at him, his stormy eyes were always on me. It made me feel uneasy.

When I did manage to forget about the boy for a while, I became intensely bored. I stayed locked all day in the prison, with nothing to do, nothing different to see, and nothing to eat. I was hungry by noon because of my deprivation of regular, good meals over the past ten days, but no one ever came with any food. As an elf, I could go for almost a week and a half without food, but regardless, I had become ravenous.

I sighed and absently fingered a rough stone. Coarse and gritty, it provided some distraction from monotony, but I soon got tired of fiddling with it. This heavy dose of boredom was taking its toll on me; to escape it, I even dozed throughout the day several times.

⁊

When night came, I reluctantly resigned myself to the hard floor again, wishing fervently for a blanket, at least. As I lay motionless on the cool floor, I wondered about the boy again. He had said nothing the entire, gruelling day, but then, neither had I.

I felt sort of a connection to him since we were both stuck in this god-forsaken prison with no food or water, and we were both away from our homes. I just wished I knew his name. I sighed and closed my eyes, letting all thoughts empty from my mind.

"Who are you?"

The question was barely audible in the silent expanse of our confinement, but I heard it. My eyes flew open, unsure if he had actually spoken, or if I was just imagining it. But I knew I had heard it.

I supported myself on one elbow as I sat up. "I'm Elysia. What's your name?"

A long, deafening stretch of silence followed and then: "Yaron."

I looked over at the cell that Yaron was supposedly in, but I could not see anything. Then the boy came into the light. The only emotion displayed on his face was that of wariness and caution. It was like trying to read a stone.

I came forward until my face was an inch from the steel bars that formed two of the walls of my cell. "What are you doing here?"

Yaron watched me with suspicious and intelligent brown eyes. Then he answered my question: "I'm locked up here until I'm old enough to join the queen's army." He brushed a lock of gold hair from his face. His eyes were wary.

"Why?"

He gazed at me guardedly. "Because I can fight. I can use a sword better than most people in this troop, but it's only been recently that I've been able to beat them all, and I have. Of course, it's only thanks to my extra training outside of here that I've been getting better. Gornhelm stopped my training here nearly a year ago, but now I can defeat all of the men here … Comundus, Phallax, Eston, Janek, Pyralus, and—"

I stopped him, confused. "Who's Pyralus? There's no one in this troop named Pyralus."

Yaron frowned, his dark eyes narrowing and becoming surprisingly flinty. "Yes, there is. He has blue eyes, and he's friends with that other boy, Veryan. He …" Yaron broke off when he realized that I had no idea whom he was talking about. "But … he was with them when they left." I could see that the fact that I had never met this Pyralus before had unsettled the boy.

I wondered who Pyralus was and why I had heard no mention of him from Veryan or any of the men in the troop. The boy seemed so sure he had been with them, and I felt that Veryan would have mentioned him at one time or another.

When I looked back at Yaron, the boy was sitting again in the corner of his cell, half turned towards me. The moonlight shone on a knotted scar across his lower back. I opened my mouth to speak, but Yaron spoke first: "Do you know how I got here?" His voice was low and emotional, and it struck a chord of pity in my heart.

"No. Tell me."

"I was captured. Right from my home. The troop, with Gornhelm at the head, came to my village to search for new recruits and demanded that I join. I had participated in the trials to qualify, and they all said I was the best they'd seen. But my parents didn't want me to go, and I didn't want to either. So Gornhelm pretended to honour our wishes and leave, but that night, they came back and attacked our home. Veryan set it on fire. Pyralus killed my mother and my father, and then they both dragged me out of the house. They left my parents to burn in the house so there would be no evidence of what they had done. Gornhelm suspected that I would try to leave to avoid being recruited, so he took me then, when I was thirteen ...

"There was a training incident soon after they captured me that convinced Gornhelm that I was not as skilled nor as strong as he thought, so that's why he keeps me here in the prison. And so I won't try to leave ... Every two months, a man from another troop comes for me and takes me to one of the army camps for two weeks of training, and then I come back here. As I said, if it weren't for that extra training, I wouldn't be getting any better. It's been like this since I came, and so it will be until I'm old enough to become a soldier. This winter, my three years of training will be up, and I'll be forced to join the army."

Yaron was then broodingly silent, and I took that to mean he would say no more on that topic.

I was stunned. *How could anyone do that to him? That's barbaric! A boy stolen right from his own house, and his parents killed!* I clenched my jaw and said sympathetically, "I'm sorry, Yaron. That's awful."

The boy grunted in agreement. Then I said, "Do you ever get out of the cell besides when you go for training?"

"Twice a week. I'm allowed to walk around outside, but only inside the gates. The only time I'm allowed to leave the tower is when I'm taken to an army camp to be trained," Yaron said softly.

I silently vowed that, if I ever escaped from the tower, I would release Yaron too.

"Elysia." Startled to hear Veryan's voice, I looked over my shoulder. He was standing on the last step, a battered steel tray of food in hand. I heard Yaron growl softly and move out of the light. I understood the boy's behaviour, but I still went over to the front of my cell, glad to see my friend.

His eyes were frosty as I came into the light. "Hello," he said gingerly.

I returned the greeting and then questioned him. "Veryan, did you really … did you and Pyralus really drag Yaron out of his home and help Gornhelm burn his house?" As much as I wanted to believe that something this awful could not possibly be true, I had a terrible feeling that it was.

Pain and steely discomfort flickered over Veryan's face at the mention of Pyralus's name. He was silent for a long time, stony eyes on me, so long that I thought that he would never answer. Then: "Yes."

I stared at him, unsure of what to think. How could people do such a thing and live with themselves? *I had no idea the world was becoming such a terrible place … but then, I've never been out of Aseamir before. What other kind of things like this are going on every day?* I wondered, feeling cold at the thought. "Veryan, how could you do such a dreadful thing?" I asked, still silently horrified.

Anger flared in Veryan's eyes, and he looked at me crossly. "I had no choice, Elysia! Gornhelm ordered Pyralus and me to do it; we couldn't disobey—"

"You *did* have a choice, Veryan!" Yaron said, practically flying to his cell door and gripping the bars with a strength that surprised me. His brown eyes blazed. "You have a choice about everything you do! It's your fault I'm here! Yours and *Pyralus's*!" Yaron snarled. I was surprised at how much anger and spite he put into the word *Pyralus*. Then he yanked his hands away from the bars and withdrew into the darkness, his energy spent. I could hear him sigh heavily as he sat down.

I looked towards Veryan, but he was gone. The steel food tray was on the floor, in reach of my hand if I stretched far enough. I looked at the small tray. The food did not look particularly appetizing, but I was so hungry that I would eat it. *At least they thought to feed me,* I thought dryly as I stretched my hand out and pulled the tray into my cell through the space under the door.

I left it on the stone floor and ate the food slowly, making a disgusted face at the taste of the stale bread. When I was done, I sighed and slumped against the wall. The moonlight on my face cooled my frustrations with the world, and I soon fell asleep.

༄

When I awoke the next morning, Yaron was gone. I guessed he had been allowed outside for the first time this week.

I turned my head towards the high crack in the ceiling above my head. Sunlight was streaming in from the tiny opening, giving a little light to the prison. I noticed that the food tray was gone. I frowned. *You'd think I would've heard if someone had come into my cell during the night,* I thought, a bit disturbed.

"Elysia!" I looked up sharply. Veryan was standing at the door of my cell. He did not smile, but I noticed that his eyes seemed a little less tired. He pulled the door open.

I scrambled to my feet. "How'd you do that?" I exclaimed. Veryan held up the silver key that Gornhelm had used to lock me in here. "Gornhelm said you can go outside if you want, but you have to stay inside the gates, obviously," he said, looking pleased with himself.

༄

Veryan led me outside of the tower, and then the two of us walked around silently. Yaron was nowhere to be seen.

I was acutely aware that Veryan's eyes were constantly on me, as if he was searching for something in my face, and I was uncomfortable under his russet gaze. I was sure my cheeks were slightly red, but I also hoped Veryan did not notice.

To distract myself from my thoughts, I said, "Do you know where Yaron is?"

Veryan's eyes tightened, and he said crossly, "No. I don't keep track of him."

I retorted, "Why are you and he at such odds? Surely he knows it wasn't your fault for what happened that n—"

"No, it was, Elysia. I was the one who lit the fire, and Pyralus dealt with his parents. Yaron was only thirteen at the time, but he fought us viciously. He killed six men before Gornhelm struck him down from behind. He didn't say or do anything the entire way back, but you could tell from the way he looked at me and Pyralus that, one day, he was going to have his vengeance."

My brow furrowed as I took in his words.

"And I will," a low voice growled from behind us. I turned to see Yaron glaring at Veryan with smouldering eyes. His arms were folded across his chest, and his torso rigid, as if the very sight of Veryan enraged him.

Veryan's eyes darkened as well, but he said nothing.

Feeling that being in between these two was not a safe place to be, I said tensely, "Yaron … Veryan … please?"

Yaron's eyes flickered to me, and the storm in them died a little after a moment. But Veryan's dark brown eyes continued to be stormy and steely.

I noticed for the first time that while Veryan was about my height, Yaron was at least a foot taller than I was, and he was a year my junior. Baffled as to how this could be, I studied his face. Like Veryan's, it was tired and worn, with circles under his eyes and no hint of childishness left. But his eyes … they were a deep brown, also like Veryan's, but contained a soft sparkle that seemed permanent.

They were the only part of his face that was not hard—in fact, they seemed rather gentle—and as he looked back at me warily, I suddenly wished that I could look into those soft brown eyes forever.

But I was drawn back to reality when I heard the jovial voice of Comundus behind us. The three of us turned to see Gornhelm's kind-hearted lieutenant striding up to us, a broad grin on his face.

Once he was before us, he greeted us heartily, "Come! Come! It's nearly noon, and lunch will be on the table! The ambassador will be arriving soon, but before that …," he paused and winked at Veryan, "comes feasting!" Comundus finished while beckoning again for Veryan to follow him. I noticed that he did not pay any attention to Yaron and me. I exchanged a glance with Yaron, unsure. But Yaron seemed amused, and so we followed Veryan and Comundus back to the tower.

PLANS

Yaron had infuriated Veryan so much that he had excused himself to his quarters after they had come back inside in an attempt to calm himself down. Partially successful, he now walked up the steps toward the common room, where the banquet was to be held. Still, his thoughts remained on Yaron. The boy acted as though his only reason to live now was to get his retribution on Veryan for what he and Pyralus had done, even though his vengeance was already partially complete: Pyralus was dead.

Now, however, Veryan was anxious to get back to the common room and out of the dank, dreariness of the lower tower. The other soldiers had set up long banquet tables and had lit huge fires in the pits for roasting the meats and stews to be served at the feast. Even from down here, Veryan could smell the warm scents of food cooking over the fires, but he was not looking forward to it at all. The very thought of it made him sick.

He ran on past Gornhelm's quarters; the door was closed and looked ominous in the dim light. But he froze when he heard Gornhelm's thick voice saying, "That prisoner, that beastly girl, she's got to go! She's a threat to us!"

Veryan exhaled softly and knew he had to listen to learn what Gornhelm's plans for Elysia were. As much as he loathed the fact, he knew that he'd also have to relay them to her, no matter what they were. His eyes burned angrily when he imagined all the things Gornhelm could come up with to do to her.

He went back to the door and pressed his ear against the smooth wood.

Gornhelm said, "Well, what do you suggest, Comundus?"

Veryan pulled away from the door for a moment, shocked that the kind old man would be helping Gornhelm in this way, but then continued listening.

He heard Comundus sigh and say, "I don't know, my lord."

Gornhelm said, "We could just have her duel one of the men. She'd be finished before she could lift a sword!"

"No, no, she's only a child, Gornhelm. And besides, you know why we can't do that! Namarii said ...," Comundus started, seeming to be pleading with the captain.

Veryan heard Gornhelm swear. Then the captain exclaimed, "That blasted fire-witch doesn't know anything, Comundus! Why shouldn't we harm her?"

Comundus answered, "She said—"

"I know what she said! It's false! Utterly false! The fire-witch was lying to us, Comundus!"

For a long moment, both men were silent. Then Gornhelm said, "We need to be rid of her, one way or the other, and my original plan for her is as good as any. There are slave traders on the coast. We will trade her for goods, maybe a horse or two!" He seemed eager to get rid of Elysia.

Comundus was silent. Finally he said, "All right. After we have our assignment, we'll take her to the coast-traders and trade her to Bijan and his lot."

UNPREDICTABLE

Rubbing my sore arms, I leaned back against the prison's stone wall. I could barely hear Yaron's light breathing a few cells down. I sighed and closed my eyes, letting my mind drift away from the confines of the stone prison.

After Comundus had come for Veryan, he took us back to our cells. Yaron and I had not been allowed to stay to see the queen's ambassador nor to partake in the feast. I did not particularly care, but I would have liked to stay with Veryan. He seemed out of place and uncomfortable with the rest of the soldiers.

I frowned, unwillingly allowing myself to approach the subject of why I was here. My mother had warned me that there were things she had not told me … and still, the question remained: What had I done wrong?

I looked down at my hands. Thinking of my mother had made me homesick again, and I put my hands over my face to try to keep myself from crying.

"Are you thinking of your family?" Yaron said softly. His husky voice calmed me slightly, and I took a shuddering breath.

"Yes. I miss my mother and sisters. I didn't even get to tell my twin good-bye before leaving," I confessed. My eyes met Yaron's brown ones, and even in the dim light, I could see the soft sparkle. We looked absorbedly at each other for a long moment, and suddenly I knew that Yaron understood my longing for my family. *At least I'll get to see my family again someday. Yaron will never see his parents again because of what Gornhelm and Pyralus and Veryan did ...*

Echoing my thoughts, Yaron sat down by the cell bars facing me and wrapped his arms around his knees, saying softly, "At least you still have your family."

I felt guilty when I heard Yaron say that. I said softly, "I'm sorry, Yaron. I didn't mean to remind you of your parents."

He grunted and said nothing. I was not sure I had ended the conversation on a good note, so I said, "What were your parents' names?"

"My mother was Saula, and my father Jevon."

"Did you have any siblings?"

"No." Yaron shifted to where he was leaning up against the stone wall. I thought I could see tears welling up in his gentle brown eyes. *I feel so sorry for him*, I thought. *I wish there was some way I could cheer him up.* But I could not think of anything that would put a smile on Yaron's face. For a long while, silence filled the prison.

I was about to speak again when Gornhelm came plodding down the stairs. I quickly scooted away from the cell bars, hoping that Gornhelm would not suspect I had been talking to Yaron, but the burly man was not paying attention to what I had been doing. He seemed harried and a bit frustrated. His forehead creased in annoyance when he saw me staring fearfully up at him.

"Girl," he said impatiently, "come. I've a job for you in the armoury." Gornhelm jammed a key into the lock and turned it so hard I thought it might break. He then threw the door open, stomped in, and yanked me to my feet.

I was half pulled, half dragged out of my cell. I looked helplessly over my shoulder at Yaron. The boy was watching me from the door of his cell, his brown eyes shadowed.

꙳

Gornhelm shoved me through the door, and I nearly collided with Veryan, who grabbed my arm to keep me from falling. "Help the men get armed. When you're done, clean and polish the excess armour,"

Gornhelm ordered after me. He slammed the door behind him, and I stared at the door with anger, strangely furious with Gornhelm for making me do this.

I was dimly aware of Veryan beside me. Ignoring him, I stomped towards the racks of armour. There was a rag and bottle of polish for the armour on the bench nearby.

I sat down with a huff, waiting to help someone with his armour, but no one seemed to need my help. *Or else they just don't want to bother me*, I reflected sullenly. Most of the men got all their armour on just fine, but occasionally, a man would ask a fellow soldier for help lacing his greaves or bracers.

Veryan came over and sat down beside me. He wore a leather jerkin over a chain mail shirt and leather bracers were strapped to his forearms. Gold greaves were tied around his shins.

I leaned back and drew a sword from the racks and handed it to Veryan. "Thank you," he said softly, taking it.

"Where are you going?" I asked.

"The queen's ambassador has a mission for us in Dontae, farther down the coast," Veryan replied, avoiding my eyes, "We'll leave at dawn in one week."

"Why are you getting ready now?" I asked.

Veryan shrugged. "All of us are going outside to do sparring practice, and Gornhelm wants us to fight as we would in a real battle."

"Will I ... will I go too? With the troop to Dontae?" I asked, almost inaudibly.

Veryan looked at me, and I was slightly startled to see anger in his eyes. I suddenly had a tight feeling in my throat; I did not want to hear Veryan's answer.

But he replied, "Yes. Gornhelm has ... plans for you." Suddenly Veryan snapped his gaze to mine. "Elysia, I must tell you something." He paused and rubbed his face. "Gornhelm is going to sell you to a band of slavers camped on the coast when we go to Dontae. I-I overheard him telling Comundus before the feast."

I stared at him in stunned silence. *He's going to* sell *me?! To a group of slavers?* I searched Veryan's face for any trace that he was lying.

I don't know why he would, though, I reasoned miserably. There was no lie in Veryan's eyes. He was telling the truth, and I hated him for it.

I looked at the floor, oblivious to the sounds of the men grabbing swords and buckling armour.

Veryan said softly and harshly, "At least he didn't decide to kill you outright."

I stared at him. Kill me outright?

Gornhelm entered the room and announced loudly, "Be outside quickly, or you'll get no food tonight!" He turned to go, but not before grumbling, "You're almost half an hour late as it is."

The men scrambled to gather their things and follow their captain. Veryan slowly picked up his sword and followed the men without a backward glance at me. One of the soldiers, however, remained behind as a guard, stationed at the door. He stared vacantly out at the room and paid no attention to me whatsoever. It was Janek, one of the more unskilled swordsman and one who rarely spoke.

Sighing and feeling lonely, I looked forlornly at the armour for a long while. I then groaned and buried my face in my hands. "Get to work," Janek said in a bored voice.

I sighed again, removing my hands from my face and loathingly took the rag and polish. I took a sword from one of the racks and began my work slowly, drawing upon what little I had read about swords and cleaning them—which was not much.

A hand was suddenly laid on my shoulder. Startled, I turned swiftly to see Yaron smiling down at me.

"Remember, lad, Janek is watching you and the girl, so don't try to run off or anything," I heard Comundus say. I looked over my shoulder to see the kind old man at the door beside Janek. He looked unsure at the sight of the two of us, but after a moment, he said, "I'll come for you two in a few hours; get as much as you can done and don't dawdle." He then left, leaving Janek to guard us as we polished armour.

For the next three hours, the two of us spent our time cleaning and polishing all the metal armour and swords. It was tiring, and soon the muscles in both my arms and Yaron's were burning. I began to wonder if Comundus would remember that we were still there.

I grunted as Yaron tossed me another sword. "Remind me, again, why we're doing this?" I said, glaring at the sword.

Yaron rolled his eyes, a bit of tightness returning to them. "Because Gornhelm, everyone's favourite captain, has commanded us to do so, and we must obey his every whim and desire, for why else would we be here if not to wait on the courageous, kind, and beloved captain?" he said, snorting as he reached for another sword. It was obvious Yaron hated the man as much as I did.

When he was done with the swords I had told him to clean, Yaron grunted and tossed his cleaning rag onto the floor, then leaned back against the wall, and picked up a dagger, eyeing it with an unreadable expression. The steel blade glinted in the dim light, reflecting the gleam in Yaron's eyes. I glanced at Janek, but the soldier had wandered out into the hall, locking the door to the armoury behind him. "Yaron?" I said.

"Hmm?" His eyes never left the dagger.

"What are you thinking about?"

"What? Oh. I was just noticing the inscription on this dagger. Look at these. They must be at least seven centuries old!"

He leaned forward and pointed at the gracefully curved writing running around on the hilt of the dagger and over the cross-guard. They looked like dunes of sand or waves running along a smooth bank. "They're beautiful," I commented, not really understanding his fascination with the markings.

But Yaron continued on, his voice excited. "But don't you see, Elysia? This dagger is not only from seven centuries ago; it's not even *elven*! I think it must be from ancient Greece." He shook his head in amazement and leaned his head back against the wall. "A real Greek dagger, here in Yaracina. What do you think it's doing here? Unless it got here during the War of the Red Moon ... but that still wouldn't explain how it got *here* ..." He continued to puzzle over this for a while. I listened with amusement as I sat down beside him. His brown eyes glittered with excitement as he rambled on.

Finally, I interrupted by saying, "Yaron? I hate to interrupt—"

"No, you don't," he snorted and hefted the dagger to the other hand. "I can tell when you're lying, Elysia. It's not that hard to tell."

He chuckled and got to his feet. Yaron strode over to a rack of swords, pulled out one, and examined it carefully. Then he smiled and shoved it back in. I watched him with interest as he walked to the room's window and sighed, putting his hands on the rails. After a few minutes, he seemed to grow uptight again.

I thought he looked almost worried. His muscular shoulders were tense, and his torso rigid. His hands gripped the black rails tightly. Yaron's golden hair fell over his face, obscuring his eyes, but I could still sense that he was restless. His mood had changed so abruptly, and I speculated as to what had brought on this new, uneasy frame of mind.

"Yaron." I walked up beside him and watched him closely. It concerned me to see him so agitated.

He said nothing but stared out at the Salquessaé Plains, stretching for miles before us. The golden-haired boy sighed and then stared down at the ground.

"What is it?" I asked, touching his shoulder gently. He tensed slightly at my touch, and I felt hard muscle flex under my fingers.

Yaron looked up at me, his brown eyes shadowed. I blinked in surprise at the pain and unfathomable knowledge of something in his eyes that I could not understand. I suddenly felt my heart go out to the boy, and I put my arm around his strong shoulders. I was slightly surprised he did not shrug me off, but he did tense. *He just seems so alone …*

Then, to my complete surprise, a tear rolled down Yaron's cheek, and he bowed his head. His body trembled slightly, and his shoulders tightened. I frowned and said softly, "Yaron? Are you all right?" I looked over my shoulder to make sure Janek had not come back, and he had not.

The boy took a shuddering breath and then wiped away his tears with an angry swipe of his hand. "I'm fine," he said, his voice cracking. "I …, " he began, but then he shrugged and broke off.

I knew he was not. I did not want to crowd him, so I removed my arm from his shoulders and took a step back. *His parents were ... killed by the people who are now holding him captive,* I thought, puzzling yet again over the strange word, *and they'll force him to fight for them this winter. He must have so much anger inside him and so much hurt. I just hope that won't make him too unpredictable in the future.*

I gazed out at the plains and heard Yaron sigh. The boy leaned against the window's frame and crossed his arms. His tears were gone now, and his eyes held the only emotion on his face. I wondered how close he was to losing control.

Moving closer to Yaron, I touched his shoulder. He did not respond. "Yaron," I said, "I know you're angry with Gornhelm and Veryan and all the others about your parents' death, but you can't keep your anger pent up inside you. If it keeps building, eventually there'll be too much for you to contain, and one day, it'll just all explode. And when it does, you won't have any control over it, and it could really hurt you and others around you. Anger is often more hurtful than the wrong that caused it. Don't let anger rule your life, Yaron. It'll destroy you." I gazed at him intently, hoping he was thinking about what I had said.

The boy slowly turned his head until our eyes met. I was slightly scared by the expression I saw there. His brown eyes now held an unmistakable look of smouldering fury, like a blazing bed of red-hot coals. Then, just as quickly, the look vanished, and there was no expression in his eyes whatsoever. The boy then walked across the room to where the Greek dagger lay. He picked it up and then looked back at me. The same unreadable expression returned to his face.

"I may need my anger someday. If I let it go, I'll wish I had it later." Then he whirled suddenly and flung the dagger with incredible force at the door. It lodged with a solid thump less than half an inch above the door's latch. Yaron glared at me for a long moment. Scared, I stared back.

Janek came back inside, apparently having heard Yaron's dagger hit the door. He pulled it out of the door and tossed it to the floor, where it clattered to a stop beside the racks of swords. "Hey, get back to work," he grunted in an uninterested voice.

"We're done," Yaron said stiffly, moving his eyes off me.

"Then get back to your cells. Come on." Janek motioned for us to walk, and we did, all the way back to our cells. Janek locked us back in our iron prisons and then disappeared up to the common room, leaving Yaron and me alone, surrounded by simmering silence.

꒜

I groaned as I let my head thump back against the cell wall. Yaron refused to talk to me, no matter how hard I tried, and sat in the corner of his cell farthest away from me. The boy's impassive face irritated me, but I knew that he was still seething over what had happened earlier.

"Yaron, please talk to me. I'm sorry if I offended you earlier, but I was just trying to help."

"Well, stop trying!"

I blinked in frustrated surprise. "Well, I would think it would make you glad that *someone* cares about you!"

"I can take care of myself!"

"Oh, I can see that; that's why you're still locked up here," I retaliated. I instantly regretted that remark. *It's not his fault he's imprisoned here*, I reminded myself, *and he* can't *do anything about it.*

As I had expected, the boy did not reply but merely shifted to where his back was facing me. My breath caught when I noticed the scar on his lower back again. It almost made tears come to my eyes. *He's so young, and yet he has already suffered so much … I wish there was a way I could help him, but he seems so distant and so … inaccessible.* I pulled my knees up to my chest and rested my chin on them. I tried again. "Yaron … I know that remark was cruel, and I'm sorry. I didn't mean what I said; I was just venting my frustration."

"Yeah, right!" Yaron muttered.

I continued, undeterred, "But I just want you to know that I do care about you. You've suffered more than anyone should have to at your age, and I'm sorry. You don't deserve this."

"Everyone gets things he doesn't deserve." His hand traced his scar. "See this? I got it when I was six years old."

Though he did not give details, I could see his jaw muscles tighten with pain at his memory of it. I felt a pang of sorrow for the boy, and I said quietly, "Neither of us should be here."

"Veryan should be," Yaron muttered. "He deserves every hardship that befalls him."

I started to admonish him but then stopped myself. I had just spoken out in frustration a moment ago, so I carefully considered what to say before I began. Then I said softly, "Perhaps, but I wouldn't know. I don't know anything about him, so I'm not going to judge him. Not yet."

"Are you going to judge me?" Yaron asked sardonically, his face still hidden from my view.

I hesitated. "No, Yaron. I'm not going to judge anyone, least of all you. To form an opinion of people without knowing all the facts would be to elevate myself above everyone else, and I won't do that. I don't know everything that has happened; therefore, I could not be an accurate and fair judge."

Yaron turned to look at me, his eyes watching me with incredulity. I looked back at him for a moment and then lowered my eyes, uncomfortable under his gaze. "So how, then, can you say that we don't deserve to be here, since you said yourself you don't know everything? Could there not be a reason that we are locked in this god-forsaken prison?"

I shrugged, feeling as if I was under attack. "I suppose there could be a reason, but ... I don't know what it is."

Yaron snorted. "Of course you don't. No one knows the reasons for things that happen to us until they are in the past ... and sometimes not even then. I suppose ... everything is linked; everything is either the cause or effect of something else ... but only once we are wise enough to take a step back can we see the whole grand tapestry."

I smiled a little. "Yes, I suppose so."

Yaron let out a long sigh. "It's going to be a long time before I'll be able to see all of it. Right now ... I can't even see the purpose for today."

"You'll be able to, with time," I reassured him. "It takes millennia for many to find the purpose for their life. And as for today's purpose ... it may have some small significance that will be impossible to see for a long time. Who knows?"

Yaron looked at me again, brown eyes thoughtful. For a long time, he was silent, just looking at me, and I at him. Finally, he asked, "What about you? Why do you think you've been captured by these soldiers and locked up in here to be sold to slavers?"

I moved my eyes to study the floor, not wanting to hear about what awaited me in the coming months. "I don't know, Yaron ..."

"Well, it must be something important and impressive if you've got to go through all that first," he commented, and despite myself, I laughed. "I dearly hope so," I said.

We were silent for a long time then, each mulling over our own thoughts. Finally, after what seemed like hours, Yaron spoke again: "I know there's a point to what happened to me ... my parents getting killed and my imprisonment and all, but ... for the life of me, I can't imagine what good could come out of it ..." He looked over at me as if seeking my advice.

I said softly, "As I said, it will probably be many years before we will be able to see the tapestry that will be woven from the tangled threads of our lives. Just be confident that something good *will* come from the bad."

Yaron was about to respond when we both heard light footsteps from the stairs. A moment later Veryan appeared, holding the small steel tray of food for me. I smiled ruefully, but Yaron let out a low growl and turned his back to the approaching elf. Veryan scowled but said nothing to him.

He came over to my cell and unlocked it. Veryan grimaced as he handed me a tray. I sighed grimly when I catalogued the contents: a stale piece of bread, a hunk of cheese, an onion, and a tin cup with rather dirty-looking water. "Well, they certainly don't overfeed us, do they?" I said dryly.

A ghost of a smile flickered over Veryan's lips. "No. We don't get much either." He shrugged and waited as I set the tray down on a stone and then walked back to him.

I smiled at Yaron, who was now watching me behind strands of golden hair. When he noticed my eyes on him, his eyes darkened, and he turned away abruptly.

Veryan noticed and remarked sarcastically, "He seems happy."

"Veryan. Don't," I rebuked him quietly. "You should not make fun of him." My eyes fixed on him with an admonishing look.

Veryan's eyes narrowed, and he said coldly, sounding none too apologetic, "Sorry. I just don't like him much."

"Why?"

"I don't know," Veryan said mockingly.

"Because I don't like *you*?" Yaron hissed. His brown eyes smouldered like red-hot coals.

Veryan took an involuntary step backwards at the viciousness in Yaron's eyes. Then he glanced anxiously up at the stairs and turned to me. "I'd better go. Gornhelm wants all the men to be readying for the trip next week."

"I guess *you* can't go then," Yaron muttered.

"I don't see *you* coming with us," Veryan shot back, clearly angry.

I sighed. "Veryan, it was good to see you again, but I think you probably should go if Gornhelm needs you."

He looked at me with an unfathomable expression that contained a hint of steel and then shrugged. "Okay." Veryan cast one last angry look at Yaron, and then he left, motioning imperceptibly for me to follow.

I glanced at Yaron and then hurried after Veryan, anxious to talk to him. I followed him to a small corner of the large prison, where the dim light made it difficult to see the details of his face.

I stood in front of him and crossed my arms to try to abate the dull chill that was spreading over my body. It made my limbs ache, and my mind felt tired.

Veryan blinked and shifted as he said, "Are you well, Elysia? You look … tired."

I sighed and hugged myself tighter, trying to stop my involuntarily quivering muscles. *I haven't felt this tired in all my life*, I thought grimly. I sighed heavily, and my ribs hurt as I drew in my breath.

I remembered how, last night as I lay asleep in my cell, haunting visions of wounded and bleeding men had tormented my mind and how previously unknown feelings of intense pain and anguish for the soldiers' fate had besieged my heart, making me want to scream out my grief for all the world to hear. My very soul had seemed to shake as raging, bloody battles had gone on in my mind, the men outlined by a black sky and a blood-red moon ...

Then I had seen the horseman. His very being blacker and darker than anything that was natural in the world, his soul had been filled with plots of supernatural power, and his mind was overpoweringly cobwebbed with strands of a black and inauspicious magic that felt profoundly wrong, as if the rotting remains of some blood-thirsty, ravenous animal with an insatiable appetite.

I remembered how I had seen him galloping on a monstrous, blacker-than-night horse down the path of my mind, his black cape billowing behind him like raven wings. His eyes had been the only thing I could see, save for his black form. They glinted with a disgustingly evil fire that sent racking chills up my spine every time I thought about it. A ruby-coloured moon had floated in the sky behind him, but while it illuminated everything else in a reddish light, the horse and his rider had not even cast a shadow on the ground. It was as if he was some sort of ancient demon, come to haunt my dreams.

The horse's eyes burned into my mind too. Red, like fresh blood oozing from a wound, they had filled up my mind's eye as it had come closer and closer. I remembered how I had thought the horse was not going to stop and felt terrified that I was going to be trampled by its hooves. I had screamed, I remembered, both with my mouth and with my mind, and just before the rider had reached out his hand to grab me, the dream had ended as abruptly as if I had opened my eyes, but I had not. I remembered that too. I had not woken up after the horseman had nearly grabbed me. Instead, my thoughts had turned to a green forest though I could not see it very well. It had been indistinct and hazy, as if seen from a dirty looking glass. But then I had seen a young woman dancing in the forest. I had been puzzled but had watched the young woman with interest. Her face was lacking clarity as well, but I could tell she was beautiful. Black hair fell in splendid waves down her back, and she wore a dress of deep red satin. A laugh broke from the young woman's lips, and it sounded like birdsong. Golden light illuminated her form, but her face remained hazy, as if hidden behind a veil.

The dream of the young woman dancing lasted for several minutes, and then numerous dreams that were cloudy in my memory had come. I remembered a few details, such as another fleeting glimpse of the black rider and a glance of another, different young woman whose face had much more clarity than that of the woman dancing.

Then my dreams had slowly stopped altogether, and I had woken up. I had lain awake in a sort of trance for a while, trying to work out what my dreams meant and where they came from. I wondered if they were premonitions of something that was to come. I shuddered to myself. *I hope not. I have absolutely no desire ever to meet that black rider, or his horse, for that matter. I wouldn't mind meeting either of the women, though. The woman in the forest looked like a creature from a fairy tale—what I could see of her, anyway.* I tried to remember what I had seen of the other woman, whose face I had recalled fairly well, but it was beginning to fade from my memory now. I tried to hold onto the memory, for I had a nagging suspicion that the people I had seen were important, in one way or another, although I did not want to think about why the rider could be important.

But the thing that puzzled me the most was that I had never seen any of the men that had been bleeding or the young woman dancing in the woods or any of the places that had flickered across my mind's eye as I had slept. I was also certain I had never before encountered the black horseman. Everything in my sleep had been foreign to me. And when I had woken from my vivid nightmares, I had felt a horrible feeling of dread at the thought of seeing the sun come up and of having to face the new day. That had perplexed me as well because whenever I had had nightmares or premonitions before, I had always looked forward to the coming of the light, but this time, I had dreaded it. I recalled that it had almost felt as if the thoughts and feelings were not my own. It was almost as if I had seen someone else's memories and had experienced that person's feelings in my body.

I shivered again as the confusing emotions pushed at my consciousness again. This time, I felt an overwhelming and paralyzing fear, and I suddenly felt as if I was going to be sick.

I looked up at Veryan's face and saw his faint concern. I suddenly realized why he had cause for worry. I had not been outside in over a week or been given an opportunity to wash, so I must look pale and dirty. My face must have had an expression to match my roiling emotions. I grinned quickly to try to hide my discomposure.

"I haven't been sleeping very well for the past few nights, but it's nothing to worry about; it's probably just the discomfort of sleeping in an ancient cell with only mouldy straw and ill-tempered rats for company."

A ghost of a smile flickered over Veryan's face. It occurred to me that I had not once seen him truly smile.

"Whatever else Gornhelm has done to break your spirit, it seems you have retained your sarcasm," he said, dark eyes gleaming in the pale light.

"Maybe." I shivered as another wave of emotions washed over me, this time filling me with a heavy, aching exhaustion. I shifted in discomfort and then said, "How have you fared? You seem to have a new air of weariness about you. Has Gornhelm been working the men into the night to prepare for the trip to Dontae?"

Veryan's eyes clouded. "It's nothing I can't handle. It's just ..." Here he sighed and ran the fingers of one hand through his curly hair. "I ... I just wish I could free you and Yaron. Neither of you deserve to be here, especially you. Yaron, I can understand because of his skills with a blade, but you ... The only reason you're here is because Gornhelm saw fit to have an eighteen-year-old boy, whom he hates, try to prove himself by capturing an innocent girl riding past, who had never done him any harm, and then decide to sell her to a band of slavers because he didn't want to be bothered with her."

Veryan sighed and cast a glance at Yaron. "Every time I see him or hear his name, I feel so guilty about what Pyralus and I did. I still can't quite believe it myself … the things we did to his parents and him …" He sighed again. "I doubt Yaron will ever forgive me for what I did, even if he does get his score settled. I wouldn't, if I were in his position."

I stared at the ground, my arms still wrapped around my middle. I could think of nothing suitable to say to reassure Veryan; he was probably right about Yaron. I shrugged and then groaned as another coursing emotion pulsed through me, this one full of a burning eagerness and excitement, though I did not know what the cause of it was.

Veryan looked at me with a perplexed expression. Then he walked me to my cell and retrieved the piece of bread from the steel tray he had brought me, motioning for me to eat it. I accepted it with a word of thanks and hungrily began eating the bread, shocked to discover how hungry I was. Within half a minute, I had finished it.

I sighed, my hunger only barely sated, but the bread had at least eased the empty feeling of hunger gnawing inside me. As I glanced at Yaron, I suddenly felt all of my previously roiling emotions come to an abrupt halt. I staggered slightly, feeling as if something had just been ripped out of my mind.

I felt nothing now except the calm peace of my mind. No more pain or regret or fear. I felt nothing. Confused, I put the heel of my palm to my temple in an attempt to stop the slight headache that was forming over the confusion of what had just happened.

Veryan noticed and asked, "Are you all right, Elysia?"

My lips parted slightly, as if in a silent gasp, as I regained my composure and said, "I think so. I just … have a bit of a headache, that's all." Then the room began to spin as my headache worsened. I threw out my hand to touch the wall to support myself.

Veryan's eyebrows narrowed. "Do you need to sit down?"

My vision blurred slightly. "I … That would be good." I walked forward on shaky legs, gripping Veryan's forearm for support. I could see Yaron's face partially illuminated by the light as he watched.

I grunted as I sat down on a roughly hewn block of stone inside my cell and leaned my head back against the wall. Veryan knelt beside me, gripping my arm with a firm but gentle grip. His russet eyes burned into my face with unease as he watched me.

I took a deep breath as my racing heart began to slow down. A layer of sweat filmed my brow, and I felt hot.

"Elysia. Don't lie to us; I know something's wrong," Yaron said from behind the iron bars, facing me. His husky voice calmed me, and my headache lessened some.

"I feel better now," I rasped, my throat feeling hoarse. "Sitting down … helped …" I closed my eyes.

I heard Veryan stand, and I sensed Yaron's eyes on me. "What?" I asked, eyes still closed, "I didn't lie."

"I know," Yaron said, but I was aware of a faint note of quiet apprehension in his voice.

That, more than anything, scared me.

FOREIGN EMOTIONS

I sighed and shifted on the floor of my cell yet again. It was night—two days since my strange headache and near collapsing—and I could not sleep, no matter how long I closed my eyes or attempted to soothe myself with calming thoughts. No dreams plagued me, but I felt a sort of ... presence in my mind, as if I had brushed up against something and it had attached itself to me. However, when I tried to reach out to it, the contact vanished like morning dew under the sun. I was beginning to doubt that it was there at all.

I sighed again and moved into a place closer to the crack high above my head where the moonlight shimmered down. The night air let in from the opening cooled my face, and I closed my eyes once more. I could hear Yaron's light breathing in his cell. My thoughts wandered back to my dream of the young woman dancing in the woods. Though I had only seen it once, I remembered it well. The dream was as clear as a memory, and I wondered if it was. Though I had no idea where I could have seen the young woman, I had a small feeling nestled deep in my consciousness that the woman was important in some way.

I felt a sudden emotion roil up in me. Mostly comprised of weariness and mental exhaustion, it also carried with it a sudden and unexplainable ache deep in my muscles, almost as if I had been sparring for several hours. I felt incredibly and utterly tired.

Then it was gone.

Puzzled and frustrated, I sat up and leaned my head against the wall. *Are these my feelings? Or someone else's? I don't know where they are coming from. I don't know how someone else's memories and thoughts and feelings can be in* my *head and heart … I suppose it's possible, but I can't figure it out. After all, I'm certainly not the brightest person in Yaracina.*

The fatigued sensation abruptly returned but along with it a mood of bright enthusiasm. That anticipation made some of the exhaustion lift from my weary muscles, and I suddenly felt the intense desire to move, to get out of this cramped little cell and run and jump outside under the warmth of the sunlight! I sighed heavily; after all, it was nighttime, and I was still stuck in the prison, regardless of how much I wished to be free.

"Elysia? What's wrong?" Yaron said from his cell, watching me carefully with his brown eyes.

I gasped as the sensations disappeared as if I had shut the door to my mind, and every foreign emotion and thought receded from my consciousness. I pulled my knees up to my chest, wrapped my arms around them, and sat in the corner of my cell, terribly bewildered by everything that was happening to me. I had been taken from my family, locked up in this desolate prison far from home, soon to be sold to slavers, and now this … What was happening to me?

⸎

I could not sleep for the rest of the night. Emotions and feelings beset me constantly but at uneven intervals, and by the time the sun came up, I was exhausted from frustration and lack of sleep.

The next morning, neither of the boys wanted to be near me, for I refused to give more than a one-word answer, and if I did, it was a snappy, short-tempered response. Yaron kept quiet, watching me broodingly through the cell bars, his soft brown eyes evaluating me.

Privately, I was glad that they gave me my space and that I could be alone with my thoughts. I wanted to figure out where all the aggravating emotions and surreal dreams were coming from. But any answer I came up with did not make logical sense. I puzzled over it and examined my predicament from every possible angle, but eventually I decided not to worry over it, thinking, *The answer will come soon enough. I just wish it would come sooner than later.*

Some time later in the day, Yaron and I were let out for the second time that week. It was not Veryan but a young man that I had not met before who came to take us outside.

As the soldier unlocked my cell, I flicked my eyes over to Yaron who was pacing impatiently in his iron prison. His eyes were flashing like a forest cat's, and the golden strands of his hair were tangled and unkempt. For a brief moment, he looked up, and our eyes met, and then Yaron quickly looked down again. I shivered. His eyes had held some sort of almost feral anger that burned like smouldering coals, and even the ever-present spark seemed hard. I wondered why he was so agitated.

The young man swung the door open and waited for me to come out. I faintly smiled at the man and murmured, "Thank you," as I stepped out of my iron cage. The young man bowed slightly and then proceeded to unlock Yaron's cell. The boy paced anxiously, keeping his eyes on the key turning in the lock, looking as though he was silently willing it to turn faster.

The instant the door was unlocked, Yaron shot out of the cell, past the bewildered young man, and up the stairs. His legs pumped with muscle as he bounded up the stairs.

The young man turned his eyes on me, and I shrugged in reply. "Does he always do that?" the man asked.

⌁

I breathed in the fresh air and felt it fill my lungs with a satisfying rush. I walked over and stood beside Yaron. His shoulders and torso were tense, making him radiate an air of stress. His eyes had a flinty look in them and golden strands of hair hung down in his eyes. I sensed he was deep in thought, so I wisely did not intrude on the silence. Warm sunlight washed my face with golden rays, making me feel like singing. It had been several days since I had been outside, and while it warmed my heart to be standing under the light-filled heavens again, my spirits were a little dampened by Yaron's dejection.

We stood together silently, watching the sun spread its golden canopy and embrace the world with warmth and light. The turquoise sky was breathtaking, and it made me feel more hopeful just looking at it. As I watched the fluffy, white clouds float by overhead, I felt as though I was in a huge, cloud filled bowl.

"It never ends, does it?" Yaron said in a quiet voice, gazing up at the sky.

I felt myself smile, and I looked over at the young boy. He had such an innocent look just then, gazing up at the blue sky with wide eyes, that I momentarily forgot the so very jaded expressions and angry emotions he had so often displayed at other times. At this moment, none of that existed. He was just a young boy whose heart had been captured by the beauty and mystery of the heavens. "I wish I could fly," he said wistfully, longing filling his brown eyes. "I would fly far away from here."

I felt a lump form in my throat. *How I hate Gornhelm for imprisoning Yaron! How could he do such a horrible thing? Doesn't he understand that Yaron is just a child, alone and lost in the world?* Then a realization struck me. It made the lump in my throat grow larger. *Just like me. We're both alone ...* I moved my gaze up to the sky, trying to keep myself from crying. That thought raged inside me, tormenting my consciousness, as had the thought that I might never see my family again.

I suddenly recoiled as I felt the foreign consciousness touch mine. I felt it briefly examine my emotions, and then I sensed a feeling of gentle pity emanate from it. Curious, but extremely cautious, I pressed my curiosity toward the unfamiliar consciousness, hoping it would understand. I tried to make it understand that I was interested in it.

I felt a tentative reply, one of similar curiosity, but underlining it powerfully was an emotion of extreme caution, like mine, but much stronger. I got the feeling that the being did not trust people easily.

Strengthened by my resolve to make the being trust me, I concentrated hard on feelings of friendship, but they, too, were laced with caution. I had heard of people who were able to break into other's minds and control them, causing vast amounts of destruction. I fervently hoped this was not one of those kinds of people, if it was a person at all. I could not tell yet, but I had always thought that a person would communicate with words instead of emotions if their minds could connect.

A reply came very slowly, and I felt a hint of pain joined with the feeling of dim understanding that I had offered friendship. I sensed that the being knew that I was hesitant to trust it also. I did not blame it. *Caution is good.* Feeling a stronger emotion of pain from the being, I sent the emotion of curious concern for the being's pain.

There was a mental sigh, but no reply to my worry. A fuzzy, grey picture flashed through my mind, but it was too quick and too distorted for me to make out any details. I sent a questioning thought.

I jumped slightly as Yaron touched my arm. The contact with the being vanished, and I was suddenly aware of my surroundings again. Nothing had changed.

"Yes?" I said, my voice slightly shaky. I cleared my throat and then asked again with a steadier voice.

"Nothing," Yaron replied. "Your eyes just looked distant, and you looked as if you were seeing something I couldn't." His eyes were gentle and questioning.

"Oh, I was just thinking …" *What should I say I was thinking about?* I thought with some panic. *What would sound right?* "About my family. About my sisters and my mother."

"Ah." Yaron turned so that he was facing the plains in front of him again, gazing out through the tall iron bars of the courtyard fence. He sighed, his tawny skin rippling as his shoulders dropped slightly. I cast an admiring eye over his wiry arms. *I wonder how strong he is and how good a fighter he'll be in the coming years.* I shivered at the thought of what Yaron could become.

My spine stiffened slightly as I felt a questioning thought from the being. As I blinked in surprise, it occurred to me that the being must have been quietly sensing my whole conversation with Yaron and was now enquiring as to who he was. I also realized that, though the being might have experienced my emotions, it might not know what Yaron looked like, so I held a picture of the boy in my mind and pressed it at the general direction of the being, unsure as to whether it would be able to visualize the image. *After all, I couldn't see the details of the picture it sent to me. It was just grey and incredibly fuzzy.* I cast a quick glance at Yaron, who was now walking the circumference of the circular fence. He seemed lost in thought. I gave a faint smile, still waiting for the being's reply.

It came as a dim acknowledgment about the picture. I still sensed a bit of slight confusion from it, so I sent the image again, stressing the details. I felt the being examine the image carefully and then give a mental nod of satisfaction. Pleased, I decided to try something else. I formed an image of myself, trying to make it look accurate, but before I could send it toward the being's mind, Yaron called out to me, "Elysia! Come!"

A small wave of irritation swept over me, and I hoped the being was able to sense it as my thoughts turned toward Yaron. I sighed and ran quickly to where Yaron was standing by the courtyard gate. A smile crossed my lips as I ran. The sun warmed my face, and the wind brushed my hair with gentle fingers. My feet were silent as I streaked over the grass, and I felt as if I wanted to lift off the earth and soar far above the world, raised by the wind on a pair of great white wings ...

I came to a stop beside Yaron. He was standing in front of the great gates at the entrance to the Tower of Orlena. I peered up at the massive, iron gates with some sense of awe, wondering how long it had taken to build such monolithic gates. I dimly sensed the being's agreement with my awe. "What is it?" I asked, glancing at Yaron and then out at the plains.

He pointed.

My eyes followed his gesture. They widened slightly as I beheld the sight before me.

A pack of Salquessaé wolves, about twenty strong, were streaking silently across the plains, their glossy coats shimmering under the sun's gaze. Some had grey fur, others had black, some had brown, and one or two even had white fur. They were nowhere near the size of the massive wolves that had attacked us but were the size wolves should be. Their eyes held a fierce determination—to hunt and survive, to care for their pups, and to raise the next generation to be as good a pack of hunters and fighters as they were, if not better. But their eyes lacked the indisputable intelligence that the other wolves had had in theirs, and for that I was thankful.

They streaked in front of the tower, silent except for their soft breathing and the gentle pounding of their paws on the grass. A white wolf toward the back of the pack noticed us watching, and she slowed down a little, pausing just long enough to cock her head and stare at us with curious brown eyes that reminded me of Yaron's. Then she took off again, bounding after the pack with a steady, loping pace. It took less than half a minute for the pack to sprint past the tower and then begin to fade into the distance. Yaron and I watched them go, each of us feeling differently about what we had just witnessed.

Yaron sighed and followed them with his eyes until they disappeared from sight beyond the horizon. I looked at him, studying his expression, and said, "Are you all right, Yaron?"

The boy crossed his arms and stared out at the plains. A gentle breeze tugged at his golden hair, and his brown eyes were shadowed. "What I would give to be free like them," he said. "That's something I've longed for ever since that spineless coward of a captain brought me here. Every night that's what I dream of and what haunts my soul when I'm awake. Freedom. It echoes in every thought, underlines every word, fills every man's heart. It defines who we are and what we become." He turned his head to me, his brown eyes meeting my own blue ones. "You take away a person's freedom, and what do you have left? Nothing." He faced the plains again. "You have nothing."

I felt sorrow and pity well up in my heart again and rage towards the soldiers who had imprisoned this innocent boy, taking away any joys in his life that he had experienced before his cruel captivity. Instead of enjoying a happy childhood with his parents and growing up to become whatever he wanted, his path in life had been chosen for him, and he had to follow it, whether he wanted to or not. He was already able to defeat even the most battle-hardened veteran in the troop, Comundus. *Yaron will never have the opportunity to live a normal life, not after this. His path will be that of war for the rest of his life.* I hated Gornhelm for what he had done to Yaron.

And now, to hear him talking about freedom and to see the emotion in his eyes, it was all I could do to keep myself from grabbing a dagger and plunging it into Gornhelm's heart. It made me so furious.

I shivered as a wave of anger washed over me, trying to calm myself. I received a reassuring emotion from the being who, I sensed, could understand my rage and had experienced it too. I felt my fury slowly fade away as the being continued to send me calming emotions.

I sighed and looked at Yaron. Nothing in his expression had changed except that he looked somewhat more stressed. I suddenly had the desire to comfort him, so I gently put my arm around his muscular shoulders.

I felt him tense slightly, but he did not shrug me off. He did not even blink but continued to stare out at the Salquessaé Plains. A few golden strands of hair hung down in his eyes, but a light breeze gently lifted them off his forehead. His lips parted slightly, as if he were about to say something, but no words came. Yaron blinked hard several times, and I guessed he was close to shedding tears. The being expressed some anguish for Yaron as it was sensing my own concern for him.

I heard Yaron give a small gasp, and I glanced at him in alarm. He blinked several more times, still not looking at me, but no tears came yet.

I murmured a comforting word and squeezed his shoulder gently in reassurance. Yaron turned to me, his brown eyes beginning to fill with tears, and whispered, "Thank you, Elysia. For everything."

I smiled encouragingly and wrapped both arms around him, enfolding him in a gentle embrace. He did not protest, but let me hold him.

For that moment, as the sun bathed us with warm light, Yaron was nothing more than a simple child who had seen more than he should have at such a young age and was being comforted by a person he knew and trusted.

And I was glad I was that person.

 ⌇

I rubbed my forehead in an attempt to alleviate the massive headache that had plagued me for at least an hour. It was night, and the moon shimmered down through the small, high crack above, bathing my face with alabaster light.

Yaron was awake too, sitting up against the stone wall with his knees pulled up to his chest and his arms draped loosely over them. His head was bowed slightly, his eyebrows furrowed in thought. His narrow features were tightened as he appeared to be grappling with some decision.

I leaned my head back against the wall, massaging my temples. I had not received any emotions from the being since it had expressed concern over Yaron, but that was fine with me. I did not think I could stand interacting with it along with having my headache. I watched Yaron for a while but soon grew bored and shifted my gaze to the stairs. Faint light from the moon illuminated us and cast eerie shadows on the walls. I lowered my hands from my head to shift myself to get a better view as I would likely be staring at them for a while.

I groaned as the throbbing in my head redoubled, and it felt as if a hammer was pounding away inside my head, trying to break out of my skull. I applied pressure with my hands once again and brought my knees up to my chest, putting my head on them. An involuntary tremor ran down my spine as small bursts of pain exploded along the length of my body. I felt tears swim in my eyes, and my vision blurred. I knew that something was terribly wrong.

 ⌇

Yaron stared at the wall behind the iron bars in front of him. He was dimly aware of Elysia two cells over, sitting with her back against the wall. He studied her out of the corner of his eye. Her face looked pale, but he knew that was only because of having to stay in the cell all day, every day. *We only get one hour to go outside twice a week;*

they might as well keep us locked in here forever for all the good that does. And yet he knew deep down that the time outside was what was keeping them both sane.

Yaron sighed and looked down at his hands. *She doesn't deserve to be here. Elysia's done nothing wrong; at least they have a reason for keeping me locked up in this blasted cell, even if it's not a good one.* A sneer formed on his face. *When I'm old enough and I'm let out for good, I'll kill Gornhelm the first night I'm free.* Yaron's fist clenched. *And maybe Veryan too ... although, Elysia is friends with him ...* He sighed.

He stiffened slightly as he saw Elysia put her head in her hands and heard her groan. Yaron got to his feet and silently moved closer to Elysia's cell. The shadows covered him like a black blanket, concealing him from anyone's view.

Yaron watched Elysia closely. He tightened, alarmed, when he saw her tremble with the force of the tremor that coursed down her body. Then, a moment later, she collapsed.

Yaron hissed and glided up to the bars of the iron cell. He watched with a helpless feeling as she curled into a ball, violent spasms racking her body. He could hear Elysia whimpering with pain as another wave coursed over her.

Panic flared in Yaron's heart. *What's happening to her?* He wrapped his hands around the iron bars that separated them, distressed. They leeched the warmth from his hands and made him shiver slightly.

"Elysia! Elysia, can you hear me?" he said urgently. His heart was pounding violently as his anxiety mounted. "Elysia?"

She did not reply but only groaned in pain. Worried and frightened for Elysia, Yaron lowered the fortifications from his mind and reached out to try to touch Elysia's. Yaron shuddered as the empty vortex of space swirled around him. He had purposely secured the walls around his mind to keep Gornhelm or any of the others from trying to control his mind and keep him from escaping. *But I have to do this, for Elysia's sake. If I can just figure out the source of her pain ...* He let his mind drift around the prison, touching everything in it so that he could determine if anything had changed, but nothing seemed any different. Then he found Elysia's mind.

He blinked in surprise as his mind touched hers. It was not full of pain or shut off, as he had expected, but rather felt perfectly normal as it should when she was conscious and all right. Puzzled, Yaron moved around her mind, searching for the cause of the pain she was experiencing. His mind brushed against beginnings of what seemed to be fortifications that were being erected in her mind. *So, she's learning to defend herself*, he thought with some surprise. *Interesting …*

Yaron gleaned what he could about Elysia from this experience. He absorbed memories of her family and of her home. He felt the emotions she had felt when her twin had left home without a word of warning and her heartache over wanting to return home.

He was surprised to learn the level of hate she harboured for Gornhelm. It burned like smouldering coals in one small section of her mind, and he learned it was hate because of what the captain had done to him, not herself. He halted when he came across that, having a mixed emotion composed of affection and a solemn resolve that he would free her as well if he ever had the chance. *She doesn't deserve to be here*, he thought again.

Yaron sighed. No one had taken any real interest in him since his parents' death. They had only cared because of the incredible sword skills he possessed for his age. Most of them had failed to treat him as a living being and barely more than a child at that. When he had first come to the tower, Gornhelm had made him train every day for five hours with the best fighters in the group, which left him with countless bruises and cuts every night. The men were merciless in their treatment of him, forcing him to surrender regularly because they used sophisticated moves and tactics or were too fast or too strong for him to best. He had just barely turned thirteen, and the shock of his parents' death together with the troop's cruelty weakened both his mind and his body. It was only when he had nearly died from a deep gash in his stomach dealt by one of the men that Gornhelm had ended the training and had thrown him in the prison. But he had done nothing to help Yaron during the time he lay unconscious in his cell, walking on the very edge of the cliff that separated him from death. Comundus, apparently having some unknown obligation to see that he did not die, had brought him food and water, but there had been no medicine available for his wound. Comundus had kept it clean to keep infection from setting in, and Yaron had recovered slowly, but surely. His body had had to find the strength to mend his wound, and it had taken a long time for it to do so, but it finally had.

After he had recovered fully, Gornhelm had declared him weak and had discontinued Yaron's training, despite Comundus's disapproval. Yaron had only been allowed to leave his cell twice a week since his near-fatal experience in training, and he knew that that short time with fresh air and exercise did him little good. And the man under whom he would be serving when he was old enough to join the army was apparently convinced that Gornhelm was not doing enough to prepare Yaron because he had demanded that Yaron come to him once every two months for two weeks for demanding and difficult training. Seemingly, the man had heard of Yaron's skill and had taken a special interest in him, wanting him to be prepared and in shape for when he was old enough to be a soldier. Despite the brutality of the man's instruction, Yaron looked forward to it somewhat; for a while, he could be free of the tower and Gornhelm.

But Yaron missed going outside every day. He longed to feel the wind on his face again and to run on the grass and be surrounded by nature, instead of the bare, cold stone of his cell. His fading memories of the land where he grew up haunted him, and try as he might, all he could remember of his home was the vision of it burning, which was forever seared into his consciousness.

Yaron's thoughts ceased abruptly as he ran into something completely foreign in Elysia's mind. Not only was it foreign, but it was also impenetrable and full of pain.

FOREIGN MINDS

Yaron instantly recoiled. He threw up his barriers and quickly retreated back into his own mind. His heart beating wildly, Yaron blinked several times and then cautiously lowered his guard. He drew his mind back into Elysia's and warily touched the foreign being's mind. The being recoiled as well, and Yaron sensed a subtle, almost unnoticeable change in its mind.

Who are you? Yaron asked, having to shout to be heard over the thundering waves of pain that ringed the edge of Elysia's mind.

The being did not answer.

Who are you? he shouted again. *I'm not leaving until this thing tells me why it is making Elysia endure this pain*, he thought to himself.

Very slowly, the being lowered its barriers and answered, *My name should not matter to you, Yaron.*

Yaron stiffened and replied, *How do you know my name? Tell me.*

The being paused and then said, *I have seen you before and have heard stories of your skill with the blade.*

Tell me your name.

No.

Why? What are you afraid of? Yaron was becoming frustrated with its reluctance to share its name. *And why are you making her feel so much pain? She can barely sleep anymore at night, and her mind is tormented when she is awake by the dreams she receives!*

There was a long pause. Then the being said, *It was never my intent to hurt your friend. For a long while, I didn't even know my mind had touched hers. You can't blame me for her dreams, Yaron. I assure you, I would rid them from my mind and hers if I could; I only just awoke from a terrible one. I tell you the truth.*

Yaron frowned. *What are you? Your mind feels ... different. Are you elven?*

No. Are you? The being sounded irritated.

Yes ... If you cannot tell me your real name, can you at least give a name by which to call you if we speak again?

The being was silent for a moment. Yaron sensed its discomfort and reluctantly offered a feeling of friendship and reassurance. He got the return emotion of grim amusement.

I would prefer it if only Elysia knew my name, Yaron. It would be safer for all of us.

It was only then that Yaron realized that the being's voice sounded male and very weary. He wondered at it but made no comment. Reluctantly seeing the being's point, Yaron leaned his head against the stone wall, still gripping the bars. Moonlight washed his hair silver. *Very well, then ... if you think that is best.*

The being made no reply, but Yaron sensed him beginning to depart from Elysia's mind. He made no move to stop the being. *As long as he leaves Elysia alone, I have no quarrel with him.*

AWAKENING

I grimaced as light streamed washed over in great, torrential streams. I quickly closed my eyes, protecting them from the painful rush of light. I felt faint, and my forehead throbbed. The warmth of the sun splashed across my cheeks, making me hot.

The warmth suddenly vanished as I sensed something moving in front of the sun's path. Hoping the light would not still pain my eyes, I opened them a crack. Light streamed around the figure of a person kneeling in front of me, casting me in shadow. *Who is that?* I thought, squinting to try to see better. The person's outline was fuzzy and indistinct; I felt as if I was seeing the outline from underwater. There was the even fainter outline of a second person behind the first. I grimaced as a wave of pain racked my body, shaking me to the core. Tremors followed a second later.

I winced as the person shifted, letting light hit one side of my face. I quickly closed my eyes as the bright warmth dazzled my eyes. *Ohhh … that hurt. What's happening to my eyes?* I shifted, but I could not tell if I was lying on the floor or on something else or even if I was right side up. My sense of direction and perception was completely muddled. I gasped as the person knelt down and touched my face gently, but I was more startled than afraid.

"Elysia."

I moaned and shifted again, wishing the light would dim. It hurt my eyes even when they were closed.

"Elysia."

I moaned again and felt tremors course down my body, followed by a searing blast of pain that engulfed me like an angry outburst of crimson fire. It felt as if red-hot lead was being poured through my veins. My muscles instantly contracted with the paralyzing wave, and I gritted my teeth as another surge of pain pulsed in my blood, determined not to scream. My heart fluttered like a dying bird.

Intense colours pulsed behind my eyes as the agony redoubled, and I let loose a hoarse scream that echoed strangely in my ears, as if I was in a large space that was devoid of life and pressed down around me like a blanket.

I feebly opened my eyes again and looked into my own eyes, the same eyes I had looked into the night I had watched the line of human soldiers pass by, the night I had met Veryan. I was dimly aware of a gentle touch against my mind as I slipped into unconsciousness.

꒱

"I don't understand. Say it again," I said. My eyes searched Yaron's in question. He sat beside me in my cell, arms crossed over his chest and leaning against the stone wall. His face bespoke weariness and concern, but there was something in his eyes that made me uneasy, something about the way he looked at me. The omnipresent sparkle was somehow softer and gentler than it usually was.

"He refused to give me his real name; I don't know why. He said it would be safer for all of us if only you knew. I can only guess there's something he doesn't want us to know or find out about his history or who he is."

"And you think he's the reason I've been having all these strange nightmares and unexplainable visions?" I said, fingering a round stone.

Since I had woken up from my last bout of agony, Yaron had been explaining to me what he had discovered about the human and what role he played in my foreign emotions and dreams. I was extremely sceptical of the idea that he had just … connected to my mind and that his emotions and thoughts and memories were overriding mine to the point where I could not tell which were his and which were mine. Concerning the pain, the only explanation Yaron could come up with was that he had been wounded or something had happened to him that was causing him all the agony that was also plaguing me.

"I do," Yaron sighed, running his fingers through his hair. "I don't know how, or why, but I do think he's the source of your pain."

I stared at my bare feet in silence. *This is so strange. I wonder what Malitha would say and what her opinion about this whole thing would be.* I shivered at the memory of my twin and closed my eyes, trying to eradicate the harsh feelings I had had towards her. I sighed. *I miss her.*

She's your sister, isn't she?

My eyes flew open, and I sat upright with a start. Yaron watched me with a studied expression. "What is it?" he breathed.

I exhaled shakily and replied, *Yes. Who are you?*

You may call me Lliam, but do not tell Yaron nor anyone else. My connection is with you and only you.

How do you know Yaron? I asked, bristling slightly. *And who are you?* My voice held barely contained venom after all I had been through during the night.

I've met Yaron before, he answered wearily. *As for my name, I believe I said that you can call me Lliam, no?*

Why this secrecy? Why are you trying to hide who you are? I asked, feeling guarded and frustrated yet curious and sympathetic at the same time. I did not know what had happened to Lliam, but his voice held the same weariness and caution that Yaron's did when I first met him. And the name … I had heard the name Lliam somewhere before…

It's not by my choice, believe me, Lliam said, a hint of bitterness coming into his voice. *If I could, I'd break out of this prison and ride as far away as I could and never look back. But even then, I'm not sure I could completely escape, because 'the most indestructible and ominous prisons are the ones in our minds.'*

I felt a twinge of pity and emphasized it in my next words: *So you, too, are imprisoned?*

Yes. I am. Lliam was silent for a moment, giving me a chance to mull over his words.

I blinked as I considered his words. *So ... he hates his imprisonment as much as I do. I wonder where he is being held and why.* I raised my eyes to the ceiling. *I wish I could help him.* Then I asked, *Where are you held, Lliam?*

I was unprepared for the spiteful venom in his voice when he snapped, *What's it to you? Why would you care? You don't know me! You don't know what I've done! If you did, then I think you would not be so eager to want to help me!*

And with that, Lliam withdrew from my mind with a sharp pull. Remnants of his consciousness and emotions still lingered, but the entirety of his being was gone.

༄

"Yaron, how did you get in here?" I asked in a while, as it finally dawned on me that he should not be in my cell. Yaron was stretched out on his back, hand behind his head, gazing up at the ceiling.

"I walked through the bars," he said.

I gave him a glare, knowing he was being sarcastic, though nothing in his voice revealed it. "Yaron."

He looked over at me and grinned, then turned back to his original position, and closed his eyes.

I rolled my eyes and glanced over at his cell door. The padlock was lying on the floor, badly dented, and the door hung ajar. My own door was in a similar condition. I raised an eyebrow. *Here's another display of his amazing strength*, I thought. His power was extremely uncanny for a boy his age, as was his incredible skill with all things weapons-related. *Ah well. It's not in my interest to attempt to understand his complicated mind.* I shrugged to myself. "So you punched the lock off?"

"Yes," he replied, sounding uncommonly cheerful. He opened his eyes and grinned at me, the soft sparkle twinkling at me, and then closed his eyes again.

I half-nodded absently. "Amazing," I muttered.

"Exactly," he agreed.

I rolled my eyes again and said, "Why are you so happy? Did Gornhelm finally disintegrate after looking at his reflection?"

To my surprise, Yaron actually laughed out loud. "I wish! No, I don't know why I'm 'so happy.' I just am." He glanced at me, amusement etched in his handsome features. "Do you not want me to be so happy?"

I smiled despite myself. *I have to admit, the cheerful Yaron is much more interesting to be around than the usual angry one.* I sat down beside him on one of the crumbling stone blocks. His eyes were closed, but a grin was still upon his face. I laughed, "You look like an idiot, grinning like that."

Yaron chuckled. "Oh well. Call me whatever you like; it makes no difference to me." A little while later, his face and body relaxed, and I could tell he had fallen asleep.

Yaron awoke and jerked up with an audible gasp. Sweat coated his body, and the darkness pressed around him on every side, threatening to overwhelm his senses. Every muscle in his body ached and burned, as if he had been climbing rocky terrain for two days.

He wiped the dripping sweat from his forehead and shifted to a more comfortable position, gritting his teeth to prevent a gasp as his leg muscles suddenly cramped. Yaron sat down slowly on a slab of broken rock, wanting to cry out in pain as his muscles burned.

Letting out a heavy sigh as he leaned against the wall, Yaron ran his fingers through his damp hair and closed his eyes reluctantly, hoping his dream would not reappear in his mind. He was not sure how he would know if it was the one he had just had, however, because he could not remember anything about it except the feeling of utter panic that had consumed him and the fear, the fright that this dream would become a reality.

Though Yaron had had many such dreams since that fateful night his parents had been slaughtered and he had been abducted from his home, this one was worse than usual. Elysia had been in this one, too.

He shuddered. She had been lying on what looked like a floor of ice, her face and hands very, very pale and tinged with blue, and she had been trembling. Her breath left her lips in a great, white cloud, but it was also very shallow, and her eyes were closed. He knew she was dying.

Yaron wrapped his arms around his knees and dropped his head to rest upon them. He sat silent for what seemed like hours, terrified by the images he had seen.

꙳

The next morning, when I awoke, I immediately sensed that something was not right. I could feel it in the air, crackling like lightning, demanding my attention. I raked my eyes over the prison, every inch of it, trying to discern what was wrong.

My gaze stopped as soon as Yaron entered my field of vision. I gasped. He was right next to me on his side, curled into a shivering and shaking ball. Tremors racked his body, and I saw that one of his hands was pressed to the scar on the small of his back. Moans of pain and anguish emanated from him, and I caught a glimpse of his face, which was contorted into a pained grimace.

I could have sworn my heart stopped in that moment. "Yaron." The name dropped from my lips as barely more than a whisper, softer than the murmurs of the gentle breezes of the night.

No. No. No. Yaron. No. My heart pounded like a drum, and I felt a pent-up burning energy that permeated my entire being, trying to escape the imprisonment of my body. I stalked back and forth like a cornered wolf surveying its options. *No, Yaron. Wake up. Please.*

It's in his dreams. They're hurting him, Lliam whispered gently into my mind. *Wake him.*

I slid to my knees beside Yaron. The boy cried out in pain when I gently touched his shoulder, and my heart ached with pity at seeing him like this. I gathered him up in my arms. The boy stirred slightly as I smoothed the golden hair from his forehead. I gently shook him and pleaded, "Wake up, Yaron. You're having a bad dream." *Oh, Yaron. Wake up. Please.*

To Lliam, I whispered, *What's going to happen to him, Lliam? Will he be all right?*

There was a long silence, and then Lliam answered, *I don't know. I have a friend who deals with things like this, though his are not very frequent—only once or twice a year. I don't know how often this happens to Yaron. If this is the first time, or if it happens very often, he may not be able to cope with it very well, being so young. But then, 'there is strength in being young.'*

He's strong, I agreed, but I said it with a sinking heart. Privately, I thought, *Oh, I hope with all my heart Lliam's wrong. Yaron has to be all right; he has to.* I touched his cheek gently; it was very cool, and his eyes flickered under their lids in a dreaming state.

I shook him gently, trying to wake him, but that only made Yaron groan again. *No, don't. If he didn't wake before, he won't wake now. Don't disturb him*, Lliam said quickly. *That will only make it worse. Let him be. He has to wake up on his own.*

Is he asleep?

Yes. But he can't wake up just yet. Do you remember that dream you had of the black rider? And how you could not wake? This is very similar, but it is more of a physical experience, in his case; his body feels the stress and panic your mind felt in that dream.

It became harder and harder for me, watching the boy grimace in obvious pain in my arms. I blinked back tears several times, feeling my hate for Gornhelm well up like a fountain in my heart. *He will pay for this*, I swore. *No child deserves to be treated like this. No child deserves to have such nightmares at such a young age.* I said to Lliam, *Is there nothing we can do to ease his suffering?*

Lliam sighed heavily. *If you want, I can try to enter his mind and rid him of the nightmare. I don't know how easily I'll be able to accomplish it, though.*

I considered this for a moment and then replied, *How can you? It took days for us to be able to speak, and—*

This is quite different, Elysia, Lliam said. *Entering someone's mind and forming a tangible, mental bond with someone are two different things. I can speak to Yaron with my mind, yes; I can enter his mind, yes. But I don't and never will have a connection with him as I do you. If you, one day, wish to speak to someone with your mind, you will be able to, but not with the level of comprehension and depth that we can.*

Bewildered, I thought for a moment. Then I slowly consented: *If you think you can help him, then please do. Don't exhaust yourself, though, Lliam.*

Lliam answered slowly, an expression lacing his voice that I could not identify: *Don't worry. I'm stronger than you know.*

I shivered slightly, but I did not know why. A moment later, I felt Lliam's consciousness drifting away from mine again. I lost the ability to tell what Lliam was doing after his mind separated from mine, but I watched with apprehension as Yaron began to grimace and groan again, this time with renewed vigour. Something was happening inside his mind that was causing him even more pain than the nightmares.

"Elysia."

I started at the sound of Veryan's voice. I looked up to see him standing at the door of my cell, looking concerned. "What's wrong?" he asked, gesturing at Yaron. His eyes were dark and cold, and I knew he really had no interest in what was wrong with Yaron.

I scowled, and then replied, "I don't know. I just woke up, and Yaron was in this unconscious state. He was … shaking, and …" I watched Veryan's face as he knelt down beside me and Yaron. His dark eyes searched the younger boy's face with intensity. "What is he doing in your cell?" Veryan asked in a low, steely voice.

I looked up at him with uncertainty. What was he angry about? "He came in here last night when I was having a bad dream," I said uncomfortably. "What's wrong?"

Veryan stalked over to my cell door and picked up the broken and bent lock from the floor. He held it up and looked at me with raised eyebrows, as if demanding an explanation. "How did *this* happen?"

I balked at his angry brown eyes but answered, "He knocked it off somehow, I think."

Veryan looked at me as if I were missing something very important. "Elysia," he said, "This can't happen again. You and Yaron both could get into serious trouble for something like this: Yaron leaving his cell, breaking the lock ... Elysia—"

"Okay, I understand, Veryan," I said stiffly, looking down with concern at Yaron.

Lliam touched my mind. *Who is this?* he asked, rather sharply.

This is Veryan. He's ... an acquaintance. Actually, he's the one Gornhelm had capture me. Lliam grunted in reply, seeming suspicious, and almost as if he knew something about Veryan that I did not. *Have you met him before?* I asked.

There was a long silence, and then Lliam said, *Yes.* But he refused to give me any more details of their meeting.

I opened my mouth to ask Veryan a question, but at that moment, Yaron's eyes suddenly flew open, and he began taking in rasping, shuddering breaths. His body was coated with sweat, and his eyes stared into space, but he was conscious again. I felt weak with relief.

I quickly asked Lliam, *Was it hard?*

But no answer nor any emotions or words emanated from Lliam. I could not even find a whisper of thought from his consciousness. Lliam was gone. For now.

⁂

I stared at the stone wall at the far end of the prison with revulsion. It had been two days since Yaron's strange seizure, and though he had woken briefly after Lliam had banished the dreams from his mind, he had soon fallen back into unconsciousness again. I had asked Veryan to tell Comundus of Yaron's situation when the boy did not wake after the night had passed. Comundus had asked Gornhelm to allow me to stay with Yaron so that I could tend to him, and the hefty general had agreed grudgingly. As an elf, Yaron could normally go without water as well as food for nearly two weeks, but because of the extreme stress from his dreams and the great loss of fluid through sweating, I feared he would require water much sooner. I sat beside the boy, day and night, wiping his face with cool, wet cloths provided by Comundus and hoping he would not be conquered by the nightmarish visions that haunted his mind.

Now, I was resting against the stone wall that ran along the back of the prison, tiredly watching Yaron sleep beside me. The boy's chest rose and fell irregularly, and his breathing was laboured, but he appeared to be safe from the nightmares for the moment. His golden hair was tangled about his face, and his forehead was beaded with sweat. His eyes wandered sightlessly beneath their lids.

I felt drowsy. The warm shaft of sunlight from the crack overhead illuminated a small line along the stone floor. My eyes roved lazily over the room, taking in the sun-illuminated stone and watching for anything that had changed. Nothing did change, except for Yaron's occasional tossing and turning. *I wonder what Lillian's doing right now ... and Mother and Malitha. I wonder how they are. I wonder if Father's home yet ... I wonder if I've been missed yet. I have lost track of time.* I closed my eyes and smiled grimly. *I wonder so many things ...* I opened my eyes and said aloud, "I wonder who Lliam is." *There are so many people he could be. He could be anyone, really. And I guess he probably won't tell me who he really is, considering he won't even give his right name.*

You're quite smart for such a young girl, he whispered gently in my mind.

My lips curved into a smile. *Thank you.*

Lliam sighed softly and then replied, *In many ways, you are not unlike me. We often think the same things, and that is why it is sometimes difficult for you to tell your thoughts from mine. I find myself doing the same thing as well. Our souls are linked for now and ever; just wait and see if I am not right.*

I shivered slightly. *What makes you say that, Lliam? How do you know this?*

You will find I know a great many things.

Yes, but how? *How, and why, do you know these things?*

But he did not reply, and a long silence ensued during which I contemplated what Lliam had told me. I watched Yaron without really seeing him, thinking everything over. *Everything's so different than I thought,* I said.

How so?

I don't know … I just never thought all this—I waved my arm at the prison—*ever existed, and I never thought people like Gornhelm and Yaron and you would be people I'd ever come in contact with, and all this mind-speaking and everything, really. I don't know what to believe anymore or whom to believe. How do I know you're trustworthy, Lliam? How do I know whom to trust and whom not to trust? How do I know who my enemies are and who are my friends? Nothing makes sense anymore.*

Lliam was silent; I sensed he was trying to think of something to say. Finally, he whispered, *As for me being trustworthy, you can't really know. I don't even know if I'm trustworthy or not.* He laughed harshly. *But I think if we ever meet, you will find that I'm quite different from what you will have imagined. After all, 'you shouldn't judge someone until you've walked a mile in their shoes.'*

I sighed. *Is that not true of us all? Are we not all different in the eyes of various people?*

When Lliam spoke again, I detected a hint of amusement in his words: *As I said, you and I are not so different in our thinking, my friend.*

I said nothing for a long while; I watched Yaron sleep for several minutes, my mind empty of all thoughts.

If we ever meet, I think you will also find that we are not so different in our relations to the world, Lliam said quietly.

I closed my eyes. *Maybe so; we are both prisoners of this world's evil. But I doubt we will ever meet.*

I would not count on that, daughter of Damir, he said gravely. *We may meet sooner than one would anticipate.*

I immediately opened my eyes and narrowed them. To myself, I thought, *How does he know my father? And how would he know when we'll meet?* To me, Lliam's words were making him sound more suspicious by the minute. *I'm really not sure I can trust him.*

I'm not sure you have any reason to trust me, Lliam said in a tormented voice.

I frowned. *Are you so unsure about your own allegiance?*

You would not say that if you knew who and what I am!

If you would tell me, then I could understand!

No ... no, I can't tell you. I can't tell anyone. No one would ... no. I-I can't ... no—

Suddenly Lliam stopped short. I felt a great wave of fear wash over me, almost taking my breath away. I gasped. I knew the fear came from Lliam and not from me, but it still threatened to overwhelm my senses and conquer my free will.

Lliam? Lliam, what's happening?

But he gave me no answer.

UNEARTHING

Stiffly, I sat down beside Veryan and leaned my head against the smooth stone of the tower, sore from my tossing and turning on a stone floor all night. We were outside two days later, and it was the first time Yaron and I had been allowed out of our cells in over five days. Yaron was nowhere in sight. I assumed he wanted to be left alone after the horrors of his nightmares that had plagued him every night for a week. He had been sombre and somewhat aloof ever since, no doubt weary after the ordeal.

Veryan said nothing as I sat beside him. His face looked thoughtful and weary. His eyes were shadowed and dull, and his dark hair stirred slightly in the breeze.

"Veryan," I said softly, "what are you thinking about?"

The dark-haired boy did not answer me for a long while, nor did he give any sign that he had even heard me. I watched him closely, but it seemed he would not answer me, so I averted my eyes, studying the wide, flat plains outside of the iron fence once again.

"My family."

I barely heard him speak. I turned back to him and said, "What?"

"I said, 'My family.' That's what I was thinking about," he said, not meeting my gaze.

I inspected the grass between us. "Oh." I glanced at him again. "You miss them much?"

Veryan gave a faint smile of grim amusement that did not reach his eyes. "No." He met my eyes. "They were unbearable. I wouldn't go back there, not for any reason in the world."

I thought that was strange. *He doesn't miss his own family? There's no possible way I could not miss my family. I love them all so much … I'm sure there's a good reason, though. I doubt it would be otherwise. But …*

I made no comment on his revelation. Instead, I merely gave an absentminded nod.

Veryan, however, scowled. "Don't mistake me, Elysia. If my circumstances were different, if my family were different … I wouldn't have had to leave. But that's why I'm here … because they were … intolerable." He stared out at the wide Salquessaé, taking in every inch of it.

"Where did you live, Veryan? Where is your family now?" I asked, taking into consideration what Veryan had told me.

His face clouded, and he seemed to bristle at my questions. Veryan glared at the ground. "Doesn't matter," he hissed. He glanced at me with his piercing dark eyes, changing the focus of the conversation to me. "Do you miss your family?" he asked then.

I swallowed, feeling a heavy pressure knotting in my chest. The way Veryan said it, his question almost sounded like a challenge. "Yes, of course. I miss them more every day. I haven't seen my father in several weeks. I didn't get to tell my twin good-bye before she left to be married, and my mother was heartbroken over her departure. I doubt she even lets my youngest sister out of her sight now, with the two of us gone." I laughed, trying to sound nonchalant, but it was hard. I wrapped my arms around my knees and stared down at the ground. "My mother thinks I'm on my way to Hartford City, and I wish I were, but instead I'm stuck in this place," I scowled, looking around at the tower's grounds. "I wonder if I'll ever get out of here and back home," I whispered, almost as an afterthought. I felt tears flood my eyes, and I blinked hard to ward them off. I did not want to appear weak in front of Veryan.

But to my surprise, I felt Veryan's hand laid tentatively on my shoulder. I glanced at him, and we locked eyes. Then I found I could not look away. Veryan's dark eyes held mine, betraying a hint of compassion and another look that I could not identify, but it made me feel uncomfortable. It made my heart quicken, and though I wanted desperately to look away, to be free of that overwhelming gaze, I could not make myself avert my eyes.

Finally, Veryan broke the connection as Yaron approached. The dark-haired boy blinked several times as he looked past me to watch Yaron striding up to us.

I felt dizzy. I stared down at the tan grass, trying to calm my spinning thoughts. The blood roared in my ears, and my hand trembled slightly as I snapped a seed-stalk between my fingers. I could not bring myself to look up as Yaron approached. Veryan murmured a word of greeting, but I did not hear Yaron reply. The golden-haired boy sat down beside me but said nothing.

I finally looked up, trying to avoid looking at Veryan, and swept my gaze around the tower grounds. The grasses rippled like gentle waves as the breeze caressed us, and the great iron gates stood resolute and proud, glinting in the sun.

"The Shardrock Gates," Yaron breathed beside me.

I looked at him with an odd expression. "How do you know?"

Yaron grinned. "How do I know their name? Or how did I know what you were thinking about?"

Both, I thought with a tiny shiver. "Their name. How do you know their name?"

Yaron grew sombre. "This tower," he indicated the grounds with a sweep of his arm, "used to be an outpost and a guard tower for a northern regiment of the Queen Alexandra's soldiers, one that was captained by Lady Yara for a while. It was the sight of the Battle of Alussa, which took place over seven hundred fifty years ago. That was one of the many battles that led up to the War of the Red Moon, which was seven years later. After the battle, the tower was abandoned for a century and then was made the fortress of a small town, Ruoho. Ruoho was inhabited for many years and then abandoned after a fire ravaged the town. About twenty years later, it became the Tower of Orlena, after being refurnished and having the gates restored to their former glory. It's been a guard tower ever since, and Gornhelm's men have been using it for the better part of nine years."

I nodded absently, absorbing the information Yaron had given me. "How do you know all this?" I asked him, genuinely curious at where he had learned such information.

Yaron looked embarrassed. "I ... well, on Iciar, we value education highly, though I must say I read more than the average person my age. I enjoyed it, and I relished reading books about the past wars and battles and, especially, the kings and queens of old. Oh, I could be lost in the pages of the past for hours on end and never notice the passing time. Several times, when I was younger, I stayed in the library of my father's friend Taethon all day. Once, my mother found me late at night, well past midnight, asleep with a book still in my hand." A smile spread over his face as the fond memories came back to him.

I smiled as well, pleased to see him happy. "Tell me more," I encouraged, delighting in hearing the information he was giving about his early life. I knew he might not so readily give out the information at a later time, so I wanted to hear everything he would share now.

Yaron grimaced tightly, looking a little uncomfortable. He looked pained now, as if the pleasant memories he had experienced a moment earlier had now vanished from his mind, leaving barely a thread of recognition for him to return to later. "No," he said.

I felt guilty. *Don't push him*, I reminded myself. *Just listen to what he says and don't ask for more.* I reprimanded myself silently and then said aloud, "I'm sorry, Yaron. I didn't mean—"

"It's fine, Elysia." He lifted his head and smiled at me. "I know you mean well, and besides, it helps to talk about it." And then after a brief delay, almost as if it were an afterthought, he said, "Eases the pain ..."

I frowned slightly, letting the silence stretch into several minutes. Then I asked, "Did you sleep well last night?"

Yaron shrugged. "Better."

Despite my following questions, that was the only word he uttered concerning that topic.

After telling Yaron and Veryan I wanted to be alone for a few minutes, I stood and began walking slowly around the grounds, braiding my hair as I walked. I strode along slowly, giving myself time to sort out my thoughts and resolve some of my conclusions about my fate and Lliam and other such puzzling subjects.

It worried me that I had not heard anything from Lliam since that night, now three days past. I had tried to contact him numerous times, but every attempt had only brought deafening silence to my mind. My fingers flew along my braid, deftly tying my hair as I contemplated what could have happened to my mysterious acquaintance. *He said he was imprisoned … I wonder where and why. I don't even know of any other strongholds in Yaracina. I wonder if he is just a child like me and he is being imprisoned for no wrongdoing he has committed but simply because he happened to be in the wrong place at the wrong time.*

That's the closest thing to the truth I've ever heard, Lliam said sourly.

I blinked in surprise and pleasure at hearing his voice again. I paused in my walk and leaned against one of the massive iron bars in the fence surrounding the tower. My curiosity about what had happened to him last time aroused itself in my mind, but I was hesitant to ask for fear that Lliam would get angry or would leave again.

You can ask me, daughter of Damir; it's all right, he assured me gently.

Instead of asking my original question, I asked, *How did you know what I was thinking?*

Lliam laughed. *I told you, daughter of Damir, we are becoming more and more closely connected with every passing day; soon we will be as one mind. We will know everything the other is thinking and every thought and feeling that plagues the other. And … once we are advanced enough, we will even be able to see what the other sees.*

I frowned and pondered Lliam's words. *Why me?* I wondered. *Why should I be the one to bond with Lliam? Why me? Do I really* want someone else knowing everything I'm feeling and thinking? I'm really not sure I do.

Our destinies are inexorably linked, daughter of Damir. You cannot change your destiny; it has already been laid out for you. All you have to do is find the path and follow it. But who you are is not set in stone; you can be whoever you wish, but that will not alter your destiny, nor mine. 'The way won't always be straight, but it will lead you to a good end,' or so I've read.

I wondered at his reflective words. *How do you know your destiny? How do you know your fate is going to be cruel? Could it not be magnificent and wonderful?*

Lliam scoffed, *My life has been nothing but heartache, lies, and sorrow, young falcon; there is no good left in this world to be wasted on me. Don't question me about how the world works when I am far more experienced with it than you are.*

I crossed my arms, even though I knew Lliam could not see me do so. *I was only trying to be optimistic.*

He chuckled harshly. *Well don't. Why try to be optimistic when you are fully aware of the severity of the situation? Why try to make it sound better than it is?* But he sounded as if he wanted desperately to believe that what was coming could be better than what he thought it would be.

Because it keeps your spirits up. I resumed walking, toying with my braid again. The sun beat down on my back, burning against my fair skin.

Lliam grunted. *Maybe. But you still have much to learn, young falcon.*

I half-smiled. *Why do you call me " young falcon"?*

You remind me of a very young falcon that thinks it knows how to fly and hunt for itself, but in reality, it knows very little of how to survive in the world.

I rolled my eyes. *I appreciate your confidence in me*, I said, my voice dripping with sarcasm.

Lliam laughed. *That is not necessarily a bad thing. It just means you have much to learn and plenty of room to grow. I'm sure, one day, you will be one of the wisest people in the elven world.* I detected only the slightest hint of amusement in Lliam's words.

I said nothing for a long while and continued walking around the grounds. I emptied my mind of thoughts but kept my connection with Lliam.

I lifted my eyes up to where Yaron and Veryan stood on the small hill. Yaron was a lean, lithe figure with taut shoulders, and Veryan was slightly shorter but just as wiry. I smiled. *They're my closest friends now*, I thought. *Two young boys, both of them lost and searching for their place in the world. Like me, save that I'm not as lost as they are. I have a home and a family, though I have no earthly idea what I'm meant to become.* I bent to pick a small, white wildflower by my feet and then straightened, holding the flower in one hand and stroking its silky petals with the other. *A flower is such a simple thing, yet it brings the creatures around it such joy.*

I could hear the smile in Lliam's next words: *If you think flowers bring joy, then I believe you'll find some of life's upcoming events even more exciting. A wonderful—but also heart-breaking—world awaits you, young falcon, once you learn to fly.*

I smiled. *What is one thing I can look forward to, wise one?*

Lliam smirked. *Love. Once you find that, your life will never be the same, young falcon.*

And you would know, yes?

I detected a bitter note in his voice when he answered me: *Not personally, no. But I know of plenty of people who have found happiness in love with the person destiny led them to. 'Once you fall in love, it's very hard to climb back out.'*

I pursed my lips. *If I ever fall in love, it won't be for a long time, Lliam. I'm only seventeen.*

Lliam gave a mental shrug and then said, *Maybe. I wouldn't know.*

You said people found happiness in the person destiny led them to, yes?

Yes. Why?

Do you really believe it's only destiny that decides who a person falls in love with?

What else?

Lliam's answer unnerved me slightly. Though I was not exactly sure why, I believed that involved more than following destiny. I was sure that something else decided whom you fell in love with and married, though I was not sure what. But I could not quite understand that feeling or explain it, even to myself. *I'm just sure that destiny isn't the only thing at work in our lives*, I thought to myself.

I fingered the stem of the flower for a moment, contemplating Lliam's words, and then I said, *Lliam, what is love?*

To my slight surprise, his voice and manner softened, and he said gently, *You will find the answer soon enough, young falcon. You will know it when you experience it. I'm sure you will be able to answer your own question once you know what it is in your heart.*

I gently stroked the petals with a finger as I pondered what Lliam had said. He seemed to think that I would find the answer to the question about love on my own, which I guessed was true enough. *I guess everyone has his or her own definition of love*, I decided to myself.

Daughter of Damir, I must go now. I will speak with you again soon. Lliam said his words softly and lightly, but I could tell there was some weight behind his words.

Farewell, Lliam, for now. And thank you.

ᣔ

I walked up the little hill and stood beside Yaron. The boy dipped his head in greeting, the gentle sparkle alight in his eyes, and then said, "How was your walk?"

"Uneventful," I replied, still mulling over Lliam's words. I felt slightly irked that he had left my mind without giving me a chance to discuss his words with him further. *Well*, I thought, *at least now I have a chance to think my own thoughts without his hearing them. That's somewhat unnerving.*

Veryan moved closer to us, his dark eyes probing my face. My cheeks suddenly felt warm as I remembered how he had stared at me earlier. *I hope he doesn't do that again; that makes me so uncomfortable.* I felt as if I was an interesting specimen under a magnifying glass.

"While you were walking," he said, "Comundus told us to come in. He said we needed to be in early today. I don't know why, but that's what he said."

Yaron frowned and made a face, and I felt like doing the same. *I don't* want *to go in*, I thought grumpily and sighed. Being outside after staying in the dirty, smelly cell all day and night so refreshed the body—and spirit. Outside, I could actually run and breathe in the fresh air and stretch my sore muscles.

I glanced down at my arms, the now pale skin visible beneath the torn and dirty fabric. My skin had once been a deep, golden shade, but the weeks of staying in the dim cells and the lack of sunshine had caused my skin to pale to a light creamy colour. I halfsmiled ruefully. *There's probably a lot less of me, too*, I thought, thinking about the meagre portions we were given at mealtime. While I had always been slender, I knew that the scanty scraps were not giving me the nourishment my body needed. *In fact, I'm probably* under*weight now. Those scraps they insist on calling a meal barely make the hunger pangs in my stomach ease, much less come close to filling me up. Now I know why Yaron is so lean*, I thought humourlessly.

Shaking my head, I followed Veryan and Yaron back in the direction of the Tower of Orlena. As I began walking, though, I frowned and cocked my head. I thought I heard a very faint, distant pounding behind us, much like the night I had seen the humans, but it was so soft I was unsure. I looked over my shoulder and squinted against the sun, trying to discern with my eyes what I thought I had heard.

A small black speck was streaking towards us over the plains, growing larger with every passing second. I squinted again, harder this time. *What is that? Is that … a wolf?*

"Yaron." I reached out and caught him by the elbow, bringing him to a stop. "Look," I said, pointing at the fast-moving speck.

Yaron regarded it for a long moment, and then as it came closer, his eyes widened. He sighed heavily. "So soon?"

Concerned, I said, "What is it, Yaron? What's wrong?" I glanced from his ashen face back to the black speck. *What is that?*

Then an instant later, I realized what it was. *It's a person! Riding a horse ... A very big horse, or so it looks.* Indeed, to my vision, the horse was every bit as large as those I had seen bearing the human soldiers the night I had met Veryan. I wondered what breed those horses were; Shire horses were the biggest horses I knew of, and these were large enough to be Shires, but they ran more like Arabians, swift and graceful.

I sensed Veryan glide up behind me, and I could almost feel his dark eyes probing the horizon. "Who is that?" I asked to no one in particular.

Yaron took a shuddering breath and then said, "That's the man I was telling you about, who trains me. He's very unpredictable and temperamental. Though he is not very good with the bow, he handles the sword well, and his weaponless fighting is amazing. Altogether, not the kind of man I'd want to meet in battle. He's killed many people of importance in other nations, so I've heard ... I have learned much from him, but I had no idea it was time for him to come again." He sighed even as he finished the sentence.

I frowned. *What a reputation. I hope I don't have to meet him; he sounds like someone I definitely would* not *like to come in contact with.* I shaded my eyes with my hand to watch the man's approach.

As he advanced closer to us, I began to make out details. He was garbed entirely in black—even his hair was black, black as ravens' wings. A black cloth hid the lower half of his face, to keep the dust of the road away. His horse was a great black beast with a broad chest, strong, muscular legs, a sleek coat, and a long, proud head. I had never seen such huge horses as these, but I thought them fine and fearsome anyway. *I suppose they're some sort of war-horse,* I thought curiously. The man had a great long-sword belted at his waist, and a black cloak fanned out behind him as he rode. I thought he looked like a demon. Suddenly I was reminded of my terrifying dream, and fear squeezed my heart, making me light-headed. Was my dream coming true before my eyes? I caught my breath.

As the man came closer, the two boys and I heard men shouting behind us at the tower's doors. Apparently, they, too, had seen the man and were hurrying to open the Shardrock Gates to allow his entrance. I looked over my shoulder as I heard Gornhelm's great voice boom across the grounds, calling a greeting to the approaching man. I frowned again and then glanced at Yaron, unsure. The great gates began to creak open, grinding noisily on their hinges. The sun shone brightly through the open doors, temporarily blinding everyone's eyes, and the man was hidden momentarily from our gazes as he entered.

When the gates creaked to a position that dimmed the brilliant glare, I could see the man standing inside the gates, sitting tall and proud on his great horse. His eyes raked over the grounds, surveying every square inch and every person present. He lingered on the three youngest elves—Veryan, Yaron, and me—for a long while, watching us for several minutes each. He dipped his head to Yaron, who followed his lead and did the same. I noticed that, despite what Yaron had said about the man being a formidable warrior, they had mutual respect for each other. I wondered at it.

He looked at me again, then seemed to hesitate slightly at the sight of me. I felt weird inside, as if something was about to happen but what, I had no clue.

Then he grunted and swung down from his huge horse, landing lightly and smoothly, with the obvious grace of an elf. Yet something about him made me doubtful of his elven blood. He seemed … unlike any other elf I had ever seen. Almost as though of royal blood, he carried himself differently, as if he were some superior race and it shamed and disgusted him to be among the lesser elves.

I watched with interest as Gornhelm strode up to the man, bowed humbly, and then took the horse's black reins and led the stallion after his master. The man walked smoothly across the grounds with the grace of a wildcat, never looking to his right or left, but staring with burning eyes at the massive tower rising before him. From Yaron's description of him, I had expected him to be much older, but when he removed the black cloth covering his face, he appeared to be around my own age, or maybe slightly older. Though his face was weary and his light eyes exuded an expression of eternal aloofness, he still looked young.

"You, girl!"

I started as Gornhelm called me. He beckoned me over with a wave of his hand and then tossed me the horse's leather reins. "Take the horse to the stables, girl," he said, less curtly than usual. I guessed he was too distracted with the arrival of the black-clad man to be cruel—which was fine with me. *I wish this man could've come sooner,* I thought as I caught the leather reins. I turned them over in my hands. They were embossed with small swirling patterns and scenes, and while they held no meaning for me, I knew that only the wealthier riders had the wares to have that finery on their horse's reins. As I gently tugged on them to urge the horse forward, I noticed the same designs on the saddle. *Whoever this man is, he must have plenty of goods to trade to have this done,* I thought. While nearly every family in Yaracina had horses, very few had enough to trade to get their horses' saddles embossed.

Then I realized I did not know where the stables were. *Blast it,* I thought crossly.

"Excuse me, sir?" I said as politely as I could bring myself to sound.

"What?" Gornhelm said gruffly, sounding distracted.

I bit my lip, hoping my question did not make him angry. "Where are the stables, sir? I ... I haven't seen them before," I said, hoping to sound apologetic for not knowing something so basic.

"Behind the tower, girl!" he said grumpily. "Don't you know anything?" Gornhelm grunted and sidled away, following the man in black.

I rolled my eyes and then said to the horse, "Apparently, I *don't* know anything." The horse stared at me with liquid brown eyes. I sighed and began walking.

The horse, big as he was, moved gracefully with smooth steps. His giant hooves left prints as big as both my hands together with room to spare. I ran my eyes over his muscular legs and his shiny black coat and then put a tentative hand on his broad neck. The stallion snorted softly and nudged my shoulder with his big nose.

I smiled at the horse and then thought, *I wonder what his name is ... He's a beautiful horse.*

The horse snorted again, and much to my shock and surprise, I received an image of solid black from the horse. *Black?* I asked. *That's your name?* While the horse could not understand everything I said, I was fairly sure he understood the general idea of my words.

I felt the stallion's displeasure, and I realized there must be more to his name. *Tell me*, I urged.

An image of a pool of black water came next. Puzzled, I thought, *A black pool?*

Then I understood. *Black-pool? Is that it? Is that your name?*

The stallion bobbed his head in pleasure, and I smiled, pleased that I had figured out the horse's name.

Black-pool followed me to the stables amiably, occasionally sniffing the tan grass below him and trying to take a bite, but I gently rebuked him, telling him that better food waited for him in the stables and that he could graze later. Black-pool obliged grumpily but then resumed his happy attitude.

I led Black-pool into the small stables behind the tower and chose a large stall near the back for him. Then I gave him a pile of sweet hay and oats and a small amount of water.

I let out a little squeak as I turned to see Black-pool's master right behind me. The man stared down at me, and I muttered a word of apology. I could see his eyes now: They were a blue-grey colour, the colour of heavy mist and of grey clouds before a storm. The colour contrasted starkly against his ebony hair, a few strands of which hung over his eyes. They were my eyes.

Stunned, I stumbled back a few steps. Was this the same man I had seen that night as I had watched the human troops unseen from the misty shadows of the dark forest? My heart pounding, I stared up at him unabashedly.

He glanced at Black-pool, who snorted at his master. Then the man looked back at me, and said, "I trust my stallion has been given the proper comforts fit for a travel-weary horse?"

I blinked and nodded, puzzled by the man's strange, slight accent. His voice was light and rich—different than I would have expected—but the accent caught me off-guard. I could not tell where he was from, or even if the accent was elven, but I rather liked it and the rolling, lilting melody to his words. He was not from Yaracina, I suddenly knew, but I could not identify his accent. However, he spoke with the same accent of the blue-eyed soldier I had heard talking in Aseamir, so I presumed they must all be from the same place.

The young man nodded and then left after another quick glance at me. I watched him go, feeling strangely curious about the man with the accent who had my eyes.

৵

Later that day, after Yaron and I had been escorted back to our cells, there was a feast in honour of the blue-eyed man in the common room. Yaron and I could hear the revelry from our stone prison, and it kept us awake long into the night. There was much laughter and carousing among the men, but I instinctively knew that the accented man was not among those making such a racket. He had seemed to me too aloof and refined to join in such foolishness.

I sat silently against the stone wall, tired and frustrated with the din coming from the feast. Yaron was equally silent, sitting motionless in the shadowed corner of his dark cell. Neither of us wished to intrude on the tense silence between us, and so we sat soundlessly in our cells, each brooding over his or her own thoughts.

Soon my mind began to drift, and I instinctively connected to Lliam's mind but sensed that he had not noticed my presence. *Lliam?* I said softly.

A few moments passed before he answered. *Elysia*, he replied tensely, obviously not paying much attention to me. *I can't talk now; I'm busy.*

Doing what?

If I wanted you to know, I would tell you, he answered curtly.

I sighed. *I'm sorry, but I'm terribly bored right now and frustrated, and I wanted to talk to you.*

About what? he asked uninterestedly.

Nothing in particular, I answered. *I just wanted to talk.* I sighed again and brushed aside some of the mouldy hay that was lying beside me, curling my lip at the damp feel.

Lliam snorted. *Well, let me know when you have a good reason to interrupt me, will you? Goodbye, Elysia.* And with that, his mind moved away from mine, causing me to feel more lonely than ever.

I reluctantly lay down on the stone floor, staring out at the darkness of the prison blankly, listening vacantly to the sounds coming from the common room upstairs. I thought for a long while of my family and wondered again if they had any idea what had happened to me. I wondered if Malitha was home yet or if she actually had stayed with Alqua and, if so, how Aubryn was handling it. I wondered if Lillian missed me much yet, and I wondered when Father would be home …

Eventually I fell asleep, comforted and lulled by thoughts of my family and the hope of seeing them again soon. I did not dream, thankfully, and I slept soundly until long after the feast was over and the last of the drunken men had been helped to their quarters.

ॐ

"Elysia."

Startled, I awoke swiftly and sat up at the sound of Veryan's voice. I rubbed my eyes at the bright halo of light that was outside my cell door; he was standing nearby with a torch.

It was a long moment before my eyes adjusted to the light, but when they did, I looked over to Veryan, curious. "What is it?" I asked him.

He slipped a small key into the lock on my cell and opened my door, beckoning for me to follow him. I did so hesitantly, uncertain. He began walking up the stairs, the torchlight casting long, eerie shadows on the walls. I followed him slowly. What could Veryan want at this hour? Surely it was already well past midnight.

"What?" I asked again softly.

Veryan paused and turned to face me, his eyes gleaming in the torchlight. He looked almost angry, I realized, as he spoke: "Gornhelm and that man that arrived earlier today are talking about you. I think you need to hear what they're saying."

I frowned. That was why Veryan had come to my cell during the night and gotten me out? "Veryan, couldn't you have just *told* me what they said in the morning?" I asked tiredly.

Veryan shook his head, as if he was trying to rid himself of a bothersome fly. "No ... As I said, I think you need to hear what they're saying. Come." And with that he grabbed my wrist and pulled me along after him hurriedly.

༗

We quickly and silently glided to the top of the stone stairway that led up from the prison. Once there, we moved until the shadows completely hid us behind one of the marble columns that encircled the circumference of the common room. The torches had long since been extinguished, and the only light came from the moonlight, which streamed in through the high, open windows. I heard soft voices, and though I watched for the people who were speaking, I saw no one. We waited for several minutes, and I stiffened as I saw two men come out from the shadows. It was indeed Gornhelm and the man with the accent. They stepped into the moonlight, and began speaking in low, hushed tones. I strained my ears to hear what was being said but could make out nothing but a few words here and there. From what I could piece together of the conversation, I gathered that they were discussing where I would be given to the slavers, and a few words about someone named Namarii.

I decided to move to where I could see the ebony-haired man's face and possibly hear a bit better. "Elysia!" Veryan hissed very softly in disapproval.

As I moved, however, I bumped into something unseen in the dark and gave a little gasp. I instantly clamped my hand over my mouth.

Immediately, the man with the accent stiffened, and his conversation with Gornhelm abruptly ceased. He motioned with his hand for Gornhelm to remain silent. Then he strode outside of the moonlight and melted into the shadows.

Frightened and angry with myself, I scooted farther back, hoping he would not see me. I heard a very faint rustle as Veryan escaped into the darkness, leaving me alone in the common room.

I started as I heard something else behind me. I darted a quick glance over my shoulder, but realized it must have just been the wind blowing through one of the small, high windows that were set in the walls of the tower.

Relieved, I turned back around and then let out a gasp. The man with the accent was standing right in front of me, his blue-grey eyes glinting. With a start, I suddenly realized he had appeared without warning … *How had he gotten here? I swear I would've heard him!*

The man grinned, making me feel even more uncomfortable. Though his face was obscured by shadows, his eyes glinted in the moonlight so that I felt I was looking at a mirror.

"Greetings, young falcon."

My whole body went rigid, and I let out another gasp, mouthing *Lliam.*

Then with a cry, I turned and fled, disappearing into the darkness.

FINDING A LIGHT

I thought back to that moment again and again, thinking of Lliam's gleaming blue-grey eyes and his knowing smile. *That can't be him, it* can't! I thought over and over, trying to convince myself it was not true. But then I would remember the sound of his voice in my head, and I would rethink my conclusion. *It sounded exactly like Lliam. He had that same ... mocking tone, and it just ... ah, it had to be ... Who else? And strangely enough, I think that's probably what I imagined him looking like.* I shuddered again and shifted against the cool stone wall of my cell.

You imagined me well, daughter of Damir. I could hear a sly grin in his voice, and that only made me more frightened and reluctant to associate with him.

Leave me alone, Lliam! I hissed in reply. *I want nothing to do with you!* Could he not just leave me alone? I put a hand against my pounding heart, wishing I could slow its frantic beating, for I knew he would be able to pick up on my fright through our connection.

As you wish, my young falcon, Lliam said mockingly, his voice laced with contempt as he withdrew from my mind.

I sighed with relief and sagged against the stone wall. While I had grown fond of Lliam over our many long and painful conversations, I was not so sure I wanted to be affiliated with him anymore after what Yaron had told me about him. It made me alarmed just thinking about how little I really knew about him and about what I *did* know of him. By all rights, I should not even *want* to keep associating with Lliam; he was of such a terrible reputation! And yet ...

I sighed again and shook my head to clear my thoughts, wishing none of this had ever happened. *Yaron made him sound like a monster,* I thought, shuddering. From the way I had heard him described and from what I had experienced myself, I knew that he sounded dangerous, he looked dangerous, and he was dangerous.

And yet ... after all that I had endured with him and everything I had seen from his mind and heart, now to have him gone ... just seemed wrong somehow, as if I were missing part of myself. *I don't want him to leave ... and yet ... I don't want him to stay either. I don't know what's right,* I thought miserably. I wrapped my arms around my knees and stared up at the moonlight sifting through the crack above. I sighed heavily, expelling the air from my lungs and then taking in a deep breath to refill them.

I wish Mother were here, I thought. *She'd know what to do.* Yet even as I thought that, I was glad my mother was not here. I did not want my mother to see where I was, and I did not want her to know I had a connection with such a man as Lliam.

Turning my thoughts back to Lliam, I continued to battle over this with myself. *Oh, what should I do? Should I continue to speak to him ... or should I terminate all contact with him? I don't want to do either, really; it'd just be easier if I'd never met Lliam. Argh, this is so ridiculous! I should be focusing on how to escape, not on whether or not it's safe to be associated with someone! After all, I heard them talking about where to meet the slavers.*

I leaned my head back against the stone, feeling the cool, moist night air caress my cheeks with a tender touch. A few curling tendrils of mist snaked over the prison floor, pausing to touch my bare feet with their damp fingers before moving on.

I know how you can escape.

I stiffened, my shoulders tensing. *Lliam ...* I said warningly.

Well, I couldn't help it, he said in retort. *You think so loudly it's impossible* not *to hear you.*

That's no excuse! I said fiercely, determined to break the contact with him as soon as possible.

Actually, if you think about it, yes it is, he replied smugly.

Did you hear everything? I asked, bewildered, already knowing the answer. Could I not even think without his hearing anymore?

As I said …

I sighed and said tiredly, *I don't mean to be rude, Lliam, but I really don't know if I can trust you—*

You can't.

Displeased and annoyed, I broke the contact grumpily, not wanting to talk. I just wanted to think, to reason, to muddle through this great big mess I had somehow gotten myself into since I had left Aseamir. How had all of this happened? How I gotten myself so tangled up in the world in such a short time? Was there any way I could get myself *un*tangled?

I know how to escape.

I shifted uncomfortably, irked that he kept talking to me. *I don't care.*

Lliam laughed, sounding harsh. We both knew I was lying, and he told me so: *I know you're lying, young falcon.*

Just go away, Lliam, I said miserably.

No. I can help you. I know how you can escape. The men are all drunk, no one's awake, there are no guards … Must you give up this opportunity for freedom simply to keep your pride from being injured? 'Often our greatest mistakes come from the smallest sources,' after all.

Furious, I spat, *Why would you want to help me? I know what you are; Yaron told me everything. He said you've killed people and that you are extremely unpredictable and likely to cut a man in two when you are angry. Why should I trust you? Tell me.*

Lliam's voice took on a low, growling quality. *He knows me well. He is a good student … very observant*, he said, his voice soft and muted.

That made me even more disconcerted and distrusting; my mind instantly told me not to count on Lliam to get me out, however much he claimed he could, for I knew next to nothing about him and what I had heard was not promising … How could he expect me to trust him, anyway? *Don't trust him!* every instinct screamed at me, making my mind and heart whirl with confusion.

And yet …

Lliam was silent, giving me time to contemplate what he had said to me. I tried to pick up on his emotions, but none met my probe, no matter how deeply I searched. He was concealing his feelings perfectly, giving me no warning at all what he was going to say, which unsettled me massively, making me feel as if I was walking on the edge of a very sharp knife, one that was cutting my feet even as I balanced upon it.

Tears filled my eyes as I thought about what he offered. *Home. I want to go home! I want to leave behind this god-forsaken prison and go home*, I told myself, hoping these thoughts were private. *But I just can't trust Lliam! If this fails, I could lose not only my freedom forever but also even my life. Is it worth that? Do I trust him and forfeit my life to him?*

I can give you what you want, his voice whispered, gently and softly. *Freedom … it can be yours. All you have to do is trust me …*

Feeling tortured, I replied, *Why would you want to help me? What have I done to earn this help from you?*

Lliam was silent for several long, agonising minutes. Then, *Those reasons I will keep to myself, young falcon.*

I started to protest, but he hushed me by saying, *But I may tell you someday, if we ever meet again.*

I took a haggard breath, thinking everything over in my mind. I thought about Lliam's words: "*I can help you. I know how to escape. The men are all drunk, no one's awake, there are no guards … Must you give up this opportunity for freedom simply to keep your pride from being injured?*" Feeling tormented with fear and uncertainty, I cast my glance to Yaron, sleeping silently two cells down, and I remembered the oath I had taken that if I ever escaped, I would take him with me.

Then a memory of Lliam's menacing and chilling grey eyes flashed through my mind, and I shuddered, all my previous doubts washing over me yet again, making my heart sink with fear.

You must trust me, Lliam insisted, *despite how I may appear.*

But Yaron said … and you agreed … and—

Yes, I know. But if you want to escape, daughter of Damir, blast it, you will have to trust me! All I ask of you … is your simple trust. He sounded so desperate, so earnest, so urgent … Maybe I could trust him. Maybe he really did want to see me freed.

I looked at Yaron, thinking, *If I do take Lliam's offer, I will be trusting my life to a stranger.* I blocked Lliam out of my mind for a moment, and I thought, *I must take Yaron and Veryan with me as well; I swore I would if I ever escaped, but … I don't know what Lliam will think when the time comes …* for I did not intend to tell him just yet.

Lliam resumed our connection and gave a tight mental smile. *Am I such a stranger to you, young falcon? 'Those who understand us best are sometimes those who have known us for only a moment.'*

I shuddered, knowing his words were true. But despite that we had so often shared dreams and emotions, I knew little of him outside of what he had revealed in our conversations. He *was* a stranger to me, and yet I knew him better than I had ever known anyone before. I knew him almost as well as I knew myself, which both frightened me and relieved me.

I pondered the offer again, over and over, weighing the odds, knowing what could happen if we were caught, and then, finally, slowly …

Fine. I accept. I will come with you, and you will help me escape.

STEALERS OF FREEDOM

Feeling uncomfortable, I sat across from Yaron in his cell, the silence stretched out between us like a thick spider web, weaving its way into every nook and cranny. I watched him breathlessly, waiting ...

Veryan had come down to the prison to see if I had made it safely back without being discovered in the common room, which I greatly appreciated. I had told him of my urgent need to speak to Yaron face to face, and he had reluctantly gone and lifted the key from Gornhelm's ring while he lay sleeping. I had just told Yaron of Lliam's offer of freedom, and I had insisted earnestly that we both take it.

Now I waited awkwardly for his response. His brown eyes focused on the stone floor, taking in every square inch of it as he deliberated. Strands of golden hair hanging in front of his eyes only partially covered his creased brow and a mind deep in thought. Sitting with fingers laced together, he remained still and silent, as he had for many minutes.

Finally, after what seemed an eternity, he slowly lifted his gaze to meet mine, looked at me a while, and then said softly, "You're gambling our lives for a prize that doesn't exist."

Confused, I said, "What do you mean? If Lliam's plan works, we'll have our freedom—"

"No," he said, cutting me off and rising, "Freedom does not exist."

I stood as well, bewildered by his strange reaction as well as a little nervous. "Yaron," I said, "if Lliam's plan works, you'll get to go back to Iciar, to your people, to your home—"

He again cut me off. "That's a big *if*, Elysia."

"But—"

"Besides, I have no home. I have no people. Remember? Gornhelm and his men murdered my parents and burned my home to the ground! I wander this earth alone, Elysia, and I have no room for if's and maybe's." He began to walk past me, but I clamped my hand down on his arm, holding him in place. I stared at him furiously and pulled him around so that he faced me, forcing him to look at me.

"Has all this time down here confused your brain, Yaron?" I said more harshly than I meant to. But I was upset and angry with him, and I felt he needed to hear the frustration in my voice. "Have you been locked up down here so long that you've lost all hope? This is our chance for freedom, and we *have* to take it! Do you hear me? This could be our only chance; we have to go!"

The boy clenched his jaw, and his eyes smouldered. "Do you hear *me*, Elysia?" he spat angrily. "While my physical self may gain its freedom, my inner self never will! Even if I go back to Iciar and live there for three thousand years, the memories of what Gornhelm did to my family and me will never be gone from my mind! *Never!*" He jerked away furiously and began stalking around the cell, working himself into a frenzy. Fear touched me when I realized how close to losing control he was.

"The memory of these blasted months here will ever haunt me, stalking my dreams and hounding my soul!" He was shouting now. "I can never be free. Do you hear me? Freedom does not exist in *my* world! I can never forget what I have endured here!" He shoved out his hand, revealing a recently burned and scabbing brand, one that I could tell had been seared onto his hand recently. "Look at that!" he shouted, eyes blazing. Then he snatched his hand away swiftly and said, "I got that not three nights ago, Elysia. Gornhelm *branded* me with his own hand!"

Then to my alarm, he sank to the floor and covered his face with his hands. Shaking sobs racked his body, and tears flowed down his face, leaving pale streaks in the grime that coated his cheeks. "I *can't* do this again, Elysia," he said, nearly inaudibly. "I *can't* have another false hope. I *can't* … I'm not strong enough …" He wept for another moment before whispering, "I'm not strong enough …"

Pity and anger stirred in my heart, and I knelt swiftly beside him. I held Yaron close to me, saying nothing but just letting him shed tears. I stroked his golden hair and leaned my head against his, wishing I could do something to alleviate his suffering.

I must get him out of here.

༄

I took my borrowed sword from Veryan and smiled grimly. The dark-haired boy said nothing but inspected me silently as I secured it on my braided leather belt. Veryan had retrieved my dagger, bow, and quiver from the armoury earlier that night. That they were now restored to me alleviated some of my tension.

Veryan looked away uncomfortably. Then he said softly, "You know you're laying a bet on our lives for something that may not exist."

I did not look up, but my fingers flew even faster over the buckle. "Yaron said the same thing. But …," I finished and looked up at him, "just because freedom may not exist in your world or his … doesn't mean it doesn't exist in *my* world. I made a vow that if I ever had the chance to escape, I would take you both with me, and I intend to keep it." I walked past Veryan to stand at the door of my cell. Yaron stood a few steps away, partially hidden by shadows, his hand clenched around the hilt of his Greek dagger, also restored to him by Veryan. The only emotion now displayed in his cold eyes was that of burning, unwavering hate.

I met his eyes, then Veryan's, and saw my own unspoken fear reflected in them. *Now the time has come to see if we can become stealers of my freedom*, I said to Lliam.

Veryan sighed, grasping the hilt of his sword in his fist, and said, "If luck is on our side, the clouds will stay over the moon. We need to be swift, and we can't let anyone see us. I ..." He faltered suddenly and then fell silent.

I let out a small sigh and said to the boys, "I don't want to lose either of you. Stay close to me, and Lliam will see us out of here." I briefly embraced both of them, and then I led the way up the stairs, never looking back, my heart hammering in my chest.

I kept my mind very carefully filtered, making sure no thoughts of the fact that Veryan and Yaron were coming with me entered my thoughts; I did not want Lliam to discover their presence beforehand and change his mind. Then we would be truly ruined, for if Lliam backed out, we would probably have no more chances to escape for a very long time, and I did not intend to spend any time as a slave on the coast. I just wanted to go home, and with luck, Lliam could get us headed that way.

I led the way silently up the staircase, the light from the torch Yaron was holding flickering on the walls. My badly worn leather boots made no noise on the damp, stone stairs, and I kept one hand on my sword hilt to keep it from hitting against the narrow walls. The tower was deathly quiet, and no guards were anywhere in sight. I guessed they were all still in a drunken stupor, and I hoped they would not rouse until long after we had escaped.

I quickly reviewed the plan in my head. Once we came to the common room—where I had so recently come face-to-face with Lliam—he would lead us from there to an abandoned passage that would, I hoped, lead us to our freedom. While I was unsure if Lliam was going to meet with us physically or mentally—for he had not said which—I knew that I would feel safer either way. Yaron was an extraordinary fighter to be sure, but somehow, even that did not give me much comfort.

We stole silently through the dark hallway that led to the common room, none of us speaking or making any noise whatsoever. At that moment, I was thankful I had so finely honed my skills of walking silently that you would never know I was there if not for your eyes. All my years of noiselessly stalking deer and other game came to my aid, enabling me to glide along the passageway like some otherworldly spirit. Yaron and Veryan stepped equally soundlessly behind me.

I paused a moment as a sound met my ears. Stiffening instantly, I held out a hand to stop the two boys. They halted without question, and Yaron snuffed the torch. Freezing for what seemed like an hour and upon hearing nothing else, I finally began walking again, my heart beating wildly in my chest.

We emerged like ghosts into the common room, slipping into the moonlight from behind the great marble pillars that circled the open space. Feeling like a bird within a great stone cage, I felt reluctant to expose myself to anyone's sight, but I realized it was necessary for our plan to work.

Once we were all ready, I opened my mind, and said to Lliam, *I'm here, Lliam. In the common room. I'm ready when you are.* I still had not told Lliam I was bringing Veryan and Yaron with me, however.

"Good."

I resisted the urge to gasp as I whirled around to see Lliam right behind me, his ebony hair washed silver by the pearly moonlight. Yaron and Veryan were startled as well as they both turned at the sound of his almost inaudible word. Yaron's hand clenched his dagger, and he looked uneasy as he inspected Lliam with a critical eye. Veryan glared at him suspiciously as well.

Lliam did not seem to notice, though, for he kept his gaze on me. His blue-grey eyes glinting in the light, he ran his eyes slowly down the length of my body and then back up. Then his eyes strayed to the side and landed on Veryan and Yaron. He snapped his gaze back to me angrily. "I did not agree to help *them* escape!" he hissed, pointing an accusing finger at the two boys.

"Lliam—" I started.

"Elysia, I will not take them with us, especially Yaron! His skills are valuable to the army, and he is sought after by many of the high-ranking officers; I'm not going to help him escape, and that's final." He glared at me, as if insulted that I would ask him to do such a thing.

I tentatively took Lliam by the arm and pulled him farther away from Veryan and Yaron, into the shadows where they were less likely to hear us. Lliam stood tensely and angrily in front of me. "Lliam," I said pleadingly, "those two *need* freedom, more than I do! Do you even know how Yaron got here? What happened to him—"

"Yes, yes, I know," Lliam interrupted in exasperation. "But all the same, Elysia, I haven't been taking that boy to train him for the past *year* just so I can help him escape and ruin everything that he's been trained for!" His blue-grey eyes appraised me scathingly.

"Lliam, I swore that if I ever escaped, I would take Yaron with me," I said softly, feeling intensely uncomfortable under his heavy gaze. "I will not just let this chance pass him by; he *needs* to be free, Lliam." I paused, hesitating over what I was going to say next. Finally, after considerable effort, I whispered, "If you won't help them escape as well, then I won't go either. The three of us will stay."

Lliam growled in frustration, obviously very displeased. After a long, angry moment, he said, "Do you have any idea how much trouble I'll be in if they find out that I had a hand in this, Elysia? Any idea at all?" His blue eyes bored into mine powerfully.

I shivered slightly, remembering his nightmares and the experiences of his pain. I did not meet his eyes, suddenly ashamed that I was asking him to risk so much more when he was already risking everything to help me. But I had made a promise.

Just as I was about to say something, Lliam hissed, "Blast it, Elysia; you'll be the death of me someday. I'll take them, but know that anything that happens to me because of it will be your fault."

Then he shoved past me, motioning with his hand for us to follow. I breathed a silent sigh of relief and followed him, trailing Yaron and Veryan. Lliam disappeared to my eye as he stepped out of the moonlight, but as I hurried after the others, he became visible again once my eyes adjusted to the inky blackness. When we were away from the common room and out of the hearing range of the soldiers, Yaron used two broken rocks to start a spark and relit the torch, providing pale light for us as we went.

Lliam led us stealthily along a narrow, spiralled passage, which, I presumed, was heading up higher into the tower. Then he took us step by step up a stone staircase, so narrow that both of my shoulders touched the walls at once. Feeling claustrophobic in the tiny, cramped space, I shivered and kept my mind linked with Lliam's for security as we ascended. Once we came up to the next floor, the wall ended, and only a thin black rail separated us from the air next to the stairs.

It was as black as night on the stairway, broken only by a spot of pale golden light from the torch. The tower was obviously falling into ruin on the higher levels. We occasionally passed dark rooms that circled the outer circumference of the large, open rooms, and their once grand doors were crumbling and rotting. Long extinguished torches sat draped in cobwebs in their brackets on the walls, and even a few decomposing ladders stood against walls where the mortar under the stone was visible, as if they had never finished the tower up here.

I wondered how Lliam knew where to go, and briefly, a fear that we were lost touched me. But I kept reassuring myself that he must know where he was going or else he would not have asked me to trust him.

However, as we kept going and going—we had been walking for over half an hour by now—I began seriously to doubt we were ever going to find a way out. *There's no way the tower is* this *big*, I thought with a sickening dread.

It is, Lliam said sourly in my mind.

Lliam, do you even know *where you're taking us?*

Of course, he said, sounding miffed. *Do you doubt me so much as to imply that, young falcon? Trust me; soon you … and your friends … will be streaking over the plains on your way to wherever you wish to go.*

Will you come with us, Lliam?

A harsh laugh sounded in my head. *If you knew my predicament, young falcon, you would not be so quick to say something as ridiculous as that.*

Well, then, never mind. But I had another question, one I had wanted to ask since I had first seen him … *Lliam, when I saw you outside the tower when you first arrived, why did you say nothing to me about who you were?*

Because I was not ready for you to know me yet, he answered. *As I told Yaron the night our bond was created, it would be best if you know as little of me as possible. I don't want anyone to know we are associated in any way. If we ever meet again after this in the presence of either my fellow soldiers or anyone else, we must be as strangers to each other.*

I sighed and broke the contact, feeling lonely. I found that even though I still mistrusted Lliam on a certain level, the fact that he was actually here, trying to help us escape, made my gratitude to him soar immeasurably. Even if we did not escape this time, I knew I would always be grateful to Lliam for going this far to help us. I wondered what his motive was.

Yaron hissed, "How much farther? We've been walking for a *very* long time!" I winced in sympathy; he had been very irritable and extremely jumpy the whole time we had been walking.

Lliam said grumpily, "We've only been walking for a half-hour, Yaron. What have I told you about being patient?"

Yaron answered grudgingly, "'The more you long for something, the longer it takes to get it.'"

"Yes," Lliam acknowledged. He veered off to the left into a dark passageway. "And if you would have patience, the way out would not seem so long in coming." Veryan and I followed the two others into the passage, and sensing we were in a large room because of the feeling of openness, I said, "Where are we?"

Lliam flashed me a quick, triumphant smile, which created an eerie effect with the flickering torchlight and his blue eyes, so much like mine. "We're at the bottom of the tower," he said in a slightly hushed voice.

Confused, I opened my mouth, but Veryan voiced my thoughts first, "The bottom? How is that possible? We've been going *up* the whole time."

Lliam's expression changed to that of someone keeping a heavily guarded secret, and he said, "Yes, so we have. But 'illusions are tricky things.'"

Then he turned back to face the large room and lit the two torches on either side of the entrance. Instantly a halo of light shimmered into space around us and illuminated a small portion of the room. I could see, with what little light we had, several doors along the length of the wall in both directions, and I guessed they continued around the wall of the room in the darkness as well.

Lliam walked around the room, lighting torches as he went and thus revealing many more doors. I gasped in astonishment as— once Lliam was finished—I counted nigh on fifty doors spanning the circumference of the room. It was immense in size, nearly five times bigger than the common room. The walls were hard-packed earth, reinforced with scattered rocks plastered into the walls and coated over with clay.

The three of us watched with fascination as Lliam counted the doors, pointing at random ones—or so it seemed to us—and muttering a pattern under his breath. His brow furrowed in concentration. He counted for several minutes and, then finally and with a satisfied expression, went over to a very ordinary-looking, seemingly random door. He pushed it open gently—because it was starting to rot—and inspected the inside carefully.

Then he turned to the two boys and me, who were gathered behind him with curious and—in Yaron's case—impatient expressions. "Do any of you remember how to get here?"

Completely disoriented, all three of us shook our heads "no."

Lliam turned back to face the door, examining it once more. "Good."

He faced the three of us again, the lights from the torches flickering eerily over his face. Lliam's blue-grey eyes scrutinised each of us in turn, turning over one last thought in his mind. Then he gestured at the dark doorway gaping before us and said, "Inside that door, there is a stairway. Go down it, and then follow the tunnel and do not turn right or left. If you do, your journey will end most abruptly." He held each of our gazes, emphasizing his warning.

I glanced at Yaron, anxious.

Lliam began again: "Once you come to the end of the tunnel, you will find a white stone ledge protruding from the wall. Stand on it, and lift the covering from the tunnel. You will come out on the south side of the tower, roughly three miles from it. Once all three of you are out, run. Don't turn back, don't *look* back, and don't stop for *anything*. Understand?"

Three heads nodded, focusing intently on his instructions.

Lliam grunted, appearing fairly satisfied, and handed a torch to Yaron, who took it solemnly and entered into the dark doorway, where he waited for Veryan and me to follow. Veryan did so a moment later, followed by me, but I hesitated. Before descending to the shadowy staircase, I turned to Lliam, unsure of what to say but wanting to say something.

I looked at him solemnly, unspoken gratitude in my eyes. We held each other's gaze for a moment, and then I said softly, "Thank you, Lliam … for everything."

He said nothing.

"I …" I paused, unsure of how to continue. "I … Well, thank you for listening … and for helping us. It means a lot to me." Then I added a nearly inaudible afterthought: "You've been a good friend."

Lliam grunted, displaying no emotion. "I'm not your friend, daughter of Damir. If we meet again someday, I can make no promises that I can treat you kindly; my situation places me in that position."

Confused and uncertain, I nodded slowly. "Thank you, nonetheless, Lliam."

Then I turned and plunged into the tunnel of inky darkness behind Yaron and Veryan, leaving behind all sense of reality.

THE TUNNEL OF MIDNIGHT

I shuddered as darkness closed in around me, threatening to consume every thought and emotion, leaving only the withering remains of a person's mind that would soon enough be consumed by the most deadly enemy of them all: time.

The torchlight was strangely subdued in the crushing darkness, which threatened to devour every last particle of light, leaving us alone and lost in the world of utter night. I could only see Veryan's outline ahead of me, but when he glanced back at me, I could see the sparkle of his dark eyes, highlighted by the dim torchlight.

Silence pressed around us like a constricting snake, making every noise sound strangely hushed and smothered. Yaron's faint shape ahead of me seemed rigid and tense, as if he were extremely ill at ease in the deep underground vault. *Which*, I concluded, *he probably is. I certainly am.*

We groped our way down the winding staircase, putting our hands on the cool, damp walls to steady ourselves as we descended. I felt extremely unstable as I moved down because I could not see well at all, and my touch had to make up for my sight. While I could see perfectly on any regular night, my eyes could not pierce this smothering, utterly light-consuming darkness, save only for what the light of the torch fell upon.

Suddenly, I gasped as I stumbled slightly in anticipation of the next step and not finding it. We had finally come to the end of the stairs and were now faced with the tunnel. I moved closer to Yaron and Veryan until our shoulders almost touched. I wanted to be as close to the light as possible. I felt Yaron's hand brush mine comfortingly as I shifted impatiently.

Then Yaron held the torch aloft, trying to see the way ahead. We were faced with three tunnels, one directly in front of us and one on either side of the middle one. "Well," Veryan said, "Lliam said to go straight, so I guess the middle one it is."

No protests were given, so we resolutely started down, moving slowly and silently into the tunnel of midnight.

_ు_

About an hour later, I broke the lingering silence and said uneasily, "How long is this tunnel? We've been walking for an awfully long time."

Veryan said nothing but merely glanced back at me, his own misgivings mirrored in his eyes. Yaron sighed heavily, and said, "I don't know, but I can't take much more of this. This darkness is driving me insane." He swung his arm, as if trying to clear the blackness. Veryan murmured a word of agreement. I shuddered and walked faster, moving closer to the boys.

_ు_

A few minutes or hours later—I could not tell which—it seemed to me that the darkness was becoming less heavy, as if, bit by bit, the layers of gloom were being peeled away by an unseen hand. I squinted, trying to gather all the light to my eyes. The light from the torch flickered briefly, making shadows dance over our faces. I trailed my fingers along the moist walls of the tunnel, wishing I could get out.

Suddenly Yaron cried out with a hoarse shout and fell to his knees, dropping the torch. Then it seemed a convulsion gripped him, for he fell to the floor and writhed in pain, his face screwed up in anguish. The torch sputtered out as soon as it hit the damp ground, casting us into utter blackness. The only thing that could be heard was Yaron's groans and cries.

As soon as the light had left us, I had grabbed Yaron's upper arm so that we would not be separated or lost in the blackness and to keep him from hurting himself. I remembered when he had last been like this: the night he had had a similar seizure in my cell and had been unconscious for two days. I felt Veryan's hand on my shoulder, and I squeezed it with my own, reassuring both of us.

I gently stroked Yaron's face, trying to calm and reassure him, but he paid me no mind as I suspected. His nightmares—as well as the pain from his branded hand and scarred back—were hurting him again, and the current situation made it no better.

I felt Veryan move closer to me, and he breathed beside me, "What happened?" He seemed almost afraid to speak, as if his words might further aggravate Yaron's pain.

I said back just as quietly, "Something made Yaron have a sort of … seizure. It used to happen back in the cells sometimes." I reached out and took Veryan's hand, trying to reassure myself, but he pulled it away almost instantly.

Veryan exhaled agitatedly, and then he fumbled around for the torch. There was a slight noise as his hand rammed into the wood, and I flinched. Then he picked up the wood and breathed, "Are there any rocks nearby I could use to relight this? I hope it hasn't gotten too wet; this … tunnel is awfully damp."

I groped around for a moment and then found two small stones that would be perfect for igniting the torch. I fumbled in the dark for Veryan's hands and placed the stones in them, and he began striking them together. Loudly the grating strikes echoed throughout the endless tunnel, building upon each other and magnifying the harsh sound. Veryan froze instantly, and I flinched again and moved closer to Yaron, feeling unsafe.

BREAKING THE SILENCE

U ncertainly, I sat down beside Veryan, who was holding the relit torch. The light was dim and pale in the dark, but we both knew even the slightest light in that midnight tunnel would draw followers like moths to a flame at night. We were risking everything just by staying in one place, but Yaron was unfit to keep moving at the present.

I was worried about him. He flickered in and out of consciousness a few feet away from the torch, and he would not respond to anything I tried to do for him. His forehead was damp with sweat, as were his limbs, and the brand on his hand was inflamed. I hoped that this was just a temporary ailment and that he would soon be able to rid himself of the haunting fears and apparitions the visions brought.

I sighed dejectedly. The crushing darkness made me nervous and tense, and I scooted closer to Veryan. The tiny flame of the torch was comforting, to some degree, but it could not abate the impending feeling that we were just one turn away from some disaster, whether falling down some lightless pit or being caught by soldiers. While I told myself that the soldiers could not have possibly followed us, that did not do much to convince me. *And Lliam could have led them to where he took us.* Though I had no idea why he would do that, I felt I had to consider everything, logical or not.

I heard Veryan take a shuddering breath, and I knew he was having the same thoughts I was. I glanced at him and saw that he was staring dismally at the torch. His usually emotionless eyes were uncertain, and he looked exhausted. I paused and then said, "Veryan. Are you all right?"

He blinked and looked at me swiftly, as if startled. Then, just as quickly, he glanced back at the fire flickering at the head of the torch. He swallowed and said in a low voice, "I'm afraid."

Pity, as well as surprise, twinged at my heart. He had lived his life in fear of the tomorrow every day and had never had a place in which to feel safe. He had been alone ever since I had met him, and I guessed even long before then. *I wish I could help him*, I thought regretfully. *I wish there was some way I could.* I sighed and then conceded, *He needs a friend, someone whom he can count on. I can at least be that person for him. He deserves that for all he's risked for me.*

I gently took his hand and laced my fingers with his. Veryan did not respond—except for flinching slightly—so I agreed, "So am I." Veryan loosened my hand a little and answered icily, changing his tone. "Don't be, Elysia. I'll see you out of here, no matter what it takes … I promise."

I sat up slowly, and then looked at Veryan purposefully, saying, "Veryan, you've already done so much for me." His eyes locked with mine, and I again felt heat rise in my cheeks. I hoped he would not notice. His gaze was so piercing and soul-searching; it discomforted me and made me feel naked and exposed, as if all my thoughts and emotions were laid bare for him to scrutinise. I suppressed a shiver. I smiled at him gently and murmured, "Thank you. For everything …"

Veryan gave a grim, tight half-smile, and he swiftly pulled his hand away from mine.

࿇

Several minutes later, I was sitting beside Yaron when I heard him groan. Instantly, my gaze snapped to his face and waited, hoping he would wake.

A few more minutes passed before his brown eyes opened, and when they did, I smiled in relief. *Thank goodness*, I thought, so glad he was all right. Yaron passed his gaze blindly over me and Veryan, and then he closed his eyes again.

I frowned. *He needs to wake. We need to keep moving.* I glanced at Veryan, who was still sitting, holding the torch, and then back down at Yaron. I placed my hand on his shoulder and shook him gently. "Yaron," I breathed.

He groaned and opened his eyes again briefly. I whispered, "Yaron, are you all right?"

He murmured drearily, "I'm fine. Where are we?"

"We're still in the tunnel."

He grunted and then said, "Help me up; I can walk." Yaron resolutely and slowly sat up, gritting his teeth.

I stood and took his arm. Then I put it around my shoulders and wrapped my arm around his waist. Yaron stood shakily, while leaning heavily on me. He exhaled forcefully once, and I glanced at him in concern. He shook his head, indicating it was nothing, and righted himself.

He walked stiffly over near the torch with me still supporting him in case he needed aid. Yaron glanced once at Veryan, who was watching us with shadowed eyes. His eyes narrowed, and he said harshly to Veryan, "I'm not weak."

Veryan's eyes tightened, but he replied stoically, "I never said you were."

"No, but you were thinking it," Yaron accused.

Veryan had no expression, so it was difficult for me to tell what he was going to say next. I took a small step back, unwilling to take a side in this argument. I wished Yaron and Veryan could either come to an agreement or just not speak to each other at all. That would simplify things significantly, I knew.

Finally, Veryan sighed and said to Yaron, "Yaron, when can we ever settle this? I've told you, I'm sorry for what Pyralus and I were ordered to do. I didn't enjoy it, and I'm sorry for what Gornhelm has done to you—"

Yaron cut him off, snapping, "Saying you're sorry doesn't change anything, Veryan! It doesn't undo a second of what I've endured nor what I think of you. I will firmly and always hate you."

Then Yaron stalked away, leaving me dazed. I glanced after him, and he was standing—hands on hips—several yards away, just inside the dim halo of light the torch emitted. He looked tense and angry.

I gave a small sigh and then walked over to Veryan, who was staring crossly at the fire flickering on the torch. I put my hand on his shoulder and murmured, "You tried." Veryan gave me an angry glare and shrugged my hand off. I opened my mouth and was about to say something, but Yaron cut me off by saying in a low voice, "We need to go."

I glanced up at his dark silhouette and then at Veryan. We traded quick looks, and then Veryan stood, holding the flickering torch aloft. Yaron walked tensely back to my side, a scowl still on his face.

Veryan led the way with the torch, and the flickering shadows on the walls returned. I shivered, unwilling to begin the dark trek again, but I knew the sooner we got moving, the sooner we would get out. *Or die*, I thought dismally, thinking again of what could befall us in this midnight tunnel. I shuddered at the thought of Yaron or Veryan lying still and lifelessly like those men that had been slaughtered by the wolves on the way to the Tower of Orlena.

Yaron walked behind me. We started slowly at first as our fear of the darkness rushed back to us, but as we progressed further along the tunnel, we moved faster, hoping to make up some of the time lost. I stayed close to both the boys, feeling vulnerable and frightened. Yaron sensed this and moved closer to me, his hand brushing mine to reassure me.

※

A while later, Veryan held up his hand to signal the two of us to stop. I peered around him to see what had made him stop. I gasped and moved back closer to Yaron.

A monstrous, gaping hole lay before us, taking up the entire tunnel floor, wall-to-wall. It was utterly and profusely black and lightless, and there was no telling what was at the bottom of that cavernous mouth. Veryan took several steps back and glanced at Yaron and me. "There's no way around," he said in a hoarse whisper. His eyes showed traces of unease and fear, and I put my hand on his shoulder. He did not shrug it off this time. Yaron exchanged glances with Veryan, and I was pleasantly surprised that neither of the boys had a harsh word for the other.

Yaron glanced at the cavern and then back at Veryan and me. "We'll have to jump it," he said, saying what I had hoped would never come to mind. I was deathly afraid of what would happen if one of us fell down there and did not even want to come close to risking it. *I don't want to lose either of them, and I'm scared I will if we try this.* "There must be some other way," I murmured apprehensively, knowing there was not, but still hoping. Veryan sighed, agreeing, but said, "There's not. Yaron's right; we'll have to jump it." He refused to meet my eyes. "I'll go first."

I wanted desperately to stop him, but I knew I could not. "Here," I said, gesturing to his torch. "Throw that over first, and see how large it is. If you know you can't make it …" I looked meaningfully at Veryan, "then don't go." He sighed shakily and nodded.

Veryan was about to throw the torch when Yaron said, "Wait!" He grabbed the torch from Veryan and set it down on the ground, careful to the keep the end away from the damp earth. Yaron picked up a couple of sharp rocks nearby and then rolled the fiery end of the wood under some water that was dripping from the high ceiling. It promptly sputtered out.

"What are you doing?" Veryan hissed.

Then came the sound of a rock striking against the wood. After several hard, strong hits, the wood split into two. I then heard Yaron strike the sharp rock against another, and sparks flared into life on the end of the torch. Another light followed it soon after. We now had two smaller torches, one for this side and one to throw.

Yaron stood and handed one of the torches curtly to Veryan, who scowled at him. "Now you can throw it," Yaron said.

Veryan gripped the torch tightly and then threw it as hard as he could across the cavern. It clattered to the ground a moment later, and we could see it was barely four yards from here to there. The torch was close to the edge of the other side, illuminating the area where we were to land our jump. I sighed in relief. That was an easy jump for any elf, and I knew I would be able to make it. I nodded slowly to Veryan, and then Yaron and I stepped back to make room for him to jump.

Veryan took several steps back, paused, and then took off running. I barely had time to see him before he leaped.

I heard him breathe a sigh of relief from the other side after he landed, and he cried, "It's easy! Come on!"

I looked back at Yaron, and he motioned for me to go next. He moved to the edge with me so that I could see where I would begin my jump. I slowly took off my quiver and looked at it, thinking. I could not throw it across; the arrows and the bow would most likely fall out, and I doubted they would stay in if I jumped with them on my back. If I tried to shoot them across the hole, even softly, they would likely skitter into the darkness and be lost, and it would be dangerous for Veryan. I very reluctantly set my quiver down on the ground, knowing I would have to leave it there. I hefted the borrowed sword Veryan had given me, evaluating it. "Veryan!" I called then. "Can I toss my sword to you? I don't really want to jump with it."

He nodded, and after a moment's hesitation and aiming, I threw the weapon across to him. Veryan caught it deftly and set it down by the torch, out of the way.

I tried to quell the nervousness and fear that was roiling in my heart as I stepped back several feet. I tensed, reluctant to begin running. I stared at the ground, taking a moment to compose myself before starting.

Suddenly, to my surprise, Yaron stepped in front of me and embraced me with his strong arms. Even though he was only sixteen, he was taller than I was and much stronger. He crushed me against him tightly for a long, breathless moment—making my heart rate climb massively—and then released me. "Be careful," he murmured and stepped back.

Momentarily stunned, I blinked, and then without even giving time for the fear to return, I ran.

My feet flew along the ground as if wings were attached to them. All I could hear was the blood roaring in my ears, the sound of my own breath, and the whistle of the damp cave air. I barely saw the edge of the ground coming and just scarcely remembered to jump.

Flying over the cavern was terrifying. I could sense the gaping black chasm beneath me, just waiting to swallow me and keep me from the daylight forever. I felt weak.

The next thing I knew, I was in Veryan's arms, safe on the other side. Shaking badly, I took a few seconds to just gulp in air and try to slow my heart, which was beating so hard it hurt. "Are you all right?" Veryan asked vacantly, and I nodded fiercely. He grunted in approval and left me, walking back to the edge of the monstrous hole.

I shakily stood up, still uncertain if I would be able to walk. I made my way over to where Veryan was standing on the edge of the chasm, and we waited for Yaron.

I could see him on the other side, a small, dark shape holding a faint light against an enormous blanket of blackness. Yaron set the light down a moment later, and it lay forlornly against a rock near his feet. I watched breathlessly as he tensed, ran, and leaped …

At first, I thought he was going to make it, but then I promptly realized that he was just the tiniest bit short on his leap. Casting a panicked look at Veryan, I stepped closer to the edge, terrified. Veryan, sensing my alarm, moved closer too. "He's not going to make it," I whispered hoarsely.

Half a second later, Yaron crashed into the side of the cliff on the edge of the massive pit. I had been right; he was just barely off. He yelped and scrabbled at the rocks, trying to gain a foothold. Then Yaron yelled in pain as he held onto the edge of the rock with his branded hand; I could see blood starting to ooze out from under his gripping fingers.

I instantly and automatically kneeled and grabbed his arm, my heart pounding in my chest. Veryan seized his other arm, and we both pulled, trying to get him up.

But Veryan's hold slipped as Yaron's weight brought him too close to the edge. Veryan gasped and let go for the briefest instant before scooting back and regaining his grip on Yaron's arm.

In that fleeting second, the torch had sputtered out, and the curtain of night swept over us, enfolding us with its clenching arms. There was a very dim, faint light from the other side of the chasm where Yaron's torch remained, but I knew it would burn out soon. All three of us instantly froze, and all I could hear was my heart fluttering like a dying bird and the heaving gasps of Yaron. "Yaron? Veryan? Are you both all right?" I whispered, afraid to break the silence.

"I'm fine!" Veryan replied, sounding as panicked as I felt.

Yaron gasped, "Get me up!"

I paused and then began pulling him up again. I could feel Veryan do the same. Yaron helped as best he could by not struggling, and I was proud of him; I knew he was terrified.

A moment later, he was up. He gasped and scrambled as far away from the edge as he could and then fell in a heap against the ground like a dead thing. Terrified for him, I began to make my way over to him.

I scooted over to Yaron. I could hear his laboured breathing and followed it until my hand bumped against his. Yaron sensed me beside him and then slowly sat up, still breathing heavily.

Without giving it a second thought, I wrapped my arms around him and pulled him into a tight embrace. It scared me how close I had come to losing him, and now I did not want to let him go.

It surprised me how frightened and panicked he seemed. I could feel his tears wet my cheeks, and he was shaking badly. "It's all right, Yaron," I whispered over and over. I kissed his golden hair and his face and leaned my head against his, feeling my heart pound so hard I was afraid it was going to burst out of my chest. I did not ever want to come this close to losing him again.

Then I was aware of Veryan beside me, and I looked at him fondly over my shoulder, barely able to see him in the pale light from the torch across the pit. I was so thankful he was there too. *If I had lost either of them … I would've lost part of myself*, I thought. Veryan sighed, and I was aware that he was shaking too, though not nearly as bad as Yaron. Then I wrapped one arm around Veryan and hugged him as well. He stiffened, but he did not pull away.

We stayed in this embrace for several minutes, all panting with the fright of nearly losing Yaron. I did not ever want it to end.

꒰꒱

Later we resumed our trek and walked for what seemed like an hour before we finally came to the end of the tunnel. The torch remaining on our side had been so small and damp that we could not manage to relight it, so we went on, very slowly and uncertainly, our hands on the walls to give us some idea of where we were going. We took every step with extreme care, as we were terrified that we would encounter another pit and, this time, would not discover it until we were falling.

We did not know we had reached our destination until Veryan, who had positioned himself in front, called back to Yaron and me, "I can't go any further! There's a rock wall in front of me!" And we could see that there was a dim glow of pale light shining out from behind the bend around which Veryan had gone. Staring in relieved wonder at the thing that had evaded us for so long in the tunnel of midnight, a smile instantly formed on my lips and my heart skipped a beat in anticipation of our freedom. Surely it was close now ...

I glanced at Yaron to see if he was as comforted by the sight of light as I was. But in that brief look, I saw no excitement in those brown eyes but, rather, fear and shame, and he mostly avoided my eyes. I put a hand on his elbow to stop him. "What's the matter?" I asked softly.

Yaron smiled harshly, staring down at the ground. "I *am* weak ... aren't I?" He shook his head disbelievingly. "I can't believe I lost control like that back there. I ... I don't even know why I did ...," Yaron snorted. "I wonder what Veryan thinks of me now."

I could not believe I was hearing him say that. After all that he had been put through, how could he *not* lose control sometimes? "Yaron," I said, "how can you think that you're weak?"

He did not answer me.

"Yaron, look at me," I said gently. He would not, and he resolutely kept his eyes on the damp ground. I reached out and turned his face towards mine, but still he did not meet my eyes. "Yaron," I said again. "Look at me."

Finally, slowly, he did, his brown eyes tired and fearful. "You are *not* weak," I said firmly. "You have every right to lose control sometimes, Yaron, after what's happened to you! What does it matter what Veryan thinks? There's no reason, none at all, to be ashamed, do you hear me? You are strong, Yaron, the strongest person I know ..." His brown eyes held mine for a long moment, and then they moved back to the ground. "And no one can lose his family and be imprisoned and mistreated and come out unscathed, so don't think you have to ..."

Yaron looked at me again, blinked a few times, and then slowly nodded and pulled out of my grasp, continuing to walk. I followed him.

Veryan was standing next to a large white stone that was protruding from the wall, looking with a frown upon the solid, earthen wall in front of him. He turned to us. "Did we go the wrong way? Lliam never said anything about a dead end."

No one spoke for a moment, and then Yaron said tiredly, "Yes, he did. Remember?"

Veryan looked at him, appearing as though he was trying to remember but not able to do so. I quoted, "'Once you come to the end of the tunnel, you will find a white stone ledge protruding from the walls.'"

Yaron pressed, "Remember now?"

Veryan's frown deepened a little, as if frustrated that Yaron had remembered when he had not, and jerked his head in a nod. "Yes, I do recall that now." He turned to the white rock. It glittered like a thousand stars under the light of the sun filtering in through several crevices, and it was so brilliant that it hurt my eyes. Veryan tapped it experimentally, and a dull, heavy sound echoed in the tunnel, making us freeze as the noise reverberated loudly. All three of us stared at each other, and when the noise had died, Yaron said hastily, "Don't do that again."

Veryan nodded quickly, looking disturbed. Then he glanced up at the ceiling, which was surprisingly low. "'Stand on it, and lift the covering from the tunnel.' That's what Lliam said …," he murmured to himself.

Yaron motioned for Veryan to get down, and he took his spot on the white stone. He studied the roof for a few minutes. Then he placed his hand on the dirt-packed ceiling and began applying pressure to different areas. He pushed against the imbedded rock as hard as he could several times, but the rock did little more than shudder slightly. Veryan and I watched with apprehensive eyes.

Yaron pulled his hands down, seemingly thinking. He was silent for a few moments. "Well," he said, mostly to himself, "I can't lift it off …"

"I'll help," Veryan offered.

"No," Yaron growled, glaring at him murderously. "I don't need your help or want it."

I frowned at him, but he did not notice me. Veryan and Yaron glared intensely at each other for a long, heavy moment, and then I finally could not bear it anymore. "Stop it," I said in exasperation. "This is not getting us anywhere. Can I help, Yaron?"

He slowly moved his powerful gaze off Veryan to look at me. "Fine," he said shortly.

I jumped onto the rock and put my hands on it, feeling its gritty, moist surface on my fingers. I shuddered a little. On Yaron's count, we both pushed as hard as we could.

As soon as we began pushing, the rock trembled and groaned. We paused to regain our energy and then pushed again. The rock gradually began loosening from its hold. Three more times, we struggled, and then we finally pushed the rock up and off the hole it had sealed so securely.

BROKEN TRUST

After the deadening darkness, the light that streamed down from the outside world blinded us. Yaron yelped and jumped down from the white rock, which now glared back the sun's rays. I followed him quickly, shielding my aching eyes. It took several minutes before any of us could even open our eyes. But when I did, I gloried in the light after all those hours of blackness, and it made my heart leap with genuine hope. For the first time since this whole escapade had started, I felt as if we might actually escape after all. I gave a relieved laugh and stepped forward into the streaming light. It covered me like a warm blanket. The curtain of darkness had been drawn back, and the stage of light revealed, again, its formal splendour times a thousand.

I laughed again and looked back at the boys. They were now staring up at the world outside the hole, at the brilliant azure sky above our heads.

Elated, I hugged Yaron. "Well done, Yaron," I whispered to him, smiling in delight. We were almost free! Yaron's arms wrapped around me, and I heard a smile in his voice as he said, "You too, Elysia."

I pulled back, grinning up at him and then hugged Veryan. He exhaled shortly and pushed me away firmly, but I did not mind. I smiled at him happily; he was free now.

Then I drew away and looked at both of the boys. I took a deep breath, excitement and anxiety rising together in my stomach, and said, "Ready?"

Veryan and Yaron exchanged glances, and I saw an adventurous spark in both their eyes. When he looked back at me, Yaron said, "I've never been more ready for anything, Elysia."

～

Yaron climbed out first. He disappeared outside our vision once he was out of the tunnel, and we waited eagerly for his return.

Veryan looked at me, and he said, "Why don't you go next, and I'll follow. That way, you'll have a better chance of escaping if someone sees us."

I looked at him affectionately and said, "No, Veryan, you should go fir—"

Veryan cut me off, his brown eyes darkening strangely: "Elysia, just go. Don't argue; you're going first."

Bewildered, I opened my mouth to protest, but he moved away, allowing me access to the rock. I sighed and jumped up on the rock. Looking up at the cloudless sky, I took a deep breath of the clear, sweet air, put my hands on either side of the hole, and hoisted myself up into Yaron's waiting arms.

He helped me up, and I sat down beside the hole to wait for Veryan. He came a moment later, dark eyes sweeping over the plains.

Then all three of us stood and looked at the sight before us: Lliam must have been correct on his estimate of how far away we would come out for we could not see the tower. I remembered he had said we would come out south of the tower, so I supposed that was where we, indeed, were.

We had emerged in the middle of the day. The sun shimmered fiercely down on our shoulders, and I was already almost missing the coolness of the tunnels. But, no, in truth, I was extremely relieved to be out of there and back into the world of light.

Yaron breathed, "I already looked, and there are no soldiers anywhere around here. I'm guessing they're all still drunk from last night."

I frowned. "It's only been a few hours since we left the common room, but it seems as if it's been days ago that Lliam led us through the tower … doesn't it?"

Veryan murmured in agreement, but Yaron was silent. I glanced at him and noticed that he had tensed. I heard him give a low growl, and I questioned, "What is it?"

He pointed. A lone horseman was coming into view on the horizon, gazing around the plains as if he were looking for something. He carried a spear in his hand and a horn at his hip.

Veryan, Yaron, and I immediately froze. If the soldier saw us and alerted the others, whether the men were clear-headed or not, there could be trouble. I knew at least one formidable fighter was not drunk, and while I fervently hoped Lliam would not turn on us, he *had* told me that next time our paths crossed, I should not hope too greatly that he would treat me kindly. *He wouldn't betray us now*, I thought optimistically. He *couldn't*. But I was unsure.

A twig snapped behind us, sounding to us as loud as a crack of thunder. The three of us whirled, and we saw a deer bound away, frightened by our sudden movement.

However, the movement also unfortunately drew the attention of the soldier. He found us with his eyes instantly. A slow smile crept over his face, and he seized the horn at his belt and blew. An instant later, the bellowing notes rang out on the plain. Anyone within a mile could have heard that note easily.

Yaron shot a panicked look at me and cried, "Run!"

I took off without a second thought and was dimly aware of Yaron and Veryan running beside me.

At first, I thought we were going to get away without any pursuit. The soldier had galloped back in the direction of the tower, still blowing his horn, but thus far, no men had come. *Maybe we'll get out of this after all*, I thought.

I looked back over my shoulder. Horsemen were now pouring into sight over the horizon, armed with bows and spears. They were riding hard and fast, and I knew they were bent on catching us. I noticed the outline of a man standing at the edge of the horizon, arms crossed. He yelled something to the troops, and their speed doubled. I could barely make out a smirk on his face. *Who … ?* Then it hit me as I noticed the man was dressed in black and had black hair. *Lliam.* The shock of what was happening made my legs stop working, and I felt weak. I skidded to a stop and felt the pang of betrayal engulf me. After all he had done for us and after all I had told him … *I hate you,* that was my only thought to him.

Lliam sneered and retorted, *You are far too easy to fool, Elysia, and far too trusting.* I savagely severed my contact with him.

Dimly, I felt Yaron grab my arm and pull me onward. I continued to stare at the man who had betrayed me and felt as if I was seeing the world from under water. Everything seemed hazy and indistinct, as if a misty cloud had descended on my mind, making everything vague and blurred. I could faintly hear Veryan call my name, and I was dimly aware of an arrow flying past me in slow motion.

Then, in a flashing instant, the world regained its normal speed, and I felt the ground beneath me. "Elysia!" Yaron said forcefully beside me. I felt his hand grip my arm with bruising strength. "Go!" he snapped and shoved me into Veryan. A spear zinged past Veryan's arm, and he turned me around and pushed me in the direction we had been running. I stumbled slightly, but then my legs remembered the urgency of escaping, and I began pumping my legs as fast as I could, desperate to get away from Lliam.

I looked back again, and to my alarm, saw that the soldiers were steadily gaining on us. I cast a fearful glance at Yaron, who was running swiftly beside me. I saw my own fears mirrored in his eyes and also the fierce determination to escape.

We must get away.

LOST

I looked back again. The soldiers were even closer now, and I could hear Lliam barking his commands to the troops, spurring them on. Hate roiled in my chest, and I spat at the ground.

"Elysia! Yaron!" We both looked at Veryan, who was barely three steps behind us. "Stop," he said.

I did so automatically and without thought, subconsciously knowing he would not have asked such a thing if there was not a good reason. Awareness of what I had done finally hit me, and I realized I had stopped moving. Growling, Yaron stopped too. "What?" he shouted, clearly angry with Veryan for making us stop when the soldiers were obviously gaining on us. I hoped this did not take an ill turn.

Veryan hesitated, and then said to Yaron, "I'm staying behind. I want you to stay with Elysia and keep her safe, no matter what."

Even Yaron looked surprised. He was silent for a moment and then looked Veryan in the eye and said, "I will. I promise you."

I burst out, "Veryan, you can't—"

"I'm going to, Elysia. You and Yaron need this more than I do. At least you have a place to go to. Maybe I can buy you a little time," he murmured and then shouted, "Go, before they catch up." He glanced over his shoulder and then turned back and said, "Don't wait for me or try to come back for me. Promise me you'll run and not look back."

I was about to protest, but Yaron grabbed my arm and said, "We promise." He looked at me. "Come," he said grimly.

I exhaled, wrenched my arm away from Yaron's grip and then threw my arms around Veryan and whispered, "Be safe, Veryan ... and thank you for everything."

Then I pulled away and shot off running, not looking back because I knew if I did I would cry.

We flew through the endless tan stretch, and the miles melted away before our feet. I hated leaving Veryan. Every time I thought of him and remembered the fear in his eyes, I nearly turned around. I knew this would haunt me the rest of my life, and I hated myself and him for having to endure this. But the steady breathing of Yaron beside me kept me going. I focused intently on running, looking straight ahead and marvelling at how the landscape passed in a uniform blur. It was the only way to distract myself from the burning pain that was mounting in my heart because of what Veryan had done for us.

For the rest of the day, Yaron and I sprinted across the Salquessaé Plains, covering ground in half the time that it had taken Gornhelm's men to traverse. Yaron kept up with me perfectly, our legs moving in synchronicity as we ran. We said nothing to each other; I, out of fear I would break down.

As the day slowly became night and the miles vanished like mist under the morning sun, I began to lag a little. No matter how hard I tried, I remained one step behind Yaron and could not even our paces. It frustrated me, but the muscles in my legs had begun to cramp and prevented me from keeping up with him.

Finally, when the moon rose in the velvety sky and we had the cover of the night, I had to stop. I was now breathing harder, but still, my breaths could hardly be heard. My legs ached, and my mind felt fuzzy. I stopped suddenly and bent over, hands on my knees, staring at the ground in an attempt to distract myself from the burning, numbing pain in my legs.

Yaron stopped too, and he seemed puzzled as to why I was stopping. He stood beside me, looking up at the moon. I noticed he was not breathing hard at all.

I eyed him strangely and straightened. *I don't know why he's not tired by now. We've been running for* hours. Yaron flicked his eyes to mine.

"Why have we stopped?" he said, clearly not ready to do so. I exhaled heavily, feeling my ribs ache as they swelled with my intake of air. Putting my hand against them, I leaned over, trying to catch my breath.

"I'm tired, Yaron. My legs burn, and I can't think straight," I said feebly. Yaron stared at me in disbelief.

"You're ... tired." To me, it sounded as if Yaron did not fully understand me. I nodded and sat down in the grass. My legs burned as I tried to make myself comfortable.

Yaron sighed and looked around. He noticed a dark band on the horizon and squinted to see better.

"They're trees," he said softly. I looked up at him strangely. *Trees?* I thought. *But we couldn't have possibly come that far yet. There's no way we could have already travelled such a distance in this amount of time* ... I stood up and looked at the horizon. The black band definitely was a forest.

I could feel Yaron's eyes on me, his unspoken question on his face. *Do we go on?* I looked up at the sky, thinking. Yaron shifted impatiently beside me. I knew his mind was made up; he was going on.

I turned my eyes on Yaron and said, "We go on." He nodded in approval and began running again. I followed, taking a heavy breath, and wished my legs would stop aching. We streaked across the plains as swift black shadows under the moon's pale light.

Minutes later, we came into the forest. The trees—immensely tall and cast dancing shadows on our faces in the moonlight—gave me an uneasy feeling. I could sense that they were very old and were probably unused to people wandering through their forest home. *Are trees really alive?* I wondered with a shudder.

Old and gnarled, the trees looked like dead spirits, reaching to the heavens and begging fate to have mercy on them. I heard them sway slightly in the wind, making a nerve-racking, creaking noise that sounded similar to metal scratching against metal. It hurt my ears, and I moved closer to Yaron.

He took my hand with his strong fingers, looked at me carefully, and breathed, "I'm sorry, Elysia. About Veryan. I know he was your friend."

Instantly, I felt the pain squeeze my heart. It just did not seem fair. After all Veryan had been through and after all he had done to get to that point, he had forfeited everything so that we could escape. *I wish I had been the one*, I thought. *I should have … Veryan and Yaron are the ones that really deserve freedom.* "He was," I agreed and then silently rebuked myself. The way I said that, it sounded as if he was dead. "He *is*," I corrected myself.

Yaron was silent for a moment and then said, "I admire him for what he did. It couldn't have been easy. I know I couldn't have done that."

I squeezed his hand. "He's better than you give him credit for."

Yaron sighed and murmured, "I know … I promise, though, Elysia, that I'll never desert you. I'll always be here for you." He met my eyes, and I smiled fondly at him.

The two of us walked through the woods, both now silent. Far off, we heard a wolf howl. Yaron drew his dagger and gripped it tightly.

"You know," he said after a while, "that soldier knew we were going to be out there. He was looking for us; you could tell … which means that the others must have been alerted that we had escaped because there's no earthly way they could have responded so quickly to the horseman's horn call. Lliam told them we escaped, Elysia. That's the only explanation. You know that, right?"

"Yes, I know," I whispered. "He told me I couldn't trust him … He was right." I gave a shaky sigh, disbelief still prominent in my mind and heart. How could he have done that to me?

꒰꒱

Yaron and I walked deeper into the forest, looking for a place to make camp for the night. We were both thoroughly exhausted, not only physically but mentally and emotionally as well. This journey had taken much more of a toll on me than I wanted to admit.

The moon shone brightly, and we had seen no animals, but I was still fearful of the great wood. I calmed myself with several deep breaths, but that did little to abate my feeling that something—or someone—was watching us.

Eventually, after walking for what I guessed the better part of an hour, we came to a glade. Only bare earth covered the area. And around the glade, grew trees thin and willowy, much slimmer than the broad, tall outer ones that circled it. I breathed a soft sigh of relief to be out in the open again and leaned my head against Yaron's shoulder, taking comfort in his presence.

He looked at me gently, compassion in his brown eyes. "Still tired?" he asked.

"Exhausted," I replied.

Yaron laughed softly and said, "We *have* had a pretty exhausting two days. Come on; I'll build a fire, and then you can sleep." He led me into the glade, and we sat down close to the trees ringing the clearing. Yaron wandered around the area, looking for firewood. He would pause occasionally and pick up a few sticks, but most of them that he found were not good for fuel.

My eyes followed his outline in the moonlight, as if in a drowsy trance. Already Yaron seemed to be more relaxed. His posture and face showed less tension, and the omnipresent sparkle in his eyes seemed more gentle now, as if being free at last had finally softened some of the hardness left in him. My eyelids began to feel very heavy, and I knew I would not be able to stay awake much longer.

Finally, Yaron had enough wood for a fire and came back over to me. He sat down beside me and arranged the pieces into a rough pyramid before striking two small rocks together. A flurry of sparks immediately flew up and latched onto the tinder, hungrily devouring it with a ravenous appetite.

Yaron then looked over at me, and after a moment, he sighed. "So what now?" he asked.

I was silent, staring drowsily into the bright orange flames before us. Despite the pleasant night air, I felt cold, not from the chill of the air, to which we were immune, but from a sort of dread creeping along my spine. I shuddered and held my hands out to the fire, wishing there was some sort of internal fire I could light that would restore my soul.

"I don't know," I said, looking at him wearily. "Will you go back to Iciar?"

Yaron frowned thoughtfully and stared at the ground for a while. "No," he said after a long stretch of silence. "I … I was hoping I could go with you." He glanced up at me, questioningly.

Surprised and pleased, I answered instantly, "Yes, of course, but … what is there for you where I'm going?"

Yaron frowned again. "I don't know, but I'm not going to Iciar … There's nothing for me there now."

"You don't have any family left?"

"No. All my family is dead," he said tightly. Yaron absently stoked the fire with a loose stick.

I stared into the leaping sparks without seeing them, tired and unwilling to devote much thought to our futures right now. My eyes suddenly closed on their own accord, and I opened them again immediately, startled.

Yaron chuckled. "You're still tired; go to sleep, Elysia. We'll worry about all this tomorrow." He put an arm around my shoulders and hugged me for a long moment before standing and saying, "We're going to need food; I'm going to hunt." And with his hand on his dagger, he melted into the shadowy darkness of the forest.

⁓

When I awoke the next morning, the ashes in the fire were cold, and Yaron was not there. I knew something was wrong, and it frightened me.

I scrambled to my feet and felt my heart start to pound. I kicked dirt over the ashes, buckled my sword to my waist, and then began walking away from the glade, determined to find Yaron. *What could've happened to him?* I thought with a touch of fear. *He's such a good fighter, and I doubt he would have gotten lost.*

I walked for a long time, looking everywhere, pausing at every sound. But there was no sign of him anywhere. After nearly an hour, I went back to where we had camped and sat down on a mossy log. I put my head in my hands and tried to calm myself, but it was incredibly difficult. Tears soon began running down my face, and I took a few minutes just to cry. It helped me immensely, and once I was done, my mind felt clearer. I took a steadying breath. *Oh, what should I do? Did Lliam find him? I doubt he would have been pleased to capture only one of us ...* That made tears spring to my eyes again, and the lump in my throat made it hard to breathe. I blinked furiously, determined not to cry. That would no longer help the situation.

I took a shuddering breath and then resumed pondering my situation. *A town. I need to find a town. I can find the nearest one and someone to help me look for Yaron. Once we find him, we can go to Hartford City, and from there ... home.*

I took another long breath and then stood. I fetched my things and covered all traces of the fire in case someone was looking for us.

Sunlight poured down in great rivers through the tree canopy. I now noticed that ferns covered the entire forest floor, in some areas, rising as high as my hip. The bright, vivid green somehow refreshed me and made my long walk more bearable. Birds even began to sing, darting through the air and chirping loudly. *This forest looks so different in daylight. I don't know why some people are afraid of it.* I reached out to touch one of the massive trees.

As my fingers brushed the wood, I jerked them back slightly. I had felt a pulse. The tree was alive. Tentatively, I laid my hand back on the wood. A low vibration could be heard, and a deep pulse throbbed under my fingers. Captivated, I put my ear closer to the wood to see if I could hear any better.

An arrow's low whine filled the air and struck the tree right beside my face, and then I heard a loud curse. As I turned around, the soldier fit another arrow to the string. Stunned, I stumbled away from the tree, and then tripped over an unseen rock and fell into the ferns. Green leaves closed in over me, blotting out the sun. I lay perfectly still, hardly daring to breathe. I knew that if I moved, the soldier would find me. I could hear him now, tramping loudly through the ferns and poking them with his crossbow. I closed my eyes and exhaled slowly.

Shouts came from a distance. More of the troop had come to help their comrade. They began kicking at the leaves, searching for me. I slowly got onto my hands and knees and began crawling away. But my movement through the ferns gave me away, and the soldiers easily spotted me. With excited shouts, they chased after me.

I threw away all thought of caution. I stumbled to my feet and ran. The forest streaked by me in a vibrant blur. I could dimly hear the men following me, some on horseback and some on foot. Arrows zinged past me, narrowly missing their mark. One grazed my arm but luckily did not break the skin. Horses' hooves pounded close behind me.

I looked over my shoulder. A man on a great grey horse was pulling up beside me. I turned my eyes back to the path in front of me and ran harder, but the horse kept steady pace with me. I began to grow desperate. How could I escape them? No doubt, Lliam had sent them for me, as I was the only free one left. The soldiers already had Veryan, and I was almost dead certain that they were the cause of Yaron's disappearance as well.

Suddenly I was on the edge of a steep, rocky hill. I yelped and tried to stop myself, but it was too late; I lost my balance and toppled forward over the edge.

Every time my body slammed into the ground somewhere on the descent, the force drove the breath from my body and bruised another rib. When I finally came to a stop in the tall ferns below, I was bleeding and soon faded into unconsciousness.

MENELTAURE

I dreamed of Yaron. We were standing in a golden forest bathed in the morning light, warm, soft scents wafting all around us. He stood before me silently, brown eyes looking at me gently. All signs of weariness and abuse were gone from his face, and he looked like nothing more than a young man, as he should. My heart rejoiced at the sight.

I gazed around the forest, entranced. It seemed to stretch on endlessly in every direction, teeming with colour, light, and beauty. The golden lights streaming down from the sky above caught on the falling leaves, making a shimmering silhouette around them and bearing them aloft until they gently touched the ground. A layer of newly fallen leaves covered the earth, allowing only glimpses of the soft, fertile brown soil, rich and earthy in colour. A single green shoot emerged in front of my bare feet, its tender leaves beginning to unfold.

I looked back to Yaron, who smiled affectionately at me, all traces of anger, bitterness, despair, and loneliness gone. He looked calm and relaxed. I had never seen such a look of peace on anyone's face, and I suddenly longed for it.

He held out a hand to me, and I took it instantly. Yaron smiled at me and then turned and pulled me along behind him. We walked through the forest for what seemed like years, but I think only a few minutes had elapsed. I was in such a haze, inhaling the intoxicating scents and soaking up the light of the forest, that I barely noticed the passing of time.

Suddenly, I noticed the trees were thinning, and then they disappeared altogether, leaving us standing in a field full of white and pink flowers, interspersed with long, waving green grass. It was simply the most beautiful, tranquil place I had ever seen, and it took my breath away. The brilliant blue sky overheard, filled with billowy clouds, stretched endlessly over the field. Grey mountains were to our left in the distance, capped with pure white snow. Before us, a single peak rose into the sky, a silken waterfall cascading down its precipice, creating a silvery ribbon against the grey rock. This place was paranormal, I knew that. Magic pulsated in the ground, grew with the trees, and rose with the mountains. It fell to the earth with the waterfall and reached to the sky with the flowers. It was as if this whole world was made solely from magic. In comparison, I felt out of place, shabby and tattered.

I looked to Yaron, who was gazing out at the mountain peak before us with unfathomable eyes. "What is this place?" I asked in a hushed voice, afraid to disturb the silent beauty of the field.

Yaron turned his gaze to me and smiled gently. "This is Paradis, where virtuous souls come after they've died. I've been chosen by Menel to come to you in this dream and prepare you to come here once you awaken."

"This is a dream?" I asked with bitter disappointment even though I had known there was no possible way this could be real. But Yaron had said I would come here once I woke up. I frowned. How would I get to this dreamland? And why was I dreaming about it when a few sketchy myths and fanciful tales were all I had ever heard of it? Perhaps if this all really was a dream, Yaron's message was too.

Yaron's smile lessened minutely, and he said softly, "For now." Then he began walking forward, his hand pulling on mine. I followed beside him, feeling dazed. The palpable magic of this place was beginning to seep into my soul, making it feel renewed and fresh. I breathed in deeply, letting the intoxicating air fill my lungs. A thrill ran over my spine.

Yaron said to me, "When you awake, Elysia, you will find yourself in Meneltauré. Do you know where that is?"

I nodded; it was south, close to the Altai Mountains and about eighty miles north of Rielture, where my father was. Meneltauré was one of Yaracina's most beautiful cities—so I had heard—and was rumoured to be the first home of Yara when she came to our continent from Europe. I had dreamed of going there when I was younger; Malitha and I had loved to imagine attending elegant balls and meeting high-standing nobles and courtiers. I smiled at the memory.

"Victoria Ar-Elle, the daughter of Lord Riyad, who is the leader of Meneltauré, is to bring you back here, to attend the Gathering of the Kinds here in Paradis," Yaron went on. "The Gathering of the Kinds happens once a year, usually, but this year, it is different. The Kinds are being summoned here to attend to a matter of utmost urgency. Menel himself with be attending the Gathering."

"So …," I said, unsure, "why am *I* going?" This was striking me as quite bizarre; maybe this really was only a dream.

"Menel has a task for you," Yaron said, looking at me gently, the sparkle in his eyes softening.

I snorted and pulled him to a stop. "Yaron, this is a dream, and I know that. But even for a dream, this sounds strange. Who are these people who are going to meet here, and why would Menel—if he is real—choose me for a task? Doesn't he have someone to do things for him?"

Yaron shrugged. "I don't have answers to your questions, Elysia. All I know is that once you awake, you will find everything as I have said. I promise." He kept walking.

But I pulled my hand out of his and stood still. He paused, sensing my cynicism, and looked at me. "If this is real," I said, "then tell me this, Yaron: Where are you? Where did you go? What happened?" I looked at him desperately.

He shifted his gaze to the ground. "Elysia …," he began. Yaron sighed and then said softly, "Menel told me specifically not to tell you anything if you asked about that. I cannot break my word … I'm sorry." He glanced at me guiltily.

But this did not surprise me. I knew this to be a dream and, therefore, Yaron just a fabrication of my imagination. None of this was real, and this disappointed me inconsolably. I wished with everything in my being that I really could see Yaron again and know he actually was well.

I said quietly, "That's what I thought. This is all just a dream. You're not really here." Then I started speaking faster, suddenly desperate, "You said you would always be there for me! You promised you would be! You said … you … would always be there … so why aren't you?"

He did not answer, and I took a shuddering breath. The perfumed air gusted against my skin, brushing my cheeks and tossing my auburn hair back over my shoulders. The flowers rippled in pink and white waves at my feet. Painful aches that grew stronger and more tender every second formed in my heart. How I longed for this to be real.

Yaron finally said, "It's time for you to go back now, Elysia. As I said earlier, when you wake, you'll be in Meneltauré. Victoria will bring you back here at the next full moon, which is in two days … I'll not see you again." He came forward and stood only a foot away from me, his eyes full of sorrow, and he started to say something else, but did not.

I looked back at him mournfully. "You're just in my dream, Yaron. You're not really here," I repeated, the aching growing in my heart. Tears unexpectedly threatened to spill out of my eyes, and I stated mournfully, "I miss you, Yaron. I miss you so much. You and Lliam and Veryan …" The magical world blurred before my eyes, including him. How my heart longed to see him again. "I *miss* you …"

The colours of Paradis smeared together, fading into a hazy, faint image of what had been before me only moments before. My dream was disappearing gradually, and Yaron with it. I did not want it to end, but it was not up to me. I closed my eyes and let myself fall back into reality.

A warm, fragrant breeze was blowing over my face. Wherever I was, it was balmy and slightly humid, and though my eyes were closed, I could sense that I was lying close to an open window.

I was so tired. My body felt numb and achy, despite the fact that I was lying on a bed and knew I had just awakened from sleep. But I did not want to open my eyes. I felt tremendously fatigued and wanted only to sleep. Again, I tried to drift off but found I could not. I was awake now.

After lying there for what I guessed to be another half hour, I finally—reluctantly—opened my heavy eyes, resigning myself to the fact that I would not be getting any more sleep right now.

Golden sunbeams streaming in from the high windows in the room highlighted the dark mahogany of the ceiling. Swirling carvings of astounding skill and elegant style were set in the wood, capturing my attention. I had never before seen a ceiling carved so intricately or so beautifully. It bespoke wealth, prosperity, and an obvious display of fine taste. I wondered where I was.

I began to sit up, but sharp pain suddenly exploded in my left ribs and my right shoulder, forcing me to fall back in the bed with a gasp. The pain ebbed away slowly, and now I could feel that I was very sore and stiff, no doubt from falling all the way down that rocky hill in the forest.

I sighed and laid my head against the white pillow, thinking. I wondered briefly about Lliam. An image of his face flashed through my mind, and I sighed once more. I was filled with longing to see him again and to hear his voice. I hated it. Tears of anger filled my eyes as I remembered all that we had been through together—all the dreams and discussions and revelations of our souls—and then he had betrayed me. Deliberately and easily. And yet, I still missed him. I smiled wryly through the tears in my eyes. What a strange world I lived in!

I turned over on my side, wincing as my tender right shoulder began to throb. Warm sunlight washed my face, and I was met with the sight of a very tall, completely open window before me, revealing a beautiful landscape. Tall, verdant trees from a forest along with a nearby apple orchard, its trees bowed with the weight of their fruit, made up the breathtaking view outside the window, which extended all the way to the grey cliff several miles away. Birds flew by the window, chirping cheerfully and zipping by with remarkable speed. The sun shone on the canopy of the forest and illuminated the leaves with stunning, intense colours. I smiled, the dull ache that was pulsing through my body easing a little. I had never seen any scene so beautiful and elegant as this one before me, save only in my dream.

My dream. I gasped unexpectedly, memories instantly flooding back: Yaron, the golden forest, the field of flowers, the single peak and the waterfall, Yaron's strange message … it had all seemed so real to me … but it was not. I knew that.

Sighing, I closed my eyes, an intense yearning for my dream to have been true filling my mind. It had been so lovely, and Yaron had been there, alive and well. Where was he now? Was he even alive? Or had he been captured by soldiers from the tower? I longed to know.

Suddenly, quiet tears filled my eyes, a hard lump forming in my throat, overwhelmed as I was by feelings of despair and a desperate desire to go back in time when everyone I cared about was safe and there with me, when I was certain that they were all still alive and well …

After nearly an hour of weeping softly, my cries began to lessen, until they were finally silent. I lay still for a long while, just staring at the magnificent forest out the window and trying desperately—willing myself—to forget Yaron, Lliam, and everything else for a while. After almost two hours, I began to fall asleep again, my face warmed gently by the sun's golden rays.

ᘔ

I woke once more when I heard the door to my room quietly creak open. I was still facing the window, but nighttime had moved in. The white moon was shining brightly over the now-silvery forests, and the sky was clear and a majestic shade of indigo.

I shifted so that I was lying on my back and forced myself to sit up, trying unsuccessfully to ignore the stabbing pain in my ribs. I faced the girl before me with surprise.

She held a candle, which illuminated her face with orangish-gold light and gave her blue eyes a weird tint. Her elegant blue dress, a silver circlet resting on her brow, and her confident stance gave her an air of importance, but who she could be, I had no idea. I uncomfortably remembered Yaron telling me in my dream of a girl named Victoria Ar-Elle, and I hoped desperately that that was not her name because then the rest of the dream would probably be true as well …

The girl smiled warmly at me and said, "So you're awake. How are you feeling?" She came and sat down on the edge of my bed, setting the candle down carefully on the nightstand.

I assessed myself quickly and replied, "My ribs and shoulder hurt terribly, and I'm quite sore and stiff, but other than that, I feel fine." I shifted into a more comfortable position, and I did not mention the hurricane that was spinning inside my mind.

The girl said sympathetically, "Yes, well, it's a wonder your ribs aren't broken after that nasty fall you took, and your shoulder too. I imagine you'll be sore for a few more days, but don't worry; you had no serious damage done to you." She smiled.

I was beginning to like this girl, whoever she was. "Thank you for tending me," I said. I rubbed my aching shoulder absently, wishing for the pain to go away.

She smiled again. "It is my pleasure; I'm glad you're awake now. My name is Victoria Ar-Elle. A scout brought you here last night after travelling for two days with you all the way from the Blackwood Forest up north. I must say, I'm a little surprised at how quickly you woke. You were unconscious all that time, after all."

I flinched. Her name was Victoria Ar-Elle? Was I still dreaming? *How could that be possible?* I wondered, a little fearfully. *How could I have heard her name in my dream before I even woke? That's odd …*

Victoria noticed my sudden alarm and asked me, "Are you okay? You just turned quite pale." Concern lined her face.

I took a shaky breath, not entirely sure this was not still a dream. "Your name is Victoria?" I asked, just to be sure I had not misheard.

"Yes, that's right," she replied, looking at me carefully. "Why?"

I hesitated. Should I tell her about my dream? Would it sound terribly ridiculous? But I had brought it up, so I might as well tell her, I decided.

"I ... had a dream ... just before I woke ... and I heard your name in it. It just ... caught me offguard ... when you said that was your name. I didn't expect that dream to have any reality to it." I paused, realizing how utterly absurd my words sounded. I wondered if Victoria would laugh.

But she did not, to my surprise. She grew earnest and questioned me, "You did have the dream? Did anyone in the dream tell you about the Gathering?"

My eyes opened wide in surprise. How on earth did she know about my dream? "Yes ...," I said slowly and disbelievingly. "How did you know about it?"

Victoria laughed at my expression. "My father knew you were going to have it, and he has instructed me to take you there in two days. I'm looking forward to it greatly." Her smile returned, and she beamed at me. "I get to go every year with my father, and it's one of my favourite places to be! Last year, Fray took me to the Varjo-murhajat camp, and I got to meet more of the tyrises. It was one trip I'll never forget; it was *incredible*." Victoria's blue eyes were alight with excitement, but I did not know what she was talking about.

"What?" I asked. "What are tyrises? Who's Fray?"

Victoria waved her hand nonchalantly. "You'll meet him at the Gathering. But now, I'll wager you're hungry. Am I correct?"

I was not starving, but there was a faint ache in my middle, so I agreed, and Victoria left to get me something to eat. I waited until she was gone, and then I hauled myself slowly out of bed. I walked to the window. The cool moonlight shone down on my face, and the shimmering autumn leaves and last fruits of the season tossed perfumed scents into the air. I inhaled deeply, missing the smell of magic in the air from my dream. I laid my hand against the marble sill, staring out reflectively at the moonlight-washed forest below. How I wished for the sight of my own home instead of this foreign, fairy-tale land. I yearned to see my parents and sisters again, as well as Yaron, Lliam, and Veryan. I missed them all so much ...

"Here, Elysia," I heard Victoria say as she returned. I turned and took the proffered bowl of thick soup and piece of bread. I lowered myself carefully to the bed, wincing because of the pain in my ribs, and slowly ate the food. Victoria stood at the window, her blue eyes searching the outside view.

She asked, "Who did he send to you?"

Puzzled, I looked up. "What?"

Victoria looked at me apologetically. "I meant, 'Who did Menel send to you in your dream'? He always sends someone that is particularly close to the person to whom the dream is given ... and I just wondered who carried the message to you."

My throat constricted as I remembered seeing Yaron in the golden forest and the familiar soft sparkle in his eyes and his smile. Oh, how I wished he were here! "A friend," I said. "A very close friend. We were travelling together, but we got separated recently, and I don't know what happened to him. But ... it was good to see him again ... even if it wasn't real." I struggled not to let the tears escape my eyes in front of Victoria; I knew most people would not be so saddened by the loss of a friend they had known for such a short time.

Victoria sombred and said regretfully, "Oh. I'm sorry. I didn't know that—"

"It's fine, Victoria," I replied wearily. I rubbed my forehead tiredly and set the bowl down on the nightstand, next to the candle.

A long silence ensued. I let all thoughts leave my mind, and I just sat there silently, enjoying the peace. I felt emotionally, physically, and mentally exhausted right now; all I wanted was to be able to rest.

After a long time, Victoria said softly, "I imagine you're still tired so I'll leave you now. I'll check in on you in the morning, and then, if you're feeling well enough, I'll show you around my city. There are some beautiful sights—"

"Where are we, exactly?"

Victoria looked surprised but told me, "Meneltauré." She continued, "My father, Riyad, is anxious meet you. Perhaps I shall take you to see him tomorrow." She smiled warmly at me, and then she took the candle and the bowl from the nightstand. As she left my room, Victoria shut the oak door behind her, leaving me alone in the darkness.

I sighed heavily into the gloom. How could I have dreamed of Victoria and this place before I was even awake and aware of anything? How was it possible? *Was* it possible? I stretched out on the bed, flinching at the eruption of aches that my motion caused, and tried to make sense of everything that had just happened to me.

The next morning, Victoria came to see how I was doing. I woke unwillingly, still feeling sore and tired, but she persuaded me that walking around would help the stiffness. I grudgingly swung my feet off the bed and stood laboriously. I hobbled after Victoria, who stayed close to me in case I needed to lean on her for support.

I was surprised to find that immediately outside the guest quarters was a narrow but graceful bridge, its walkway dusted here and there with autumn leaves and fallen flowers. Slender, six-inch thick columns rose on either side of the bridge and melded in a graceful arch at the top, making an elegant awning over us. Golden sunlight splashed in dappled patches over the pearlescent floor, and shifting shadows from the waving trees played over the ground hundreds of feet below us. The very air seemed to be bursting with life, and it was rich and fragrant, like the forest smells after a spring rain.

I peered out of one of the tall openings in the bridge archway and up at the majestic crags that shot high above the valley floor where Meneltauré was situated. Vegetation covered most of their faces, but a few sparse patches of rock were visible in the midday light. Long, spindly waterfalls, streaming like silken threads over a verdant backdrop, rumbled in the milieu of gently swaying emerald trees and cliff faces.

The forests were several hundred feet below us, and their green and golden tops stirred lightly in the fall breeze. A silvery creek wound its way through the forest, making a small break in the canopy.

I gazed to my right, awed at the sight of a sheer, exceptionally steep cliff-face shooting to the heavens a few hundred yards away, flocked with golden trees. Ethereal waterfalls streamed from its peak, falling to the earth like a wayward strand of silk. It was as if I had walked straight back into my dream.

Victoria smiled at my expression of wonder and led me on across the picturesque bridge. When we came to its end, she led us down a long, stone stairway, which took us to three more bridges a few hundred feet down. Each one led to another large hall, which had been erected atop massive pillars of natural rock rising from the valley floor. The bridge that Victoria chose to take led us to what looked like a huge banquet hall with a long, stately table and high-backed chairs on either side. From this hall, there was a connection to several other bridges, all leading to other rooms in the palace. I could have easily gotten lost if Victoria had not been guiding me. Enchanted, I gazed around in a daze, feeling that the only thing that was missing for this to be my earlier dream was Yaron.

Victoria said beside me, "First, I shall take you to meet my father. He's going to meet us in the library. Then, if you like, you can stay there for a while. I have to help him prepare for the feast tonight. We have one every year at the beginning of the Gathering of the Kinds. Everyone in the palace attends. I'm sure you'll enjoy it very much." She smiled widely at me, obviously anticipating the day's coming events.

I was not so enthusiastic. A giant feast sounded more like a set-up for an evening of misery for me. I hated large crowds, especially when I had to endure them for extended periods of time. In that way, I differed from Malitha and Lillian, who both—especially Lillian—adored parties and socializing in sizeable crowds. In fact, such surroundings seemed to rejuvenate my sisters, whereas they always completely drained my energy. I murmured my agreement, resigning myself to the fact that I was going to have a less-than-favourable evening.

Victoria led me to a spacious, attractive brown structure that was resting on top of a gargantuan rock face with two waterfalls streaming down on either side. A thousand tiny droplets of water sprayed my face as we approached, and it felt cool and refreshing.

Victoria pushed the giant door of the library open, and it slid ajar on well-oiled hinges. Although dimly lit, at the far end, it had an open window at a balcony, which cast a long rectangle light on the marble floor. I stepped in behind her and looked around in fascination. I had never cared a great deal for reading, but this library caught my attention. Shelves and shelves of books and old, musty scrolls filled the great room. A long mahogany table dominated the middle of the room, and two torches flickered softly in their brackets on the wall. But it was the vast amount of books that enthralled me. Hundreds and hundreds of books, all crammed tightly against one another, filled the tall bookshelves. Some lay on top of the rows, some in stacks on the floor, and still more piled on the long table. I had never seen this many books in all my life.

Victoria took my arm and led me through the enormous library to the end where the open window and balcony were. Here at a large, mahogany desk sat a man, silently reading an ancient, yellowing scroll. Another dozen or so were piled around him, and even more books were strewn on the floor beside him. Furrows of intense thought lined his pale brow, and he did not notice our approach. His clothes were of the finest make. Silver threads shimmered throughout the blue cloth, caught in the light's rays and glowing like streaks of stars. His brown hair was the same colour as Victoria's, and everything about him reminded me of her.

Victoria waited patiently for a moment for her father to notice us, and when he did not, she said a little impatiently, "Father."

The man instantly looked up and, seeing us, smiled warmly. He deftly rolled up the scroll he had been poring over and stood to embrace Victoria and then me. His startlingly blue eyes seemed to extract all my secrets and then sift through each one with great interest. They reminded me of Lliam's, and I winced.

"Ah. You are awake at last, my dear," he said, smiling at me charmingly. He seemed to radiate friendliness and acceptance, and I immediately felt at ease with him, despite his soul-searching eyes. "I am glad to find that none of your bones are broken; that was a rather nasty fall you took, dear," he said kindly.

"Yes, sir, but thanks to Victoria, I feel I'm healing well," I replied, smiling at Victoria, who responded in kind.

Her father smiled warmly. "Well, that's good, my dear; I'm glad to hear it! Oh, where are my manners? Forgive me; I am Lord Riyad, Elysia, and as I'm sure you know, Victoria is my daughter. I am most pleased to have you here in our humble city." He gave a bow, which surprised me.

"Th-thank you, sir," I replied, stuttering a little. Why would a lord of such a magnificent city bow to me? "I appreciate Victoria's tending to me, and I'm quite in love with your city already, sir; I've never seen a place so beautiful."

"Yes, my city has long been proclaimed the most beautiful city in Yaracina, but too few are able to see it anymore ..." He shook his head sadly. "Too few ..."

Puzzled, I asked, "Why is that, sir?" I had not heard of any trouble in Yaracina—save those patchy rumours about black ships—especially not trouble so great that it would keep people from travelling here.

Lord Riyad looked at me unhappily. "The arrival of the humans here has changed many things, my dear. Many of the main roads are no longer safe to travel upon, and our people are often robbed and killed and their bodies left to rot along the byways when they do venture between cities. It is a shameful practise—led by that boy Lliam, you know—and I am mortified that Queen Elisheiva is doing next to nothing to prevent it. We just don't have enough Yaran soldiers to protect our people. Of course, no one knew a few months ago that we would need them!" He shook his head again, lines of worry creasing his forehead.

I flinched at the mention of Lliam. I hated it that Lord Riyad spoke negatively of him. Conflicted feelings stirred in my chest with reference to him; while I longed desperately to see him again, I remembered all too well the victorious smile that had crossed his face when he had crested the hill with his men as we were fleeing the tower.

Lord Riyad waved his hand. "Ah, enough talk about such depressing things! You, my dear, need to be educated about the Gathering of the Kinds, which you and my daughter will attend very soon." He rested his hands on the desk, blue eyes searching mine with intense earnestness. First, he asked me, "What do you know of Paradis, Elysia?"

I thought about his question. I had only heard fanciful stories about the place and had dismissed them as mere fairy tales. My mother had often spun wondrous tales about the magical land when my sisters and I were much younger, and they had enchanted me. Even then, I had known they were just fantasy. But after the dream … I was not so sure anymore.

I shrugged. "Hardly anything, sir. All I've ever known about it were just myths and fantasies, tales my mother made up as bedtime stories for my sisters and me when we were young."

He looked at me gravely, and there was no mistaking the sincerity in those blue eyes. "Then everything you know is about to change, Elysia. Despite what many people think, Paradis is a real place, a very real place. It's an entirely different world from the one we know here, and so are its creatures—tyrises, genesis, vardis—ones you could never have imagined. Menel lives there with his son and presides over these Paradisian beings, as well as those of us on Earth. The world there exists in a whole different realm from Earth, Elysia. Magic, mystery, divinity … Much that happens there cannot be explained here on Earth. Paradis is a perilous place for ones such as ourselves to venture."

I thought back to my dream and how even the air seemed to emanate magic and how everything growing there radiated something supernatural. But in my dream, Paradis had not seemed perilous at all … in contrast, it had seemed to be the most tranquil and beautiful place I had ever been. So if it was really so dangerous to people like us, why did Yaron tell me that Menel wanted me there for the Gathering? I asked Lord Riyad this question.

He sighed heavily and did not reply for several minutes. I shifted uneasily, glancing at Victoria, hoping maybe she would answer, but she did not. She merely looked at me and then averted her gaze.

Lord Riyad finally said, "Menel believes you … to be adequate for a task he needs doing. He has reasons for choosing you; that I promise you. But I'm not at liberty to address them with you … And, Elysia, when you go to Paradis, you must promise me that you will stay with Victoria at all times. There are some creatures there, ones I'm well familiar with, who would not hesitate to take advantage of your elven naiveté and ignorance of their world. Victoria knows their tricks and will keep you safe from them. Do you promise?" His blue eyes bored into me, searching for my reply.

"Yes, Lord Riyad … I promise," I answered, slightly disturbed. What kind of world would I be entering, exactly? From the way Lord Riyad described it to me, it did not sound quite as inviting as Victoria had described earlier.

Satisfied, he straightened, removing his hands from the table. A sparkle of amusement returned to his deep azure eyes, making him suddenly seem years younger. "But worry not about the danger, dear; your journey to Paradis will be one you will never forget, that I can assure you. Very, very few of our kind are fortunate enough to see that wondrous land, much less attend the greatest gathering of Paradisian creatures in all their land. The Paradisians are normally fairly hostile and competitive with each other; however, the Gathering is the one time of year that all the kinds meet in peace. Menel's son often spends much of his time visiting among the various species, and as such, he is very valuable in retaining that peace at the Gathering. Victoria, I think, is particularly fond of the tyrises. I would not be surprised if she forced you to come with her to one of their camps while you are there." He smiled fondly at his daughter, and Victoria looked shyly at me, clearly considering the idea.

She then urged her father, "Don't forget about the feast, Father! Tell her about that."

"Ah, yes!" Lord Riyad said. "Tonight, I am hosting some important nobles and aristocrats of some of our country's smaller cities—Nélia, Belterra, and others like them. We invite them to come every year at this time." He waved his hand, indicating that the fact was irrelevant. "They are going to join us for a feast tonight. We shall discuss some business matters of course, but the main purpose of this meeting is to celebrate our friendship and alliance against the humans." His blue eyes sparkled merrily. "And Victoria and I would like it very much if you would attend with us, as our guest of honour! I know you will enjoy it very much," he added, smiling at me kindly.

Despite the fact that I knew I would not enjoy the great number of people Victoria had told me would be in attendance, I also knew that I could not refuse, even if I wanted to. So I forced a smile and said, "It sounds lovely, Lord Riyad. I'd be honoured to come."

"Excellent!" he said happily. Lord Riyad glanced at his daughter and then said, "Well! Since I've discussed the Gathering and the feast with Elysia, I do believe I need to be getting back to business elsewhere." He looked back to me once more, his soul-searching eyes boring into mine. "It's been wonderful to meet you, my dear Elysia. I will look forward to seeing you at the feast this evening."

And with that, he left us.

A Familiar Face

We stayed in the library for quite a while after Lord Riyad left. I wandered aimlessly among the high shelves, looking at the books but not with great interest. Some of the books in the library looked positively ancient, and I could not help but pause and examine those a bit closer. Bound with leather, stitched together by hand, and having pages yellowed and stiff, the books could easily have been well over a hundred years old. Fascinated, I reached out with careful fingers to touch one of the leather-bound books. My fingertips brushed over the now brittle cover cautiously, and the scent of the worn leather and musty pages filled my nostrils.

I moved along the shelf, my fingers trailing over the spines of the books as I walked. I could see Victoria on the aisle a few feet away; she was pondering over a very thin and fragile-looking scroll, her brow furrowed in concentration.

Leaving that aisle, I moved to another towards the back of the giant room where there were fewer books and scrolls, all of which were covered in a layer of thick dust. Many were draped with spider webs as well. I walked around slowly, wondering why these books had been cast aside. I knelt beside a shelf and picked up an antique-looking book. A storm of dust billowed off it when I lifted it, and I resisted the urge to sneeze.

I opened up the book slowly, and its binding cracked and popped noisily as it folded back. It fell open to a page with faded black ink written in fine script across the length of the page in a language I did not know. But somehow, I felt if I tried hard enough, I would be able to understand it. I cocked my head and stared at the page long and hard. I had a strange feeling in my brain, as if a part that I had never used before was waking up and starting to work. After a while, the words seemed to float before my eyes, and I blinked hard several times. Then they blurred, some of the letters rearranged themselves, and I suddenly found I could understand the script, even though I was not familiar with the language. There were several lines of verse in the middle of the page, and they read:

> From the ashes of a ruined hope,
> in the dying twilight of a long-dead day,
> seven fading candles flicker,
> holding the choking shadows at bay.
> Fire and shifting shapes swirl in the mist,
> twisted, pale, and grey.
> Small and wavering on the edge of night,
> they stand unaided, their flames threatening to sway,
> giving a desperate fight.
> Two candles stand close together,
> sheltering each other from the dark whispers around,
> small and tentative, unsure of their forever,
> but through their combined faith, strength will abound.

Unsure, I read the verses again. What on earth was this poem talking about? The beginning of some ancient elaborate epic, no doubt. I looked at the rest of the text on the page and found that, while it was the same language as the poem, I could not read it. When I looked back to the verses, I also discovered, to my disappointment, that my brief ability to read them had vanished. I could not understand them anymore. Perplexed, I sat back on my heels, staring unhappily at the book.

"Elysia, what are you doing?" Victoria asked curiously from behind me. I turned and showed her the book. "Trying to read this, but I can't. I mean, I could for a moment, but now I can't anymore … Does that sound terribly ridiculous?" I asked, looking at her with some embarrassment.

However, Victoria did not appear to have heard my question. She merely cocked her head and studied me with fascination, blue eyes scrutinizing. "How curious," she said, so softly I could barely hear her.

"What's curious?"

Victoria quirked her lips and handed me the book again. "Can you read it now?"

Unsure, I stared at her for a moment and then looked back to the book. The fine script was still indecipherable to me. I looked at it intently for a second, hoping it would change as it had done earlier. All the same, nothing happened this time. I frowned and closed the book. "No," I admitted. "I can't … I don't how I was able to read it earlier."

Victoria said, "Hmm. Well, I'm not surprised. It was only your first time, after all, but I've heard of people like you—"

"What do you mean," I asked, alarmed, "'people like me'?"

Victoria shrugged and answered thoughtfully, "Well … there are people I've met—mostly in Paradis—who have what Menel's son calls Instinctive Speech. They're able to use a part of the brain that is normally not used, and it allows them to understand pretty much every language there is, whether spoken or written. Their brains see or hear the words and automatically translate them into their own language, and they can speak or write in that foreign language. It's really quite a fascinating thing; Menel's son knows a massive amount about it."

Completely confused, I asked incredulously, "You think I can understand languages I've never heard before or studied? That's impossible."

Victoria shrugged again. "That would be my guess. Had you ever seen this language before?"

I frowned down at the grimy book. "No …"

"Well, I'm not sure, Elysia. I'll ask Menel's son about it when we go to the Gathering," Victoria said confidently, trying to reassure me.

"Why don't you ever say it?" I asked then, my mind on something else. I had already dismissed Victoria's theory as impossible and, frankly, quite ridiculous. A part of my brain that translated words of other languages into my own and let me understand it? That was impossible.

Frowning, Victoria asked, "What do you mean?"

"His name. You just say 'Menel's son'; he has a name, doesn't he?"

"Oh," Victoria said, looking surprised. "Of course, he does. I just—"

"Then why don't you just say it?" I asked, trying not to sound too abrupt.

Victoria hesitated, looking a little unsure, and then she said, "Well … I suppose it wouldn't hurt anything. His name is Nathaniel.

"Now, come. I've got to go help prepare for the feast, and you simply cannot go in that old dress!" she continued, a spark of mischievousness illuminating her blue eyes as she looked at my muddied, worn green dress. "While I'm helping with preparations for the feast, you can get cleaned up. Then we'll find something simply stunning for you to wear!" And with that, she grabbed my hand and pulled me to my feet and out of the library, leaving the dusty book lying open on the floor.

꒲

"This one," Victoria said, beaming proudly as she laid out a gorgeous black dress trimmed with red.

Once we had come back from the library and I had washed and bathed, Victoria had insisted on finding a dress for me to wear to the feast. It was the most lovely thing I had ever seen, but even so, I was unsure. "Red and black?" I asked. I had always hated those colours; red was the colour of blood and pain, and black the colour of night and dark things.

Victoria looked surprised. "Of course! With your red hair and pale skin, it will look absolutely divine," she assured me with a happy smile. "And it will make your blue eyes stand out as well. Wear it, Elysia," she urged, a pleading look on her face.

Hesitant, I touched the silk fabric gently. It *was* very lovely ... despite the two colours I detested so. "All right ...," I said reluctantly. "If you really think—"

"Put it on!" Victoria encouraged, bouncing with excitement.

Smiling at her enthusiasm, I traded my shabby green dress for the red-and-black one and found that Victoria was right; it did go well with my red hair and pale skin.

Once Victoria had arranged my hair suitably for the feast, she led me once again from my guest quarters across the narrow bridges and platforms to another large building that was situated on a massive cliff from which a roaring, mile-high waterfall surged, falling thousands of feet to the valley floor below. It was magnificent. Even though the narrow bridge that led to the building had railing for support, walking over it with the rushing torrent of water just below us was quite as terrifying as it was awesome. But Victoria walked confidently before me, and that granted me some reassurance.

We entered the building a few moments later, and I stopped, speechless, at the sight of the most breathtakingly beautiful, most elegant interior I had ever laid eyes upon. Marble columns, capped with glittering gold, lined the perimeter of the hall. Colourful rugs of finely dyed wool covered intricately in-laid, solid, mahogany wood floors. Deep crimson silk curtains hung from massive windows, which reached from ceiling to floor. On the walls, exquisite tapestries and paintings depicted angels and elves with wings and clouds and beasts of the hunt. A long table in the middle of the hall, draped with an eye-catching tablecloth woven with golden threads, held perfectly arranged, delectable foods that tantalized the senses. The utter magnificence overwhelmed me, and I wondered if I had not fallen asleep and walked back into my dream once again.

Victoria laughed at my expression. "Welcome to Meneltauré, Elysia. For goodness' sake, don't look so awestruck! You'll see grander things than this in Paradis," she informed me with a playful grin.

"Elysia, Victoria! How good to see you, my dears," I heard Lord Riyad say, and I tore my gaze from the magnificent sight before me to smile at him as he approached us. Dressed in blue silk robes—like his daughter—he seemed at home in the lavish surroundings.

"Ah. I see that Victoria has found a dress a bit more suitable for the occasion than your old one, hmm?" he said, winking at me. "You look very nice in it, my dear."

Smiling politely, I agreed. "Yes, sir, thank you. That one was a bit … worn. I'm thankful she allowed me to wear this one; it's the most beautiful dress I've ever seen." Victoria beamed at my feigned enthusiasm.

Lord Riyad nodded at me, smiling, and then said, "So, did you discover anything of interest in our little library? Victoria mentioned that you might have."

I looked disapprovingly at Victoria but answered him, "Just a few lines of poetry in an old book, my lord."

Lord Riyad raised his eyebrow in amusement. "Is that all?" he questioned. "My daughter told me otherwise."

I sighed. "Well … I'm not sure, sir. Victoria did seem to think it was something, but I don't know … What she described as instinctive speech sounds so impossible …" I shrugged, uncomfortable with the conversation.

He looked at me with his piercing, blue eyes. "All things are possible, Elysia. Sometimes, though, they may just be smothered by our unwillingness to believe in them. Remember that," he said kindly.

Then he said, "Come! I do believe it is almost time for the feast to begin. Victoria will show you to your seats." And with another benevolent smile, Lord Riyad left us to greet a noble-looking man and his pompous wife.

Victoria stifled a giggle at the sight, and she whispered to me, "That's Lady Antella and her husband, Othello. They're quite a ridiculous pair, really, but they are ever so amusing. The way Lady Antella talks about herself, you'd think she was a goddess."

I chuckled. Just from their appearance, I could tell that what Victoria said was true. We had to stifle our laughter and adopt a serious manner as Lord Riyad brought them over to introduce to us.

Victoria curtsied politely and said, "Greetings, Lady Antella, Lord Othello. It's a pleasure to see you again; I trust you are enjoying yourselves tonight?" She smiled pleasantly at them, her eyes alight with amusement.

Lady Antella spoke: "Indeed, child. 'Tis a lovely evening, and it is always an honour to be invited here. It's so tranquil, and you know Othello and I rarely have time to unwind. We're extremely busy running the estate and travelling for various conferences! It's just so exhausting," she said in a sad voice, one that did not make me feel sorry for her whatsoever.

She turned her attention to me with interest as if just now noticing me. "And who is this lovely creature? Heavens, child, but you do remind me of my sons! You've got the same shape to your face and everything ..."

Unsure of how to take this, I just smiled and replied, "My name is Elysia Ar-Aubryn, milady, and it's a pleasure to meet you."

Lady Antella beamed, obviously pleased. "Yes, it is, isn't it? You have lovely manners, child; if only my sons could have learned as well. Where are you from, dear?"

"Aseamir, milady."

"Ah, a country girl, then!" she declared, looking at me pityingly, a look I despised. Aseamir was not in the country; it was larger than many of the cities near it! "So tell me, what do you think of this wondrous city then?"

"It's quite the most fascinating city I've ever seen, milady; I'm greatly enjoying my stay here," I said politely, wishing she would go away and stop looking at me as if I was a poor, unfortunate orphan.

Lady Antella nodded. "Indeed, child. Well, you should be honoured that Lord Riyad invited you to this feast; I doubt many little country girls like yourself have been so privileged!" She looked at me primly, obviously expecting me to rave about how great an honour it was and how humbled I was to be invited and to enjoy the company of sophisticated ladies such as she.

But I simply said, "Yes, milady; I know," and smiled sweetly.

Lady Antella, obviously satisfied with my meekness, smiled back and then said, "Sweet girl," before waltzing off, her husband trailing behind her.

They were hardly out of earshot before Victoria started giggling. Lord Riyad shot her an amused but disapproving look, and she half-heartedly attempted to regain her composure.

I said to Victoria, "Why did she tell me I looked like her sons? Is that a compliment?"

Victoria frowned. "Well, her sons disappeared a few years ago. No one really knows what happened to them, but apparently you reminded her of them." She shrugged.

"Hmm. That's odd …," I murmured, staring after Lady Antella for a moment. "But I suppose with parents like that, I would run away too," I said blithely.

Victoria giggled again. "I suppose so," she agreed.

Then Lord Riyad announced sternly, "Victoria, if you would please stop laughing at other people and take Elysia to her seat, I would most appreciate it." But he winked at her after saying this.

Victoria grinned and hurried me off towards the table, where we were seated on the right-hand side of Lord Riyad's place at the head of the table. Victoria greeted and spoke with some of the others already seated, leaving me to sit awkwardly beside her.

After a few minutes, all the guests that were still conversing and mingling about the hall came to the table and were seated, including Lord Riyad. As soon as he took his place at the head of the table, the conversations quieted. Victoria's father paused at his seat and held up his arms as a motion for silence. The other elves stopped their talking and gave him their undivided attention.

"Greetings, my friends and allies. Thank you all for the sacrifices you made to attend our feast this evening in this potentially dark time," he began. "It has been a long while since we last gathered together in peaceful conversation. As you all know, there has been talk of black ships on the coast, with flags bearing a blue dragon, as well as the attacks and murder of our people on the roads by Zoser's young assassins, Lliam and Roman, and his soldiers. There has also

been an alarming increase of human soldiers in and around our cities. I'm sure most of you remember the War of the Red Moon and
that the men we fought there years ago bore flags with blue dragons.
And … Neron and our dear Yara." He paused, and the elves seated
broke out into quiet murmurings and soft words of disapproval. I
felt my face flush with humiliation as I heard Lord Riyad mention
Lliam and associate him with such a terrible thing. Surely it could
not be true. I felt sick.

But who was Roman? If Zoser had another assassin working for
him, why had Lliam not said anything to me about him? Frowning,
I listened carefully, hoping to hear more about this Roman character.

Lord Riyad continued, a grave expression on his face, as if he
were mourning some great tragedy. "But now our own soldiers are
being posted on the coast and around all the smaller cities that cannot defend themselves. Just today, the village of Evodia, one of the
smallest of the cities in Yaracina and one of the most vulnerable, was
reinforced with one hundred of the queen's best soldiers."

Cheers broke out among the elves at the table. Lord Riyad's
sombre expression did not change, but he merely nodded his head
and went on speaking.

"And tonight, we are honoured to have the Lord Aakin, who
joins us from Queen Elisheiva's court in Atlanta. Tell us, my lord,
what plans does the queen have for eradicating these black ships and
the foul beings aboard them?"

The stately lord stood and inclined his silver head toward the
governor of Meneltauré. I watched the noble man in awe, knowing
that he must be some great warrior or philosopher to be considered
one of the queen's closest counsellors and friends. *I wonder what
makes him so special … I* thought curiously. *I suppose he's probably
done something great or saved somebody important.*

"My Lord Riyad of Meneltauré, I have been told by the queen
herself that she is sending emissaries to every town and city in Yaracina
to gather able-bodied young men and women to form an army, to
prepare for war if these humans continue to invade Yaracina and do
not stop their attacks. Queen Elisheiva wants those men to understand

very early on that they are not welcome here and never will be. The queen is prepared to declare war as soon as an army is gathered."

Uneasy murmurs circulated around the table. The elves looked anxious, but I could also see a steely determination glinting in their eyes, and I knew that they would be ready to supply their queen with their best warriors immediately.

"Thank you, Lord Aakin," Lord Riyad said then. His blue eyes swept over the seated elves. "I believe I speak for all of us present this evening when I say that my best warriors will be prepared to join the queen's army the moment she calls." A hearty agreement came from each of the high elves.

I felt an anxious knot form in my stomach, and my heart ached at the thought of my people fighting against Lliam and trying to hurt the humans, even though they deserved it. Surely there was another way.

However, Lord Riyad went on to say, "I think we all can share in the sorrow and regret that is besetting us as a consequence of Neron's betrayal, and this being not the first but the second time ..." He let out a heavy sigh and then resumed speaking, "It will take all the strength we can muster to keep him out before he wreaks havoc and death upon our cities once more, as he did at the War of the Red Moon."

Confused, I turned to Victoria and asked her softly, "Who is Neron?" I had heard the name before, and I knew he was someone associated exclusively with the War of the Red Moon; there was no record of his existence before or after the war. It was as if he had vanished off the face of the earth once the war was over.

Victoria frowned, her face becoming serious. She leaned towards me and said very softly, "Neron is the one who initiated the War of the Red Moon. He led the human armies here and laid siege to Hartford City for almost two years. He cut off their food supply and killed any Yaran supporters that tried to go to Hartford City. Nobody really knows why he attacked us, and I've heard so many theories, but I think the most popular is that he was after Yara for some reason ..."

Interested, but unable to ask all the questions I had without disrupting the meeting, I turned my attention from Neron back to Lord Riyad, who was standing silently in simmering frustration.

Then he composed himself and once again thanked Lord Aakin for his report on behalf of the queen.

At last, he turned the topic of his address to the fine progress of Nélia's silver mines. I listened with interest. Nélia was a small town in the Salquessaé Plains that was renowned for its abundant silver production. A large cavern under a huge spurt of rocks near the town had yielded huge amounts of silver that was later transported to cities all over Yaracina.

After that, another lord from Atlanta, though not as high-standing as Lord Aakin, gave the news that Queen Elisheiva's younger daughter, Hanna, had celebrated her fifth birthday about two weeks past. The guests applauded dutifully.

Finally, Lord Riyad held up his hand to silence the chatter and stood with a raised goblet. The others stood as well, and Victoria nudged me to do the same. We each held the goblet that was placed beside our plate and raised it in a toast. I stared at mine curiously as I held it aloft. It was golden with rubies inlaid in a swirling pattern across the face of the cup, and Yaran runes lined the lip of the goblet. The runes told of a hunting party led by the legendary Yara. I frowned slightly at the runes, immediately dismissing their authenticity, and then turned my attention back to Lord Riyad.

"Tonight," he said, "we have a special guest who joins us from Aseamir." He smiled and nodded to me. I smiled back, despite being embarrassed and feeling an instant blush warm my cheeks. "Elysia Ar-Aubryn is our guest of honour. She has endured the harshness of captivity and was nearly sold as a slave. But thanks to one brave young man, she and another prisoner were freed and made their way to Meneltauré. Regrettably, the young boy she escaped with disappeared the night they were freed and has not been seen again, though we fear he may have been recaptured or killed by the humans."

How does he know about Yaron? I thought in surprise. I had told no one but Victoria about my friend, so I had no idea how he could have learned about him. I assumed that Victoria must have told him.

Lord Riyad continued, "And as a memento of her visit to our city, I would like to present her with a sword, forged especially for her by my own sword smith. In future narrow fixes such as the one she has bravely survived, may it serve her well."

I gaped at him. A sword? But I was terrible with the blade! *Oh, surely not ...*, I hoped. But in disappointment, I saw one of the guards hand a long, wrapped bundle to Lord Riyad, which I knew had to be a sword.

However, I hid my uncertainty and frustration as best I could and stepped shyly away from my seat to stand before Lord Riyad. He smiled warmly at me and handed the long sword to me. It felt awkward and heavy in my hands, and I desperately wanted to give it back, to tell him that I could not use a sword ... but, of course, I could not.

I slowly unwrapped the cloth from the blade and after laying the material aside, I gaped at the sword in my hands. The hilt was wrapped with black leather, and two falcon heads decorated the crossguard tips. A large ruby set in the pommel glittered brightly in the light from the torches. With a flash, I remembered the premonition I had had at Alqua's house: the young soldier on the bloodied battlefield clutching a sword with a ruby in the pommel ... But who could it be, if this was my sword?

I tentatively touched one of the falcons, thinking of Lliam's name for me: young falcon. How could Lord Riyad have known? Or did he? And the black hilt and the ruby ... the same colours of the dress I was wearing. With a wry smile, I concluded that that was the reason Victoria had chosen this dress for me tonight.

I turned to face Lord Riyad and said with genuine gratitude, "Thank you, my lord; this is ... an invaluable gift. It's beautiful ... thank you." The guests at the table expressed their approval by breaking into thunderous applause.

Lord Riyad then leaned over to me and said softly, "I know you find yourself inadequate with the blade, my dear, but perhaps with some practise ..." He winked at me and smiled warmly.

I did not have time to say anything else, for he placed his hands on my shoulders and addressed the crowd at the table, "Come. We have talked long about both pleasant and unpleasant things. But now, a feast awaits us! What do you say we get started?" The elves at the table responded with cheers of agreement, faces beaming. Lord Riyad chuckled, and then motioned for the feast to begin.

It was quite merry, and food and drink were consumed in large quantities, but I barely touched my fare. The smoke from the kitchens and the smells of all the different foods, as well as the heat of the room and the volume of noise, were making my head ache and caused me to lose what appetite I had had.

I sighed and looked up at the little window far up the stately wall. The stars twinkled brightly through the window's square frame, and I could see the edge of the white moon.

Then I pushed the thoughts from my mind and settled on a thick slab of honey roasted meat. The tangy spices made my mouth tingle, but I could not enjoy it. I felt slightly sick, thinking again of the last time I had eaten game like this: the day I was captured by Veryan's troop. Trying to swallow the meat past the lump in my throat, I gazed up at the small window once more, bringing to mind my last memories of Yaron and Veryan. All around me, elves laughed heartily and ate merrily, oblivious for a while to the very real threat on their lives and their homeland by the humans. But I was faced with devastatingly real memories of the three closest friends I had ever had. *I don't know what happened to any of them, and Yaron may well be … dead …* Tears rushed to my eyes at the thought, and I suddenly had to get out of the warm, jolly feast-room. I had to be alone. It would not do at all to lose control at a feast such as this. I stood shakily, tears blurring my eyes, and walked unsteadily out of the room, ignoring Victoria's questioning call. I had to be alone.

ॐ

I escaped the windowed hall, leaving the merry feast behind, and walked out along several platforms and down staircases, not really planning to go anywhere, but going where my feet led me. Presently, after descending countless staircases having golden rails, I found myself on the ground level of the city nestled in the peaceful valley. After meandering down several streets, I ended up at the stables. I pushed the door open, and went inside. I could see the horses in the soft flickering of torchlight, all of them quiet.

I walked over to one of horses' stalls and stroked the mare's velvety cheek. The horse snorted and nudged my shoulder. I closed my eyes, the lump in my throat making it difficult to breathe. A few hot tears spilled from my eyes, and I brushed them away angrily, not wanting to cry, but needing to in order to release my pain a little. I missed them both so much …

For a long while, I just stood beside the mare and cried silently, not willing for anyone passing to hear the sounds of my sorrow. The horse would occasionally bump my cheek with her velvet nose and nicker softly, seeming to realize my distress. I looked up at her gentle brown eyes through my teary ones and said unsteadily, "You are fortunate not to have feeling such as this, my friend." I scratched her forelock, and she gazed at me steadily. "You are fortunate that you have not been left to muddle through this journey alone, losing the two best friends you've ever had, not knowing … what's happened to them …" Tears quickly filled my eyes again, and the lump in my throat rose once more, but I choked out, "Or whether they're alive or … *dead* …," before breaking down again.

"Hey, now, what's this?" I heard a soft voice say behind me. I froze, and my heart started beating harder. *I know that voice.* Slowly, disbelievingly, I turned around and looked into the dark eyes of the boy who was now in front of me.

"Veryan! Oh …" I threw my arms around him and hugged him tight. Veryan exhaled heavily in protest. He did not pull away, but neither did he return the gesture. I held him for a long moment, and I felt as if a rainbow had just streaked across my stormy sky.

I pulled away a second and laughed through my tears. "What are you doing here? I thought … How did you get here, Veryan?" Tears blurred my vision, but I blinked them away, focusing delightedly on his face. *He's alive! And he's here!* I rejoiced silently.

His characteristically cold eyes softened a little, and he replied, "After I helped you and Yaron escape, I finally managed to get away from the troop with the help of Comundus since they were more concerned about capturing the two of you anyway. I had nowhere else to go, so I decided to come here. Lord Riyad had been kind to me when our troop had passed through once before, and ...," he shrugged, "I supposed he would be again. And you're here." He eyed me calculatingly. "Why are you here? I thought you were going to Hartford City."

I smiled, wiping away some of my tears with the back of my hand. "I was headed that direction, but I got sidetracked. Again." I forced a laugh, my heart tightening at the thought of my close brush with the soldiers. After Yaron and I left, we went into the Blackwood Forest for cover. That night Yaron left the campfire to go hunting, and when I woke up the next morning, he wasn't there ... and I haven't seen him since. Have you ...?" Breathless, I watched his face for any sign of hope.

Veryan frowned. "No."

Despair crashed over me, and I exhaled hopelessly, feeling all of my previous worry and hurt return. I continued sluggishly, "After that, soldiers from the tower discovered me and gave chase. I fell down a steep, rocky hill. The soldiers either left me for dead or didn't bother to look for me. I guess someone from Meneltauré found me and brought me here; I don't actually know. Victoria hasn't told me."

Veryan cocked his head. "Victoria? Victoria Ar-Elle? I've met her before. Her father is Lord Riyad, right?"

"Yes. They're having a feast right now, but the smoky air and the heat was giving me a headache, so I left ..."

"To come here and cry?" he asked unemotionally. I bristled a little, defensive, but I knew it was only his way. He had not meant to offend me.

I let out a shuddering sigh and nodded. "Yes." I looked at him then and asked, "Why don't you come back to the palace with me? I'm sure Lord Riyad could find somewhere for you to stay tonight, if you want ...," I shrugged.

Veryan hesitated. He looked as if he would agree, but then he said doubtfully, "I don't think so, Elysia. I don't want to presume upon his kindness."

"No, he would be glad to see you, Veryan, and you know it. Come. We'll go together," I begged.

He scowled irritably, all his characteristic coldness and indifference returning, but Veryan finally said, "I don't know …" Sighing, I motioned for Veryan to follow me back to the palace. He trailed me slowly. I still could not believe he was actually here. I smiled again as he quickened his pace to walk beside me, and I said with a wobbly laugh, "I'm so thankful to see you here, Veryan. I thought … well, I wasn't sure what would happen to you when you left us on the plain. You risked your life for Yaron and me, and I will forever be grateful to you for that. I'm relieved you finally got away from the troop. You didn't enjoy it, did you?" It was not truly a question; I knew the answer.

Veryan's eyes tightened. "I did enjoy seeing all the different places we went. Pyralus …" Here his voice broke slightly, but he stopped and started again. "Pyralus and I, we would always find time to slip away from the rest of the men and take a look around. Meneltauré and Nélia were my favourite places to visit, but we never got to stay in one place for long."

"What was Nélia like?" I asked. Even as a child, I had always loved hearing about other towns and cities far away and had often badgered the traders to tell me about their travels and the places they had seen.

Veryan glared at me, but answered obligingly, "It's a quiet place where all the people are friendly and welcoming, a good town in which we could relax. It had a couple hundred houses, stables, a blacksmith's shop … and the silver mines. It was about twenty miles from the Van'edhel Mountains and was surrounded on all sides by the Salquessaé Plains. Nélia is one of the most beautiful places I've been, barring Meneltauré, of course."

I glanced up at the star-littered sky as we ascended the stairways back to the palace. "It sounds interesting," I said, recalling what I had heard Lord Riyad say about it earlier, before I had left the feast.

"It's probably not as interesting as Aseamir," Veryan said, a slightly mocking tint to his voice making clear his foul mood.

I chuckled, intent on keeping the conversation light. "Everything was so boring in Aseamir. It was basically just the same routine every day. We never did anything new or exciting. There were never any new people or opportunities until Mother told me Father needed me to go to Hartford City … I was so ready to leave …"

Veryan's scowl turned darker. "If you had been to the place *I* was from …" His face clouded over immediately, and he fell silent.

I frowned to myself. *I wish he wouldn't do that. I want to know where he's from, but I guess if the memories are too painful for him … I wonder what could have happened there. Nothing terrible has happened to any of the Yaran towns I know of …. Maybe it's just a personal matter. In that case, I should probably be quiet now and stop thinking about it.* I wrinkled my nose and said, "So what happened after Yaron and I left?"

Veryan seemed to be relieved that I had steered away from the subject of his home but shook his head, eyes still frosty. "I'll tell you later—"

"Veryan!" I said, cutting him off. "You know I want to hear about it now!"

He snorted, still in a bad mood. "Then that will make it even more exciting later," he said sourly.

I frowned at him, and he eyed me strangely, as if challenging me to keep staring at him. "Well, you haven't gotten any less aggravating since I saw you last."

Veryan narrowed his eyes warily. "And you haven't gotten any less blunt."

"Thank you," I said, trying not to be offended. It was just his way; I was sure it was not meant to be a cruel comment. So I moved off that obviously sensitive subject and lamented regretfully, "Oh, I wish Yaron was here. He would have liked this, I think." I crossed my arms over my chest, wishing I could ease the ache that mentioning Yaron's name had brought back inside me.

"What happened to him, exactly?" Veryan asked, sounding none too interested.

I shrugged, now falling into a dark mood myself. "I don't really know any more than I've already told you. We ran for the entire day after we came out of the tunnel onto the plain. We kept on running into the night so that we could reach the cover of the Blackwood

Forest, and then we camped out in a glen. He went hunting while I slept, and he never came back. The next morning, I woke up, and he wasn't there ..." I shook my head and shrugged, afraid to say more and that emotion would overwhelm me. I wiped away the tears that were already forming, feeling ashamed of acting like a child in front of Veryan. But how I loved Yaron! Then, startled at the realization, I blushed and pressed my lips together in a tight line. I could picture Yaron in my mind, grinning at me, a mischievous glint underlying the omnipresent sparkle that lighted his eyes, and I wished with all my heart that I knew what had happened to him ... and that whatever it was, it had not happened. I wanted him back here with me ...

Veryan glanced about us without interest and asked me absentmindedly, "Did you hear anything?" With disgust, I concluded that he did not truly care what had happened to Yaron; he was just asking because he knew I did.

"Nothing," I answered harshly. "I don't know what could have happened to him, Veryan."

"Maybe the soldiers found him," he suggested, his voice telling me that his mind was only partially on the topic we were discussing.

"Maybe," I said angrily, glaring at him.

Veryan swayed suddenly and grasped the rail of the stairway for support. I looked at him with concern, all of my previous anger dissipating instantly. "Are you all right?" I asked.

Veryan inhaled sharply as he sat down on one of the steps and grimaced. He glanced up at me with a frustrated expression. "I'm just sore. That's all."

I sat down beside him on the step and eyed him carefully. "How long have you been on the road, Veryan? You look as if there's more troubling you than just soreness." My eyes bored into his dark ones; there was no way he could escape answering under my probing gaze.

"I ... had some trouble with Gornhelm because of our escape," he answered slowly, glaring back at me with all the crossness he could muster.

"What do you mean?" I asked.

He shook his head irritably, like a dog that was shaking away a bothersome fly. "It's nothing," he said.

I was starting to become frustrated with him, and I knew I would not get an answer about his trouble with Gornhelm, so I simply said, "Veryan, please stay here, for tonight at least—"

"Elysia, I *can't* stay!" he said as he stood up, anger flaring in his dark eyes. "I need to be moving on. Gornhelm's soldiers will probably be looking for us, at least for me, and I don't want Lord Riyad to have to be concerned for the safety of his people because of having a fugitive staying in his city. I'll be fine; let me go."

"Is there somewhere you know of, where you can go to be safe and not have to worry about the soldiers finding you?" I said, feeling determined that I could not let him go without at least having a decent meal and a good night's sleep. *Could I even let him go then?* I wondered, uncomfortable with the thought. *I just found him again …*

Veryan started to answer but then faltered and looked at the ground. "No," he admitted harshly.

To his surprise, I laughed. "Then why must you leave? You said you have been here once before. Didn't you say that you enjoyed it? I thought that was the reason you came," I reasoned.

Veryan glared at me for a long moment and then said, "Why are you so intent on keeping me here, Elysia? Aren't you going to Hartford City anyway?"

I frowned a little. "Yes, eventually, but I'd like to enjoy my time here as well, and I want to make sure that you're strong again before you take off to who knows where. Besides, you're avoiding the question," I said pointedly.

"So what?" he snapped.

"I'd just like my question answered," I countered, trying to hide my amusement. I knew I was successfully persuading Veryan to do what I wanted him to do: stay the night.

He sighed heavily and irritably. "Fine. My answer is yes, but only for a few hours. And regardless of whether I like this place or not, the reason for my not choosing to stay here, I believe I already explained to you, did I not?"

"Yes, you did, but I don't know why you're worried about Gornhelm finding you here. I don't mean to be offensive, but why would he want you back? I thought he hated you; he's probably happy to be rid of you," I asserted. Though I was trying to lighten his mood and make the conversation continue as long as possible, I was genuinely curious as to why Veryan was so opposed to staying in Meneltauré. *I wish Lord Riyad would come out here. Veryan couldn't possibly refuse an invitation to stay from* him.

Veryan huffed impatiently, "I'll explain all that later, all right? I need to get a few things for my journey, and then I'll be on my way—"

"Veryan, please don't go yet!" I pleaded, my eyes searching his. "Stay for tonight at least. I haven't seen you since Yaron and I escaped, and I want to hear what's happened since. At least come to the feast. I know you need to eat, and I'm sure you need some rest as well." I added, running my eyes over his wearied form.

He sighed. "Elysia, I can't—"

"Veryan." I said his name quietly, but watched him carefully with my eyes.

He looked at me for a long, conniving moment, but then he thought better of it and surrendered, "All right; you win. I'll stay for *one* night; then I'm leaving tomorrow."

I grinned in delight and hugged him again, truly thankful he had decided to stay for a little while. I did not want him to leave so soon after having him back again.

Veryan exhaled deeply and grudgingly let me embrace him for a moment until he gently but firmly pushed me away.

⁓

The feast had ended by the time we got back, and we found Lord Riyad and Victoria in a small courtyard outside the banquet hall.

"Ah, Elysia! Welcome back, my dear!" Lord Riyad said kindly as we entered the courtyard. "Victoria told me that you had left to get a breath of fresh air. Is that right?"

I looked at him uncomfortably. That was not entirely a lie. "Yes, my lord. I went for a long walk and ended up at the stables down below, and I found Veryan there ...," I turned to him and grinned widely, unable to contain my glee, "and, after some persuasion, brought him back with me."

Lord Riyad turned his eyes on Veryan and smiled. "Veryan! Yes, we were expecting you. I'm glad to see that you've arrived safely."

Veryan looked at me in faint surprise, and said, "You ... knew I was coming, Lord Riyad?" He looked slightly baffled, but the hardness of his eyes did not cease.

Lord Riyad put his hands on Veryan's shoulders and laughed. "I know many things, Veryan. I have seen you here before, when you came with your troop, and it wasn't difficult to see that you enjoyed your stay here. And, I would also like to thank you for your help with Yaron and Elysia's escape. I'm sure they are both very grateful to you, Veryan." Lord Riyad's eyes twinkled, and he smiled contentedly. "Now, how would you like to join us for a walk in the palace gardens and tell us what has befallen you since Elysia's escape?"

Veryan looked glaringly at me, and I smiled reassuringly. But, in truth, I was also anxious to hear what had happened after he had left Yaron and me in the Salquessaé.

He exhaled and nodded resentfully. "All right."

Lord Riyad led the four of us around to the gardens, which adjoined the palace, and found a bench for us to sit on while we listened to Veryan. I looked around the garden in wonder at the dew-webbed petals and leaves that were bathed in silvery moonlight. Veryan's face, despite the mythical settings, retained all if its usual lack of emotion and warmth.

"So," Lord Riyad began, sitting back on the bench with his hands clasped behind his head, "tell us your tale, Veryan."

Veryan paused, trying to figure out where to begin, and then launched into the story, but not before casting an irritated look at me, as if it was my fault he was having to relate his story.

"While Elysia, Yaron, and I were fleeing, Lliam's soldiers were chasing us and trying to shoot us with their arrows. They were gaining on us quickly, so I decided that Elysia and Yaron would have a better chance if I slowed the soldiers down by allowing them to capture me. Sure enough, several of Lliam's soldiers overtook me and one of them hauled me back to the tower. Gornhelm was furious with me, and he asked Lliam to do something to punish me for escaping and for helping Yaron and Elysia."

I closed my eyes tight with a sigh, not wanting to hear what was next, but knowing where this was going.

"So Lliam had me shackled, and then the same soldier—the one that had taken me to the tower—whipped me. Thirty lashes. Then he put me in a cell and didn't give me any food, water, or medical attention for five days. I should have died," he said broodingly, brown eyes dark. Then he looked over at me slowly. "But on the sixth day, Lliam came himself. He ... brought me food and water and even tended to my lashes, but he never said a word ... I shouldn't even have been able to travel yet, but he used some kind of odd medicine, one I've never seen before, on my wounds. They're not nearly healed yet, but they're far better than they should be by now.

"Lliam told Comundus to get me out, and he did that very night. Came to my cell, unlocked it, and took me out the front gate himself. And before he let me go, he turned and looked at me, as if he wanted to be completely certain I heard what he was about to say, and said, 'Lliam said to tell you that he helped you only for Elysia's sake.'"

I felt my heart break, torn between whether or not I should still hate Lliam for what he had done to us. But how could I hate him? He had risked everything to help us escape, and he had helped Veryan ...

I felt an agonising disgust with myself for causing Veryan all this pain. *He went through all of that just so we could be free. And we don't even know what happened to Yaron; his escape could have well been in vain.*

I took his hand, entwined my fingers with his, and said, "Veryan ... had I known that would happen to you, I would have never tried to escape. I swear. I never imagined that you would be punished so severely. Can you ever forgive me for causing you that pain?"

He instantly jerked his hand away from mine and did not reply right away. But after a long while, he muttered reluctantly, "I never blamed you, Elysia."

Lord Riyad sighed heavily and clasped his hands. "Veryan, you have paid a great price for your friends' freedom, and I believe I am right in saying that they will not soon forget it. You have showed more consideration and devotion to your friends than I would have thought possible at such a young age. If you continue on that path throughout your life, your reward will be great, my son."

Veryan seemed a bit surprised at the praise but accepted it gratefully, I could tell, though he did not reply.

Victoria echoed her father, "I think I speak for us all when I say I'm thankful you were able to withstand the hardships you endured and choose to come here to us. I doubt very many could have suffered such a great burden at your age."

"Yes," I agreed. I smiled at Veryan. "I'm so glad you are here, Veryan."

He only eyed me expressionlessly.

We talked for another half-hour, and Lord Riyad asked me to share once more my time with the soldiers and how Yaron had disappeared the night we had escaped. Victoria was particularly interested in that part and peppered me with questions. Veryan was quiet the entire time, sitting motionless next to me on the bench.

Finally, Lord Riyad held up his hand to conclude our conversation. "Much has befallen the two of you recently, and you both are in need of more time to rest. Elysia, you have already been given guest quarters, which I hope you are finding quite adequate. Veryan, if you will go with Victoria, she will show you to a guest room where you may rest tonight."

The boy nodded before following the lord's dark-haired daughter back to the palace. I started to follow, but Lord Riyad said, "If you will wait a moment, Elysia."

I turned around obediently and looked at him steadily. "Yes, my lord?"

Lord Riyad smiled, his warm blue eyes twinkling in the pale light, and said, "Elysia, you said earlier that it took some persuasion to get Veryan to stay tonight, yes?"

I smiled as well, nodding. "Yes. He didn't want to stay because he was afraid Gornhelm, the leader of his troop, would come after him and that it would cause havoc for you and—"

"Ah, yes. I know all about Gornhelm," Lord Riyad said, his expression becoming grave. "A rather tall, stocky man, correct? With black hair and an untidy beard and a wicked looking sword?"

"Yes, my lord. How did you know?" I asked curiously.

Lord Riyad sighed. "I met him when he brought his troop to my city. He was here to receive an assignment from me from the queen. The way he treated his troops quite appalled me, in particular, one young boy with dark hair."

"Why does he hate Veryan so much? Is it just because he's young?"

Lord Riyad looked at me with an odd expression. "I believe Veryan will tell you that when he's ready, if ever."

Hmm. It seems Veryan has a lot of secrets, I thought, feeling a bit suspicious. *I wonder what he could have possibly done to have earned such extreme loathing by Gornhelm ...* "So ... do you think he should have left tonight instead of waiting until tomorrow? I mean, so you think there's a chance Gornhelm could actually find him?"

"Anything's possible, my dear," Lord Riyad replied, a twinkle coming back into his eyes. "But no, I don't think there's much chance of Gornhelm finding Veryan."

Lord Riyad motioned to me with his hand. I followed him over to a stone bench, and we sat down. "May I see your sword, Elysia?" he asked, looking at me with kind, blue eyes.

I quickly unsheathed the new sword from its scabbard and handed it pommel-first to him. His face brightened as he took it, and he then gazed fondly at the sword, like a father who was proud of his only child. He tapped the ruby in the pommel with a finger and then said, "My finest smiths made this sword for you, Elysia. It took them a day and a half to craft it."

"I've never seen another sword like it, my lord. It is by far the most beautiful thing I've ever seen, much less had the privilege of owning."

Lord Riyad seemed very pleased. "I'm glad you appreciate it, my dear." He gazed at the two falcons with an expression that was hard to read, perhaps a mixture of pride or sorrow or, even possibly, joy. I watched his face closely, trying to figure it out. I was about to say something, but he began first.

"Do you know the name of this sword, Elysia? It took several attempts to get it right, but I think I finally found one that works appropriately, considering the runes engraved on it and its owner."

"What is it?" I asked eagerly.

Lord Riyad smiled, obviously enjoying my enthusiasm. "Zan'dúril," he said.

Zan'dúril ... I like it, I said to myself and then aloud, "Does it have a meaning?"

"Indeed it does. 'Zan'dúril' means 'light,' as in the light in the darkness," Lord Riyad told me.

I smiled, feeling the satisfaction well up inside me. *Light.* "Why did you choose that name for my sword?"

"I have my reasons," the lord responded, content with my positive response. "And ... because it has a nice sound to it."

I laughed. "That it does. Thank you so much for Zan'dúril, Lord Riyad. I will treasure it always."

"Don't thank me, Elysia. It was my pleasure. It has also been my pleasure to offer the services of my household and of my people. I hope you have enjoyed your stay here in Meneltauré."

"Very much so, my lord. It's the most magnificent place I've ever seen, and ... well, I'm looking forward to going to Paradis again ... It was so beautiful in my dream, and ... well ..."

"You want to see Yaron again?" he asked gently.

I started at this statement because it took me by surprise and because it embarrassed me that Lord Riyad could so easily read my thoughts. But I agreed, "Yes, sir, I do." I sighed miserably, remembering how I had felt in my dream when Yaron had told me it was exactly that—a dream and nothing more.

Lord Riyad was silent for a moment, gazing at the stars, and then he said softly, "Do not be embarrassed that you miss him so, Elysia. You were close to him, and he to you, despite the short time you spent together. I know you desperately long to know where he is, but I cannot help you find the answer, nor do I think you will find it in Paradis. Be strong, dear; you may yet see him again."

I sighed again, wishing it were so. However, another thought came to me: "Lord Riyad, do you know where Veryan is going to go?" I asked him.

"I do," Lord Riyad answered gravely, "but I cannot tell you that, Elysia. That knowledge is for Veryan, and him alone."

"Then how can you know of it?" I asked, my face clouding in disappointment. *I would like to know where he is going. Then, when I go to Hartford City, at least I'll know where he is and if he's in a safe place.* It seemed I was going to lose him once again, and so soon ... I sighed miserably.

Lord Riyad attempted to comfort me by saying. "If you become ruler of Meneltauré one day, Elysia, then you can know those sorts of things. But until then, you will simply have to wait like everyone else." The lord told me this gently, but firmly.

Then he stood and said, "Now, I believe it is far past your bedtime, is it not, my dear?"

I stood also. "I suppose so," I said ruefully. "I enjoyed the conversation we had, Lord Riyad. It was good to have someone to talk to again."

He put his hands on my shoulders and looked directly into my eyes. "You will never be alone, Elysia. No matter where life takes you, you will always have friends by your side."

"Thank you, my lord."

He nodded and removed his hands from my shoulders. "Good night, Elysia."

I dipped my head respectfully. "Good night, my lord. And again, thank you for everything."

Lord Riyad leaned over to me and spoke a soft sentence in a language I did not know, and yet, I found that I understood his words. Then, as quietly as a shadow, the lord walked past me and disappeared into the night.

THE GATHERING OF THE KINDS

The day of the Gathering dawned bright, clear, and cool. Victoria came into my quarters just after the sun began peeking into my window and cheerfully roused me, her eyes shining with excitement. I, however, was drowsy, still stiff and sore from my fall and, I'm afraid, much less enthusiastic.

Victoria had brought me a light breakfast of some fruit, a hard biscuit, and some milk. I sat on the edge of my bed, bleary-eyed and still half-asleep, and slowly ate my food while Victoria waited patiently.

Finally, when nearly through eating, I noticed that Victoria was holding a simple red dress, trimmed with black. Annoyed, I wondered why she was so intent on choosing these colours for me to wear. But I obediently changed into the dress after finishing my breakfast. I sighed as Victoria began chattering non-stop about how excited she was to be able to see Fray and the other tyrises and Nathaniel and all her friends. I still wondered what tyrises were.

Victoria told me we would be leaving for the Gathering as soon as she returned for me. She then took the empty breakfast tray and left me for a while, probably taking care of some last minute matters. She was gone for at least half an hour, during which I fell asleep on my bed once more, still not feeling refreshed. Perhaps the magical air of Paradis would revive me.

I woke with a jolt as Victoria gently shook my shoulder. She smiled down at me. "Ready?" she asked, blue eyes still brimming with eagerness.

I rubbed my forehead wearily, still groggy, but I resolutely stood and followed Victoria out the door. We were on the narrow bridge again, and the sun's golden rays were spilling over the edges of the sheer cliffs, tinting the waterfalls with fiery gold. Meneltauré really was the most splendid place I had ever seen.

But as we came to the place where the other bridges joined ours, Victoria led me down a very narrow staircase I had failed to notice before. The steps had only a very thin, black, metal rail, and it led us down a very steep incline, which made me feel more as if I was on a ladder than a staircase. The stairs were positioned alongside one of the massive waterfalls, so close, in fact, that by the time we were half way down I was utterly drenched. I was thankful then that elves could not feel the cold; my aching body told me that if I could have, I would have been freezing.

The staircase went down for what seemed like a mile, always very close to the waterfall. I looked down as far as I could, but I was not able to see where it ended. It just faded mysteriously into the mist below my feet and gave me no clues.

After nearly thirty minutes of descending the stairs, Victoria finally came to a stop, and I craned my neck to see below us. I was surprised when I realized the stairs came to a very abrupt end in the middle of the air, falling away to nothing but the billowing spray of the water. Confused, I thought, *Well, what now?*

Victoria turned to me and said, "Now we have to jump—"

"Jump? How far down is it?" I asked with a bit hysteria. Was she mad?

Victoria reassured me: "It's only about ten feet down to the water, and the water's very deep. And besides, you won't even have to swim; you'll just float up. It'll be okay; I promise." She smiled encouragingly at me and then leapt off the narrow staircase. Grasping the cool, wet rail desperately, I watched her disappear from my sight, swallowed up by the swirling foam below me.

But, I decided, if Victoria had done this before … and she had reassured me it was not very far down … I closed my eyes and let myself fall off the staircase.

Falling was terrifying. I dropped swiftly past the roaring waterfall, which thundered so loudly in my ears that it almost deafened me. My stomach ached with a clenching pain, making me wish I could curl into a ball. Brilliant light, reflecting from the water, surrounded me, blinding me. Spray flew into my face and my eyes, which I closed in desperation.

And then, I suddenly crashed into the water. It slammed into my stomach, knocking the breath out of me, and I had no time to take a breath before I was surrounded by millions of foamy bubbles and the massive pressure and weight of the water, pushing me down, down, down … I soon lost consciousness, succumbing to the intense pain and the frightening sensation of the water utterly suffocating me.

Suddenly, I could breathe. I gasped, the air rushing into my lungs with exhilarating speed. Instantly, my headache lessened, and I felt my heart begin to beat strongly again. It was the most amazing thing I had ever experienced.

I opened my eyes and saw an incredibly blurry scene before me. I realized I still had water in my eyes. Groaning, I blinked and wiped my eyes with the back of my hand. When I pulled my hand away, I jerked back a little in surprise. Two piercing black eyes were looking down at me from above, looking anxious.

I jolted up, surveying my surroundings. I was lying on a lush bank with a myriad of blooming flowers and waving green grasses. The sun was shining brightly overhead in a brilliant, cloudless blue sky. But the air I breathed in was the most fantastic—Paradisian air, fresher and more magical than even the air in my dream. It was intoxicating, invigorating, and extremely revitalizing. I breathed it in for a long moment, closing my eyes. I could almost feel it seeping into my bones and muscles, extracting the exhaustion and inferiority of my world and replacing it with some kind of deep, healing magic.

"Are you all right? You look a little … waterlogged," said a very smooth, charming voice beside me. Astonished, I turned. It was a voice unlike any I had ever heard before, one that captivated you and held you at its mercy, a voice that painted pictures in the air.

The boy it belonged to had the palest skin I have ever seen, as if he had never seen the sun. His eyes were in stark contrast, an exceedingly dark black, but his hair was light brown and pulled back into a ponytail. A silver medallion around his neck caught my eye, but before I could take a closer look, he said, "Forgive me; you must be wondering where you are."

I just stared at his pale face for a moment, mesmerized. Then I blinked and regained my ability to speak: "Oh, no; I'm in Paradis, right?"

His black eyes bored into mine, searching my own blue-grey ones. For a long moment, he was silent, and then he finally said, "That's right. I'm Nathaniel. My father's been waiting for you for quite some time. Elysia …" He said my name slowly, knowingly, meditating over it. His piercing eyes never left my face. "You would have probably drowned if I hadn't fished you out. Or one of Fray's tyrises would have found you, and that would have been worse." His eyes were locked with mine, holding me in my place. I found that while he was strangely charming and enigmatic—almost like Lliam, in a way—he was at the same time very frightening, and he made me feel that, if he chose to, he could hurt me at any moment.

"Well … thank you, then …," I said slowly, dropping my eyes from his pale face.

Nathaniel gave a low chuckle and then said something that almost made my heart stop: "You're welcome, young falcon." He stood, taking my arm and pulling me to my feet with surprising ease and grace.

It was then that Victoria reappeared; she hurried down to us from where she had been standing on a slope at the edge of the green forest nearby. "Elysia!" she exclaimed, coming over to me with a smile. "Are you all right? No broken bones?" Her eyes sparkled with amusement, and I could already tell that the Paradisian air had added a bounce in her step.

"I'm fine," I assured her, glad to see her; her presence eased some of the tension I felt around Nathaniel. The three of us started walking down the lush bank. Nathaniel gave no indication that he had even noticed Victoria's arrival, and he almost seemed subconsciously shy of her; he fell back behind us and stayed there, giving us plenty of space. Slightly puzzled by this, I glanced over my shoulder once and studied him briefly. He was tall, well over a foot taller than I, and he moved with a refined elegance that vaguely reminded me of a dancer. But with those inscrutable black eyes and alluring voice, perhaps a better description would be a snake.

Victoria gasped abruptly, and with a quick glance at me, she pointed straight ahead of us, where I could see some people far off in the distance. "See that group?" she asked me, and I nodded, curious about them. They looked both dark and pale, as if made from shadows, and a moment later, Victoria confirmed that my speculation was correct

"They're vardis," she explained. "They're shadows that can take elven form, and one of them, November, is my good friend; she visits Meneltauré often."

"Shadows?" I echoed, my head spinning. There were beings who were made of shadows? How was that possible? But then, I supposed, many things were possible in Paradis that could not be recreated on Earth.

Victoria looked after the vardis another moment, and then she asked me meekly, "Elysia, would you mind terribly if I go ahead and catch up with them? I haven't seen many of them in over a year …"

Alarmed at the thought of being left alone with Nathaniel but not wanting to deny Victoria, I winced inwardly and affirmed, "Sure; go on. You look as if you're about to run off anyway." I forced myself to give her an encouraging smile. She grinned and took off towards the strange group ahead of us, making me feel very uncomfortable as I was once again alone with Nathaniel.

As he resumed his earlier position next to me, the silver medallion around his neck flashed in the sunlight, and I glanced at it again. It bore a tree on its face, and one-half of the tree had leaves and the other did not. It was a very strange picture, I thought. Nathaniel noticed me looking at it and suddenly, before my eyes, it vanished, leaving no indication that it had ever existed.

I immediately stopped, stunned and perplexed. "H-how did you do that?" I asked, staring at him.

Nathaniel also stopped, turning to face me with a knowing, uncanny smile on his pale face, eyeing me carefully. "I'm the son of Menel, Elysia," he reminded me. "I am not without power of my own." Then he winked, sending a shiver down my body. Nathaniel's smile widened, and he laughed.

"I don't trust you," I said before I realized I had been thinking it.

Nathaniel looked faintly pleased. "Good," he stated, black eyes staring into mine even more intensely.

"And you're actually quite intimidating, you know that?" I went on, feeling oddly at ease with saying these things. I stopped then, noticing that my head felt strange, as if there were someone else inside it. It was not Lliam, I knew that …

I glanced at Nathaniel again, suddenly realizing what was happening. He was inside my head, toying with my thoughts and causing me to feel at ease. A queasy sensation overtook me, and I thought I was going to be sick. I instantly shoved Nathaniel's mind away, feeling repulsed by the fact that he had been in my mind.

Nathaniel gave a low, amused chuckle. "I know that, Elysia," he said in a soft, toxic voice. "And one lesson you should learn quite well before you take another step into Paradis is this: We are different here from you who live on Earth. Not only are we different, but we're also dangerous to mortals like you." He was suddenly right before me, though he did not appear to have moved at all. Giving a small gasp, I stepped back, shrinking from his piercing gaze. But he took another step forward, a noxious smile on his face. "And so before you go to the Gathering, where there will be *hundreds* of people like me … ones who would do you harm and take advantage of your … naiveté and ignorance of our world … I suggest you remember that and stay very close to Victoria or me because if you don't … you will not make it out of this place alive." His eyes were deathly serious, and

I remembered Lord Riyad saying almost exactly the same thing to me earlier.

Nathaniel was suddenly behind me in a movement so swift it was not possible, and I cringed. I could sense him hovering over me, but I stared resolutely at the ground, refusing to be intimidated. However, I began to feel his presence in my mind again, urging me to calm down and give in, to let the intoxicating air of Paradis fill my lungs and relax me ... and I wanted to, but ...

I shook my head. "I don't know what you're doing to me, but stop it," I said in a shaky voice, fearful now. I blinked hard, trying to rid my mind of the calming haze that was settling over it. I was so scared I almost wanted to cry. What kind of devilry was this?

Nathaniel chuckled, low and soft. "Don't worry, young falcon"—I flinched as he said it again—"I won't hurt you. But it's not often we get ... visitors from Earth. Forgive my curiosity." I paused, entranced by his captivating voice. I blinked again, feeling slightly faint.

Then he was suddenly five feet in front of me. "Come," he said. "Victoria is already in the pavilion, and my father waits for you."

Feeling as if the world was spinning around me, I hesitated, afraid I was going to collapse. I did not know if it was from my calamitous leap from the staircase or the magic-filled air of Paradis or some effect of Nathaniel, but it frightened me awfully.

As I reluctantly trailed him, I looked around, curious. Like the most glorious, perfect spring day imaginable, trees that were so violently green it almost hurt to look at them sprang up along the bank, even though back in Yaracina, winter was about to come. Luxuriant grass formed a soft covering beneath my feet; flowers of every colour grew up amid the grass; the rushing, crystal-clear river hurtled along with brutal and breath-taking force to my left; and birdsong filled the golden air with divine music. Magic permeated the air so fully that it was starting to make my head hurt a little. Almost overpowering, it still felt incredible to breathe air so fresh, so revitalising, so ... pure. I took a deep breath, trying also to lessen the trembling that had come from my encounter with Nathaniel. I shuddered. If there were going to be hundreds more like him at the Gathering, suddenly, the idea of attending did not seem so appealing.

I paused, hearing a continuous low, beating sound. I listened hard, wondering what it could be. It almost sounded like wings ...

Nathaniel turned around, looking up at the sky, his pale skin like ivory in the sunlight. His black eyes latched onto something, and a wry smile came over his face. He looked at me and said, "You remember those I mentioned who would harm you and take advantage of your ignorance? Well, here they come." He grinned at me and pointed at something behind me in the sky.

I turned slowly, afraid of what my eyes would see. But as soon as I did, my mouth dropped in amazement.

There were at least ten winged people flying above, with massive wingspans that I guessed were nearly seventeen feet across. They were plunging towards us with tremendous speed, getting closer every second.

As I watched them descend, I was suddenly aware of Nathaniel behind me, and I instantly felt uncomfortable. "Remember what I said about staying close to me," he said in a low voice. "Fray is very ... unpredictable around people like you, and so are the rest of the tyrises. But don't worry; they won't do anything ... too extreme with me here."

I turned to look at him. His dark black eyes looked seriously into mine. I said the first thing that came to my mind: "Why should I trust you? You've given me no reason to."

Nathaniel leaned forward, so close that his face was mere centimetres from mine. I found I could not look away from his hypnotic eyes, though I desperately wanted to do so. He said in a very soft, persuasive voice, "Trust me for the same reasons you trusted Lliam at the tower, Elysia."

I looked down at the mention of Lliam. He was right; I had had absolutely no reason to trust Lliam when all he had given me was his word, but I had done so, nonetheless, though I was still not convinced that I should have. Now I was even more reluctant to trust Nathaniel, but with the tyrises fast approaching, it seemed I had no other choice.

Nathaniel smiled a tiny bit and replied, "Don't worry, Elysia. You'll find you can trust me. I promise."

A sudden gust of wind buffeting me from behind told me that Fray and the tyrises had landed, and I turned slowly to face them. Nathaniel stood close behind me.

Surprised, I regarded them with a mixture of fear and awe. Fifteen males stood behind Fray, all of whom wore nothing but a loincloth. Brown, black, or white, not one of their wingspans was under sixteen feet, and their arms and legs were extraordinarily wiry, save for one younger boy who looked as if he had not quite grown into his wings yet. They appeared wild, and I immediately felt unsafe, but at the sight of Nathaniel, they seemed to relax a bit.

Fray, the tyris at the head of the pack, stepped forward to greet Nathaniel, who walked around me to do so. They clasped forearms for a moment, and then Fray said something to Menel's son in a foreign language. I found I could understand a few words here and there, even though I knew I had never heard them before. With a feeling of fear in my chest, I listened. Maybe Victoria was right after all ...

Fray then turned his green eyes on me and cocked his head, looking at me with a strange fascination. "So," he said with a thick, unidentifiable accent, "this is the little elf girl Menel has brought to our land. How ... intriguing." His face was suddenly only centimetres from mine, and I was almost overwhelmed by the scent of pine needles and some other strangely pleasant aroma. I shied away from him, however, seeing the fierce tint to his eyes. Fray studied me for a long moment—I hardly dared to breathe—and then he walked in a very slow circle around me, appraising me carefully with his green eyes. One of his dark wings brushed against my back as he came back around, and it sent a shudder down my spine.

All Fray said was, "Hmm." Then he grinned at me, showing abnormally sharp teeth, his green eyes sparkling with some peculiar light.

"Fray," Nathaniel said warningly, his face swiftly showing an expression of disapproval, "none of your tricks, now."

The tyris smirked at me, eyes locked with mine. He said in a low voice, "Regrettable that you'll be leaving after the Gathering, elf.

You could've come to my home, and I could've … shown you around."
He gave a soft chuckle that made me shiver.

Nathaniel said sharply, "Enough, Fray. You're frightening her."
He moved swiftly to my side and took my arm, turning me around
and making me walk again. I was thankful for his intervention.

We walked swiftly down the bank, Fray and the other tyrises
trailing us. I had no idea where exactly we were headed. "Where are
we going?" I asked Nathaniel as he pulled me along.

"To the Gathering, which is in the pavilion farther down the
river. It's built on a small cliff, overlooking the water. My father loves
the water; it's one of his favourite things in the world, but personally,
I prefer fire." He grinned at me charismatically over his shoulder,
dark eyes glimmering.

Then Nathaniel said something to Fray in that foreign language,
but this time I could not understand any of it. Fray answered back, his
green eyes grown solemn. I wondered what they were talking about.

They talked for a long time as we walked, completely ignoring
me, so I focused my attention on the mythical surroundings, breathing in the rich, uncontaminated air of Paradis. I longed to see Yaron
again here, even though I knew he had just been a dream. I sighed,
feeling gloomy. I missed that boy. And Veryan and my family.

Nathaniel put his hand on my elbow, pulling me to stop. When I
looked at him questioningly, he pointed to the cliff that had suddenly
appeared through a clearing in the vibrant forest ahead of us. Blue-
green waters lapped at its base, making a frothing, pulsing sound that
fascinated me. I found it both comforting and relaxing, and some of
the tension created from Fray and Nathaniel's presence drained away.
I looked longingly at the cerulean water, wishing I could swim in it.

But it was the massive white pavilion on top of the cliff that really
drew my attention. Marble columns and gleaming white steps were
only a few hundred feet from the edge of the cliff, and the columns
supported a graceful marble ceiling. Spanning the front of the roof on
the exterior were carvings that were patterned from Greek mythology, and I even recognized such figures as Zeus with his lightning
bolt, Achilles with the arrow in his heel, and Orpheus with his lyre.

Nathaniel steered me into the clearing where a well-worn path led to the cliff. But before moving on, I paused and turned to watch the sixteen tyrises flare their huge wings and soar into the air, pumping strongly, each thrust shooting them dozens of feet higher as they winged their way towards the pavilion. I watched them in awe, starting to realize just what a magnificent and awesome place this really was. They flew across the sun, blotting it out for a brief moment, and then disappeared behind the cover of the trees.

"Pretty incredible, aren't they?" Nathaniel said behind me, his voice strangely flat. I looked at him questioningly, and he gave me a dry smile. "Just don't ever make a tyris angry with you; they're very dangerous with those wings."

I looked at him for a long moment, and he at me. His black eyes suddenly grew incredibly sad, and he moved them away from mine to stare at the ground. "What?" I asked, seeing something other than his self-assured side for the first time.

Nathaniel sighed. "Nothing. It's just … What's it like living on Earth?"

Surprised, I did not know what to say. That was like asking me what it was like to be alive; I had no idea how to respond. I wondered why he wanted to know, and I asked him.

Nathaniel's brow furrowed, and he hesitated. "Well … I lived there once … but I don't remember it."

"What do you mean?" I asked, fascinated.

Nathaniel sighed and waved his hand. "Never mind, Elysia. Forget I said anything." He frowned, dark eyes looking troubled, and began walking up the trail to the pavilion, leaving me no choice but to follow and wonder.

~

It was even grander once I was standing inside of it. The pavilion could have easily held five to six hundred people, and by the look of it, may have had that many then. Dozens of different creatures, including Fray's tyrises and the strange group of vardis, filled the columned pavilion, making for a very odd sort of gathering. Elegantly carved chairs lined the perimeter, engraved with curling vines, leaves, and

Greek gods and goddesses. In fact, the entire setting reminded me of a Greek myth.

Nathaniel stayed very close to me, steering me away from various groups of Paradisian creatures, every one of them pausing in their conversations to stare at me. I felt very uncomfortable, especially when I heard whispers in foreign languages trail behind us. Nathaniel's black eyes narrowed threateningly at some of them, and they quickly averted their gazes from me.

"Elysia!"

I looked to my right to see Victoria, grinning with delight like a child with an especially good secret, come bounding up to me. Her blue eyes alight with joy, she said excitedly, "Isn't this fantastic, Elysia? Isn't this the most magnificent place you've ever been?"

"I-I suppose …," I stammered, unsure about how I really felt about this place.

But Victoria beamed anyway and asked excitedly, "Have you met Fray and the tyrises?"

I cast a swift glance at the tyrises, most of whom were clustered around Fray and looking about themselves warily, as if expecting to see some enemy lurking silently in the bushes. Fray caught my eye and grinned, the look in his green eyes making me shiver and drop my eyes.

Victoria raised her eyebrows and said, "Not a pleasant encounter, I presume?"

Nathaniel answered sourly, "Not exactly," his black eyes glaring at Fray.

I looked at him, a bit surprised. I had not thought it had been that bad, but apparently he had. All my encounter with Fray had yielded, in my opinion, was my determination to avoid him if I ever came back to Paradis.

Victoria frowned, looking irritated at his response, and then left us to go talk to the tyrises, who greeted her with wide grins and enthusiastic words in their thick accents.

Nathaniel and I stood together awkwardly for a moment, just listening to the soft babble of the conversations around us. Nathaniel's black eyes flickered thoughtfully to my face occasionally, but he never said anything. Finally, I asked him, "Why did you call me 'young falcon'? No one but Lliam calls me that."

Nathaniel's pearly white teeth reappeared, and he grinned lazily at me, saying, "I know, but I've heard him call you that before, and I liked it. So I decided to call you young falcon as well. Do you mind?" His midnight eyes suddenly had their old, mesmerizing charm back, and his mouth curved into a magnetic smile.

I stared at him for a second and then shook my head, smiling ruefully. "I suppose I don't mind … it's just that when I hear you call me that … it makes me miss him even more." My heart felt heavy with sorrow and pain, remembering that moment when Lliam had crested the hill and smiled victoriously as his soldiers chased us. Despite the intense feelings of hurt and betrayal that came with that memory, it also conjured up very unwelcome feelings of longing to see him again. I loathed all those feelings and the conflict they created in me.

Nathaniel looked at me curiously, black eyes searching my blue-grey ones. "I thought he betrayed you, Elysia," he said casually, eyeing me carefully.

"Yes, well … he did, but … oh, I know it makes no sense at all, but I miss him anyway, Nathaniel," I offered pitifully, feeling ashamed of admitting this to a stranger. But then Nathaniel got a very sad look in his eyes, almost as though he longed for someone to miss him too.

He looked away for a long moment, eyes veiled. "I'm sure he misses you too, Elysia …" Nathaniel sighed shakily and did not say anything else. I suddenly felt sorry for him; I had not noticed it before now, but he really seemed quite uncomfortable among all these different Paradisians, and there actually seemed be a slight air of vulnerability about him, cloaked beneath his attractive and elaborate disguise. He cocked his head at me, eyes thoughtful. "You're very perceptive, aren't you, young falcon?" he asked wearily.

We looked at each other absorbedly for a moment, and I answered weakly, "I try."

Nathaniel suddenly frowned and warned, as if realizing he had unwittingly let down his guard, "Well, don't try so hard at figuring me out … I'm … a bit complicated, you see, and … there are things I would prefer you not know."

I reminded him, "I can't read minds, Nathaniel. I can just tell things about people by their facial expressions and by what they say and how they say it." I studied Nathaniel for a moment, and noticing some tension in his face, I asked, "Is there something bothering you … about what I said?"

He frowned and started to answer, but just then there was a stirring in the pavilion that increased the noise level drastically, and all of those inside it began to drift towards the circle of chairs on the perimeter of the floor, taking seats. Nathaniel steered me to where Victoria was seated and left me there with her, slipping out of sight as he blended in with the other Paradisians.

Next to me, Victoria was joyful, blue eyes alight and an effervescent smile lighting her face. It was obvious she was ecstatic at being here once more, and some of her excitement spilled over to me, easing my initial trepidation of the dangerous people I had encountered here earlier and soothing my anxieties.

"Oh, isn't this terribly exciting?" she asked me merrily.

Smiling at her enthusiasm, I replied, "If you like. But tell me, how have you come to be such good friends with Fray and his tyrises?"

Victoria shrugged. "They intrigue me, and Fray and his pack have always been good friends with my father. I—"

She was cut off, however, by Nathaniel, who had reappeared at the head of the pavilion. His polite and sophisticated air had returned, making me question the vulnerability I thought I had seen in him only a few minutes earlier. Now he stood tall and confident, his face composed, black eyes serene, commanding attention. I noticed that the silver medallion was back on its black chain around his neck, and it shone brilliantly as light reflected off its surface.

"Welcome," he said, the sound of his voice instantly silencing the few whispers that were still floating around the masses of creatures. Their eyes were drawn instantly to him. He paused and smiled, taking pleasure in it. "I am Nathaniel, son of Menel, as I'm sure all of you know. And you also know that this Gathering is taking place several months earlier than usual. My father believed that it would be best to convene now and not delay because the problem would only become worse in the months to come. And what is the problem, you may ask? Of course, my father knew this was going to happen and allowed it to happen, but that in no way means that he feels no sympathy for those involved. Humans," said Nathaniel, pausing to eye the crowd before him, "have come again to Yaracina. I know that nearly all of you, save some of our younger kinsmen here, remember well the last time humans were in elven territory and how tragic the losses. The War of the Red Moon was a bloody showcase of how badly the elves had underestimated the strength of the humans since the Great Plague, and I fear it will be much the same again. The humans are advancing at an incredible rate. Their weapons and armour will very soon surpass those of the elves, and I'm afraid their numbers will too. I think I am correct in saying that all of us, barring my father, of course, have severely misjudged the capabilities of the human race, and it is something that, in hindsight, we should have paid much greater attention to, especially since we barely overcame them in the War of the Red Moon."

I sat silently beside Victoria, taking in every word. The details I knew about the last time humans had been in Yaracina were sketchy to say the least, and I was relishing the opportunity to learn more about it. Aubryn had always avoided telling us too much of the humans or the war, except that the elves had won, because she feared it would frighten us, but now I wished I had pressed her to tell me more.

Nathaniel clasped his hands behind his back for a thoughtful moment and then continued, "Zoser led the humans to Yaracina the first time, and he is responsible for bringing them again. He is fully human, but it is because of Yara's antidote to the plague so long ago that he is as strong and immortal as the elves are. And now he has a personal assassin who is very nearly as skilled as he is, having been trained by the only known Seren-Apparate crossbreed alive. Two years ago, as all of you remember, this assassin murdered Eshen's king in cold blood and poisoned his infant son, leaving only his wife and daughter to rule their kingdom of Guó Xī, from the capital Chéng Fèng."

I let out an involuntary gasp, and Nathaniel's eyes instantly sped to my face. They were filled with scorn, as if daring me not to believe him. I closed my eyes and took a shaky breath, willing my mind to think about anything but Lliam.

Nathaniel went on: "Together, Zoser and his assassin, as well as the nearly fifty thousand humans who have been shipped in to serve Zoser, have made a formidable enemy for us. Zoser is even now bringing in several thousand more soldiers from the human countries to serve him. My father has devised a plan to give the elves a better chance to fight back for, right now, they have no organised army, and even though they are attempting to muster one, they have no one to lead them. They have dangerously underestimated the humans, thinking that their races' natural superiority would protect them against any threat the humans would pose. And for a time, they were right. After Zoser's defeat at the War of the Red Moon, he and his soldiers fled back to their far away countries, crushed, humiliated, and weak. But Zoser is clever; we all know this. He bided his time, gathered his army back to him, and has come upon the elves again in a time when they believed themselves invincible and, therefore, unprepared and unsuspecting. All he needs now is that extra weight to tip the scales, that additional force that could win it all for him." Nathaniel paused and then began pacing slowly around the room, hands still clasped behind his back, continuing to hold the rapt attention of everyone present.

He walked past Victoria and me, past Fray, past the shadow-people, silent. Nathaniel was brooding over something, waiting. A few moments later, as whispers began to swell again, I suddenly realized why he had stopped talking. His time was up; his talk had only been the introduction.

There was a person standing in the spot where Nathaniel had been originally, and he, too, was silent. I found I could not tear my eyes away from him; he was infinitely more commanding and regal than Nathaniel could ever be. His very presence seemed to cause an astounding change to those in the pavilion. All seemed to sit up a little straighter and tried to look a little more noble themselves. A respectful and almost awed silence fell over the creatures assembled. Out of the corner of my eye, I noticed that even some of the trees were flowering at an incredible rate, their blossoms unfolding in mere seconds, and the birds redoubled their cheerful trilling, apparently heralding the arrival of this person of honour. Other trees rustled their leaves even though there was no wind, and I could have sworn I heard gentle, breathy whispers coming from the trees themselves. It was as if nature itself was rejoicing at the mere sight of this man.

Though he did not look particularly extraordinary, I knew he was. Dressed in simple sky-blue robes, the man was of average height with light brown hair much like Nathaniel's and eyes that were a rather odd combination of green and blue. He had a kind, compassionate face that also held a surprising strength, and his eyes were the kind that seemed to sift through your soul and extract every secret.

The man took a few steps forward, his robes swishing softly against his ankles, and then he paused and said in a deep, rich voice, "Welcome, one and all, to the Gathering of the Kinds. It has been nearly a year since I have physically seen some of you, and others I have seen often, as of late, as we have been discussing important matters together. These are ... potentially dark times for our brothers and sisters on Earth, and it grieves me to know some of the upsetting things that are to follow these upcoming weeks. With us today are two young ladies who have been and will be witness to some of these terrible things, and I wish you all to welcome them warmly. Victoria Ar-Elle, you all know; she is the daughter of Riyad of Meneltauré. And Elysia of Aseamir." He paused, his kind blue-green eyes resting on me and scrutinising my face gently. I felt queer inside, as if my soul recognised the presence, only a few hundred feet away, of a being who was not elven nor human nor any other race I had ever encountered but a god. I felt as if my world had just changed with one look into those omnipotent, knowing eyes, and a part of me became whole for the first time.

I was suddenly aware of the eyes of everyone in the pavilion upon me, including Victoria's and Nathaniel's, studying my face with uncomfortable intensity. Whispers were also spreading like wildfire amongst those around me. My face burning with embarrassment at their scrutiny, I lowered my eyes and stared at the toe of my boot without seeing it.

Menel went on to say: "Elysia has come here for a special purpose. Normally, as you know, most mortals are not allowed into Paradis unless they have died and are coming here for an eternity of peace and happiness, but I have allowed Elysia to come because I have chosen her to do something for me … something that will give her people a chance to fight back against Zoser."

I looked up then, knowing everyone's eyes were back upon Menel. His rich, resonant voice filled every inch of the pavilion, entrancing us and causing us to listen to his every word. "But before we get to that," he said, "I would like to address another issue; that of Zoser's young assassin. I believe that there are some things about him that I need to tell you."

Feeling my heart flutter and a thousand different emotions fling themselves at me with the mere mention of Lliam, I sank lower in my seat, wishing that Menel had not chosen to talk about him.

"Firstly, Lliam is not innately evil, as I know many of you believe. Though he had a trying childhood and many of the events of it were undesirable, the boy is merely lost in a world that is too big for him right now. I know that he chose to join Zoser's army, but that was merely on a whim. He has deeply regretted it ever since." A profound sadness came into Menel's sea-green eyes, and he suddenly looked very weary. "Lliam was trained to fight and kill callously on Zoser's orders, and he has become extremely skilled at it. His assassinations of King Naoko and of various nobles and people of importance in Naoko's court over the past few months have demonstrated this. His teacher is exceptionally gifted and taught him how to gain trust and to kill cleanly and without drawing suspicion.

"However, I believe this boy can be won back if we fight hard enough. Of course, the choice lies ultimately with him, but there is a very good chance that he can be brought back to the side of the good and just. He suffers at Zoser's hand daily, and while I detest this, it must continue because of Lliam's choice to serve Zoser. Lliam's mistreatment will help shape his character, though whether for good or for evil, only time will tell; Lliam's destiny lies ultimately with the choices he will make in the next few months. But I know there to be good within him still, and it is not out of reach, though I fear it slips farther and farther away with every day."

"But he betrayed me," I whispered, not intending to say it aloud, but it slipped out before I knew it. Instantly, I pressed my lips together, hoping no one had heard me. But to my horror, Menel turned his blue-green eyes on me, looking at me with profound understanding and sorrow.

"Yes, he did," he agreed softly, and as he said this, I could feel the Paradisians' eyes turn back on me. "But he did not do it willingly, my dear Elysia. You and Lliam, you share an extraordinary connection, though you do not know its origin. Tell me, have you no idea why you and he are bonded thus?"

Bewildered and wishing fervently I had not said anything, I shook my head despairingly. How my heart ached to hear all of this about Lliam, whom I had trusted so deeply such a short while ago and was now resolved never to trust again.

Menel glanced for a moment at his son, who was standing at the other end of the pavilion, arms crossed and black eyes expressionless. Nathaniel glanced at me with a vacant stare, but I was unable to discern what he might be thinking from his blank face.

"D-does Lliam know the reason, sir?" I asked timidly, avoiding Menel's eyes meekly, afraid to look at him and let him see the conflict that was roiling inside me.

"Does he know why you and he are connected? Yes, Elysia, he does. But I'm afraid he will not tell you for quite some time," Menel answered kindly, but I could tell that there was weight to his words.

I was both relieved and disappointed at his answer, but I longed for the subject to move off Lliam. I was not sure how much more my heart could stand.

I realized Menel had probably sensed this because he proceeded to say, "And now I believe it is time to come back to the real reason Elysia is here in Paradis today. Nathaniel and I have been discussing this strategy for some time, actually, and we are both convinced that his plan, along with some other key factors, will give the elves a significant boost in the fight against the humans, and as such, I am allowing Nathaniel to test his idea, and Elysia is to help him. A rather large part in the success or failure of my son's plan will depend upon her ability to carry it out. Lliam shall also play a crucial part in this war, though because of the complexity of what will happen in the next few months, I cannot say whether he will choose good or evil, nor when his final choice will be made."

I sucked in my breath. Why did he have to keep coming up in Menel's discussion? Why couldn't I just have been able to leave him and all thoughts of him behind forever after what happened at the tower? He had betrayed me and Veryan and Yaron. Because of him, Veryan had lost his freedom nearly as soon as he had gotten it and then was flogged unmercifully and left unattended for days. And I had no idea what happened to Yaron. For all I knew, he could be dead. A fierce ache began pulsing in my heart with these troublesome thoughts. How much simpler life had been in Aseamir!

"Nathaniel," Menel said to his son, his deep voice with an almost ominous tone, "It is time. Bring out the hope of those of a world long silent."

I looked at Nathaniel, wondering what his father could have meant by that. The hope of those of a world long silent? Who could Menel be referring to? But when I glanced at Victoria, hoping she would be able to explain the god's words to me, I saw that she looked equally perplexed.

I shifted my eyes back to Nathaniel and saw that he was staring at me too, his black eyes full of indecipherable meaning. Then he turned slowly and disappeared into the trees, leaving me feeling fragile inside, as though he had just discovered a secret of mine without my knowledge.

"Isn't he incredible?" Victoria breathed beside me, watching the place where Nathaniel had disappeared keenly.

A little surprised by this question, I just simply stared at her. I knew I certainly did not look at Nathaniel the same way Victoria did; I barely knew him. And besides, he was the son of a god; of course he was going to be incredible. A bit miffed by Victoria's question—though I did not know why—I simply answered, "If you say so." There was something almost familiar about Nathaniel that kept me from thinking about such absurd things; perhaps it was because he vaguely reminded me of Lliam.

But I was saved from hearing more about how incredible Nathaniel was, for although Victoria had opened her mouth to say something more, he returned just then, gliding through the trees into the pavilion, his pale face indifferently blank. He was holding a large rock.

However, as he came closer, I saw that it did not look like an ordinary rock. It was lumpy and rough looking, and while it was the greyish colour of a normal rock, there were small, intermittent streaks of a brilliant green, polished substance on the rock's face as well, as if the grey rock had partially grown over the green. The green was a violently bright shade, similar to that of the trees in the forest surrounding the pavilion.

It was not particularly big—about the length of my forearm, not including my hand—and neither did it look especially heavy. *This is Nathaniel's plan?* I thought incredulously. *Giving the elves a* rock? I had expected something … more impressive, something grander. Frankly, this looked pathetic.

Nathaniel caught my eye and looked at me solemnly, his black eyes staring with incredible intensity into mine. After cradling the rock in his arms for a moment, he handed the rock to his father, who took it gently.

Menel looked at the stone with an incomprehensible expression for a moment, his sea-green eyes unfathomable. Then he looked up at me, and I felt an involuntary shiver when my eyes met his soul-searching ones.

Nathaniel suddenly stood beside me, not appearing to have moved at all. He put a gentle and vigilant hand on my shoulder and guided me forward. I felt exceedingly vulnerable as I walked in front of him toward his father; I knew the eyes of every Paradisian in the pavilion were on me. Butterflies trembled in my gut for a moment, and then I felt an outside force enter my mind and calm me, making me feel almost drowsy. Nathaniel. I glanced over my shoulder at him irritably, but his black eyes did not meet mine.

I stood only a few feet away from Menel, in between a god and his son. I shivered. Could this be real? Could I be certain that I had not simply hit my head on a rock when I had jumped off that bridge? Or had that been a dream too? I remembered the first dream of this place I had had: Yaron and the light-filled forest and the field of pink and white flowers … Oh, how I missed him.

Menel looked at me kindly, his fatherly face gentle. Then he asked in his deep, resonant voice, "What do you see in my arms, Elysia?"

I looked at the grey and green rock, wondering if I was supposed to be seeing something astonishing. "Just … a rock, sir," I mumbled.

"Yes, it does rather resemble an ordinary rock, doesn't it? If one came across this on the road, one might think it was a rock containing traces of emerald, or jade. However, it is much more than that, my dear Elysia. You see …," and he paused to run his fingers tenderly over one of the bright green streaks, "within this stone, there is a pulse of life. A tiny heart has formed and lungs and limbs. This is no ordinary rock, Elysia. It is a hope, for you and your people. As Nathaniel said earlier, Zoser is very much interested in gathering people or things that might tip the scales in his favour. You see, he has a large and efficient human army, but he will need more than that to defeat the elves. Caught off-guard though the elves have been, they are not helpless. Zoser knows this. He knows that he will need every additional force he can acquire to aid his cause. This … just might be one of the things that could give him that extra edge."

"So …," I said, struggling to piece this all together, "it's an egg, then, sir?"

"Yes, it is, Elysia. But this is not the only thing that could give Zoser a better chance of achieving his goal, oh no! You mustn't think that. There are some … particular people he is very much interested in gathering to his cause, people I highly doubt you have heard of." He looked at me keenly. "This egg's inhabitant will serve a purpose in this war, not a large one, you must understand, but it will lead to events that will be tremendously important, that will ultimately give you elves an exceedingly great advantage."

"So, why, sir, are you giving it to me?" I interrupted, unsure.

"Because," Menel said, "this egg involves you and Lliam. You both have significant parts to play for your respective sides in this war, and this egg is vital in that."

Feeling more and more that this was a dream, I looked over at Nathaniel, who to my surprise had his jaw tightly clenched and an intense look in his midnight eyes. I could practically feel the fury radiating from him. Momentarily forgetting Menel was there, I asked him, "What's wrong, Nathaniel?" Out of the corner of my eye, I noticed that the engraving on the silver medallion around his neck had changed from the odd tree to a storm cloud, from which silver bolts of lightning were actually flashing.

"Nathaniel," Menel said in a startlingly stern voice, making me jump slightly. "I told you, we will discuss this later. Now is not the time!" His sea-green eyes seemed strangely abrasive as he looked at his son. I felt unsafe between the two of them. Nathaniel merely looked away, jaw still clenched and eyes tight. Menel sighed and turned his attention back to me, looking resolute. "Now," he said, "here you are." He handed me the egg, and I took it gingerly, then more firmly, surprised that it was heavier than I had expected it to be. It felt rough and awkward in my hands.

"I want you to take this to Rielture, Elysia," Menel went on, an enigmatic look coming into his eyes. "You must give it to Rielture's governor. And keep it safe."

I just stared at him. Rielture was at the opposite end of Yaracina from Hartford City, where I was supposed to be going. In fact, it was nearly six hundred miles directly south of Hartford City on the maps

I had seen of Yaracina. To the west of Rielture was a small plain and, beyond that, the volcanic, barren land of Emen Cahútomec, the only unpopulated part of Yaracina. The only possible habitable area in Emen Cahútomec was along the coast, where a small strip of forest and cliffs looked out over the sea. "B-but ...," I stammered, "my father needs me to go to Hartf—"

"Yes, well, your father's papers will have to wait, Elysia," Menel said gently but firmly. I quieted instantly with his reprimand. Feeling that this was all truly surreal, I glanced sideways at Nathaniel, who was still staring resolutely and stiffly off to the side. His eyes moved in my direction for a brief second, as if knew he knew I was watching him. I wondered what had upset him so.

"And now," Menel went on, "my business with you is done, Elysia. You must be ready to leave Meneltauré at first light tomorrow. Nathaniel, you will now escort our guest home, please." He looked seriously at his son, who was still looking extremely irritated. "Victoria will join you later; she is going to stay for the rest of my meeting with the Paradisians."

"May I please stay too?" I asked timidly, looking around me at the other creatures I had forgotten were present around us, inspecting me with intense eyes. I felt very uncomfortable under their scrutinising stares. It felt as though they were evaluating me, comparing me to some unknown standard, but I wanted to stay regardless.

"We are going to be discussing matters I do not wish for you to hear, Elysia, nor do they concern you. Nathaniel will see you safely back to Meneltauré. Remember, Elysia, keep that egg safe. In your hands, you carry the hope of your people." He smiled warmly, his blue-green eyes once again kind and amiable.

I felt Nathaniel's hand on my shoulder again, and he turned me around and guided me out the way we had come in, to the small forest path at the south end of the huge pavilion.

To my surprise, Nathaniel did not remove his hand from my shoulder. He still seemed upset, so again, I asked him what was wrong. Fuming, he answered, "I hate the way they look at you—as if you're some kind of thing on display to ogle at. It makes me sick.

Just because you're not from here, and you—" He suddenly stopped and fell silent, black eyes full of anger.

I was taken aback by this statement. I definitely had not expected Nathaniel to feel so protective of me. I wondered why he did. He explained this, almost as if he had heard my thoughts. I shivered. "I wouldn't usually care about such a thing, but you're … different," he said heavily. "They have no right, especially considering what my father's asked you to do for him ... They're so thoughtless. To them, mortals are just like toys, something to play with and toss aside when they're done with them." He shook his head, clearly furious.

"You said 'mortals,'" I pointed out tentatively. "Elves aren't mortal. 'Mortal' means they can die, right?"

Nathaniel snorted. "Well, they can die if they get stabbed, can't they? Elves *can* die, Elysia; they just typically don't because there's been nothing to threaten them for a few hundred years. Paradisians *can't* die; there's nothing on heaven or earth that can kill them because they were never alive. Yes, there are some elves who have died and live here now, but they are few in comparison to the others here, the ones native to Paradis, and to Paradis only." His eyes suddenly seemed very emotionless. "When you die, your soul either comes here to Paradis or goes there." He pointed beyond me. I turned and looked where he was pointing. Beyond the clear, rushing river and the eternally green, lush banks, there was a dark, ugly smear of land at the edge of the horizon, but it was so far off I could make out no details about the miserable place. The thought of spending eternity in such a place was not a pleasant one, however.

Eager to change the subject, I looked back at Nathaniel. "Earlier you said that you had lived on Earth once," I reminded him softly. "What did you mean?"

"I'm the son of Menel," Nathaniel said stiffly, bristling at my question. "I've been to Earth before." But then he fell silent and would say nothing more about his days on Earth.

We left the green forest and silently walked along the bank of the rushing river, each mulling over different thoughts. Once, I glanced at Nathaniel's necklace and saw that the lightning, which earlier had been savagely discharging from the storm clouds, had now subsided. The clouds were slowly dissipating, allowing silver rays of sunshine to break through. Nathaniel's rage was fading away too, I realized suddenly. The necklace reflected his mood. *How odd*, I thought, intrigued by the concept. I had never seen anything like it, and I wondered briefly what the original picture of the half-dead tree had meant.

Almost as if he knew I was wondering about it, Nathaniel said suddenly, "The image on my necklace changes depending on my mood. It was a gift from November, one of the vardis, on my fifteenth birthday." He absently touched the silver face of the medallion, and the storm clouds faded away completely to a cloudless sky, which hung over a single, tiny tree in the distance. I took that to mean he had calmed down considerably.

He unclasped it and handed it to me. I reached out with my hand, shifting the egg in my arms so that I could take it. The metal was warm from being next to Nathaniel's chest, and the medallion itself was about the size of a large coin. A fine black chain dangled from the pendant. I rubbed my thumb over it once, and the picture changed from the peaceful day to a feather pen hurriedly scratching something onto a piece of parchment, writing, apparently, by itself. Amused, I wondered what it meant and asked Nathaniel.

When he did not answer, I looked up and was surprised to see him looking thunderstruck, mouth slightly open in shock, paused in his steps. Alarmed and bewildered, I asked, "What is it?"

He merely shifted his gaze from the medallion to me, black eyes wide. Nathaniel instantly snatched the necklace away from me, and it disappeared a moment later, his movements abnormally swift and agile. I stared at the space that the medallion had occupied only a moment earlier, wondering what on earth had shocked Nathaniel so.

A moment later, Nathaniel held out his hand to me, a blank medallion exactly like his on his palm. "Take it," he said urgently.

I did slowly, unsure. Unlike his, however, the medallion was cool, and there was no picture upon it. But when my fingers took it from Nathaniel's, lines began to form in the silver, bunching together to form ridges that soon became the image of a person sitting on a rock, chin resting in hand, a pondering expression on the face. I assumed this meant I was confused. I looked back at Nathaniel to see his reaction.

He reached out tentatively and took the necklace from me and then yelped in surprise when another engraving formed, jerking his hand back quickly and dropping it. The medallion fell into the grass with a soft *plop.* Nathaniel stared at it with disbelieving intensity.

I bent down and scooped the necklace up in my hand, the image returning to that of the pondering person. "What is it, Nathaniel?" I asked again, thoroughly convinced there was something he was not telling me about these necklaces.

He shook his head agitatedly, like a dog trying to rid itself of a bothersome fly. "It doesn't matter. Take that necklace and wear it always. Don't ever lose it. If anyone else touches it, it should become blank. If it doesn't …" He looked at me with bewilderment, silent for a long moment. Then he finally concluded: "Keep your eye on that person."

He started walking again, farther away from me than he had been previously, as if he was afraid of me. He kept shaking his head, lips moving silently, as if he was trying to convince himself of something. I watched him with growing concern as I fastened the chain around my neck. The metal was cool against my skin, and I was uncomfortable with its weight. It felt like a mental and physical burden because of Nathaniel's reaction to it. Oh, how tired I was becoming of secrets!

Nathaniel's next question threw me off-guard; it was the last thing I expected him to ask. "What is Lliam like?"

Tensing, I braced myself as my heart began to ache with a flurry of different emotions. The image on my necklace turned to that of two different scenes: a dark, rainy day with storm clouds and lightning on one half and a clear, sun-drenched day on the other. I clearly had conflicted feelings about Lliam; I knew that much without the medallion. I struggled to find words to describe the enigmatic boy I was bonded with so closely. How does one describe the mirror image of her own soul?

"He's …," I started tentatively. "I … we're exactly the same."

Nathaniel raised an eyebrow. "Apparently not, for, if I remember correctly, you are on *our* side, and he is on *their* side."

I bit my lip. There was that one, rather … significant detail … "Well," I amended, "except for that …"

Nathaniel smirked, looking bitter. Though his eyes still held their lethal, mesmeric power, they had turned harder and more cynical than I had ever seen them. "What does he look like?" he asked then.

I shrugged. "He's got black hair, and his eyes are blue-grey, just like mine. He's eight or nine inches taller than I am, though."

Nathaniel nodded, his eyes searching the ground with strong concentration. I wondered why he wanted to know about Lliam.

We had reached the place where I had come up from the water and found myself beside Nathaniel. I saw now that there was a waterfall here also, though significantly smaller than the one the staircase had been beside, and the pool the water fell into was a little, circular one, only a few feet across. The waterfall streamed from a lower part of the cliffs that the pavilion sat upon and fell about five feet down into the sparkling pool, which was frothing and bubbling from the intrusion. I stared down at it with aversion, remembering the crushing feeling that had swept over me when I had been underwater earlier.

"I wish I could go with you," Nathaniel voiced mournfully as he, too, looked down at the pool beside me.

Surprised, I looked at him. "Why can't you?"

Nathaniel's necklace changed back to the storm clouds and lightning, and his eyes tightened. "My father doesn't think Earth is safe for me. 'It's too dangerous,'" he sneered angrily. "He thinks I'm not capable of protecting myself there and it's not safe for someone like me to go wandering around a place like Earth right now." Nathaniel dug the toe of his boot into the sandy dirt, fuming. "He has no faith in me. I'm not a child! I can take care of myself."

"Maybe you need to have some faith in him," I said softly, thinking to myself that while Nathaniel probably could take care of himself, his father would have had a better reason than that to keep him from going to Earth.

Nathaniel fell silent, frowning, the lightning flashing with increased ferocity on his medallion. He gave a heavy sigh and gestured to the water before us. "Just dive in and relax; let the water carry you back to where you need to go. My guess is that you'll come up next to the bank by the waterfall you came through."

I shifted the egg in my arms, looking uncertainly at the frothing water. How would I be able to hold on to the valuable egg underwater? I had almost been torn limb from limb the first time, and I did not relish the prospect of having to try to keep myself *and* the egg intact this time. "W-will I be able to hold on to it?" I asked hesitantly, trying not to think of what would happen if I lost it in the water.

Nathaniel quirked his lips undecidedly. "Well …," he said, and then was silent for a long moment. "My father just agreed to let me go with you to Earth make sure nothing happens to the egg, but I have to come back here as soon as you're delivered safely." He looked mournfully at the small pool.

"Well, at least you can go to Earth at all, even if only for a little while," I pointed out optimistically, and Nathaniel nodded reluctantly. "Here," he said, "I'll take the egg. You had enough trouble coming the first time without it."

Feeling a little embarrassed, I handed him the rough egg. He took my hand then, explaining, "It'll keep you from getting separated from me." Nathaniel held the egg very tightly in his other hand. I wondered how it did not break from the force of his grip but realized it must be awfully dense.

Nathaniel took a deep breath and stepped to the very edge of the grassy bank, his intense black eyes looking down at the water eagerly. I knew that he understood that he was only a few minutes away from finally getting to Earth. And then, without warning, he suddenly stepped forward into the pool, pulling me with him.

The water closed over my head, and I shut my eyes tightly, instantly feeling paranoid and vulnerable in the water. The only thing that gave me any sense of security was Nathaniel's hand clasped around mine, hauling me along through the millions of tiny bubbles that were ramming into my face and body, causing me to lose all sense of direction. I had no idea which way was up and which was down. I just held on to Nathaniel's hand with all my strength and prayed I would not be swept away by the whirling current.

Suddenly I could breathe again. Before even opening my eyes, I opened my mouth and gasped in air. My eyes flew open and through the watery blur that coated them, I saw that we were a few hundred feet from a dull green bank. Blue-white water swarmed around us, but I realized that neither of us was wet. My auburn hair was perfectly dry about my shoulders, and even my clothes were dry as a bone, despite the fact that we were floating in water. *How very odd,* I thought vaguely as I swam weakly towards the shore, Nathaniel beside me in the water.

I scrambled up on the bank and then lay in the soft grass, shivering and out of breath. I never wanted to see that much water again; I was frightened out of my wits right now. Being under the water at that depth caused my heart to hammer painfully in my chest and my head to pound. I had always dearly loved swimming in the Avarii River back in Aseamir, but this was quite a different experience.

Nathaniel sat beside me, looking as if he was in a daze himself, his eyes taking in every inch of the scene before us. We were on the eastern bank of the massive waterfall by which the staircase had run, and I could feel the spray on my face from the falling water even from here, several hundred feet away.

Panting, I finally sat up, immensely relieved to see the egg still in Nathaniel's hand, but he was not paying attention to it. Nathaniel was looking about with an enraptured expression, black eyes wide with ecstasy, and a beautiful engraving of a rising sun over a field of gently swaying flowers emerging upon his medallion. I had no idea why he had wanted to come to Earth so badly; it was nowhere near as beautiful and wondrous as Paradis. And had he not been here before? Having the distinct feeling that Nathaniel must have lied to me about having been to Earth before, I shifted uncomfortably. Most of my shivering having subsided by now, I gazed at him curiously. His father was a god, and yet he had never even been to Earth. I briefly wondered if Nathaniel was supposed to lie; after all, his father presided over the place where righteous souls lived for eternity after death. Nevertheless, I dared not ask him and disrupt his obvious delight at being on Earth.

"It's so beautiful …," he whispered, setting the egg down in the grass and wrapping his arms around his knees, staring up at the monolithic waterfall like a child that had just discovered the night sky.

"I didn't expect it to be so beautiful, after all I've heard about Lliam and the humans and all," he said in a small voice. "How can such a beautiful place harbour such evil?"

Surprised, I said, "Paradis is so much more beautiful than Earth, Nathaniel … And wasn't everyone telling me how dangerous Paradis is? Are the two places really so different?"

Nathaniel smiled bleakly, his white teeth blending in with his pale skin. In fact, I noticed, he looked even paler here than he had in Paradis, if possible. His black eyes stood out drastically from his white face, and he seemed almost to shimmer. I knew it came from the magic in his blood, that of Menel's son. Different from any other person I would ever encounter, he awed me just with his presence, this son of a god. It was exceptionally difficult for me to believe, and yet, there he sat, near enough to touch.

"No, I suppose not," Nathaniel admitted, his usual charismatic manner returning. His mouth curved into a cocky smile, and his black eyes narrowed with a knowing, entrancing glint. I knew why Victoria thought him incredible but counted myself fortunate that I did not think the same. I understood him too well to be so thoroughly entranced by him as she was, but I must admit that he did have some power over me.

I averted my gaze to the mysterious egg beside me. Its green streaks glimmered even more magnificently here, and in contrast, the grey parts appeared all the more dull and plain. I stroked one of the bands of emerald with a finger and marvelled at how smooth and flawless it felt, as if not a single grain of it was raised. "What kind of egg is this?" I asked Nathaniel.

He studied it for a moment and then answered, "It's a dragon egg."

I scoffed, "Dragons aren't real; everyone knows that."

Nathaniel shrugged nonchalantly, seeming strangely mild about my protest. His eyes wandered over the falling water for a time, a peaceful and happy expression on his pale face. "I know you thought I was lying when I said I've been to Earth before," he said, stretching out in the grass beside me and toying with a blade of it, "but I wasn't."

Surprised, I waited for him to continue. "I *have* been here before, but only twice. The first time ... I remember nothing whatsoever of it. I was very young." He stared down at the grass a few inches below his face. Silver raindrops began falling from the silver clouds on his medallion. "The second time, I was allowed to be here for only two days, and it was the two best days of my life ... but it was over six hundred years ago." He smiled ruefully. "It's been a very long time—too long—since I've been here."

"Six hundred years?" I asked with disbelief. "How old are you, Nathaniel?"

He laughed at my incredulity, white teeth flashing a smile. "I'm only twenty-seven, Elysia, don't worry. Time works differently in Paradis than it does here. For instance, you left Earth to go to Paradis only a little after dawn, and now after only an hour or two in Paradis, it's nearly sunset here. It can be opposite at other times; it's not something that is predictable. But then ... is anything really predictable?"

I had not noticed the lateness of the day here until Nathaniel pointed it out, and when I looked up at the sky, I saw that he was right. Pink, yellow, orange, and indigo streaked the fading blue of the sky, and the sun had already dropped behind the steep walls of the valley. "Wow ...," I said softly, realizing that this was the reason the grass and the forest behind us had looked so muted and dull. But even if it were sun-high, I reckoned that Meneltauré would still pale drastically in comparison to Paradis, what little I had seen of it.

Nathaniel murmured a soft word of agreement, flipping over onto his back to stare up at the sky. The scene on his necklace was that of silver waves washing soothingly onto a silver beach, and it made me drowsy just watching it. I looked at my own necklace and saw that it too had rhythmic waves rolling over a beach. Still amazed by the medallion around my neck, I touched the warm metal with a finger. What a wondrous gift it was.

"So," Nathaniel said then, "how did you like your sword?"

I looked up from my medallion at him calculatingly. "How did you know about that?"

He grinned devilishly at me, black eyes narrowing in amusement. "I was the one who told Lord Riyad to have it made. Actually, I let him know through my friend November, the one who gave me my medallion—she's a regular visitor to Meneltauré."

"*You* were the one who had it made?" I asked in disbelief.

Nathaniel grinned, looking very satisfied at my astonishment. "Yes. Did you like the falcons? I thought it was a nice touch, personally."

A little unsure of what to say, I said slowly, "Yes … I suppose I did."

Nathaniel's grin widened. "Good," he said, looking smug.

He suddenly sat up. "My father wants me home," Nathaniel explained gloomily, standing and looking sadly at the huge waterfall and its pool. I stood too, lifting the egg in my hands, and followed him back to the edge of the water.

Nathaniel looked at me for a moment undecidedly. Then he reached out and lifted up my medallion, examining it ruefully as its picture changed yet again. After a moment, he let it fall and said, "Keep that safe."

"I will," I promised, and he smiled at me again, this time genuinely, as one would smile at a friend. "Good luck. And don't worry so much about Lliam; he'll come around," Nathaniel said softly and then turned and dove into the pool.

PROOF

Collapsing on my bed back in my room, I stared with bleary eyes up at the mahogany ceiling. How could I really be sure that what just happened was not a dream? Could Nathaniel and Menel and Fray all have been nothing more than part of some wild reverie that my weary brain had thought up in the wee hours of the night?

I sighed and turned my head. The egg was lying next to me on the bed. I turned over to my side, propping my head up with my hand and leaning on my elbow, staring at it. I touched it, just to make sure it was really there. It was. And my necklace … I smiled and stroked the smooth metal, thinking again what an extraordinary gift it was. With these two very tangible objects with me, I had to admit my time in Paradis could not have been a dream.

I flopped onto my back, taking a deep breath and closing my eyes. I knew there would be no way I would be able to sleep tonight; it just was not possible. I needed something to occupy my thoughts and keep them from all that had just happened. A thought occurred to me: I could go back to the library and find that little book I had read earlier, the one that had led Victoria to believe I was developing the ability of Instinctive Speech. I snorted softly. Though I thought that idea absurd, I must admit that it intrigued me too. I rocked to my feet and left my room quietly, but not before shoving the egg under my bed out of sight.

ᔐ

I had forgotten I would have to cross the narrow bridge outside my quarters in order to get to the library, and with my all-too-recent experience underwater, going to and from Paradis, the massive, roaring waterfall under the bridge did nothing to reassure me. The memories of my two encounters with that huge waterfall earlier made me nervous about going over the water even on the bridge. I shuddered as I remembered the feeling of hundreds of gallons of rushing water crashing onto my back and pushing me down, down, down …

I let out my breath slowly and began walking across the bridge. I felt especially uneasy on it after sundown, and I purposely kept my eyes up and off the waterfall raging beneath me. Though I was hesitant as I crossed the bridge, to my relief, I got over it without incident. I hurriedly stepped onto the pathway that would take me to the library and rushed to the building as quickly as I could.

I opened the door and slipped inside. The library was eerily silent and dark, the only light coming from the small window across the room from the door. I walked quickly and breathlessly over to the darkest corner of the room, where the book had been earlier. Though my elven eyes see fairly well in the night hours, it seemed to me that tonight was even darker than usual.

I knelt down by the shelf and saw that the little book was still lying on the floor where I had left it earlier. I picked it up and brought it over to the table by the window where there was more light and sat down, flipping through the pages slowly. I was looking for any familiar words that I knew or could understand, but as I expected, all the words were and continued to be foreign to me. I found the page with the odd poem and stared at it for a long moment, but none of the words became comprehensible. Though I had expected nothing less, I must admit that I was a little disappointed.

I touched a finger to the page and stroked it over the words absentmindedly, wondering what language the words were from. *Latin*, I suddenly knew. Startled, I almost knocked the book off the table. How did I know that? I had heard of Latin and knew that it was a language from long ago, but I had never studied it nor seen it written nor heard it spoken. And even as I looked back at the book, I was able to understand some of the words from their similarity to English. I shook my head, trying to grasp this new concept. Surely this could not be real, and yet this was the second time it had happened. In fact, the first time, I was able to read an entire section of a poem before my understanding faded. I just closed my eyes and took a deep breath.

No one in Yaracina spoke Latin; that language had died out along with the Great Plague so many years ago along with many other ancient languages. Even though I now recognised the similarity of Latin to English, how had I been able to read the poem so easily before? I shook my head. *This is so bizarre*, I thought. *Maybe Victoria was right …* I shuddered at the thought. *Instinctive Speech? Really?… How* could *that be possible?* But then I remembered that only a few days ago, if anyone had told me that an afterworld existed and that there were people with wings there, I would have laughed to his face.

I looked down at my medallion and saw that it again had the engraving of a person lost in thought and seated on a rock. I smiled unconsciously. My gaze drifted back to the book as my thoughts wandered back to Paradis. "*Et magnus factus super insula secum trahit validis ventis unda alta et …*"

I started involuntarily translating the text I had just read, my brain buzzing, stumbling over some of the words, "And a … storm came … over … the island, bringing with it … mighty winds and … high waves … and …"

Suddenly, gasping, I realized what I had just done. How had I just understood that entire sentence? *This … is not happening to me! This is impossible!*

Suddenly I heard footsteps nearby, and I grabbed the book and ducked behind a bookshelf as quickly as I could. I clutched the book to my chest and watched through the slots of the shelves. But I heard nothing. Puzzled, I watched and listened for a long time, heart hammering. Whom had I heard?

"Isn't it a bit past your bedtime, my dear?"

I jumped and whirled around to see Lord Riyad behind me, hands clasped behind his back, eyes watching me with amusement.

"L-Lord Riyad …," I stammered, suddenly embarrassed to have been caught, "I was just looking at this book because—"

He raised his finger to his lips for silence and then smiled at me. "I know why you are here, Elysia," he said softly, "but do not speak so loudly for there is another here besides the two of us, one who I do not think would like to be disturbed."

He motioned to me to follow him, and I did slowly, still clutching the book. When I saw who was standing at the balcony beyond the window, my heart suddenly constricted in sorrow and compassion. I had never before seen Veryan looking so vulnerable.

⤳

Veryan stood silently on the balcony of the library, watching the pale stars emerge. He sighed and shifted his gaze downward to the trees. Their silent black shapes in the night offered him no comfort now.

What am I doing here? he thought once more, looking with loathing at the shimmering waterfalls across the valley, roaring far in the distance. He had never intended to stay this long; he wanted to go to Eshen, across the Atlantic Sea. It was much farther away from Ascension than Yaracina was, and Veryan wanted to be as far away from that hateful place as he possibly could. Detesting the memories that the name aroused, Veryan gripped the rail under his hand tighter until his knuckles were white.

What reason did he have to stay in Yaracina anyway? Pyralus was dead, Elysia was leaving, and now that he had left the troop, he truly had nowhere to go. *Why did Pyralus have to die?* he wondered yet again, silently grieving for his dead friend. *He was only nineteen* …. Angrily, Veryan punched the rail with all the strength he possessed, and the flaming pain it brought felt good somehow. So much better than the hurt inside his heart. Bowing his head and panting with the effort it took to keep his emotions stuffed inside, Veryan glared crossly at the softly swaying trees below. It was not fair.

And now Elysia was leaving him too. He had just found her again. He had been so worried that something had befallen her while she and Yaron were running … it had plagued him often in the days when he was alone in the dark cell in the tower's prison. Something had happened to Yaron—Elysia did not know what—but Veryan could not care less. *She's better off without him, anyway*, he thought bitterly. *He's so impulsive.* Shaking his head and feeling the customary guilt that came with Yaron's name, Veryan longed to know what Pyralus would have thought of all this.

Furious with himself for causing Pyralus's death and enraged with his circumstances, Veryan let out a hoarse cry full of anger, pain, and longing. Then he sank to his knees and let the tears fall, feeling numb and disbelieving inside. Hot tears coursed down his cheeks, but he was barely aware of them. Veryan closed his eyes and tilted his head back, facing the heavens above. He let out a shuddering sigh and thought helplessly, *What's the point? Why is this happening to me? What did I do?...*

He opened his eyes and looked up powerlessly at the cold stars twinkling in their distant halls above. He did not know where the words came from, nor did he know to whom he directed them, but he whispered, "If you're up there, if you're really there … give me proof. Prove to me that there is purpose to this life. Just … give me some sort of proof …" He bowed his head again, letting his tears fall once more. "Give me proof that there's a point to all this … Please …" He closed his eyes and began to weep, softly and desperately.

⁂

I instantly felt my heart go out to Veryan, and I felt a lump form in my throat as he began to weep, shedding tears that he thought no one saw.

I walked out from the shield of the wall and slowly toward Veryan. I faintly heard Lord Riyad whisper rebukingly, "Elysia!" But I did not heed his reprimand. I had to go to Veryan. I had to help.

I paused behind Veryan, unsure of what to do next. After a moment of hesitation, I said softly, "Veryan …"

He instantly scrambled to his feet and whirled around, anger blazing in his russet eyes. "What are you doing here?" he shouted, cheeks flushed with embarrassment.

Startled by the anger in his words, I stammered, "I-I couldn't sleep, and—"

"Go away, Elysia!" he yelled furiously. Tears continued to stream down his cheeks even as he said this. "No one asked you to come here and spy on me!"

Horrified, I protested, "I wasn't—"

But he cut me off, shouting, "Go *away*! Leave!" He pointed furiously at the doorway that I had come through, and with all the anger and pain in his eyes, he looked as if he wanted to hit me. "*Go!*"

Feeling my own eyes tear up at the obvious loathing in his eyes as he glowered at me, I turned, dropping the book on the floor, racing through the library without pausing to notice Lord Riyad, and fled out into the night. I kept on running down the path, across the bridge, until I was back to my quarters. I slammed the door shut behind me, trembling with the force of hurt emotions inside me, and stalked to my window. I glared up at the stars glimmering merrily in the black sky and took a deep breath of cool, crisp, night air. Once I had filled my lungs, I exhaled slowly and unsteadily, trying to calm myself and forget the absolute hatred on Veryan's face when he saw me behind him ...

But still the memory lingered.

⌇

I awoke deep into the night, my eyes searching around the room for the source of my disturbance, but they met nothing. Dappled silver light from the moon and the shadows of trees swayed over my bed, and the wind wafted through the branches quietly. Surely, there was no cause for my wakening.

And yet ... there was a stiff and evident tension in the air that crackled like lightning, noticeable from the moment I had opened my eyes. I shifted to the edge of my bed, pausing for a moment when I thought I heard a sound, and then slipped out from under the covers and walked silently to the window. I moved aside the sheer, silk curtain and peered out at the sleeping city, several hundred feet below my window. Nothing moved; no one stirred … there were no lights or any sounds, save that of the wind rustling through the foliage. So what had caused me to wake?

I let the curtain fall back into place and took a few steps back toward my bed, mulling over what had awakened me. I had not been having any dreams, that I recalled, nor had I heard anything unusual … I sank down on the edge of the bed, staring at the marble floor beneath my feet, looking for answers in it.

A moment later, my attention was drawn to the candle by my bedside, its pale halo of light filling the darkness beside my bed with gentle, luminous fingers. I stared into its small flame for a while, feeling some sort of strange identification with the little fire: I, too, was like a tiny, wavering flame, threatened by the looming darkness around me but fighting not to go out as I so easily could by one fatal breath of air.

Uneasy with the foreshadowing resemblance to myself that the little candle represented and longing to make myself feel better, I went to the nightstand and pulled out another candle, striking the match and lighting the second one, setting it beside my little candle. *Now I'm not alone anymore*, I thought with a wry smile.

I suddenly stiffened as I felt Lliam's mind brush against mine. He did not speak, but his mind radiated emotions of sorrow, remorse, and grief. I froze, all of the familiar feelings of betrayal, anger, and hurt rising to the forefront of my mind once more. Because of him, Veryan had stayed behind, instead of escaping with us, to divert the soldiers from chasing us … Because of him, Veryan had suffered in the tower at Gornhelm's hand for days … Because of him, I was alone now … Because of him … I had my freedom. Closing my eyes, I reluctantly opened my mind and touched Lliam's. He recoiled for a moment, and I sensed guilt stemming from his thoughts.

Lliam …, I said gently, trying not to let him hear the uncertainty in my voice, *Why haven't you talked to me before now?*

His answer was long in coming. Finally, he admitted, *I ... didn't think you would want to talk to me, after ... what happened at the tower.* He waited tensely for my reply.

What he said was true, I realized. But, despite his betrayal, I found I had been longing to speak with him again; I had missed him in the long days we had been apart. I spoke timidly, saying, *You're right ... but I've missed you all the same.*

He replied gingerly, *And I you ...*

Then I asked Lliam, *Why do I feel as if something's about to happen? It woke me not long ago, but now I find that there is nothing amiss here.* I got up and walked back to the window, pushing aside the curtain once more.

Lliam was silent for an indecisive moment. I sensed he was debating about what he would say. Eventually, he revealed, *Those feelings come from me, young falcon. I'm sorry they woke you; I've been ... restless this night, and I suppose my feelings were strong enough that they touched you because of our bond.*

Oh? ... What's wrong?

Lliam gave a weary mental sigh, and I gathered emotions of sorrow, exhaustion, and loathing from it. *Young falcon ...,* he began softly. Lliam was silent for a long while. I grew drowsy as I waited and leaned against the window's frame tiredly. After what seemed half an hour, Lliam continued, *Do you trust me, Elysia?*

Surprised at his question, I answered hesitantly, *Well ... you got us out of the tower, didn't you?*

Then do you trust me enough to do as I tell you now?

Bewildered and doubtful, I asked, *What do you mean, Lliam? Tell me plainly what you're talking about.*

He faltered and then went on to say: *There is another under Zoser's control, like me. He is called Roman.* His voice took on an edge of bitterness. *Roman and a contingent of two thousand men are at the top of the cliffs that drop down to this valley, as I tell you this. They are going to set fire to the city, slaughter everyone in Meneltauré—including the women and children—and burn it to the ground.*

I let out a gasp and clapped my hand over my mouth. I looked out the window up to the high cliffs that shot up from the valley's floor, creating two impossibly steep walls on either side of the city, which was nestled at the vale's floor. I strained my eyes to see the tops of the cliffs, but in the darkness, they were far enough away that I was unable to make out anything. *But,* I asked, my heart drumming in my chest, *Why?*

Lliam sighed. *Zoser is upset with Lord Riyad's refusal to cooperate with him. So … he's going to destroy the city.*

Fighting back the panic rising in my chest, I asked, *So, then, why did you tell* me? *What am I supposed to do, Lliam?*

I told you because I want you to get out of here! Go to the stables, Elysia. I will meet you there—

You're here? I gasped.

Impatiently, Lliam agreed and then instructed me, *Get what you need and leave immediately. Don't worry about anything or anyone else … and hurry!*

I hesitated. *But, Lliam, what about Veryan? And Victoria and Lord Riyad—*

They'll be fine, Elysia, I promise you.

How do you know? I almost shouted, and Lliam winced mentally before answering, *Do you trust me, young falcon?*

I did not answer immediately. *Do I?* I asked myself, feeling tortured inside. Lliam had given me very valuable information, and I knew that if I did hurry, I could possibly get Veryan, Victoria, and Lord Riyad to safety as well. But … Lliam had said they would be okay … I shook my head. How did he know? I hesitated again, thinking—

Elysia! Lliam snapped angrily. *I promise you, your friends* will *survive! None of Roman's men will harm them, I swear it. Just please, leave* now! *You don't have much time.*

Lliam … I whined, dread and indecision filling my mind. *I can't just leave them—*

Elysia, yes, you can. Please *do this. You* are the most important *person here; you* need to escape first and foremost. *Do you hear me?*

He sounded desperate and truly concerned for me, so I, hardly believing I was saying it, agreed, *Very well. If you* swear *Veryan and the rest won't be harmed.*

Do you trust me?

I paused yet again, weighing my options, and then I finally replied, *Yes.*

Then come.

TRUST

C arefully, I lowered the egg into my satchel, tucking it into the bottom of the bag, and then eyed it disapprovingly because the odd shape of the egg made the satchel lumpy. I rotated it several ways, but discovered that nothing I could do would make it less noticeable, so I slung the bag over my shoulder. I had traded in my nightclothes for a simple blue dress I had found in the closet, knowing I could not go traipsing around in a nightdress.

I buckled my sword and my dagger to my belt next. Then I took a dark blue cloak from one of the racks of the closet, and put it on slowly, knowing that this was stealing but thinking that neither Lord Riyad or Victoria would mind later if they knew it had saved my life. I needed the cover of its dark colour so that I would not be seen. I ran my fingers over the dagger at my hip, making sure it was there and then surveyed the room for anything else I might have forgotten. My eyes found nothing, so I silently went to the door and opened it, peering out to see if the way was clear.

When certain that it was safe, I closed the wooden door behind me and then walked swiftly and noiselessly across the narrow bridge, not even aware of the rushing waterfall this time. After hurrying down endless stairways and across countless bridges, I came to the end of the stairway, hundreds of feet below in the city. All the while, I forced myself not to think about Veryan and the others I was leaving behind while I was about to escape. As I looked back in the direction from which I had come, I could see one single torch waving in the breeze on the far side of the cliff. I instinctively turned to see another torch above on my side of the cliff. Lliam had been right. I paused, my hand on the golden rail, and said to Lliam, suddenly hyperventilating, *I can't do this. I can't leave all these people behind to die while I get to escape this tragedy. It's not right, nor is it fair ... I can't do this.*

I started to turn back, but Lliam told me savagely, *Elysia, you may not think yourself important, but what about the favour you carry for Lord Riyad? Did you not tell his daughter that you would get it to Rielture safely?*

Yes, I answered haltingly.

Then you must do this for him and Victoria—and everyone. That egg is vital to you elves, if you intend to have any chance at all of striking back at Zoser! As one of my favourite writers said, 'It's just the matter of taking advantage of our chances and making things happen'! Please, Elysia ... don't throw this chance away, he said pleadingly.

Remembering what Menel had said about this egg having much to do with Lliam and me, I asked him suspiciously, *Why should it matter to you if the elves have their chance? You serve Zoser; you are his personal assassin. Why should any of our lives be of importance to you, Lliam?*

A good question, he admitted, *but I have my reasons. I'll not share them with you now, but I promise you, young falcon, one day I will. Now please—time grows short. The stables are not far off. Go, Elysia.*

I faltered for a long moment, trapped in my indecision. Surely this was not the right course of action. *There must be another way,* I thought desperately, *some way they can all be saved ... Oh, Lliam, I can't do this.* I sank down on the last step, leaning against the rail heavily. Sweat dampened my forehead, and my heart pounded painfully in my chest as I searched frantically for another option that could save more lives.

I jumped back with a muffled cry as a house not far away suddenly exploded in a burst of billowing fire and smoke. I could feel the smouldering heat on my face, and the fiery blast momentarily blinded me. I heard the dull creaking of timbers and splintering of wood as the house toppled to the ground and continued to fan the ravenous flames sent down by the soldiers from the cliffs.

I scrambled back against the rail again as another house, this one closer to me, caught on fire from the first explosion's flames and was instantly engulfed. The thatched roofs and wooded walls succumbed without any hope to the fire's angry and famished appetite. The heat waves chugged across the streets, blasting me in the face when it reached the stairway, and I coughed hard to get the smoke out of my lungs. I heard the first screams, loud and confused, begin to sound in the streets, but I could not move. I was paralysed, staring with empty eyes into the ravishing fire that swallowed the two houses in only an instant ... and the people inside ...

"Elysia!" And then there was Lliam, running down the street toward me. He reached me in only a second and took my arm, tugging me to my feet. I automatically flinched away; the last time I had seen him face-to-face was just before we had plunged into the tunnel underneath the tower ... before I had lost Yaron and Veryan. I was not prepared for this. He was a stranger to me.

"What are you doing?" he hissed. "Run! You're lucky you haven't been blown to bits yet!" With that, he shoved me hard in the back, in the direction of the stables. My legs refused to work for a moment, and then my brain had control again, and I ran, Lliam by my side. As we sprinted down the street, I was uncomfortably aware of him ... of how little I knew about him ... of how much he had not told me. And yet, here he was, a servant of the enemy and their leader's personal assassin, helping me escape from what would be one of his races' victories. *Why?* I wondered for the thousandth time.

The ground suddenly rocked beneath our feet, pitching us forward. A fantastic blast of roiling fire and smoke erupted in the house we had just run past, and the searing heat rippled over my face. I threw up my arm to protect my eyes from the blinding flash of light.

"Come on!" Lliam growled, catching me by the arm and pulling me to my feet. I heard him mutter something about how idiotic the soldiers were, but I did not catch any more after that.

The stables were not far away, but with all the confused and frantic people running through the streets, looking desperately for shelter from the raining fire, it slowed us down considerably. Lliam kept a firm and almost painful grip on my arm, hauling me through the panicked crowd and towards the stables.

Suddenly, up ahead, I saw something that nearly made my heart stop. The first of the human soldiers had reached the city, and they were armed with crossbows, swords, spears, and axes. They were cleaving a bloody path through the crowded streets, their stone-like faces impassive and unaffected by the foul slaughter they were committing. While I knew that elves should be far superior to these large, slow humans, it did not appear to be so, for every elf that a human soldier came across fell by one of their blood-spattered weapons. Women, men, and children alike; none passed before the humans and lived. Fire and smoke painted a foul backdrop against the sky, and the billowing clouds of poisonous fumes blotted out the twinkling stars that I had watched from my window only a few hours earlier.

I gasped as Lliam suddenly yanked my arm so hard that I fell forward into him. We both toppled to the ground as an ear-shattering blast rang out, consuming another house and sending a massive wave of sulphurous heat over us. I coughed as hard as I could, trying to get the fumes out of my system. As soon as the explosion subsided, Lliam hauled me behind a house across the street and for a long, slow second, Lliam and I sat behind the cover of the house, panting and attempting to suck in clean air instead of the nauseous vapours that were creeping over the city. Another explosion sounded not far off.

I glanced at Lliam and saw that a small trickle of blood was rolling down his temple. He gave me a grim, half-hearted smile, his blue-grey eyes impassive, and then he stood. I did the same, rubbing my side, which was sore from where I had landed on the ground.

He looked out at the chaotic streets for a moment and then said to me, "The stables are just a few yards away. Once we get there, find tack for the first horse you see, get on it, and ride hard." His eyes bored into me earnestly. "You mustn't stop for *anything*, Elysia. You ride for the mountain pass to Rielture. As you ride away from Meneltauré, the mountains will be south of here, on your right. The pass is hard to find, but you can do it." He paused, exhaling shakily, wiping the blood off his forehead, and then questioned remorsefully, "Are you angry with me?"

"For what?"

"Everything. Everything you think I've done to you ... sending the men after you once you escaped the tower? Elysia, I wasn't the one who did that! I promise you it wasn't—"

"What?" I asked, not sure I was hearing him correctly. Who else would it have been, if not he? I saw him; I heard his thoughts in my head! How could he truly expect me to believe that it was not he who had chased after us?

Lliam sighed heavily, raking his fingers through his hair, looking hesitant at going on, but I eyed him suspiciously long enough that he decided to continue. "It was Roman, Elysia, who chased after you and the boys at the tower, not I."

I blinked in incomprehension. Roman? "But ... it looked just like *you*, Lliam ...," I said slowly.

"I know, but ..." He sighed again, avoiding my eyes. "It *wasn't*. Roman's my brother, Elysia; he's my twin. We're identical."

My eyes flew wide in shocked disbelief.

"He came to the tower that night, and ... well, he figured out what had happened when I came back so late. He was the one who sent the scout to look for you, and he was the one who took my men to recapture you. But you couldn't tell it was Roman because we look exactly alike ..." Lliam still avoided my eyes, as if ashamed that he was admitting this to me.

Stunned by the implications of this—Lliam had a twin brother!— I was silent, just trying to process, trying to understand ... a twin brother. I certainly never would have guessed that ... Why had he not told me before now? Why had he let me think it was he all this time, he who had betrayed me? And if it had been Roman who had come after us, how had he been able to say something in my mind as Lliam was able to? We did not have any connection. Putting a hand to my aching head, I struggled to take all of this in.

"I didn't tell you because I was afraid you would be angry at me. And as for Roman speaking to you, he did it using his and my connection; all he had to do was find our link and latch on to it," he said softly, replying directly to my tangled thoughts.

A heavy boom and more wailing screams sounded in the distance, but I barely heard them, so wrapped up was I in this newest revelation of Lliam's. My brow furrowed as he admitted that he thought I would have been angry at him, however. "Why would I have been angry at you for that, Lliam?" I demanded. That did not make sense.

Lliam shrugged mildly, looking embarrassed. He did not reply for a moment, giving me time to try to process it all. When he did speak, he said quietly, "You never know how people will respond to things like this, Elysia. I ... didn't want to risk it. I'm sorry I didn't tell you, it's just ... I couldn't. Not then, anyway. I was too scared of what you would say. Don't hate me, please, Ely—"

"Hate you?" I looked up at him carefully, into his light, unfathomable eyes, and told him sincerely, "Lliam, I don't hate you for anything. How could I? You're a part of me now ... And no matter what you do or say, I will never hate you." And as I said it, I knew, without a shadow of a doubt, it was true.

He looked away for a moment, as if overwhelmed, and then gazed back at me resolutely. "Come," he said and darted back into the streets.

I followed him without question, keeping close to him as we sped through the frenzied streets. I resisted the urge to scream as I tripped over the body of a young child, barely two years old from his appearance. His sightless eyes stared up at me, his features expressionless in the face of death itself. Shocked and numb, I barely felt Lliam take my arm again. Now only pure will kept my legs moving, nothing more.

The stables came into view, and Lliam pulled me to an immediate stop. They were already on fire, burning swiftly and at a dangerous rate. Dying screams of horses trapped inside resounded in the air around the collapsing building. "Lliam! What do we—"

He ignored me and called out to a human soldier riding past on what looked to be an elven horse, not one of the monstrous, unnatural ones I usually saw humans straddling. The man, a few years older than Lliam, instantly noticed him and swung down from the horse. It was a speckled grey stallion with a frosty, silvery mane and eyes wide open in fright. He tugged at the reins, but the human held them tightly in his fist.

"Jakob, can you give her the horse?" Lliam asked, his eyes darting to the side as part of the palace burst into flames above us.

Jakob glanced at me briefly and then once more. He protested, "She's an elf—"

"I know that!" Lliam snapped, "Give it to her, please! And I swear, if you tell anyone about her, I will kill you and whoever is unfortunate enough to hear your words." He spoke with such conviction that it was impossible to doubt his words. And Jakob did not. He grudgingly handed the stallion's reins to me and then said to Lliam, "You have my word that no one will hear of her from my mouth." His black eyes met mine for a moment, and he sneered at me.

Angrily, Lliam shoved Jakob on in the direction of the palace, saying something in a rough, coarse language that I did not know, but its meaning was clear. Jakob cast one more demeaning look at me over his shoulder.

Lliam took my satchel and securely tied it with several knots to the saddle of the stallion, whose frantic pacing made it difficult. The horse's ears pointed ahead, and his eyes took in everything around him. Every explosion, no matter how far away, made the frightened horse rear up and back away, making it hard to hold the reins. I put a gentle hand on the stallion's warm neck, but it did little to calm him.

Lliam came around the horse to me and said in a low voice, "This is Thibilon. He'll keep you safe, and he's swift." He glanced for a split second at some human soldiers running past, and then back at me. "Go now, young falcon. Ride hard and don't look back." And with that, he motioned for me to mount Thibilon.

I looked at the horse reluctantly, wishing with all my heart that I knew Veryan and Victoria were safe. I could not bear it if they were harmed or killed because of my selfishness in taking Lliam's offer to save myself. Thibilon paced back and forth with a skittish air about him, and lashed his tail with anxious unease. I swung up on the stallion slowly and then looked back down at Lliam.

Screams still echoed around me, and I could hear the creaking of burning timbers as they were beginning to collapse under the fire's blazing hunger. The heat of the countless fires was intensifying throughout the devastated city. As I gazed down the street, I saw a human soldier stop to shove his spear into an elven father as he was attempting to lead his fleeing family to safety. He then beheaded one of the small children and continued down the street, leaving the mother wailing with grief that was heart wrenching to hear. She gathered the limp, bloodstained body of her child and fell in a heap beside her dead husband, sobs shaking her shoulders. Numb, I could only gape at her.

"Elysia." Lliam's warning word tore my gaze from the vicious scene of death I had just witnessed and back to him. His eyes were admonishing, and I knew from that look that it was time for me to go.

"What about you?" I murmured.

Lliam's face became a cynical mask void of emotion. "What about me?"

"Will you be all right?"

"I'll be fine, Elysia. Just go."

I held his gaze for a long moment, until he dropped his eyes. "I don't believe you," I whispered.

His eyes lifted back to mine. "Do you trust me?" he asked yet again.

"Yes." I answered slowly, and this time I knew that my word was true. I did trust him. He had proven that to me now.

"Then we will meet again, Elysia. Now go." His gaze strayed to the side as another section of the palace caught fire, sending fiery clouds of smoke spewing into the sky and blotting out the oxbow moon with the blackened haze.

Lliam looked back to me for an instant and then slapped the horse's flanks, sending him skipping forward with surprise as he bolted ahead through the streets. Leaning low over Thibilon's neck because I could not bear to see the utter destruction of the once idyllic Meneltauré, I let hot tears fall from my eyes. *Why have they done this? What have we done to deserve this terrible massacre?* Thibilon rode past a flaming house that was beginning to collapse on itself, and from it, I could clearly hear a blood-curdling scream that made shivers run down my spine. There was someone still inside. I closed my eyes and felt more tears streaming down my cheek. *How could this have happened? … How could we have been so blind?*

Thibilon darted through the streets with alarming speed, anxious to be away from the flaming buildings and frightening explosions. I held the reins with all my strength, hoping desperately that none of the homes we were riding past would suddenly explode, for that would surely kill both of us. People ran frantically out of the way, human and elves alike, as Thibilon thundered down the street, dodging the network of falling timbers, burned rubble, and discarded weapons that had missed their mark. I crouched forward on the stallion's back as if in a trance, not wanting to hear the dying screams of people whose lives were being viciously ended by the cruel strokes of the stone-faced, raven-haired humans nor the slow, dull groaning of timbers and walls that were being engulfed by the ravenous, poisonous flames nor the clashing of weapons nor the tearing and burning of flesh.

A massive, billowing cloud of fire erupted from the house beside us, and Thibilon reared, throwing me to the ground. I rolled away as swiftly as I could as the horse crashed to the ground beside me, squealing with a grating pitch in fear. Oily plumes of orangish-black smoke pumped into the sky and filled the air around us with noxious fumes, making my lungs burn and my eyes water.

I coughed hard, and then staggered back to Thibilon, who had managed to get back on his feet, terrified but uninjured. I grabbed his reins and climbed back on him, urging the horse on towards the city's exit. It did not take much prodding for the stallion to bolt off once more.

We rode to the path that led out of Meneltauré, canopied by swaying trees that threatened to fall victim to the roiling flames. I spurred Thibilon on, and he eagerly obeyed, his hooves flying over the well-worn path. The road eventually led to the end of the valley and out Meneltauré. The high cliffs to the right of us would give way to mountains and curve to the south, joining the peaks that contained the mountain pass to Rielture.

I did not stop Thibilon until we were well away from Meneltauré, going at the greatest speed the horse could give me, never looking back. I had to get away from the destruction, the suffering, the death, the fate of Meneltauré tonight …

FIRES

R eining Thibilon to a stop, I turned back for one last look at
Meneltauré. We were standing on top of a low shelf that protruded from one of the cliffs, and since the path that led from the city
ascended from the valley, our position provided me with an unparal-
leled view of the burning city. It was barely recognisable because of
the smouldering rubble and collapsed dwellings, together with the
toxic haze, which blanketed the entire valley. I could still see what
remained of the palace from our perch, and it was in total disrepair.
Every now and then, another random explosion occurred sending
a fiery blast into the night sky. The trees and vegetation around the
city were ablaze with fire, their leaves and branches turning white
and crumpling into a soft, grey ash as the fire devoured them. All
the massive waterfalls of the city had been helpless to save it, and the
air was heavy with great billowing clouds of steam, smoke, and fire.

It was such a beautiful city, I thought with bitter remorse, feeling
intensely sad at the destruction of a place I had known for less than
four days. Why did this have to happen? And, even up here, I could
hear the dying screams of men, women, and children. The sound
frightened me, and I felt a sudden, powerful fear bloom inside me,
unlike any I had ever experienced before. It struck me for the first
time then how big the world was and how little I really knew of it. I

paused as fearful tears streamed down my face, unsure of what was going to happen next. If the world really was so big and harsh, what chance did I have against it, alone and vulnerable and naïve as I was?

Thibilon jerked his head, eager to be off. I tore my tearful eyes away from the city and looked behind me. I could see where the cliffs came to an end to the south and joined with the Altai Mountains, where lay the mountain pass that would lead me to Rielture. I took the horse's bridle and said to him softly, gazing out at the forest and mountains before us, "No, Thibilon. That journey is for tomorrow. Now … we must try to rest, and at sunrise, we will brave what lies before us."

With the fiery cloud of the burning city still visible in the distance, I had a difficult time focusing on getting Thibilon unsaddled and myself bedded down for the night. I imagined that it would take several days for the fires to burn out completely, and the thought once again scared me. What would all those people do in the meantime? How would Lord Riyad reassure them? How would he maintain order in the city? Would the humans continue to kill the elves, even after the last fire bombs had burned out? Feeling burdened with these heavy, unanswered questions, I put one hand on my forehead and one on my hip, tilting my head back to stare at the smoke-smeared sky.

After a while of intense contemplation, I roused myself and searched around for some small rocks to using for starting the fire. Seeing as there were no sticks up on the ledge, I half-walked, half-slid down the slope that led to the ground from the rock shelf. I picked up a few long sticks, breaking them in half, and then returned to the ledge and made a small fire. Thibilon snorted and moved away from it, folding his legs underneath him and lying down a few feet from the fire, his eyes wide at the sight of it. His ears twitched nervously. He had endured a frightening few hours and had trouble settling down, as I was sure I would too.

Once the fire flickered into existence, I sat down next to it and held out my hands over its warmth and the protection of its flames against any creatures that might be lurking nearby through the night.

How strange it was to think that, not a few hours ago, a fire very much like this had consumed the lives and homes of thousands in Meneltauré, and how very fortunate I was to be here, alive ... *Thanks to you, Lliam*, I said to him gratefully.

But he did not answer me.

Feeling terribly alone and longing to feel his comforting presence, I lay down beside the fire, staring out at the dark landscape beyond my shelf as a way of distracting myself from the agony of the night's events.

My sleep was fitful that night, to say the least. I had nightmares of myself and Lliam trapped inside one of the burning houses. It seemed so real that I could literally feel the heat scorching my flesh, I could smell the noxious fumes and smoke in my nose, I could see nothing but orange flames greedily eating our flesh. I woke up sobbing uncontrollably and did not go back to sleep, staying awake until the morning sky appeared, and it came with pale, cold sunlight and grey tones, as if cloaked in colourless clothes of mourning.

ॐ

Thibilon was grazing nearby, and in the daylight, I could see water trickling from the cliff into a small pool at the base. I led the horse over to drink before saddling him for our journey. I then rode him along the base of the diminishing cliff faces, and for a while, they cast us in their cool shadows. Still in seeming mourning, the incredibly dark, nearly black colour of the sky promised a drenching rain.

I gazed out to my left as we rode. The waving green grasses, pale in the feeble light, swayed under a stifling, humid breeze with rippling motions. Many miles away, a line of drab, brownish-grey rocks across the grassland ascended quite gradually in the ocean of green grass as the terrain led up from Meneltauré. But no more. The city was burnt to the ground, and only ashes remained. The once majestic trees surrounding the city were now blackened and dead, never to bear fruit or change their colours with the seasons again. And as for the people ... I doubted that few beside myself had survived. Veryan or Victoria or any of them ... I refused to let myself think about it, making myself, instead, focus on the swishing grasses that bowed in waves behind us as Thibilon trampled over them. But even so, a few scared tears rolled down my cheeks.

~

Rain began to pour down on us, suddenly and forcefully. The accompanying wind, which had quickly grown in intensity, whipped my hair and cloak fiercely, and Thibilon's mane snapped back and forth violently. I shielded my eyes with my hand and squinted, trying to see ahead, but unable to distinguish anything in the lashing rain and darkness.

I sighed heavily and urged Thibilon on. *We have to get out of this rain, but I can't see* anything. *We could be going the wrong way; we could be walking right into a mountain, and I wouldn't know it.* But Thibilon put his head down and continued on as best he could in the driving wind and rain. I pulled my cloak up around me to shield myself, though I was already thoroughly drenched. We proceeded on for a little while, but soon we could go no further. Thibilon was worn out, and so was I. I looked around desperately for a place that would provide us some cover from the rain. Nothing but darkness met my eyes.

Suddenly lightning flashed over the sky, lighting up the world. In that brief moment, I saw a mountainous peak looming above us just ahead. It was dark, ominous, and shadowy, but there would be shelter at the mountain's base—shelter that, as long as the rains plummeted down on the plains, would give Thibilon and me protection from the storm and a place to rest.

I tapped my heels gently on Thibilon's side, and he started forward, head bowed and ears flat against his head from the driving force of the wind. I drew a corner of my cloak over my face, trying to protect my eyes and nose from the bite of the autumn wind, which made my eyes water.

Winter was fast approaching, and so was the customary snow and ice that came with it. Aseamir never received more than a foot of snow during the winter season, but I knew that up here in the mountains, that measurement was more than doubled on any given winter day. Even now, looking up for a moment, I could see little white flecks of snow mixed in with the falling rain.

Impervious to cold weather, we elves felt only a slight chill in the strong, arctic winds. This immunity to the bitterly cold season that iced over our continent was yet another unforeseen result of Yara's antidote to the plague that had wiped out so many of our ancient world. No one had yet understood how the remedy had changed our bodies in so many ways, but clearly, modifications were supernatural. It was said that even Yara herself did not understand the alterations made, only that it was some undeserved gift bestowed by Menel.

We reached the mountain a few arduous minutes later, and I hurriedly dismounted and searched the rough surface with my hands for a recess in the rock or small cave where we could spend the night. My hands moved along the stone until I suddenly fell forward into a wide-open space. I felt dry, crunchy dirt under my fingers, and while the air inside was cool, it was warmer than the air outside in the frigid storm. With a gasp of relief, I got up and led Thibilon inside. The stallion shook off, showering me and the area around him. He walked slowly over to the back of the cave, which was about twelve feet into the mountain. As soon as I had unsaddled him, he lay down, glad to be out of the weather.

I sat down wearily beside him, and pulled the hood off my head. It was soaked, just like me. The bottom of my dress was muddy and singed from the fires of Meneltauré. I lay, panting, against Thibilon's side. My heart was pounding, and I was almost limp with relief that we had found a place to take refuge from the storm.

I took my satchel from my shoulder and rummaged through it, looking for dry food. There was none. What little food I had was spoiled. The waterskin had somehow gotten a hole in it, and all the water had leaked out. I had nothing to eat or drink and neither did Thibilon. It was nearly eighty miles to Rielture, and while I could last about ten days without food, and nearly eight without water, I was not sure if I would be able to make it to the city in time, as I would have nothing with which to hunt when my body required nourishment.

Frustrated to tears, I slumped to the ground and leaned back against the cave wall, feeling the sharp points of the stone poke against my shoulder blades. Tears flowed from my eyes, and I thought crossly,

Why? Why did I have to be chosen to take this stupid egg to Rielture? I let my head fall back against the stone behind me and closed my eyes, letting out a long, tense breath. My angry tears stopped a long while later, my irritation at the situation cooled by the sound of the now gently falling rain and Thibilon's loud panting. Where was Lliam when I needed him? Was he even still alive …?

After a while, I opened my eyes and looked out from the small cave. It was still very dark outside, and a chilly wind blew in a few, curling tendrils of air, brushing against my face before cycling back out into the storm.

Then, I pulled my thoroughly soaked blanket from my satchel, laid it down on the dirt floor of the cave, and tried to sleep. Many long, uncomfortable hours passed before sleep found me that night. I dreamed again of the burning house, but this time, Lliam was not there, and I was left alone to burn in the hut.

ॐ

I woke early and lay atop my small blanket for a long time, staring up at the roof of the cave. Then I unwillingly stood and walked to the edge of the cave and leaned against it, feeling the warm, damp air on my face. The earth smelled wet and fresh, as it always did after a rain. There were still some dark storm clouds off in the distance, promising more rain, but it was, as of yet, a long way off.

I sighed and went back into the cave. Thibilon snorted and got to his feet, shaking his silvery mane. He nuzzled my shoulder as I gathered my things up in my arms. For a moment, I paused and leaned against his warm side. I felt as if a heavy foreboding had been laid on my heart, along with a profound exhaustion unlike any I had ever known before. I tried to find Lliam's mind, hoping to speak with him once more, but I could not contact him. I sighed, feeling isolated and lonely.

I saddled Thibilon, making sure to tie my pack back to the saddle securely, and then I buckled my sword belt around my waist, slung my satchel over my shoulder, and mounted. Thibilon snorted and turned to face the entrance of the cave. He waited for my command,

and when I gave it, he walked out and trotted along the mountain's grey base.

An occasional rock broke the flow of brown grasses, and a few white flowers dotted the plain to our left. While the sky remained overcast, a few shafts of sunlight still illuminated the golden grasses in places along the way. Pearly blooms that were produced from last night's rain stood out in stark contrast to the vast, tan expanse.

Every once in a while, we would pass a few wild horses grazing on the ripe stalks of the grass. They would look up and stare at us curiously and then continue eating. I noticed Thibilon eyeing them longingly. I smiled and patted his side. "Don't worry, Thibilon," I said. "Once we get to Rielture, you can rest for a long time with other horses." He shook his frosty mane and snorted but moved ahead dutifully.

Later, we stopped for a rest. I dismounted and unsaddled Thibilon, letting him graze as I sat on a wide, flat rock near the mountain's base. The wild horses we had seen earlier were still in sight, and Thibilon occasionally glanced up at them, ears pricked. Along with Thibilon, I watched them in admiration for a moment, eyeing how their powerful muscles rippled beneath their glossy coats. I had loved horses since I was a young girl and so had Lillian. Malitha had never cared for them; their size and potentially deadly hooves intimidated her so greatly that she feared riding them. I thought them fierce and fine, beautiful and swift, and it thrilled me to be on a galloping horse's back.

I turned my attention to what was important now: food. Without my bow and quiver, I now had only my dagger to hunt with. I sighed ruefully. I was quite good at throwing my dagger and hitting the painted target on a tree, but I had no idea how I would fare with attempting to kill a moving animal. I would soon find out.

But it seemed the animals in this area were scarce. I walked for a long time without seeing anything other than the wild horses and sparrows. Although I walked a long way down the length of the mountains' baseline, I found nothing to hunt. Disheartened, I turned back toward where I had set up my little camp. The wind blew softly through the high grass, and the horses could be seen romping playfully through the fields. I sat down wearily in the tan grasses, running my fingers over the tips of the stalks.

I wondered yet again who Lliam was and why he was hiding himself from me. Surely, of the all people he knew, he could trust *me* … He had asked me to trust him so many times now, so why could he not trust me with this knowledge? I mused over the situation for another few minutes, staring out at the plains without seeing them. I snapped a few seed stalks in my fingers, needing to vent my frustration on something.

Suddenly a tawny figure darted in front of me, and I caught a glimpse of a white tail flashing. Startled, I watched the little deer bound past me. It could not have been more than a few months old, certainly not yet a year.

I just stared at it dumbly for a moment before remembering that I was going to need food, and fumbling for my dagger, I aimed and quickly threw it at the sprinting deer. I was off by nearly three feet. The deer bounded on for a few more feet and then swerved and disappeared into the side of the mountain, probably through some small passage that led deeper into the mountains. My dagger landed in the tall grass, the sun glinting off its blade.

Sighing, I trudged over, picked it up, and slid it back into its sheath with disappointment. *Now what am I supposed to do for food?* I wondered anxiously.

I debated over what to do for a moment, and then I slowly jogged over where I had seen the deer disappear into the mountain and discovered a path. Roughly worn and extremely narrow, it looked as though the only users of it were animals and possibly a few rare travellers that had stumbled upon it by accident. Lliam had told me to take the mountain pass to Rielture, but this little path was so small and sheltered that I almost doubted this was the pass he was talking about. But as I debated over it for some time, I knew that I had found no other path and would just have to trust that Lliam knew what he was talking about it.

There was only one problem, however: It was too narrow for a horse. I would have to leave Thibilon behind. That realization crashed down on me. *I can't make it all the way to Rielture with no horse! After making it through the mountains, there'll still be nearly sixty miles to go.* That realization made me question even more taking this path, but in the end, I knew that I would have to go without the stallion if I was going to make it through the mountains. *He'll be happier here anyway,* I told myself grudgingly. *Besides, it's not as if I can't walk all that way. It's just that I don't* want *to.*

I grunted mournfully and shifted my dagger to the other hand, contemplating what was to happen next in my journey. I knew that the path through the mountain chain would be roughly twenty miles from here to the other side; I could easily walk that in a few days, barring any unforeseen obstacles and problems.

So I made my way back to the camp and called Thibilon to me. The stallion twitched his ears, looking at me decisively, and then slowly came forward. I took hold of his bridle and fondly stroked his neck, saying, "You can't come, Thibilon. The mountain pass is too narrow for a horse; I'm going to have to leave you here." The stallion looked back at me with gentle brown eyes, and I knew he understood. Then I slipped his leather bridle off and let him go. He looked at me expectantly for a moment and then slowly began ambling off towards the wild horses in the distance. I watched him for a long time, wishing fervently that he could have come with me. I would have much rather ridden than walked, and he was good company. Now I felt more alone than ever.

Turning my gaze back to the mountains, I saw the jagged peaks rising like the broken teeth of some ancient dragon into the threatening sky, painting the world with an image of harsh brutality. Depressed and lonely, I sank down onto a large, flat stone.

I decided that it would be better to wait until tomorrow to start on the path and continued to hunt for food for a while. In the end, I caught a young rabbit; however, it was so small that it hardly made much of a meal. But it was better than nothing.

WOLVES

The next morning was foggy. Dark clouds loomed overhead and darkened my spirits. But, despite my melancholy, I forced myself to get up, even though I would rather have slept longer. I sighed and put a hand on my ribs, beginning to feel a slight empty feeling inside. I needed to find some food in preparation for my trip to Rielture since game might be hard to come by or kill farther in the mountains.

I slung my satchel over my shoulder, buckled my sword on my belt, and walked towards the pass. A light mist dampened my skin as I came closer to it, and though the cool water felt nice compared to the humid air, I soon became too damp to be comfortable anymore. I drew my hood over my head and wrapped my cloak tighter around myself.

After an hour or two, the crevice came into view. It was a dull, blackish colour, and strands of silver spider webs crisscrossed the upper corners. It really was not a very welcoming place. Some kind of black moss grew in the cracks of the rock and oozed the extra liquid they had collected from the recent rain.

As I peered down the narrow path, I could see broken rocks strewn along the way. The mountain walls rose on either side, and I had to look straight up to see their tops, which eventually melted into the dark sky. *Maybe this wasn't such a brilliant idea*, I reflected with a sick feeling in my stomach. I could turn back, but there was no other way to Rielture except through the mountains. I had to go on now.

I placed my hand on the rocky wall to steady myself as I stepped over a large stone at the entrance. The wall was wet and slick, so I had to grip it with my fingertips too. I curled my lip at the touch of the fungus growing on the wet walls. Stepping over the rock, I paused to look up at the dark sky. A sick greenish black lined the bottoms of the grey clouds. I grimaced and looked back at the pass in front of me.

A flicker of movement in the upper corner of my vision caught my attention. My gaze instantly snapped to where the movement had been. There was nothing there now, but I knew there had been a second ago. I had the growing feeling I was being watched as I continued walking. I kept my eyes forward but at an angle where I could still watch the place where the movement had been.

I did not see anything for the rest of the day, except grey rocks and a lizard. I kept one hand always on the dagger at my waist, just in case. I knew I was not a very good fighter, but at least with the dagger I could try to defend myself against anything hostile these mountains might hold.

By noon, the clouds had burst. Rain came pouring down in heavy sheets. Eventually, the blinding rain made it so hard to see that I had to stop and take shelter in a small cleft in the mountain wall. I sat against the back of the gap, no more than three feet from the entrance. I had to pull my knees up close to my chest to avoid getting my legs wet. I hugged myself tightly, longing to speak with Lliam again.

It was dark in the little hole and very cramped, but I knew I had to stay in there until the rain moved over the pass. I drank out of a tiny pool of rainwater just inside the hole, but the water tasted a little bit odd, so I did not drink from it again. The rain began to lessen after about half an hour. Now I could see the wall on the opposite side of the pass, but the rain was still too heavy to travel comfortably. I shivered and pulled my cloak tighter around my body. The warm air made me drowsy, and soon my eyes were closing as I succumbed to a light sleep.

⸙

When I woke, the rain had stopped, and sunlight was streaming down into the small opening. I stretched my cramped muscles and scooted out of the crevice, dusting my hands on my skirt and brushing the dirt off my cloak. My still-wet hair gleamed in the sunlight, its rays immediately lifting my dampened spirits.

I jumped onto a large rock and surveyed the narrow pass carefully. Puddles of water and mud covered the ground, and so did a few deer tracks. They were fresh; the deer must have come through after the rain while I had been asleep. I gripped my dagger pommel in frustration. *I just don't have much luck anymore*, I thought sourly, and leaped down from the rock to follow the tracks.

As I walked, I noticed the sky above was a brilliant blue, and though a few grey clouds still lingered, the enveloping darkness of the previous day was all but gone. Despite the letup of the storm, I still saw no animals, save another lizard. It was almost as if they were hiding from something, though I knew it probably was not I. The entire pass seemed to be holding its breath. It unnerved me and made me begin to doubt once again the wisdom of coming this way.

I walked and ran for almost four hours before I stopped to rest and get a drink from water trickling down from rocks along the path. It tasted better than the water from the puddle, but it still left a strange taste in my mouth.

Once the sun started down, casting long shadows over the pass, I stopped and spread out my bedroll beside a great boulder, but it was still damp, so I let it dry out in the warm air for a while before lying on it. By then, the stars had begun to appear in the night sky. Somewhat pale against the dark sky, they were still beautiful, though no stars I had seen yet came close to the grandeur of the ones in Aseamir.

Then, for a brief moment, I wondered about Malitha. I wondered where she was and what had happened between her and Alqua. If I knew my sister at all, she was still there with him, firmly holding out until Aubryn would reluctantly try to reconcile with her. And I knew that even though Malitha did not want to hurt our mother, she would not give in concerning Alqua. When she made up her mind about someone or something, she could be very stubborn. Why in the world Alqua was attracted to her, I honestly could not guess.

I rolled a twig between my fingers and frowned. I did not want to think about the troubles back home, even though they kept popping into my head like a memory I was not fond of. But I could not help revisiting them because of other things they reminded me of—like my father teaching me to shoot my bow and Laela and me dreaming about attending a fancy ball with Adonis, a boy we had both fancied when we were younger, and Lillian being born when Malitha and I were three years old. I smiled ruefully and lay down on my bedroll, wishing I could relive it all.

⌇

The next morning was hot. Mosquitoes buzzed around me, nearly driving me insane. Sweat dripped from my brow and my back and sides, but I forced myself to keep going. I hoped I would be coming to the end of the pass within a day or so, for I wanted to get out of the mountains as quickly as possible.

As I rounded a bend, I came to a fork in the pass. Bewildered and tired, I glared down each of the paths, trying to decide which to take. They looked essentially the same, which only added to my frustration. I gripped my dagger pommel so tightly that my knuckles turned white, and tears sprang to my eyes. I was burning hot, thoroughly exhausted, and ready to be done with the tiny, cramped pass that I had been traversing for nearly three days.

I sat down heavily on a stone to try to calm myself and clear my mind. I closed my eyes and focused on my breathing. In. Out. In. Out. In. Out. I felt the stagnant breeze ruffle my hair and whisper across my cheeks. I listened to the still, small voice of the wind moving through the walls of the pass and longed to hear Lliam's voice instead.

After a while, I felt calmer and more able to make a decision. I opened my eyes and peered again down the two paths. Since they both looked alike, I simply chose the right path, knowing I could always double back if I was unable to travel it for some reason.

At first, the going was easy, and I walked on for a long while. But the sun still shone down with such blistering heat that I had to stop every hour or so to rest. As I wiped the sweat off my face using my sleeve, I thought, *I bet Yaron wouldn't have stopped at all. He'd walk or run all day long and still not be tired.* I smiled regretfully at the thought of the boy I had known for such a short time and had come to love. *I wonder if I'll ever see him again.* I frowned and got to my feet, my mind shifting to Lliam. I so longed to talk to him again. I stood and walked aimlessly around for a little while, exploring the area. There was not much to see, but I was bored and not ready to continue on just yet.

A little farther down the path, I found some more deer prints in the dirt, and they were fresh. Excited and with hope renewed for finding some food, I followed them around the twists and turns and scrubby plants. They wound around the pass in no particular direction, but I followed them anyway. The thought of having fresh meat for dinner made me determined to track them. But as I rounded the next corner, I suddenly wished I had not gone exploring.

Seven monstrous wolves were feasting on three bloodied deer beside a boulder. Vicious-looking, all of them were as gargantuan as the russet wolf that had spared my life during the attack on the plains, but I knew that these would not hesitate to hurt me. With jaws stained with the deer's blood, a wild, half-crazed look had sparked in their eyes. Only one of them, a slightly smaller reddish-black wolf towards the outside of the semi-circle, looked moderately sane. His chocolate eyes looked tired and sad, but not crazed.

I stood stock-still, hardly daring to breathe. These massive, unnaturally intelligent wolves bore no resemblance to the ordinary, friendly ones my mother had always told me lived in the plains. I had no idea where these colossal creatures had come from, nor did I have any desire to learn. With a sick feeling, I remembered the slaughter of almost half of the men from Veryan's troop on the plains. Those wolves, as big and lethal as these here before me, had seemingly come out of nowhere and were gone as swiftly.

For a minute, I thought I could leave undetected. But then, the largest of the pack, a great black dog, raised his head and noticed me. He snarled and bared his bloody teeth, excitement and bloodlust filling his eyes. The others looked up then and swivelled their ears in my direction. There was obvious intelligence emanating from their eyes, but the bloodlust of the recent hunt was still raging in them.

The black wolf came closer to me, and I stepped back slowly until I was pressed up against a rock wall. *There must be somewhere I can escape!* I thought frantically. I looked around desperately for a way to escape before the wolves got to me. I could see none. I knew I had no chance of outrunning them, even if I turned and ran back the way I had come. The wolves were every inch as big as the ones on the plains had been, and I realized from where I stood that I would only come up to the top of one of their front legs. Their tails were about as long as I was tall, and their paws were many times larger than my head.

I glanced back at the wolves once I had confirmed that there was no way of escape. All seven were gathered around me in a threatening semicircle. The smallest, the reddish-black one, growled something uneasily, but the black wolf cut him off with a vicious snarl. The smaller dog shrank back, but he still looked on with disapproval. The black dog was at the head; it was clear he was the leader. My hand closed around the dagger at my belt. I had left my sword behind where I had stopped to rest. I had no idea what good it would do against such a huge monster, but it comforted me to have my hand around it. My heart pounded like a drum as the black wolf advanced slowly, his yellow eyes boring into mine hotly. *I can't do this! I can't! Nowhere to hide, nowhere to run … How am I going to survive this?* I took a deep, steadying breath, keeping my eyes firmly on his.

Two of the wolves, the ones to my far right, were glancing nervously at the rocks to their left, looking anxious and tense. One of them was the smaller, red dog. The black wolf, sensing this, turned his head and growled a snapping warning at them. He bared his bloody teeth and narrowed his burning yellow eyes.

Frantic, I turned and looked up at the rocks behind me and saw a ledge a little ways up that I had failed to see earlier. Several jagged spurts of rock which protruded from the wall allowed me to scramble quickly up to the ledge, panting with fright. I scooted as far as possible against the back of the shelf, almost hyperventilating with panic. I was about six or seven feet above the black wolf's huge head and, therefore, over twenty feet above the ground, and it frightened me.

I did not particularly like heights, and being only a few feet above the heads of a pack of monstrous wolves intent on killing me, I felt even more anxious and light-headed. The thought of what those giant, blood-stained teeth and claws could do to me raced through my head, and I slumped against the stone wall behind me, weakened with fear.

The black dog whipped his head around and glared at the spot I had been standing only moments before and then stiffened in rage to see that I was gone.

I shifted slightly, trying to get farther out of sight. A tiny sound made by my boots against the rock, however, caused the wolf's ears to swivel in my direction, and his crazed gaze found the ledge I was cowering against an instant later. Snarling, he crouched and lashed his tail angrily. Sensing he was about to leap, I tried to move back, but found myself unable to go any farther. Nevertheless, unless he was an extraordinarily good jumper, I would be safe from his reach.

He came flying towards me a second later, claws outstretched, and landed on the rock in front of me, a triumphant gleam in his demented eyes. I could not even feel a vibration from his giant paws when they landed. I screamed involuntarily as he bared his teeth at me, looking utterly demonic.

Heat began pulsing through my head, and black dots swam over my vision. I could not move or even think, so terrified was I at what could happen next. The black wolf bared his teeth again in a feral snarl and took several steps towards me, extremely agile and at ease, even with his massive bulk. I was covered entirely in his shadow. His hot breath blew over me, and the stench was overwhelming. I resisted the urge to gag, but my bile rose, and I struggled to breathe through my mouth.

Then he lunged.

I squeezed my eyes shut, waiting for the clamp of his teeth closing around my neck. But instead, I felt only the soft brush of wiry fur and heard only an angry snarl and a heavy thud. Too terrified to open my eyes, I waited for what seemed like an eternity. I could hear sounds from the wolves below me, but now it sounded as if they were fighting among themselves.

Finally, I mustered the courage to open my eyes and look down from the ledge. I was amazed to see the russet wolf, the one who had understood me on the plains, crouched over the black wolf, snarling at him. The black wolf was lying on his side whining, ears pinned back, eyes roving about desperately, wanting to be free. The russet wolf nipped the black wolf on the head and then backed up, allowing the black dog to rise.

The black wolf slouched off to the other wolves, who pinned their ears back as he passed. The reddish-black wolf snarled at the black wolf, and the black wolf lunged at him angrily. The two rolled on the ground tussling, their gigantic paws batting each other and their teeth connecting with each other's hides. The russet wolf dove into the fight and dragged the smaller wolf away, holding him by his scruff. The russet wolf then snarled at both of them, and they fell silent, ears laid flat and glaring at each other.

The russet wolf padded over to the base of the ledge where I was still trembling, and in a single, graceful leap, jumped to stand in front on me. My heart began beating wildly again. Was he going to kill me now, after he had spared my life on the plains? But no, the russet wolf lowered his huge head until we were eye-to-eye, and I saw once again the burning intellect in those dark eyes. The wolf eyed me for a long time, appearing once again to be searching for something in my face. Then, finally overcome with panic, I fainted.

꒰ꔛ꒱

The acrid smell of ash and smoke made my nose sting. I turned my head away, but still the scent was strong. My brow furrowed as I frowned, though my eyes were still closed. I felt a light touch on my arm, and I opened my eyes. Staring back at me was a pair of blue eyes set in a pale face, full of concern. I closed my eyes again, suddenly convinced I was still dreaming. After all, the last eyes I had looked into had been brown … I suddenly sat up and gasped. The wolves!

Then I noticed a person sitting beside me. It was a boy a few years older than I, perhaps, with eyes as deep and blue as sapphires, nut-brown hair that framed his face, and pale skin that resembled alabaster. I blushed involuntarily and sincerely hoped it did not show.

A quiver was slung on his back, full of swan-feather fletched arrows and made of some dark wood I could not identify. He wore a blue shirt, and there was a ring upon his left hand.

He looked at me with amusement. "How are you feeling?" he asked.

I started to respond, but then said, "I don't know … What happened to the wolves?"

He replied, "You saw them? What happened to you?"

"What do you mean …?"

"Well, I've been following a huge brown wolf for the past several days, the biggest wolf I've ever seen, and I saw him again today. He seemed to be baiting me because he would run out of sight, and then I would come around a bend, and he was there, as if he was waiting for me … I came around a turn not far from here, and he was standing over you, as if he was guarding you or something. When he saw me, though, he ran, and I haven't seen him again … Do you remember anything?" he said, blue eyes curious.

I frowned, disturbed. "He … led you to me?" I asked doubtfully.

"You could say that, I suppose," the boy affirmed.

I thought about this for a long time: So the wolf had spared my life on the plains, saved me again from another wolf, and had led someone to me while I had lain unconscious … What on earth was going on? Why was this animal helping me? I put a hand to my aching forehead and answered, "He … saved me from another wolf that was attacking me. I think I fainted—"

"You did," he confirmed.

"And after that, I don't remember anything," I said. "I don't know why he did that."

The boy was silent for a moment and then introduced himself. "I'm Efroy," he offered.

"Elysia," I returned. Then I asked, "But ... those weren't Salquessaé wolves ... were they? I've never seen any wolves that massive or agile, except for some of the same kind that attacked—" I cut myself off, realizing that I probably should not say any more. I did not know this boy or whether I should trust him yet.

Efroy shrugged nonchalantly, but his eyes became worried. "I know. Perhaps they've come from somewhere else, driven here by some ... disease or famine. I don't know. All I do know is that they've been attacking many of the incoming human soldiers and only them, none of Queen Elisheiva's soldiers."

I frowned, puzzling over this information. If the wolves had been attacking only human troops, why had Gornhelm's contingent been assailed by them? But before I could ask Efroy this question, he took his bow and his quiver and stood, stating, "I'll hunt." I looked at him anxiously, suddenly beset with horrific images of black wolves attacking me in his absence. "Don't worry," he said reassuringly, "I'll be back soon."

I said nothing but took a deep breath and watched him until he was out of sight.

⤳

Efroy could not come back soon enough. While he was gone, I jumped at every small noise, and my eyes darted around the pass continually, praying I would not see a black wolf lurking around one of the walls, his blood-lusting yellow eyes searching for me. I shivered and tried to focus my attention on the fire, but that only conjured up images of the black wolf leaping through a screen of fire to sink his huge teeth into my flesh. I squeezed my eyes tight and longed desperately for Lliam's comforting presence.

After a half hour of misery, Efroy came back, a dead deer slung over his muscular shoulders. One of his dark arrows protruded from its pale chest. To my surprise, he also had my satchel, bedroll, and sword in tow, and after setting the deer down by the fire, handed them to me, saying, "Am I right in guessing these are yours?"

I took the satchel from him gratefully, my fingers brushing the sides to make sure the egg was still there. It was, and this comforted me greatly. "Thank you," I murmured, and I buckled the sword back onto my belt with relief. Even though Zan'dúril would be next to useless in my clumsy hands, it was still a great consolation that it was back with me.

I examined Efroy closely from across the fire, hoping I was not blushing as I did so, as he slid his dagger blade over the length of one of the points of the buck's rack. Though his clothes looked as though they were of fine make, his boots were worn and dirty, as if he had used them for many years. He wore a necklace of strands of braided leather that wound around a piece of polished deer antler. A band of braided leather strips encircled his wrist. Efroy sensed my eyes on him, and he looked up and met my gaze. He ran his eyes over me and then resumed his work.

I moved my eyes down to the ground and asked, "Why are you here?"

"Why are *you*?" he replied evenly, not looking up. The sound of his knife rasping over the antler was soothing, and I found myself getting drowsy. I stirred, trying to keep myself awake.

"That doesn't answer my question."

"Nor mine."

I frowned and was silent for several minutes, listening to his dagger scrape over the antler and breathing in the cool, evening air. I wondered where Efroy was from and what he was doing way out here. But then, what was *I* doing out here? I touched the bottom of my satchel and felt the egg's bumpy surface through the soft deerskin and then gently touched the medallion around my neck. I stroked it absentmindedly, looking at the picture upon it. Medium sized waves were rolling onto a rocky beach, and small thunderclouds loomed overhead in the far distance. I frowned at it, wondering what it could mean. Perhaps it meant that I was worn out and still bothered by everything that had happened to me today; that would be a just description, I thought. I leaned back against the cool rock behind me, thinking of Nathaniel and Fray and Menel.

"I'm on an errand for Lord Riyad of Meneltauré," I said presently, my hand still clutching the warm metal of my medallion.

Efroy looked up sharply, but his handsome face revealed nothing. He examined me for a long time, blue eyes narrowed. "I see," was all he said before returning his attention to the antler point.

I thought his reaction curious, and I asked him, "Do you know something of it?"

Efroy did not answer me, nor did he pause in his work.

Annoyed, I pointed out, "I answered your question, but you haven't answered either of mine. Shouldn't you?" I ran my fingers over the small ridges on the face of my medallion, feeling the little edges of the waves pulsing with the tide.

To my relief, Efroy smiled wryly and looked up at me. He laid his dagger down gingerly and answered me, "I told you I was tracking those wolves earlier, didn't I? And as for my knowing anything about your errand, I do know something of it."

I frowned, feeling unsafe. How did this man know anything of my errand for Lord Riyad? And what *did* he know? I said uneasily, "What do you know of it?"

Efroy shrugged. "Lord Riyad was supposed to be sending someone to me with some kind of egg for safekeeping in the next few weeks—"

"Wait," I interrupted, suddenly very suspicious. "When I got the egg, I was told to take it to Rielture's *governor*, and I don't think you are he." I eyed him mistrustfully.

"So you admit to having the egg," Efroy said with a sly smile, and I hesitated, realizing that I had indeed confirmed my possession of it. I scowled at him, and he laughed.

"Don't worry, Elysia. You can trust me. Here, look at this." He pulled the ring off his finger and tossed it to me.

I pulled my hand back after I caught it and examined the ring I held it in my palm. It bore the signet of the high elves of Rielture; it was the same symbol I had often seen on sealed documents in my father's study. The signet was carved into the face of a sparkling ruby, and the band was gold. It was a beautiful ring, and I held it in my palm for several long moments before I surrendered it back to Efroy.

He took it from me. "Do you believe me now?"

"No, that doesn't prove anything," I said, still deeply suspicious and wishing I had held my tongue.

Efroy smiled. "It does, but whether you choose to accept it or not is up to you," he answered and then stretched out comfortably on his side, resting his head upon his hand.

"So you're trying to tell me that you're the governor of Rielture?" I asked incredulously, frowning at him. How could this young man be Rielture's governor? And even if he was, why wasn't he *in* Rielture? What was he doing way out here, tracking wolves?

Efroy smiled persuasively at me, reminding me for a painful moment of Nathaniel. "You're trying to tell me that you're the person Lord Riyad chose to bring such an important, rare object to me when I'm sure he had much older, more experienced messengers in his service?" he countered. I was silent, eyeing him darkly.

Efroy laughed and said, "There. We've established that neither of us is what the other expected. Are you happy now?"

"No."

He smiled in amusement at me, and I blushed self-consciously. I jabbed ill-temperedly at the deer meat that was my supper, tired and grumpy after my trying day.

Efroy also became silent, though I could still sense he was amused with our conversation. He stoked the fire for a while, his blue eyes seeming to see something in its dancing flames that I could not. I became drowsy once I finished my food, full for the first time in a few days. However, I was afraid to go to sleep, still haunted by the black wolf and the fear that it would attack me in my dreams. Therefore, I fought to stay awake a while longer, carefully studying Efroy and trying to determine why he was really here in the mountain pass.

Eventually, Efroy asked me, "So why did Lord Riyad chose you as his courier anyway?" His eyes watched my face curiously.

I shook off the drowsiness that was creeping over me and answered tiredly, "I don't know. He never said why."

Efroy pursed his lips thoughtfully. "Hmm," was all he said. "Why?"

"I just wondered … You look young; how old are you?"

"Seventeen," I answered. "How old are you?"

"I'm twenty-three," Efroy replied, adding another few dry twigs to the small fire.

I stared into the bright flames and popping embers, lulled back to sleepiness by the wood's steady cracking sounds. Once or twice, I unconsciously imagined the black wolf's yellow eyes staring at me from the fire's centre, and I jerked back to vigilance at the sight, but of course, it was just an illusion. I wrapped my arms around my middle, hugging myself tightly and wishing that I could rid myself of those unwelcome images.

Eager to get my mind off the wolf's eyes in the fire, I said to Efroy, "I'll bet Lord Riyad is glad he got the egg out of the city."

"Why's that?" he asked, blue eyes becoming hard.

"Because the humans burned it to the ground four days ago," I answered, shivering as one of the twigs in the fire shifted and caused a tongue of flame to shoot up higher than the others. "In one night … Meneltauré was gone."

"What?" Efroy asked hoarsely, incomprehension on his face. "What are you talking about?"

"Zoser's men," I answered, "attacked Meneltauré and set it on fire. They killed everyone … the men, the women … the little children. I saw one child be beheaded in the streets …" I broke off and looked away from the fire, knowing all too well how destructive it could become. How could the humans do that to us? How could people who had once been nothing but stories be real in so violent a way? What were they hoping to gain by killing us and turning us against them? Where had they even come from? Were their own countries not good enough for them anymore?

"Oh, blast it!" I heard Efroy mutter. "Are you sure the city was totally destroyed?"

"Quite."

Efroy ran his hands through his brown hair, a look of intense distress now clouding his handsome face. He muttered a long line of curses—which alarmed me—and then said, "We need to be on our way before the sun rises tomorrow morning. We need to get back to Rielture as quickly as possible … I've been gone too long."

He flipped over on his back and, covering his face with his hands, let out a long, tired sigh. Concerned, I watched him for a while, and then I slowly drifted into a fitful sleep. Several times during the night, I awoke upon hearing unidentifiable noises; another time I woke to put an end to a terrible nightmare of the black wolf. As I fell back against my bedroll after one such episode, I thought desperately, *Lliam, where* are *you?*

The next morning I woke tired from my lack of sleep, but I was ready to keep moving. Efroy was moody, and he did not say much as we packed up. I watched him carefully, a little disappointed at the new air of seriousness about him. His brow was creased in intense thought, and anything I said to him, he returned with a frown and curt reply. Eventually, I stopped trying to make conversation and fell silent, feeling snubbed unjustly.

When my bedroll and satchel were slung over my shoulder, my sword and dagger at my hip, and Efroy was likewise ready, we set out as the first pale rays of sun were falling over the edges of the high walls of the pass. The air was crisp and cool, and it felt nice against my skin, but I still tied my hair back and tucked my cloak into my satchel; it was going to get too hot for me to keep it on as the day progressed.

Efroy and I walked in silence for a long time, neither of us finding any topic suitable to speak of to the other. I spent my time wondering how such a young man could be Rielture's governor … Surely he was not yet old enough to make wise decisions? Rielture was a small city with a population of only about two thousand, but even so, I could not imagine the people trusting him to lead them well. *He must be criticised and doubted on every decision,* I thought uncomfortably, letting my eyes stray over the man beside me. I blushed again without quite knowing why, and I averted my gaze.

I touched the medallion at my neck and looked at its face. There was a rosebud, tightly folded and still nothing more than a tiny shoot, emerging from silver dirt at the bottom of the necklace. I did not even want to know what that could mean; I let the medallion drop back against my skin with a slightly queasy feeling.

I gave a little dismal sigh and opened my mind to search for Lliam's. It had been almost six days since I had heard from him, and I was beginning to worry that he had perhaps been injured in the razing of Meneltauré. I did not dare let myself think of what else might have happened to him, though I was fairly sure I would know if he was dead. My mind roved aimlessly for his, searching, probing … trying desperately to find him … but to no avail. Feeling lonely, I fiddled with the leather straps of my bedroll, wishing I had someone to talk to right now.

"What do you know of wolves?" Efroy asked, surprising me.

I thought for a moment and then admitted, "Nothing really. I've never read anything about them, and the only stories I've heard were about the Salquessaé wolves … the normal kind. Why?"

Efroy shrugged. "I was just curious. I've been fascinated by wolves since I was nine, when I saw some with my brother Ethan in the mountains. I tracked wolves before—before I became involved in Rielture's government—but I had lost interest until recently … when I discovered those that attacked you. I wonder where they've come from. They can't be from Yaracina; surely we would have heard of them before now if they were."

"I suppose so … Why were you so fascinated with them?"

Efroy grinned wryly. "Why are little boys fascinated with anything? I suppose it was just the thrill of seeing a pack of wild animals on the hunt and seeing how swift and beautiful they were that left such an imprint on me."

I smiled a little; I could almost imagine a nine-year-old Efroy watching a pack of wolves streaking past from the shelter of a tree in the mountains. "I don't like wolves," I said, my thoughts straying back to the bloody teeth the black wolf had bared at me before lunging.

"I can understand that," Efroy said kindly, looking at me with an expression of concern. "The patron animal of Rielture is the eagle," Efroy went on, seeming to have gotten over some of his previous moodiness, "because it's said that Yara put the cliff eagles in the mountains around where Rielture is now to be the guardians of the valley and of the lake. And when the first people came to Peta Valley, the cliff eagles flew to the ledges and watched over them and protected them until there were enough settlers to establish the first village, Gallagher. One winter, when some of the wolves from the mountains became angry with the settlers because they were killing the deer that the wolves hunted, they gathered to attack Gallagher, but the cliff eagles learned of their plans. They told the leader of Gallagher of the wolves' intentions, and he was able to get the people out safely before the wolves attacked. So in tribute to that legend, we have eagles on our houses, our jewellery, our clothes ... We've been known as the Eagle City for the past three hundred years."

"I never knew that," I admitted, intrigued.

"See?" he said, drawing his dagger from its sheath and showing it to me. A golden eagle's head was the pommel, and the crossguard was two golden, outstretched eagles' wings, separated from the pommel by a dark brown wood. I touched the pommel reverently, thinking of my own plain little dagger. *If I had a dagger like this, it would have a falcon on it instead of an eagle*, I thought with a wry smile. And with a lonely inward sigh—thinking of the falcons made me miss Lliam even more—I said to Efroy, "I don't think Aseamir has a patron animal; none that I've heard of, anyway. I like the idea, though ..." I cast an admiring eye over the dagger once more.

"It could be a fox," he said, tugging playfully on a strand of my red hair and grinning.

I smiled back. "Most people in Aseamir don't have red hair, Efroy. It's mostly brown hair there."

"So you're one of the lucky few then, hmm?" he asked, still smiling at me, amusement in his azure eyes.

"If you call it lucky, then I suppose so, yes," I answered, wondering what had put him back into such a good mood. But I rather liked it; the cheerful Efroy was much preferable to the moody one. I wondered again how he handled the government in Rielture and all the criticism that was bound to come his way because of his age and inexperience. I frowned. I surely would not want to have to make so many decisions, resolve so many problems, and listen to so many complaints. Why would anyone willingly subject himself to such a thankless occupation?

I asked him this, and he looked at me with some surprise and then smiled. "I've always been very interested in politics, even when I was very young. I don't know why, but … politics and government have always fascinated me. My older brother Ethan never cared much for either of them, so I think my father always planned for me to succeed him as Rielture's next governor. I took the position two years ago, and since Rielture is a relatively small city, it's been … a joy, being its governor.

"So far the worst problems I've faced have had to do with the coal mines in the mountains. Last year we nearly exhausted the coal supply, but luckily some miners stumbled onto another large mine in a nearby cave system, so we got that all sorted out. I still find time to get away from the city sometimes, like right now. My sister Anaria, who is also very fond of our family's governing history and the challenge of it all, keeps things in order while I'm gone, and so does Peter, a good friend and counsellor of mine. It … can be demanding at times, but I definitely would not call it thankless." He smiled at me, and his eyes were gentle.

I thought about this for a while but said nothing. My opinion had not changed even after hearing his account; I still thought the position as a governor an undesirable one.

"Of course, we're still required to send some of our goods to Elisheiva as taxes, and if there were ever need for war, our men would fight in her army," Efroy went on. "But for the most part, Elisheiva leaves us alone, and we are fairly untouched by the rest of Yaracina, especially the big cities and their strange ideas. It's a good system; it works for us. As long as we have the mines and our freedom, we'll be happy."

I said, "It's the same in Aseamir, though we don't have mines. Viveca is our governor, and she's a good one, as far as I know. Aseamir's fairly small too, but our economy is stable and our taxes relatively low, I think."

Efroy smiled. "Tell me more about Aseamir. I've never been there, but I've heard about it. Is it true some people live in trees there?"

"Yes, of course," I said with a smile, amused. "I'm one of them. We live in a silverwood tree on the outskirts of town."

Efroy actually laughed out loud, which surprised me. "From what my father's told me, elves haven't been living in trees for the past few hundred years. Not since the War of the Red Moon; it became too unsafe with the threat of humans invading, and … I suppose we moved into the walled cities for protection, wouldn't you say? Though until recently, I've never seen the need to live in cities … Can you describe the attack on Meneltauré for me?"

I hesitated, unwelcome images of burning homes and dead children lying in the streets surfacing in my mind. I saw my dream again, the one where Lliam and I were burning to death, trapped inside one of those little huts …"We had no warning. The humans were on top of the cliffs that drop down into the valley, and they shot fire down at us … The houses caught on fire and many of them exploded … Humans killed people in the streets, little children and mothers … I escaped only because a friend woke me and helped me find a horse, but … I doubt that many of the people survived." I stopped there, trying to keep the images of the razing from entering my mind again.

Efroy's brow furrowed in anger. "It doesn't make sense. Why would they burn the city? Surely they could have found some use for it." He fingered his dagger uncomfortably, his eyes searching the pebbly ground for answers.

"I don't know," I answered wearily, unwilling to spend much time on revisiting this painful topic.

Efroy said then, "This could be a very bad situation for us … Rielture's the closest city to Meneltauré, and I'm guessing that the humans won't be satisfied with the razing of just one city." He sighed heavily and gazed up at the pale sky. "Why did this have to happen again? Yaracina has been very stable for many years now … But I suppose it does make sense that they would come here now, when they think that we've grown comfortable and wouldn't expect it … I could have sworn the humans had become extinct!"

"So," I ventured tentatively, "the War of the Red Moon really happened? It wasn't just a myth? The humans *were* real?" I felt as if that was a foolish question to ask; I now knew the answer to be obvious.

Efroy smirked at me in amusement. "Of course it really happened. It happened around seven hundred years ago, up north, near Hartford City."

"And humans were our enemies then, too?"

"Yes."

Efroy suddenly held out his hand to stop me, and I did so automatically. He knelt down in front of me to examine several monstrous prints in the pebbly dirt, looking fascinated. I had not noticed them before, but now, searching behind and in front of me, I saw that there were dozens of such prints. I felt a sudden shiver run down my spine and wondered if the black wolf was lurking somewhere, watching us. I crossed my arms over my chest and hugged myself tightly. Efroy touched a finger to the indentation of the huge paws in the dirt and frowned. "They passed through here recently. We need to keep moving."

꒖

I could not sleep that night. Every time I slipped into sleep, my repeated nightmare of burning alive in the hut revisited me, but this time it was worse; wolves scrabbled at the frail wooden door, snarling and snapping their teeth, eager to tear my flesh. Lliam was there too, and while he was frantically trying to tell me something, I could not hear his words above the noise of the snarling wolves and the crackling flames.

After an hour or so of simply lying on the hard ground beside the dying fire, afraid to fall asleep and afraid to stay awake, I silently stood and made my way cautiously over to a large rock and climbed atop it. I sat there for a long time, looking up at the pale stars, longing to hear Lliam's voice again and wishing I had never agreed to leave my home to come on an errand for my father. For truly, what good had come of it? I had been captured by soldiers almost immediately, thrown into prison at the Tower of Orlena, knocked unconscious after a harrowing escape, separated from two of my closest friends in the same day, nearly killed by explosions during the humans' attack on Meneltauré, and attacked by gigantic wolves. And now I just wanted to go home—back to Aseamir, where everything was predictable and safe and there were no humans or wolves and where everything made sense.

I was suddenly aware of Efroy beside me, his eyes evaluating me carefully. "I heard you get up," he said softly. "Are you okay?"

I pulled my knees up to my chest and rested my chin on them noncommittally. I was reluctant to tell Efroy why I had woken. Would he think me childish for being afraid of a few bad dreams? And in any case, I barely knew him. But I said reluctantly, "I ... had a bad dream ... the wolves ... and the fires from Meneltauré ... The memories keep bothering me."

"Ah," Efroy said, looking down at the dying fire he had built, a thoughtful expression on his face. "I'm sorry," he said presently.

"I'm sure I'll get over them soon," I murmured optimistically, but in truth, I was not convinced. They had been getting progressively worse every time I fell asleep ... I longed again for Lliam's calming presence and wondered where he was ... What had happened to him in Meneltauré? What I would give to know!

"I hope so," Efroy agreed, looking at me sympathetically. I avoided his eyes, feeling childish.

"Hey," he said kindly, "everyone has nightmares at one time or another. There's no reason to feel ashamed about it." I met his gaze in doubt, but there was only gentle sincerity and compassion in those beautiful blue eyes. I felt my cheeks grow warm just from looking at him, but I could not look away. I did not want to, but I did finally, unsure what had come over me.

We were both silent for a long time. I stared up at the dark sky, missing the times I would sit out at night with Lillian and Malitha and we would look at the stars and point out constellations to each other, like Ursa, Pegasus, and Orion ... I smiled ruefully at the memory, wishing I was home again, instead of out here in this god-forsaken mountain pass.

"So are you enjoying your travels away from Aseamir?" Efroy asked a while later, attempting to change the subject.

"No," I said with a mournful smile. "Not one bit. I just want to go home. This world's too … big and chaotic for me. I prefer things the way they were back in Aseamir: simple, small, and sensible. Out here … nothing makes sense."

Efroy chuckled but offered some reassurance: "Things start to make more sense once you understand what has gone on before them. You just came out of Aseamir at an unfortunate time, I think." He lay back on the rock, folded his hands under his head, and looked up at the night sky peacefully.

⁓

A few hours later, I was awakened at dawn when I heard Efroy gathering up his things. I blinked wearily and sat up. The sky was a dark blue, tinged at the horizon with pale yellow and pink. Unenthusiastically, I yawned and sat inert for a while, in a faint haze from my troubled sleep.

"Am I really that interesting to watch?" I heard Efroy say wryly, and with a start, I realized that I had, indeed, been staring at him.

"Oh, sorry," I apologised. He chuckled, blue eyes crinkled in laughter.

Embarrassed, I turned the conversation off my absentmindedness to the weather. "The wind has picked up. It's going to be cool while walking today." And indeed, even as I spoke, the breeze gave a sudden heavy gust, tossing crisp and chilly air into our faces.

"Yes. Winter is fast approaching, and it comes even earlier in the mountains," Efroy replied, hefting his bag onto his shoulder, "Go ahead and pack up; we need to get going."

I yawned again and slowly got up, rolling up my bedding and stuffing it into my satchel. I buckled Zan'dúril and my dagger onto my belt and slung my bag over my shoulder, blinking back the last bit of drowsy fog still clinging to my brain. I observed Efroy pensively as he buckled his dagger to his belt. Before starting out, he shared a piece of bread he had left in his pack with me.

"We're going to aim for the Torrin Lake now," he said. "It's about sixty miles from here We can probably reach it by the day after tomorrow if we don't stop too often. If we had a horse, we could probably get there faster, but it's too narrow in here ..." He squinted up at the steep cliff walls on either side of us. "Well, we may not have horses, but we still have our feet. We'll run today instead of walk. We need to get to Rielture as soon as possible."

I murmured a word of agreement and groggily walked over to him, gazing around the grey pass distastefully. How glad I would be to get out of here!

Efroy hesitated for a moment, looking uncertain, and then asked, "You ready?"

"As ready as I'll ever be," I replied with a shrug.

Efroy grinned and began running. I followed him, and the two of us set out once again on the path to Rielture.

کے

We ran for nearly two hours though the going was slow because of the roughness of the narrow path. Then we stopped to rest our legs briefly before going on another hour. The maze of rocks and unbroken greyness of the mountain pass made me want to scream, I was so tired of it. *I want to be out in the wide open spaces again or at least under a canopy of green trees. This place is so dreary!* I shivered and peered up at the solemn cliff faces that rose up on either side of us. They were dark and foreboding and devoid of vegetation. Although I supposed they provided protection from the chilling winds during the winter months, I longed to feel the fresh, cool breezes I was accustomed to in the plains. I frowned and looked over my shoulder at Efroy. His brow was creased in thought.

"What is it?" I asked, breaking the silence between us. Efroy shook his head.

"Nothing. I was just wondering about ... never mind. Are you going to stay in Rielture, or immediately go on to Hartford City?" He seemed genuinely curious, which surprised me a bit.

I thought about it carefully for a moment. *What do I want to do? Going on would probably be best ... but I would like to stay for a little while.* "I don't know yet. I might stay for a while," I replied truthfully, not entirely sure what my reasons were going to be if I, indeed, stayed longer in Rielture.

Efroy nodded thoughtfully. "Perhaps you could stay for the festival. I'd like you to be there; I think you'd enjoy it." I thought he sounded almost hopeful. I smiled to myself. The November Festival was one that most of the Yaran cities—though not Aseamir—held every November to honour and celebrate Yara. November was said to be the month in which Yara was first carried to our shores from a fabled land across the sea, one that, so it had been told, had withered and died and sunk into the sea with Yara's absence. But I knew that the land did not—and never did—exist.

Autumn was the season that Yarans most often celebrated Yara, and it was said that the leaves changed colour in the fall before they fell off their trees because she had put the finishing touches on the year and was letting the colours run off the canvas to start the year anew. When they all had and left only a clean, white page, then winter came. Spring arrived once more as Yara picked up her paintbrush and first touched it to the canvas with the vibrant colours of new life and growth.

I turned my mind back to Efroy's comment. "Perhaps ...," I answered slowly. "I don't want to be gone too long, though. My family may be worried and wonder if I've gotten lost or injured ... or worse. Although ...," I hesitated, "I used to dream of seeing faraway places like Rielture and Hartford City ..."

Efroy grinned at me and asked, "So that's a maybe?"

I blushed and looked over to him, nodding. *I doubt he really cares, truly,* I told myself mournfully. *And why should he? He's the governor of Rielture.* But, though I did not want to admit it, I *did* want Efroy to care about me. So far, I liked him quite well; he seemed as if he could be a good friend.

I watched the sky turn a bright, cheerful blue as the day progressed and the sun rose higher. Soon, it was a blinding, glowing orb in the azure sky, and its warmth shimmered down on us. I could see heat rising in waves from the rocks' rigid surfaces. Eventually, it got so hot that I could not stand it any longer. I asked Efroy if we could rest for a little while, and though I knew he thought we should keep going, he consented.

I took off my cloak and stuffed it into my satchel. My forehead was beaded with sweat, and my cheeks felt flushed. I scooted up as close against the rock wall as I could, trying to find some shade.

Efroy sat down beside me, not looking nearly as spent as I felt. I leaned my head against the rock and closed my eyes. I felt utterly exhausted; I doubted I would have the energy to go on much further. We had travelled around fifteen miles, though, and Efroy was pleased with the distance. He had said if we covered twenty miles today, tomorrow, and the next day, we would arrive at Rielture.

I began to feel drowsy. The heat only added to my exhaustion, and soon I was asleep, my head tipped back against the rock. But Efroy gently shook my shoulder, waking me up, and said encouragingly, "Hey, we need to keep going. Just five more miles today, all right?"

I sighed, feeling as though I was being burned alive with the smothering, sweltering heat, but I obediently stood and dutifully ran after Efroy as we set off again.

UNCERTAINTIES AND HUMANS

The next five miles were just as blistering, but I was able to tolerate it better this time. Efroy had me run on the side of the path that was not directly under the sun, and as a result, my endurance was better. He did not seem overly affected by the heat, and that was good; I needed an incentive to keep going, and his constant steady footfalls in front of mine gave it to me.

I lost track of time as I fell into the pattern of our pace—just Efroy and I, our breath sounding in soft, almost inaudible pants; our feet pounding with steady strikes down on the pebbly ground, creating small clouds of dust; the sun's rays shimmering down in great, pulsating waves upon our heads; the straight, featureless path we were running along, its walls tall and ominous on either side. Time seemed to hold its breath as we ran, watching impassively from above, freezing everything into a slow-motion rerun of its previous scenes. Nothing else existed in that lucid hour; everything that was a dream, everything that was real was pounded out of being by our swift feet, disappearing into the clouds of dust raised by our passing.

But time did pass; I began to notice its presence after the sun began to sink behind the cliffs and cast us in long shadows. The sky grew darker, and after we had run six more miles, Efroy decided it was time to stop. We laid out our bedrolls against the side of the pass, and Efroy prepared a small fire. He had some leftover deer meat from the hunt yesterday, and he cooked it for a while. After I had eaten, I promptly fell asleep, feeling well worn and tired.

⊰

Efroy watched the stars for a long time after she fell asleep. He was tired but not ready to turn in for the night just yet.

He had a strange feeling in the pit of his stomach, almost as if he had been punched. Every time he looked at Elysia, Efroy felt it. He could not understand it. *She'll be leaving after the festival, anyway*, he told himself. *There's no use in starting anything*. Efroy frowned and stared hard at the sky, seeking answers in the bright stars.

He looked over at Elysia once more, at her face, her auburn hair tinged with a deep golden-orange glow from the fire, and thought of how her stormy blue-grey eyes twinkled when she smiled. Not what he would consider a raving beauty, Elysia was pleasant enough to look upon, and Efroy found her attractive regardless. Truthfully, however, her gentle, youthful nature and the way she gazed, deep in thought, at the blue sky, and how longing her face would become when he knew she was thinking of home were the things that attracted him. There was definitely something alluring about Elysia to Efroy, and it saddened him to think that once they parted ways at Rielture, he might never see her again. She was unquestionably unique in comparison to every other girl he had ever known, and it produced within him a deep desire to know her better.

However, he was not sure he knew what to do about his feelings for her. It bothered him to feel like this; it had always been Ethan who had been interested in girls, and he had teased Efroy about never wanting to talk to any of them. Now Efroy wanted more than anything to talk to Elysia, but for the life of him, he did not know how.

⊰

When I awoke the next morning, I was stiff and in pain from an obvious sunburn on my shoulders, the back of my neck, and the top of my head. I sighed and forced myself to sit up, feeling achy and groggy. I glanced towards the fire for Efroy, but he was not there. *Probably out hunting*, I decided and stretched my arms. So I lay back and waited, enjoying the extra time to rest.

But an hour later, he still was not back. I tried not to be worried, but I could not help myself. *The last time this happened, Yaron disappeared ... I hope Efroy will be back soon.* This made my heart twinge with pain, regret, and longing as I thought about Yaron and then Veryan and Lliam.

Another thirty minutes or so passed. Now, I was definitely worried. I decided to look for him. I grabbed my dagger, sheathed my sword, and set out to find him.

I ran down the pass, my eyes watchful for my friend, and yet I saw nothing but grey stones and scrubby bushes. Panicking, I called, "Efroy!" several times, but heard no answer. Eventually, I headed back to camp but stopped when I noticed a path I had not seen before. I hesitated, grappling with indecision, but my desperate need to find Efroy won over. The path opened up before me.

As I stepped inside, I began to think twice about continuing, but I knew I had to find Efroy, so I made myself keep going. The path was narrow, and the rock walls arched together to form a low ceiling. I looked up and shivered. Cobwebs draped across the rocks. Mist was creeping almost imperceptibly on the floor, and it chilled the air around my feet. I scarcely dared to breathe; I was afraid to disturb the deafening silence of the tiny pathway. Then something grabbed my arm, and I gasped. I whipped my head around and sighed in relief.

It was Efroy.

"What are you doing? You've been gone—" I hissed.

He motioned for me to be silent, cutting me off, and then gestured to follow him. I did so quietly, my heart still pounding.

Efroy led me behind a great spurt of rock at the end of the little path. On the other side was another, wider path, but it was one that did not lead in the direction we needed to go. Together, we crouched down where we could not be seen and listened.

Two voices could be heard, along with the sound of horses swishing their tails. The lightly accented voice of one man sounded just a few feet down the wider path. I looked over at Efroy. His sapphire eyes were alarmed, and his brow creased with worry. "Humans," he mouthed without a sound.

Oh, blast! I thought. Frustration and exasperation welled up inside me, but I forced myself to remain silent and listen while my thoughts turned dark. Why had these wretched people come to our country? Why could they not have remained as characters in fairy tales told to children rather than, literally, walking out of those fanciful stories woven by our mothers into the real world to haunt and threaten us? They had been extinct—or so we thought—for hundreds of years and had faded into our memories as nothing more than a conquered enemy in the bedtime stories told to elven children. And now ... here they were.

The man who had been speaking was silent now, and all that could be heard was the soft swishing of their horses' tails. Then he spoke again. His accent made his words almost hard to understand, not because his accent was so heavy but because I had never heard anyone speak that way before.

My gift of Instinctive Speech supplied me with the answer—American—and I understood why I recognised it. My mother had once lived in America, a place that had existed many centuries ago across the sea, though she was originally from a place called England. She had been in England when the Great Plague came about, but because she was an elf, the sickness had not killed her but had only made her very sick. Elves in the Old World were neither immortal nor impervious to the cold but merely superior physically and mentally to the humans. Nearly all the humans had died in the Great Plague, but there was some part of elven anatomy that was less susceptible to the disease that all but wiped out the Old World. Humans and elves not living in Europe contracted the disease when they traded with Europeans, and soon the pandemic had spread to every corner of the world, destroying entire populations across the earth.

The elves had been extremely sick and weakened from the sickness, though few died, and their children remained untouched by the disease, apparently immune to it. Yara had supposedly discovered an antidote for the plague, which had saved the elves and what few humans remained. Thousands of human children and adults had already died from the plague before the antidote was discovered and those who had survived it as a result of receiving Yara's antidote had long since died, being mortal. It was believed that the antidote had been lost over time and that the human race had eventually died out without the protection it provided ... or so we had always thought.

On the other hand, the effects of the antidote had changed the elven race forever, and as a result, their children—including my generation—who had been born since the plague now had superior characteristics: potential immortality and immunity to the cold, and they had retained the standard qualities of sharper eyesight, more acute hearing, quicker reflexes, and greater strength than that of the humans.

Elves—being instinctively more naturistic, even in the ancient days—had welcomed the opportunity to rid their land of all the technology and machinery that had so engrossed the humans. Once the humans had died off, the elves had simply reverted to their preferred ways of living off and in harmony with the land.

It had been said that Yara had later sailed away from Europe to escape the plague herself and had been shipwrecked for a year on the then uninhabited Yaracina. A few years after the Great Plague, Yara had returned to Europe to find utter ruin in the old lands. Very few humans were left, and it seemed evident that their race was doomed to become extinct. The elves were surviving out in the countryside, but even so, it was a difficult existence after the ravages of the plague. Yara encouraged them to migrate to her new country, and that had been the beginning of Yaracina.

Several hundred years after the elves left, legend told that Menel had destroyed the broken and abandoned lands that humans had once lived upon in Europe. But surely there must have been some mistake; if he had destroyed the human countries and the human race was extinct, where had these come from?

"When do the new recruits arrive?" I heard him say. Despite his odd speech, he sounded fairly young, but that was not what bothered me the most about the man's voice: He sounded exactly like Lliam. A cold shiver running over my spine, I listened harder.

"I don't know, my lord," the other answered.

"They were due to arrive in Rielture nearly a week ago," Lliam's voice said, a steely edge coming into it. I glanced sharply at Efroy. His jaw was clenched and his brow creased.

"Yes, my lord. But with the added time taken to burn Meneltauré, it has taken longer to get everyone—"

"Where are the men now?" the man asked.

"Camped near a mountain stream not far from here," the soldier replied.

There was a pause, and it seemed as if the accented man was mulling over something. A moment later he warned, "Make sure they are there in no more than three days if you value your life, soldier."

There was obvious unease in the soldier's voice as he answered. "Yes, my lord. You have my word."

"Good. Keep it." The horses were then spurred on, and the sound of their hooves clacking over loose stones could be heard as they departed.

I looked over at Efroy as soon as the humans were gone. His azure eyes flamed as he glared in the direction where the humans had been. His forehead was creased in thought. I waited for a few minutes to say anything. "Well? What are we going to do?" I said finally.

He glanced at me sharply. "What are we going to do? We're going to run full speed to Rielture and make sure not a single one of those human dogs sets foot in my city!" He spun around and headed back to the camp. I scrambled to my feet and followed him.

"How did they get here so fast?" I asked, wondering what Lliam was doing here and why he had said nothing to me about it.

"What?"

"I mean, they were in Meneltauré only a few days ago. Unless they were with a different troop, there's no way they could have gotten here this quickly," I said.

Efroy said with a heavy sigh, "There is another pass to Rielture, the main road through the mountains. This path you have taken is a much smaller, lesser travelled road that very few people even know about or use. I suppose they came on the main road, and that's why we haven't seen any of them all this time." His eyes were fixed on the path in front of him; he was intent on getting back to the camp.

I looked at him in confusion. So I had somehow gotten on the wrong path to Rielture? Lliam had not mentioned another mountain pass to me … Perhaps if I had heard from him after Meneltauré, he could have told me that I was on the wrong path, but as it was … I would have had no way of knowing.

I turned my thoughts back to the problem at hand: The humans were headed to Rielture.

"My mother used to tell my sisters and me stories of when she lived in a place called England," I began. Efroy did not appear to have heard me, but I went on anyway. "Until that night in Meneltauré, I thought they were *only* stories. I knew that England was a real place, but … I always thought she made up humans. I never knew they were real …"

Efroy laughed harshly. "Oh, they're real all right, as much as we wish they weren't."

I felt defensive of Lliam even though I remembered the cruelty of the humans who had destroyed Meneltauré and how Lliam and I had nearly been killed by several fiery explosions. I pictured his piercing twilight-grey eyes as he watched me gallop out of the city on Thibilon and how difficult it was to leave him. How I loved my enigmatic friend. But I had not been able to speak to him since we had parted in Meneltauré, and it was taking a heavy toll on me. I wondered hard for a moment if he was all right and where he was … and if he was thinking of me too.

The words came out before I could stop myself: "Have you ever met one? How do you know they're all cruel? My friend, Lliam, the one who warned me in Meneltauré, is a human, and yet he made sure I got out of the city while the rest of the humans destroyed it." Then I paused slightly, thinking: *Perhaps it was not the best idea to tell him of Lliam just yet.* Sighing slightly, I rushed into my next impulsive sentence: "I mean, they can't *all* be like that—"

Efroy whirled around to face me. "Can't they, Elysia? What they did to Meneltauré is what they'd do to any place! They're filth,

Elysia! Monsters and worthless dogs! They don't deserve to walk this earth! And what about your friend, hmm? I'll wager he's done some less-than-honourable things, too, hasn't he? They all have! Humans are *not capable* of goodness, Elysia!"

I stared at him, unable to believe that he had just shouted at me. Even Efroy looked as if he could not believe it. He blinked a few times, but the fire did not die from his eyes. I lowered my eyes and stared at the ground, tears gathering in my eyes in anger; how could I make Efroy see that Lliam was not like the rest of them? He was different. I could trust him. How dare Efroy insult him like that! He did not know Lliam. How could he pass such harsh judgment on my friend?

Efroy's shoulders slumped, and he looked away. "I'm sorry, Elysia. I didn't mean to yell at you." He said this so softly that I could barely hear him.

He hesitated for a moment and then resumed walking. I did not follow him. I stalked away, opening up my mind, searching desperately for Lliam's. I *needed* to talk to him.

FLIGHT

Neither of us spoke of what had happened earlier as Efroy gathered his things. I stood off to the side, my arms crossed. I had finally come back to the camp after about thirty minutes. Efroy did not ask what I had been doing, nor did I tell him.

I had tried frantically to contact Lliam, and after repeated attempts and failures, my mind had finally found his. I had, with intense relief, talked to him at length, telling him everything that had happened and discussing my concerns with him. He had seemed mildly distracted, but he had given me what advice he could, and I was vastly grateful to him for it. I felt as though a great weight had been lifted from my mind and heart; I knew now that Lliam was alive and all right, and it had genuinely comforted me to hear his voice once more.

To my puzzlement, he had also explained to me that he was not here in the pass; he was in Belterra. I had let him listen to my memory of hearing his voice in the pass, and after a moment of silence, Lliam told me that I must have been imaging his voice, for he was not there. I knew he was lying.

Efroy glanced over his shoulder at me. My eyes were fixed on the ground, turning thoughts over in my mind, and though I could feel his eyes on me, I did not look up.

"Elysia. Come. We have to get going," he said softly. I frowned but still did not look at him.

Efroy sighed and ran his fingers through his hair, looking tired and burdened. "Elysia, I said I was sorry."

Surprised that he thought I was still angry at him, I looked up sharply and replied, "Oh, I know. It's not that, it's just ... well, I'm not entirely sure. I just have this feeling ..." I broke off and waved my hand. "It's nothing. Don't worry about it." I walked over to where my satchel and dagger were lying, and I gathered them up.

"I'm just worried," Efroy explained fretfully, "that the humans are going to go to Rielture and kill my people and burn my city, as in Meneltauré, or ... I don't know ... or take control of everything there ..."

"Me too," I said, looking nervously at the ground and unwillingly remembering the great fires and swords the humans had brought to Meneltauré. Would they do the same to Rielture? Then, accompanied with a sickening realization, I wondered if they would try to kill Efroy. After all, he was Rielture's head of government ... "Efroy, what if they try to kill you?" I asked in a panic, a little unsure as to why the thought of Efroy being killed made me so distraught. "You're Rielture's governor ..."

"And it would be an easy matter to get control of the coal mines and the people if their governor was killed ...," Efroy mused, "because they would be distraught and confused without me there ..." He muttered a few curses under his breath and then said, "Well, we can't worry about that now ... I have to get back to help them."

"What do you mean, we can't worry about that now?" I demanded, unable to believe he was giving so little importance to the thought of his own death. I remembered what Nathaniel had told me about death: your body stopped working and your soul went to Paradis. I still did not entirely understand this, but after seeing so many people murdered in Meneltauré, I was beginning to grasp the concept of death for an elf.

Efroy paused, looking at me in bewilderment, and then grinned and said fondly, "Why, Elysia, it seems you almost care more about whether I survive than I do." My cheeks felt instantly hot, and my entire face flushed.

The pass was utterly silent as we progressed. Not even a breath of wind stirred. I was uncomfortable in the stiff silence, and I longed to break it.

"How much longer until we get out of here?" I asked. Efroy glanced at me over his shoulder.

"Another half-hour maybe. I'm not sure," he said.

I frowned and replied, "We're sure to be nearing the end of the twenty miles by now. It's the middle of the afternoon."

Efroy murmured an agreement, but said nothing else. We ran in silence. A dreary eeriness had settled over the pass, enclosing the two of us in its cover. Efroy led the way, staring resolutely ahead as if searching for solutions to what seemed inevitable. Though I longed to talk to Lliam, I received from his mind the impression that he could not be bothered at the moment. There was a steady unease underlying the rest of his emotions, and it bothered me, like a tiny pebble inside my shoe.

I felt tired. There was nothing more I wanted right then than to lie down and rest. My will kept my feet moving, nothing more. The greyness of the mountain pass was pressing down on me, crushing all of my hopeful thoughts and turning them to muddled, depressing ones. I did not want to keep running, but Efroy pressed me onward; I knew he needed to get to Rielture.

Suddenly Efroy held out his hand to stop me, and standing stock-still next to me, he looked straight ahead with an expression akin to dread.

I followed his gaze. Ahead of us, in the middle of the path, sat a man on a great black war horse. He wore chain mail under a black breastplate. His hair was shaggy and the colour of ebony, like Lliam's, but his eyes were a deeper, truer blue than my friend's, with no grey. With a face identical in shape and structure to Lliam's, their features were a minute bit different if only in their eye colour. In every other aspect, they mirrored each other exactly. "Lliam," I whispered, long-ing to hear my friend's voice again.

I moved closer to Efroy. I did not like the look of this black-clad man, and I had the distinct, nagging feeling that I had seen him before. Then, with another glance at the horse, I remembered. *Black-pool! I remember him now!* The gargantuan horse shook his mane at me, and I sensed that even if he did remember me, he would not show it. Ahead of me, Efroy was glaring hard at the man.

The man inspected us intently. He seemed to exude a disdainful air as he spoke. "What are two travellers like yourselves doing out here? You shouldn't be here." I shivered; the man had an American accent, identical to Lliam's, but, again, it was only because I was unused to hearing it that it made him hard to understand. This man was the one we had heard talking earlier.

Efroy spoke up. "This is the quickest way through the moun-tains. My sister and I," he glanced at me sharply, the look in his eyes cautioning me not to speak, "come through here often. We're traders."

The man snorted. "Do you think I'm stupid enough to believe your story? Your clothing is far too fine for mere traders. And as for your 'sister,' I have seen her wandering these paths by herself, as well as once before that."

I shivered, and suddenly, his impassive blue eyes met mine. I paused, slightly baffled. Could this be Roman, Lliam's identical twin? The one who had led the attack on Meneltauré? It had to be, for it certainly was not Lliam, and he looked exactly like him. And why did I feel as if I had seen him before and knew him almost as well as I knew Lliam? He *looked* identical to Lliam, yes, and I supposed that could be why he felt familiar, but somehow I did not think that explained all of it.

But as I returned my attention to the conversation between the two men, I could instantly tell from the way Efroy tensed that what the man had said had put him on the defensive.

Apparently, the man saw Efroy tense as well because his hand strayed to his sword hilt. Efroy did the same.

I quickly put my hand on Efroy's arm. "Don't," I said sharply. "It would be foolish and pointless to start a fight now. We have to get to Rielture as quickly as possible, and this would hinder us."

He gave no sign of hearing me.

"Efroy," I hissed pleadingly, "don't."

Efroy did not look at me, but his hand did loosen its grip on the pommel. I, however, did not release his arm until he began to speak.

"Fine. She's not my sister. I met her while travelling, and we joined together because there's a greater chance of getting through these mountains with a companion."

"Yes, but why did you take *this* road?" The man seemed impatient, and I heard the same sharp edge seep into his voice as it had earlier when he had interrogated the soldier about the army coming to Rielture.

"I told you: It's the fastest way," Efroy replied stiffly. The man snorted. He looked hard at Efroy and me. I shivered under his gaze.

"You shouldn't be here. Be on your way," he said. Then he turned his horse around but paused before leaving. Our eyes met briefly, and he narrowed his a moment later. "It's too dangerous out here for two children," he said softly. He spurred Black-pool back down the path, the great horse shaking his mane and moving with unnatural grace for so large an animal, and they vanished from view around a bend a moment later.

Efroy's jaw clenched, and his eyes burned as he watched the man leave. I watched him with concern.

"I hate them," was all he said.

↭

Once he was sure that Elysia and her friend had continued on their way, Roman dismounted from his stallion, heart hammering in his chest, and he sagged against the cliff wall, trying to get a grip on his emotions. He did not like his reaction to seeing Elysia again so soon; he felt completely unstable and vulnerable now that he had seen her close up, the way Lliam had told him he had felt when he had seen her for the first time.

Sighing shakily, Roman ran his hands through his hair and took a moment just to breathe, drawing the cool mountain air into his lungs quickly. What was he to do now? Zoser had ordered him to capture her and the egg as soon as possible, but could he do it now that he had seen her? What would happen if he could not? He knew Zoser would be very displeased, as he always was when Roman failed to complete an assignment, but was his anger worth it? He did not know what on earth to do next.

Roman longed to ask someone what he should do, but the only person nearby was Lliam, and there was absolutely no chance of him asking his brother for advice; that would be like admitting to Lliam's face that he was incapable of handling an assignment like this without another's help. Roman's pride balked at the mere thought. Lliam already thought that, and he did not want to give his brother even more reason to think it true. He could do this without Lliam's help.

Leaning his head back against the rough rock, he looked up at the sky, searching it for answers for a while, but when none came to him, he knew he had best be getting back to camp before Lliam sent out a search party for him. Shaking his head in exasperation and disgust at his older brother's overprotective ways, Roman got to his feet, mounted Black-pool again, and spurred the horse on, his heart still pounding within him.

⚶

We did not see any more soldiers for the rest of the day, and neither did Efroy speak again. He was still fuming. I tried as hard as I could to get him to speak, but he would not. The most he would do was shrug or grunt.

Exasperated, I finally gave up and turned my thoughts to who the man could have been and why he would have had Black-pool when I knew Lliam to have ridden the horse before. *Maybe he belongs to one of them, and the other was just riding him for a while. Or maybe Black-pool is just a horse that gets traded around from rider to rider. He's so big, though. I wonder what breed he is. Maybe it's a breed that the humans have created from others …*

I sighed and looked out at the passing grey rocks and cliffs as we continued to run. A few white flowers sprouted from the cracks of the colourless stones, defiant of the harsh wasteland around them. Mosses and lichens spiderwebbed the boulders with brown and sickly green colours, and a few ferns draped some of the smaller stones. It was definitely getting greener in here.

I longed to talk to Lliam. But when I opened my mind and found his, he repelled me instantly. Feeling alone and separated from the rest of the world, I felt a stab of loneliness pierce my heart.

෴

As we rounded a bend a half hour after we saw the man, I gasped. I could see wide open plains through an opening in the rock, unfolding like an old and yellowed map. The trail that we were now on veered sharply to the right and, from there, into the plains. Relief and happiness broke through my exasperation with the day's events, and I felt a weight lift from my shoulders.

"Efroy. Look. We've reached the end of the pass," I stated gently, tapping him lightly on the shoulder.

For the first time since we had been confronted by the soldier, Efroy actually acted as if he had heard me. He looked up, and his eyes widened. Relief and a glint of renewed determination filled them.

As we got closer, the plains spread wide before us, beckoning us. I attempted to talk to Lliam again, to tell him where we were, but as I began to speak, he said, *Elysia, stop trying to talk to me right now. I must concentrate.*

Bewildered, I asked, *On what?*

It's none of your concern.

What's your concern is my concern, Lliam.

Maybe. But not this. I must go. And please, Elysia, stay safe. Then he pulled away, leaving me feeling a little hurt and plenty perplexed. Sighing miserably, I turned my attention back to Efroy and the end of the mountain pass.

We stood before the opening in the rock, gazing out at the beautiful scene before us. Rolling plains as far as the eye could see

stretched in every direction. A bright blue coloured the sky. Here
and there, a bush or rock dotted the plains.

I looked over my shoulder at Efroy. His eyes were fixed on the
plains, a mixed expression of joy and longing on his face. He noticed
me looking at him, and he stated solemnly, "We made it."

I nodded in agreement. "Yes. We did."

ॐ

I sat before a crackling fire. The flames leaped and danced with a
mind of their own, oblivious to the two of us in front of them. *Kind
of like life*, I realized. *It's oblivious to our thoughts and wishes and has
a mind of its own.* I poked at the fire with a stick.

Efroy sat a little ways away on a large flat rock. For a long time,
we both watched the flames dance. I added a few twigs to it every once
in a while from one of the nearly bushes. A thought buzzed about in
my mind, but I hesitated to ask it and held off for a while. Finally, I
mustered the courage to ask: "When we get to Rielture, what are you
going to do with the egg?"

Efroy glanced at me as if he was surprised I was thinking about
it. "It was in your pack when I picked it up after the wolves' attack.
It's still there, right?"

"Of course. Why?" I asked, a bit puzzled.

Efroy hesitated and looked at the fire before saying, "May I see it?
Victoria was sending it to me for safekeeping, but since those humans
are headed to Rielture … now I'm not sure that was the best plan."

I frowned as I got up. I went to my satchel and carefully lifted
the egg out. Its rocky surface was a dull grey colour, but the emerald
streaks shone brilliantly in the firelight. It seemed heavier than I
remembered, but I held onto it as I handed it to Efroy.

He took it reverently and ran his fingers over its bumpy surface.
His eyes reflected the egg's glow, making them a weird, green-tinted
light blue colour. I looked on as he inspected it.

"Nathaniel said this is a dragon egg. Is that true?" I asked.

Efroy looked up at me, appearing startled. "What? Yes, I suppose." He rapped the egg lightly with his knuckles. "This is probably
the last dragon egg anywhere."

"Here in Yaracina? Or does 'anywhere' include the other territories that the humans are from?" There were several large sections of land on the continent that had yet to be explored, and I guessed that was where the humans had come from, unless they had come from a different continent altogether than the one on which Yaracina was located. Perhaps they came from lands across the sea, but from where, I did not know; surely not from Eshen! Places like England and America were shattered, ruined lands now, and from what Aubryn told me, it did not seem likely that anyone still lived in those places.

Efroy stiffened slightly at the mention of the humans, but he did not look up. "I don't know. Probably in Yaracina. But, of course, I don't know if there are any dragons in other places."

I sat down beside Efroy and stared at the egg. "There's no such thing as dragons," I said, tactlessness lacing my voice. "No matter what Victoria says. No one has ever seen one, and I firmly believe that they do not exist."

Efroy nodded. "I know." He looked down at the egg. "But maybe if this one hatches …" He shrugged.

"Well, even if it did, there would be no other dragons, and none after it," I pointed out crossly. I gently touched the egg. *I don't know why people want to believe dragons are real. They're not. I don't know what kind of egg this is really—if it even is an egg—but I'm fairly sure it's nothing more than a bumpy rock.*

I stood and gestured for the egg. Efroy handed it back to me, and I returned it to my satchel. When I came back, a question wormed its way into my head, and I asked it presently, "Are you familiar with the War of the Red Moon? My mother would never tell my sisters and me anything, except that the elves won. Do you know the story?"

Efroy laughed and playfully tugged on a strand of my hair. "Of course I know the story. The War of the Red Moon really did happen, according to our forefathers, but I don't know the full story with all the dates and names and specific details. I do know the myth that has been passed down about it. It may or may not be the truth, but I suspect it's not. Would you be content to hear that?"

"I suppose."

"All right, then," Efroy said, "Here it is, as best I can recall. And remember, this legend has been passed down for centuries so this is probably not what actually happened, okay?"

I smiled. "Of course. But I would still like to hear the story."

Efroy settled back and then launched into the tale: "Back in the days when Yara still walked on this earth, she became friends in her childhood with one of the humans, a boy called Neron. Elves and humans still cohabitated at this time—this was before the Great Plague, when the Old World was still intact—and Yara often went to visit the various human tribes and nations as queen. They were friendly with her, and she with them, but some of the elves did not approve of her mingling with a lesser race. But, of course, they said nothing because she was Yara." Efroy paused and grinned. "She could do whatever she pleased.

"Neron and Yara were especially close because she had known him since he was a child, and he was always especially fond of her. She visited his tribe more than any other and became like family to the people there. And all the while, these particular elves grew increasingly jealous of their queen's attention to the humans.

"So they set to work to destroy the humans, hoping to make Yara realize that while the humans had frail souls that could easily be shattered, the elves lasted. They wanted her to see that her allegiance would have better results if it was given to them alone, for the humans could be gone in a moment.

"Somehow they mutated some kind of rare and lethal disease, altering it so that only humans were affected by its potency. They worked on it long in secret, keeping their project from Yara, in hopes of staying the blame. And when at last it was ready, they spread it into the human tribes and nations. They sent it in with cargo traded between the two races, injected it into animals so that when the humans ate them they would contract the disease, offered it to children on playthings ... The humans had no hope of escaping the Great Plague. Yara searched desperately for an antidote to the disease, but to no avail, and in a matter of several weeks, the human race was eradicated." Efroy paused, a faint gleam of triumph coming into his blue eyes. And I knew with a sudden shiver that if Efroy had been there, he would have been one of those elves planting the Great Plague in the human nations.

Efroy went on: "The elves were victorious. They thought that everything would be right again once the humans were gone, because now not only were the frail, disposable humans gone, but now Yara could not focus on anyone *but* the elves.

"Yara was inconsolably grieved that the humans were destroyed, for some unknown reason, and she went to Menel to beg him to bring the human race back into existence and punish those responsible for destroying such precious lives." Efroy was staring beyond the fire, his eyes far away and half-closed, as if he were seeing the entire legend unfolding before him.

"And Menel did. He brought back the human race but in a way no one could have imagined. He caused the elves responsible for concocting the Great Plague to become humans; their gifts of superior speed, agility, hearing, sight, and mental capacity were stripped from them, and they were reduced to nothing more than mere humans." A note of disdain came into Efroy's voice. "And Menel also gave Yara the chance to bring back one human of those who had died from the disease to lead these new humans. She chose Neron, her dearest friend of the humans."

Efroy hesitated and let out a sigh. "And that was her greatest mistake. For Neron wrongly believed that Yara had only befriended him and his people so as to gain their trust and learn their weaknesses so that she could destroy them with the Great Plague later. He would not listen to Yara when she tried to explain to him that this was not the case, that she had had no part in the Great Plague, in the death of his children, but he would not listen. He would not even listen to Menel, who tried to make it clear that Yara had had no part in the death of his people. Stupid human," Efroy scoffed, blue eyes disapproving. "So Menel banished him and the other humans to a lonely, small continent across the sea and gave them no aid in starting afresh. He refused Yara access to them for fear that Neron and the humans—out of bitterness for their banishment—would try to harm her."

I unconsciously touched my medallion, thinking of Nathaniel and Menel and the god's sea-green eyes. Had he really had any part in the Great Plague? Or was this just exactly as Efroy had said—a myth?

"So for two thousand years, Yara and the elves had no contact with the humans. The human race passed into legend in the minds of the younger elves, giving us a reason to exalt our race in bedtime stories—"

"As we do now," I interrupted.

"As we *did* until now," Efroy contradicted, eyes sad. "But yes, it was essentially the same as these past years. Anyway, Yara remembered that the humans were no myth, but after such a long time, she began to wonder what had become of them. However, Menel had forbidden her to have any contact with them, so she abstained.

"But the humans did not forget as the elves did. Elves were never a bedtime story in the human land. The elves who had become humans—Neron, all their children—would have vengeance on the elves yet. So once they were strong again and once they again had built a powerful army, they sailed over to Yaracina from their countries—much as they're doing now—and set up a siege on Hartford City, which was the capital even then. But they overestimated their own strength; the elves were more powerful still.

"And so they fought on the Salquessaé, a human army of six thousand versus an elven army of nearly twelve thousand. It came to be called the War of the Red Moon because Menel was angry with the humans for attacking Yara's people, and so he turned the moon red while they fought. The humans could not see well in the dim light, but the elves were able to see just as well as always, thus giving them an even greater advantage. The elves, as you already know, won the battle, much to the chagrin of the humans. They fled back to their countries, humiliated, and there they have stayed ever since, passing once more into legend, a defeated foe in bedtime stories for elven children … as they should have stayed." Efroy stared into the dying flames broodingly, and silence fell over our camp.

ॐ

I awoke early the next morning. I had slept on the boulder last night, and the dawn's first rays were shining on my face. I sat up and rolled my shoulders before locating Efroy. He was stretched out near the fire, still asleep. As I looked at him, running my eyes over his motionless form, I felt a familiar pinprick of disappointment that I could not stay in Rielture long.

Oh, I'm probably wasting my thoughts, anyway. He has more important things to think about. Why would he care about me? I thought regretfully. But I could not help wishing. I folded my arms around my knees, thinking as I scrutinised his face. This was the first time I had actually studied him without his knowing. He had a narrow face, a square jaw, and skin that was pale … like alabaster. Like Lliam's. He was lean but obviously muscled, and his movements graceful, like a dancer. His sapphire eyes, though closed right now, added a sort of surreal beauty to his face, one that made me realize I had never seen anyone as handsome as he. *Beautiful,* I thought. That was the only word to describe him.

But it was not his physical features that attracted me to him, I knew. It was the way he smiled when he saw the sun rising and the way he would often make jokes during our monotonous trek, alleviating my boredom; the way he so obviously cared about his people and would do anything, even give his life to protect them, and his gentleness and insightfulness.

Then, blushing and feeling guilty for thinking about such things, I shook my head to clear my thoughts and jumped off the stone. I gathered my things together, and then prepared a small breakfast of bread and dried fruit that I found in Efroy's pack. I frowned at it, wishing for something more hearty.

I suddenly noticed something moving on the horizon far in the distance. My eyes instantly snapped to the location. A tiny figure stood on a low rise. The sun shimmered on his armour. The man seemed to be looking for something. Instantly, I recognized him.

It was Roman.

Alarmed and not willing to take chances, I quickly kicked dirt over embers, grabbed my things, and knelt down beside Efroy, waking him urgently. His eyes blinked open and focused on my distressed face.

"Be quiet," I hissed. "There's a soldier on the horizon, the one we saw in the pass. I think he's seen us."

Efroy's eyes narrowed, but he followed me to the boulder. Together we crouched behind it and waited. Neither of us spoke, afraid to disturb the crushing silence that had descended over our camp.

After a while, Efroy looked out from behind the boulder. He searched the horizon carefully, looking for any horsemen or other soldiers.

He turned back to me. "I think he's gone," he breathed. I nodded, and we both stood up. I walked around the stone and peered across the plains. Nothing but grass and rocks were in sight.

Efroy suddenly gave a startled cry and ducked away from an arrow. He landed heavily on his side and glared up at the arrow, which was embedded in the rock where he had been only seconds before. The black-feather-fletched end quivered slightly, and I looked with horror at the razor-sharp obsidian arrowhead that was fixed in the flecked stone. No arrow should be able to fly fast enough to lodge in stone.

My gaze sought out the man who had fired; he was nearly sixty feet away, behind another boulder. Another arrow was pointed directly at me.

I could hear Efroy mutter a low curse behind me. I then felt his hand grasp my arm with bruising strength, and he jerked me down behind the boulder, where I would be protected from the man's arrow. "We can't go back the other way; the river is that way, and beyond it are more mountains we have to go through. We can't afford to waste any more time." He pulled me down with a sudden jerk as an arrow zipped over our heads.

Panting behind the rocks, I listened to Efroy intently for fear I would hyperventilate with panic if I focused on the horseman. "We have to run past him, do you hear?" Efroy said urgently. "We're fresh;

we just rested. We can outrun that horse—it's so big I doubt it can go very fast or very long. Okay?"

"Run *toward* the man who just tried to kill you?" I asked, horrified.

Efroy grinned. "Why do you keep seeming to care more about my life than I do?"

I was silent.

Efroy snorted in amusement and then said, "Let's go." He darted out from behind the rock before I could protest and began running as fast as he could towards the river. I blinked a few times and then darted after him, catching up to him after a few seconds.

The man loosed an arrow at us, but it missed, and we kept running. After that, he seemed to give up on shooting at us and gave chase instead. When I looked back, he was gaining on us quickly; the soldier's black armour glinted in the sunlight as he bent low over his mount, and the horse was streaking over the plains behind us with frightening speed for such a massive animal. Undeniably, the war horse loomed larger with each passing moment.

Another arrow zinged past Efroy and me. It buried itself in the grass a few feet away. Another followed, this one hitting my right bracer. Luckily, it ricocheted off, but I still yelped involuntarily. Efroy grabbed my arm to steady me as I began to let fear take over me.

I looked back over my shoulder and moaned in dismay. Nine soldiers were now riding behind the black-clad man. They all wore quivers and held swords. One had a glinting spear in his hand. Efroy grimaced as he followed my gaze.

But then something else happened: The man at the head of the soldiers raised his right hand and a light shone from it, half blinding me. White light shot out across the plains, originating from his palm, and it covered the world briefly in snowy luminosity. It was so intense and hurt my eyes so that I closed them instantly, but the light still pained my eyes, even with them closed. When I opened them, I turned my eyes back to the path in front of me. But the world was cast in heavy shadow now, and the only thing that could be seen in the sky was the pale moon. *But it's not even midday yet!* I thought with a touch of fear. *How is that possible? Unless … maybe he's a sorcerer.*

That's what Mother calls Alqua, and he uses magic ... I glanced up at the sky. The silvery moon was high in the sky, and I gazed at it fearfully. My stomach clenched with panic as I looked at it.

Efroy scowled as he looked back at the soldiers. He knew they had to be after the dragon egg, though how they could have learned of it was a mystery to him. *Even if this has nothing to do with the egg, they can't learn we have it or get their hands on it.* He frowned and urged Elysia on beside him. "The river's not much farther," he said in a low voice. "We can make it. When we get there, just jump in, all right?"

Efroy was aware of a soldier riding up behind them. Although he was not yet even with them, every step brought him closer. Efroy could see Elysia tense beside him. Fear rushed through him as he thought of what would happen to her if they did not escape.

I yelped as a sword slashed in front of me, and I barely managed to avoid it. Efroy's grip tightened on my arm to steady me.

After that, he suddenly ducked in front of me, and I caught a glimpse of his dagger gleaming in his hand. I did not know what happened next, except that a few moments later, Efroy caught me up and placed me on the saddle in front of him, and we were streaking across the grass towards a river I could not yet see.

A broad black band appeared in front of us abruptly. I stared at it in confusion. *What is that?* It took me a minute to realize that what I was looking at was a river. *It's the river.* Relief overtook me, and I leaned forward a little bit, as if urging the horse on faster.

The horse did indeed go faster, stretching out to its full length and galloping as hard as it could with its huge hooves and muscled legs. I had never been this high up on a horse before, and though the circumstances were less than favourable, it was thrilling to be riding so far above the ground.

But my hopes of escape were dashed to pieces when I saw three of the huge horses at the edge of the water, their soldiers armed with both swords and bows. Their obsidian arrows were pointed at us as we drew closer. "Efroy!" I cried, pointing at the three men in a panic.

He cursed several times, and then said, "Can you fight with your sword?"

"No!" I shrieked. "I'm *terrible* with a sword, Efroy! I don't—"

"Maybe you should get better then!" he snapped, obviously very angry at the sight of the three humans cutting us off.

I screwed my eyes up tight and forced myself to take steadying breaths, petrified about what was coming next.

We raced closer and closer to the river with every step. The band grew wider and darker as we approached. The moon shone down a broad, shimmering channel of light, turning the lighted area silver. We were fast approaching the rocky shore now. Small fist-size rocks dotted the bank, and tough, scrubby plants grew sparsely, along with some pale purple, weedy looking flowers. A low, dull roar from the rushing water filled our ears. The horse's hooves clattered over the stones as he ran, making an extremely loud sound to announce our arrival.

Arrows whizzed past us in every direction as the three men loosed their obsidian arrows at us. We were moving so swiftly that most bounced off the rocks harmlessly. A few very nearly hit us as we came closer to the three soldiers.

But then one struck true. Our horse was hit in the chest, and with a high-pitched squeal, he toppled over. Instinctively, I jumped as best I could from the falling horse and landed on my side on the rocks. My breath whooshed out of my lungs, and for an agonising moment, I could not breathe. But the next time I gulped at the air, the oxygen was restored to my body, and I gasped with relief.

A sudden wave doused me with cool river water, making me flinch with surprise. Once the water splashed down to the ground, I sat up and forcedly coughed the liquid out of my mouth and throat. I glanced in confusion at the river; I had not thought we were close enough to it for me to get so wet. But the water churned and frothed angrily behind me, abnormally so. Waves sputtered high in the air and sprayed us with icy water. I sucked in my breath as the water doused me again, making my muscles tighten.

"Well, well, well."

Gasping, I whipped my head around and saw the man from the pass, the one who looked identical to Lliam, standing over me, his sword at my neck. His blue eyes were vaguely amused. "Look what we have here," he said softly, eyes boring into me with a strange intensity.

Panting, I was silent as I stared back.

He knelt down before me, and I instinctively scooted back a few inches, unsure what was going to happen next. "I'm sure Lliam's told you who I am, hasn't he?" he said in a very low voice, one that I doubted anyone else could hear. "But in case the name slipped your mind, I'm Roman," he said, blue eyes still searching mine.

I said nothing, though my heartbeat gained speed and began pounding against my chest like a prisoner banging on her cell for release.

I heard the sounds of a scuffle nearby, and turning my head, I saw Efroy being restrained by three of Roman's men, but they were having a difficult time, so greatly was Efroy struggling against them. They called another soldier over to help them, but Efroy fought with even greater intensity.

I turned my attention back to Roman as he said, "You got something in Meneltauré, didn't you, Elysia? Something I would be very interested in obtaining. And since you and your friend are so conveniently here with us, why don't you give it to me, and you can be on your way, hmm?"

I started to say something, but suddenly Efroy broke loose from the soldiers and in an instant was behind Roman. He jerked Roman to his feet and held the dagger to his throat. "Let Elysia and me go," Efroy hissed, the blade so dangerously close that with the tiniest movement, it might cut Roman's neck. Alarmed because he looked so much like Lliam—and I briefly forgot that it was *not* Lliam that had Efroy's knife to his throat—my heart skipped a beat, and I waited breathlessly. Nevertheless, Roman seemed strangely relaxed, as if he were merely humouring Efroy.

Roman's soldiers instantly raised their arrows and pointed them at Efroy, but he did not seem too concerned: He had Roman as his shield.

However, it seemed Roman had other plans. He jabbed his elbow back into Efroy's ribs with such an incredible force that Efroy doubled over, the dagger falling from his hand. Roman caught it and whirled around, kicking Efroy in the side of the head as he fell. Once Efroy was on the ground, Roman held the dagger to Efroy's throat.

"I think not," Roman hissed.

"Elysia!" Efroy gasped. "Jump!"

And with a flash, I remembered what he had told me earlier: *"When we get there, just jump in, all right?"* So frightened was I by what was happening that I did exactly that, without even bothering to help Efroy for I knew I could not. What could I do against Roman and nine soldiers, when Efroy was so easily defeated?

So I turned, ran for the frothing water, and jumped into the churning, black river. The inky water crashed over me, forcing me down into its murky depths, bits of moss, dirt, and pebbles swirling around me, muddled together by the unnatural turbulence of the river. I had no awareness of anything save the morbid desire to breathe and fight to the surface, and I could not see anything except utter darkness, could not feel anything other than an unearthly cold within my chest and resounding panic.

My head hammered painfully, and my lungs screamed for air. I tried to move, but my muscles were useless against the force of the brutal current. I became so disoriented that I had no idea which way was up or down, and I felt as if I was being sucked into the path of some monstrous vacuum for which my strength was no match.

A wave thundered down over me, shoving me down even farther, causing my foot to scrape the bottom of the river. Lights flickered behind my eyes, and I felt frighteningly light-headed. Panic flared up inside me again as my earlier encounter with the waterfall in Menel-tauré came to mind briefly, but I was so terrified and utterly spent that I merely stopped fighting and let the shadowy water engulf me. A moment later, however, I was slammed into a large rock, one that I had failed to notice until it was looming in front of me. The breath left my lungs with the force of impact, and I was limp, stunned, for half a second before my fingers remembered my dire situation and reached out, searching for a hold. After scrabbling at the rock for a brief, terrifying moment, I found a hold and clung to it as if my very life depended on this small boulder. Which, I reflected grimly, it probably did.

Panting, I huddled close to the rock, my satchel and the egg heavy around me, weighing me down. I closed my eyes, wishing as hard as I could that this was all just a nightmare and that I could wake up from it. But I knew that this was no bad dream.

Clutching my rock desperately and trembling from the force of the raging waters, hot tears began to fill my eyes. Where was Efroy? Had he been able to escape? What if he was dead? What if Roman had killed him . . . ? I rolled this idea over in my thoughts for a while. I tried to imagine it—Efroy with the life gone out of his body—but I could not fully envision the idea. Yet I did not have to understand the concept to know that I did not like it.

I looked up at the pale, unnatural moon, suddenly longing for Liiam to come and rescue me as he had in Meneltauré. But he was too far away to help me now. I was alone. And I knew what I must do next, even if there was no one left to help me: find a way to get out of the river without being seen and captured, assist Efroy, if possible; see the egg to Rielture safely as I had promised Lord Riyad; and then go home.